The
Accidental
Inheritance

BOOKS BY CATE WOODS

Tansy Falls

The Inn at Tansy Falls
A Secret at Tansy Falls

More Than a Feeling
Just Haven't Met You Yet

CATE WOODS

The
Accidental
Inheritance

bookouture

Published by Bookouture in 2023

An imprint of Storyfire Ltd.
Carmelite House
50 Victoria Embankment
London EC4Y 0DZ

www.bookouture.com

ISBN: 978-1-80019-067-2
eBook ISBN: 978-1-80019-066-5

ONE

When it came to making life-changing decisions on the spur of the moment, Cassidy Beeswhistle was a repeat offender. In a way, it was a shame that things had worked out so well for her the first time, because she'd got the impression that all major decisions should be taken on the metaphorical flip of a coin. And for a while it looked as though the second craziest decision of her life would end up tied in a big happy-ever-after bow as well – right up until the moment her taxi nearly crashed into the back of a tractor, thousands of miles from her home, somewhere in the muddy depths of the English countryside.

Cassidy automatically shot out a hand to protect her daughter, Nora (the glorious product of that *first* life-changing decision), who was sitting next to her on the back seat, but the seat belt had done its job. Letting out a shaky exhale, Cassidy reached down to get her phone from where it had shot into the footwell.

'Oops-a-daisy!' said the driver, his cheeriness perhaps inappropriate for the immediate aftermath of a brush with death. They had come to a halt just inches from the spikes jutting from the death-trap machinery being towed by the tractor.

Cassidy couldn't imagine a taxi driver back home in California saying 'oops-a-daisy'. Then again, she couldn't imagine them wearing a flat cap and tie, either. And what was with the weirdly narrow roads in this country? The motorway from the airport had long since given way to this single-track lane that wound and swooped through the fields, and which was now entirely blocked by the monster of a tractor.

The driver yanked up the handbrake. 'Sorry, love, looks like we're in for a bit of a wait.'

Beside Cassidy, Nora yawned. The past twenty-four hours had been a lot to ask of a nine-year-old, though her sweet girl hadn't complained once. Neither of them had slept much on the plane: excitement and back-to-back movie-watching on Nora's part; an endless, feverish questioning of her life choices on Cassidy's.

She craned her neck to try to see the road ahead, but the scrubby hedgerows rose on either side of them like canyons.

'Is it much further?' she asked.

'Oh no, we're nearly there now. Dithercott's just down that hill.' He rested his arms on the ledge of his belly. 'So what brings you all the way out here? Holiday, is it?'

'Um, no, not as such...'

'We've bought the village pub!' Nora was beaming with pride.

At this, the driver turned in his seat to look at Cassidy. She recognised his expression instantly. It was the same one people back home had given her when she'd told them about her brilliant plan.

'The Beeswhistle Inn?' he asked.

'Yep.'

The driver regarded her for a beat, his gaze lingering on her

River Cats baseball cap (which, to be fair, she was only wearing so it didn't get squashed in the suitcase). 'Do you have many Tudor coaching inns back in... where d'you say you're from?'

'Sacramento – California. And we do have some Irish pubs, but apart from that, well..."

The truth was Cassidy had never set foot in a Tudor coaching inn. In fact, she hadn't actually been to England before today. She didn't even drink alcohol nowadays, not really; just the occasional margarita if her arm was twisted and the music was right. How could she explain to a stranger that the reason she was uprooting her and her daughter's life and moving thousands of miles from their home was basically down to a combination of gut instinct and ghostly guidance from her dead father? He would think she was nuts – possibly rightly so. All she knew was that the Beeswhistle Inn, with its charming thatched roof and original Tudor beams, had shone out to her like a beacon of hope in the middle of a dark and desolate night. Cassidy knew her decision to buy it was rash, arguably crazy, but she had been convinced it would be the answer to Nora's unhappiness and her own problems. That had been reason enough then, and it had to be now.

'The Beeswhistle Inn,' the driver repeated thoughtfully. 'You know, I don't think I've been in that place for years. Not since... well, you'll know about all that business...' He said it in the way you'd refer to a sweet elderly neighbour being exposed as a dope dealer.

A cold stone of fear formed in the pit of Cassidy's stomach. She wanted to ask for more details, but it was obvious from the driver's tone that she should definitely know about whatever this 'business' was already, because she owned the place. Well, she supposed she would find out soon enough – and whatever it was, she would deal with it. There were sure to be bumps in the road, but just conjuring an image of Nora playing in the inn's

walled garden, or curled up in her new bedroom with its
panoramic view of the rolling fields, was enough to banish her
jitters and reassure her that she was doing the right thing.

'Ahhh, will you look at that sky?' The driver leant his head
out the window to look up at the expanse of blue. 'They say
there's always one day in February where you can catch the
scent of summer, and I reckon that might just be today.'

'Summer sure smells bad,' muttered Nora, pulling up her
scarf to cover her face.

The driver gestured to the tractor. 'That'll be the slurry
spreader.'

'Slurry?'

'Cow's muck, love. Farmers put it on the fields to get 'em
ready for spring.'

The smell really wasn't helping Cassidy's jet lag. 'Do you
think we should ask how long he's going to be?'

'Right you are.'

The driver leant on the horn far longer than anyone would
consider polite.

'Oh! No, I meant...' Cassidy shrank into her seat. 'Never
mind.'

Up ahead, the tractor's driver stuck his arm out of the cab
and made a circular gesture in the international sign for 'turn
around, idiot'.

'Looks like we'll have to take the scenic route.' He began
reversing up the way they came, before abruptly jamming on
the brakes, catapulting Cassidy's phone back into the footwell.
'Actually, if you don't mind a bit of a walk, you could always cut
across the fields?'

'Can we do that?' asked Cassidy.

'There's a public footpath. And even if there wasn't, right to
roam and all that.'

Cassidy looked at Nora, who was already reaching to undo
her seat belt.

'Looks like we're walking,' said Cassidy, smiling at her daughter's excitement.

'Righto.'

The driver heaved himself out of the car and went to retrieve their luggage, while Cassidy and Nora clambered out onto the verge.

'It's so cold!' her daughter gasped delightedly, plunging her hands in her pockets.

Sacramento had never really suited Nora, who reminded Cassidy of a smilier Wednesday Addams. It was a city of swimming pools and sun-baked sidewalks, whereas her daughter was at her happiest wrapped in a blanket reading a book while the rain poured down outside. You didn't get much opportunity to snuggle in front of a fire when you lived in the fourth sunniest place on earth.

The driver was already back into the car. 'Just hop over the stile,' he called out the window, 'then keep an eye out for the kissing gate on the other side, and that'll bring you straight out onto Dithercott green. Good luck!' Then he muttered something that sounded very much like: 'You'll need it.'

Cassidy shouted after him: 'Hold up, which way do we go once we've gone over the stile?'

But the taxi was already reversing at high speed, its engine squealing in protest, leaving Cassidy and Nora standing alone in the middle of the lane. They must have looked an odd pair: Nora in her Harry Potter scarf and the ski suit they'd bought because it was the warmest thing they could find in Sacramento at short notice, and Cassidy in her cap – the faded candyfloss-pink tips of her blonde hair hanging over her shoulders – dressed in her dad's treasured baseball jacket (layered on top of two denim jackets for warmth), combat pants and a pair of battered work boots. Not that there was anyone around to pass judgement. The hedgerows offered only glimpses of the farmland beyond, while overhead a flock of birds drifted and whirled like scraps of paper on the breeze. It was so still and silent that when a cow mooed nearby they started like a gun had gone off.

'Uh... any ideas what a stile might be?' asked Cassidy.

'Maybe that?' Nora pointed out what looked like a broken gate in the hedgerow.

'My little genius!' Cassidy dropped a kiss on her head.

It wasn't easy getting their suitcases – both labelled with 'overweight baggage' stickers – over the stile, and they lost their grip on one of them, sending it tumbling into a puddle and splattering them with suspiciously pungent mud.

'Ew.' Nora stuck out her dirty hands.

'Never mind, we can clean up when we get to our new home.'

They set off down the path alongside the field, suitcases bumping against their legs as they dragged them over the rutted grass. Dithercott was nestled amongst trees at the foot of the valley, the low rooftops wreathed in morning mist that mingled with the smoke puffing from the chimneys of early risers.

Their new home. Excitement fluttered in Cassidy's stomach as images of the Beeswhistle Inn came to mind: the vast stone fireplace (rumoured to have been where Charles II had hidden from Cromwell's soldiers), the tiny yet serviceable kitchen that would be the perfect place to build her new business, the garden with its vegetable beds and tubs of spring flowers. It was a place they would finally be able to build a future, Cassidy was sure of it. And more importantly, it was somewhere that Nora would be happy. Just a few minutes and they would finally see it all for real.

'Mom, look!'

The astonishment in Nora's voice made Cassidy whip her head round. She'd assumed her daughter would be pointing out something down in the village, but instead she found her gazing out across the fields away from Dithercott – and when Cassidy saw what had caught her attention, she caught her breath. She'd seen photos, of course, but nothing could prepare her for the first sight of it in the flesh. *Dithercott Manor*.

The grand house stood proudly on the crest of a hill, its centuries-old stone walls glowing in the morning light, as if even they knew just how magnificent they looked. The building was enormous: three stories tall, and so broad that Cassidy imagined it would take a good few minutes to walk its circumference. She counted four turrets, each traced with ivy, plus a large circular tower in the centre that was topped with a parapet: more than enough fairy-tale real estate to house a quartet of Sleeping Beauties, assorted handsome princes and at least three dragons.

Even from this distance, Cassidy could see the grand front door. Although, she wondered, could you really call something that large a door? It looked big enough to accommodate the tractor that had nearly squashed them earlier. And just to make the sight even more ridiculously perfect, a herd of deer was grazing near the tree-lined driveway that wound up towards the house.

'The Beeswhistle ancestral home,' murmured Cassidy.

'Sure, Mom, like, two hundred years ago or something.'

'Come on, don't you think it's incredible that your great-great-great... uh...great-grandfather lived here?'

'I guess it is pretty cool he had an actual castle.'

'Strictly speaking, it's not a castle, it's a manor house built in the gothic style.'

Nora rolled her eyes. 'Mom, it has turrets. And I'm pretty sure that's Bambi in the front yard. So, it's a castle.' She glanced at Cassidy. 'Can we go look round sometime?'

'I'm not sure – it's someone's family home...'

Nora considered this for a moment. 'What do they do with all those rooms?'

'I have absolutely no idea.'

They gazed at the view in silence, until something spooked the deer and they took off, moving as one towards the woods. At the same time, a bank of cloud moved in front of the sun, shrouding the scene in gloom. In a moment, Cassidy went from being an awestruck bystander to having the unsettling sensation that she was the one who was being watched. In this light, the crenelations along the manor's roof looked like bared teeth, warning her to stay away.

She hugged her dad's jacket closer around her. 'Let's go, kiddo,' she said.

By the time they'd reached the bottom of the field, Cassidy had shaken off whatever ghosts had briefly haunted her. The kissing gate proved even more of a challenge than the stile, but they managed to shuffle the bags through before emerging onto Dithercott green.

It had won the award for prettiest village in the county so many times now that disgruntled rivals had claimed it was a fix, but even on this freezing February morning, Dithercott was putting on quite the show. The grass was dotted with early daffodils and clumps of snowdrops, while a flock of white geese pecked for breakfast nearby. One side of the triangular-shaped green was bordered by a row of half-timbered cottages, the second by the churchyard – the squat tower of the medieval church just visible over the flint wall – and the third by the high street, which was where Cassidy and Nora were heading now.

Cassidy's research had shown her that the centre of the village was laid out exactly as it had been when Henry VIII was on the throne, a fact that blew her mind whenever she thought about it. This meant that the high street was too narrow to accommodate modern pavements, so Cassidy and Nora trundled their bags down the middle of the road. It was still early, and it looked as if they were the only people up and about. Tudor buildings with their dark lattice windows and low roofs snuggled up against more modern architecture, though even the newcomers were probably still a good few hundred years old. It was easy to see why Dithercott was often used by movie crews as a location for period dramas. Cassidy half expected Mr Darcy to appear on a horse, tipping his hat as he trotted by.

'The inn's just along here,' she told Nora.

'*Our* inn,' said her daughter, and they exchanged grins.

But as they rounded the corner, the smile froze on Cassidy's face. For a second, she thought she must have taken a wrong turn and she swivelled her head up and down the street, desperately hoping she had made a mistake. Then she spotted the sign hanging below the roof. The paint was peeling and the sign was dangling off one hinge. The crest depicting an eagle and a stag was faded and chipped, but the curly white writing was still just about legible. Her heart plummeted to her feet as she read the words: 'The Beeswhistle Inn'.

Neither of them spoke for a moment, then Nora cleared her throat. 'It doesn't look much like it did in the pictures.'

It did not. The plaster between the timbering was dull and crumbling and marked with an extravagant swoosh of algae from a leaky drainpipe. Where once the roof had boasted a full head of golden thatch, it was now suffering from severe pattern baldness. The hanging baskets (well, those still hanging) sprouted bare twigs, while attached to the front door was a length of white-and-blue tape, printed with the words: 'POLICE LINE – DO NOT CROSS', fluttering in the breeze like a streamer at the world's worst party.

Cassidy reached for the handle of her suitcase to steady herself. What the heck had happened to her chocolate-box-perfect Tudor inn?

And as she stood there, frozen to the spot in horror, she heard her father's voice, as clear as if he was standing right next to her.

'*One of these days, Cass,*' went his familiar rumbling tone, '*that Beeswhistle impulsiveness will finally catch up with you, and then you're gonna be in trouble.*'

It was one of his go-to sayings and she'd always laughed it off, telling him he worried too much. But she should have known that, ultimately, Joe Beeswhistle would end up proven right.

TWO

Panic surged inside Cassidy like a sudden bout of nausea. *You've really made a mess of things this time, Beeswhistle.*

She looked up at the inn again, hoping she'd overreacted... Nope, it was just as bad as she had first thought. Worse, in fact, as she now noticed that several of the casement windows were smashed. Cassidy glanced at the other houses in the street and their neatly shuttered faces seemed to be frowning both at the derelict inn and, by association, at her.

If Cassidy had been on her own, she would have been calling a taxi straight back to the airport, but she had Nora to think about, and her daughter's happiness was the only thing that mattered in all this. Nora had been so excited about the move to Dithercott, there was no way she could put her back on a plane again without at least trying to make a go of it here, even if their new home *had* turned out to be a crime scene. After all, hadn't she already uprooted their entire lives to move here? Cassidy swallowed audibly; she really did feel sick now. She had to make this work – for Nora's sake.

She forced out a chuckle. 'Well, it's certainly bursting with character! I'm sure it'll be really cosy inside, though, honey. And just wait until you see the walled garden, it's so lovely!'

And it may well have been lovely, but it was impossible to tell, thanks to the blanket of broken furniture, half-burned trash and heaps of rubble covering it. All that was left of the greenhouse she'd admired in the sales photos was a heap of shattered glass and some dead tomato plants.

Cassidy and Nora picked their way through the mess and found the keys to the inn under a stone by the back door, right where the agent had told her they would be (the agent, thought Cassidy furiously, who was going to get it from both barrels). They managed to force the back door open on the third attempt and walked straight into the stink of decay and a large spider's web.

Coming in from outside, they found themselves standing in the inn's bar, though if it wasn't for the fireplace, Cassidy wouldn't have believed it was the same place she'd seen on the website. The sales details had described the inn as being sold 'partially furnished', but this room was empty apart from a couple of rusty camping chairs and a single wooden table covered in scratches and cigarette scorch marks. There was a mess of fast-food wrappers and empty bottles scattered across the floor, and a scrawl of red graffiti stretched angrily along the front of the bar. Cassidy savagely added whoever 'BIG JEZ' was to her mental hit list.

She flicked each of the light switches in turn, but none worked. Standing in the gloom, her nose scrunched up against the terrible stench – *was that the drains?* – she was hit by a deadening wave of exhaustion, but then she felt a small hand slipping into hers.

'Don't worry, Mom, we can fix it up,' said Nora, clearly trying to be upbeat.

'Oh, I know, sweetie.' Cassidy squeezed her daughter's hand, smiling down at her, her heart breaking at the thought that she'd failed her. 'We'll make it beautiful again, I promise.'

That would cost money, though – a heck of a lot of it, judging by first impressions – and that was the one thing Cassidy didn't have. She had a small amount left over from her inheritance and the sale of their Sacramento apartment that she'd earmarked for minor repairs, but she certainly hadn't budgeted for a full refurb. She hadn't thought there was any need. The sales agent had described the Beeswhistle as a 'charming period inn bursting with original features that offers ample scope for a new owner to put their stamp on a unique historical gem' and Cassidy hadn't realised that this actually translated as: 'unfit for human habitation'. And then there was the question of exactly how long it would take to get the place open for business. She probably had enough money to live off for about six months, but that didn't take into account what she would now need to spend on all the refurbishments...

Nora yawned again, so vigorously that she stumbled slightly, and this snapped Cassidy out of her doom-mongering. The poor kid was exhausted.

'Come on, sweetie, let's find you somewhere to have a rest.'

There was a bed upstairs, at least – a double, big enough to fit the two of them – and by luck it wasn't in the bedroom that had a leak dripping through a crack in the ceiling. Cassidy wiped the dust off the mattress, laid out a sleeping bag and made it as cosy as she could, although by this point Nora would have probably fallen asleep standing up. She kissed her daughter and went back downstairs, determined to have got the place looking less depressing by the time she woke up.

The estate agent's phone went straight to voicemail. Cassidy left a message asking him to call her back *as soon as goddamn possible* and then rolled up her sleeves. Sure, she might be guilty of making life-changing decisions on the spur of the moment. Yes, she clearly should have done more research before moving her daughter to the other side of the world. But she certainly wasn't afraid of a bit of hard work.

When Cassidy ventured into the kitchen, however, she let out a long wail. Everything in the room, including the walls, floor and ceiling, was coated in a sticky layer of yellowish grease and dotted with dead flies. Her hand flew to her mouth. The range cooker she'd admired in the sales photos had been disconnected and now had a 'DANGER – DO NOT USE' sticker slapped across it, while the door was hanging off the fridge.

Cassidy remembered the daydreams she'd had about opening her restaurant and bit back a sob. As for the public toilets downstairs, the gents was blocked with wadded tissue (and God only knew what else), while the ladies loo had no seat, a cracked cistern and a pair of fishnet tights dangling from the light fitting.

By some miracle, Cassidy found an ancient jar of instant coffee in one of the kitchen cabinets and, risking electrocution from the old kettle, made herself a strong cup. Judging by the jitters that soon kicked in, coffee didn't go off, even two years past its 'best before' date. After further investigation, she found a stash of mops, cloths and buckets under the stairs (ironically, the cleanest things in the place) and began clearing the trash out of the bar. She was onto her sixth bin-bagful when there was a hammering at the front door.

'Whoever is in there,' came a woman's voice, high and wobbly, 'you should know that the police are on their way.'

Cassidy tipped her head back and closed her eyes. *You have got to be kidding me.*

'Reinforcements will be here any minute. You should also know I'm armed.'

'Well, I'm not,' Cassidy shot back.

There was a pause. 'Who's in there?'

'I'm the new owner of the inn.'

No response.

'Look, is it okay if I open the door so we can talk, rather than yell at each other?'

There was another lengthy silence, then: 'Do it slowly, and keep your hands where I can see them.'

Cassidy unbolted the front door and managed to yank it far enough open to reveal an old woman holding a rolling pin in both hands as if she was coming out to bat. She was short and stocky with white hair and skin as soft and pale as uncooked dough, and the apron she was wearing was dusty with flour. The only bit of colour came from the tip of her nose, which was glowing pink in the chilly morning air.

Cassidy held out her hands. 'See? Unarmed and not remotely dangerous.'

The woman slowly lowered the rolling pin. 'Who did you say you were?'

'Cassidy. Hi.' She stuck out a hand and the woman narrowed her eyes.

'Are you the American lady who's bought this place?'

'I am indeed.'

'I didn't think that was a Sussex accent I could hear.' She finally broke into a smile, her cheeks dimpling. 'Mrs Gerald Timothy – pleasure to meet you, lovey. I live above the Old Bakery a couple of doors down. Sorry about the welcome, I thought you were one of those hoodlums, back again to cause more trouble.'

'Hoodlums?'

Mrs Timothy was craning her head to look inside the inn. 'Oh, the state they left the place in! You'd never believe to look at it now, but the Beeswhistle used to be the heart of Dithercott.'

'I was led to believe it still was. Would you like to come in? I'm afraid I can't offer you much, other than a cup of stale instant coffee.'

'Thank you, dear. I'll pass on the coffee.'

As Cassidy closed the door behind them, Mrs Timothy gasped again as she surveyed the mess.

'Vandals,' she muttered, her nose wrinkling at the smell. 'Hoodlums, vandals and crooks, the lot of them.'

Cassidy showed the old lady to one of the camping chairs. 'Can you tell me what happened? I've only just got here, and this has all come as quite a shock.'

'Dreadful business it was,' said Mrs Timothy, the chair groaning rustily beneath her. 'Just awful. The problems started five years ago when Martin – that's the Beeswhistle's old land-lord – decided to retire. He sold the inn to a young couple from London called the Diaggios. You could tell at first glance they were flashy folk. Had this ridiculous car with a numberplate that read 2 R-1-C-H.' Her face puckered in distaste. 'Anyway, when they first arrived, I said to Mr Timothy – God rest his soul – I said we should give them a chance, not judge a book by its cover and so forth, but it turns out the Diaggios were every bit as awful as they looked. The first broken window appeared within days of their arrival, and it soon became clear that they had no interest in fixing it. One of Dithercott's most historic buildings, and they ran the poor old girl into the ground! From the start, there were all-night parties and illegal rave-ups, as I believe they're called – all manner of antisocial goings-on. They drove off all the regular customers, destroyed the Beeswhistle's reputa-tion and then high-tailed it back to London when the business went under. Flogged it cheap to the first fool that came along.' She glanced at Cassidy. 'No offence, dear.'

'None taken,' she managed, reeling.

'So when we heard that an *American* had bought the place – well, you can imagine there's been more than a few raised eyebrows around the village. After the trouble we had with the Diaggios, everyone had been hoping the Beeswhistle would be taken over by a local person. Someone with an understanding of our customs and standards, who could restore the inn to its former glory. You seem like a nice girl, Cassidy, but I'll wager you don't know much about traditional coaching inns. I'm afraid you might not get the warmest of welcomes from certain parts of the community.'

Terrific, thought Cassidy, wearily. She'd been moving to the English countryside for what she'd hoped would be a quiet life, but it looked like she'd walked straight onto another battlefield.

'Mr Timothy and I used to be in here every evening when Martin was in charge,' Mrs Timothy went on. 'A sherry for him and half a milk stout for me. But we wouldn't have dreamt of stopping by once the Diaggios took over, and nor did anyone else in the village. Nowadays, everyone goes to this swanky new place called the Quill, just outside the village. Very modern, it is, all cocktails and vegan nibbles. Not for me, but the young people seem to like it, and it's very popular with tourists. It's owned by them up at the big house.'

'The big house?'

But Mrs Timothy had already moved on. 'So, is there a Mr Cassidy as well?' she asked, her eyes darting around as if a secret husband might be hiding in the fireplace.

'No, just a Nora, my nine-year-old daughter. She's asleep upstairs. It's still the middle of the night for us.'

'The little angel! She must be exhausted... Where are my manners? Let me fetch you something to eat, I've just got some buns in the oven.' She patted her belly with a smile. 'Not in that sense, of course. Those buns are all grown up now, with lovely little buns of their own.'

Cassidy wasn't going to argue over the offer of food. 'Thank you, Mrs Timothy, that would be extremely welcome.'

'Not at all, lovey. Back in a jiffy!'

After Mrs Timothy had gone, Cassidy sank into the chair she'd just vacated. Her legs felt so weak it seemed perfectly possible she'd never be able to stand on them again.

She could only conclude, from what Mrs Timothy had told

her, that the estate agent must have used photos of the inn from the sale five years ago, before it had been trashed by the Diaggios. Surely that was illegal? Cassidy dropped her head in her hands. It didn't matter whether it was legal or not, she didn't have any money to pay a lawyer. What a mess this all was...

There was another knock; despite her advanced years, Mrs Timothy was clearly a fast mover.

Cassidy got up and wrenched the door open again. 'That was qui–'

But it wasn't Mrs Timothy, it was a very attractive man. Strike that – a very attractive priest. Like, *hot* attractive. Cassidy instantly felt her cheeks redden at even the suggestion of an improper thought about a man of God, although vicars really shouldn't be allowed to have such boyishly handsome faces and casually dishevelled hair, and they *certainly* shouldn't have such impressively defined shoulders.

It looked as if Cassidy's appearance was a surprise to him too, because his mouth briefly fell open at the sight of her, though she supposed the River Cats cap and baseball jacket weren't exactly traditional English country attire, plus no doubt she was now covered in dust and spider webs.

'Miss Beeswhistle?' he asked, in a voice that was pure Hugh Grant, which did nothing to calm her flaming cheeks.

'Yes, are you Reverend Keating? I'd been expecting someone... um...' *Older? More bald? Less of a dead-ringer for Tom Hiddleston?*

He reached out to pump her hand. 'It's such a pleasure to meet you! Your father and I had some wonderful conversations. I was so sorry to hear of his passing.'

'Thank you, that's very kind,' said Cassidy. No wedding ring, she couldn't help noting, as he released her hand. 'Would you like to come in, Reverend?'

'That would be very kind, if you're sure I'm not—' He

glanced over her shoulder, then inhaled sharply. 'Goodness me...'

A look of horror flashed over his face as he took in the state of the bar, but he covered it with a dazzling smile and followed her inside, ducking to get in so as not to bash his head against the low door frame. Cassidy had been led to believe that Englishmen had terrible teeth, but Reverend Keating's would pass muster in the glitziest parts of LA.

She squeezed her hands into fists, ordering herself to get a grip. What was wrong with her? Now really wasn't the right time to be losing her head over the local priest. It must be the jet lag doing weird things to her mind.

'So, we have a Beeswhistle back in Dithercott for the first time since the 1800s!' He rubbed his hands. 'How does it feel to be treading the same soil as your ancestors?'

'A little weird, to be honest. Not least because I had no idea the inn was a total wreck.'

'Yes, the previous owners ran nightclubs in London, but I'm afraid they didn't have much of an idea how to run a village pub.'

'Between you and me, Reverend, neither do I.'

He chuckled, although Cassidy wasn't joking. 'I have no doubt you'll make a wonderful success of the place. Once you've settled in, I do hope you'll visit the New Vicarage for a cup of tea? Pop round any time – well, maybe not on Sunday morning as I'll be otherwise engaged, but any other time would be super!' He laughed again, his hands fluttering at his collar.

In Cassidy's experience, handsome men tended to be confident to the point of arrogance, but Reverend Keating was blushing like a boy scout. It made her warm to him even more.

'Cooee!' Mrs Timothy's head suddenly appeared round the door. 'I brought you a few bits and bobs, just to tide you over until you get to the shops... Oh, hello, Reverend.' She looked between the two of them. 'Do you already know each other?'

'Yes,' said the vicar.

'No,' said Cassidy at the same time.

'Miss Beeswhistle and I have had the pleasure of meeting over email,' Reverend Keating clarified.

Mrs Timothy swung round to Cassidy with a theatrical gasp. 'Beeswhistle? You're not one of *our* Beeswhistles, are you?'

Cassidy smiled at her look of astonishment. 'It's kind of a long story.'

'Well, I've not got anywhere I need to be.' Mrs Timothy settled herself back into one of the chairs, rummaged in the basket at her feet and offered a brown paper bag to Cassidy. 'Fruit bun, lovey?'

THREE

SIX MONTHS AGO – SACRAMENTO

Cassidy tapped on the glass wall to the restaurant manager's office.

'You wanted to see me, Mario?'

'Ah yes, Cass, come on in. Take a seat.'

She realised she was still carrying the dishcloth she'd wiped her hands on before leaving the kitchen and slung it over her shoulder as she sat down.

'Will this take long? I've got a short rib that needs my attention.'

'I'll keep it as brief as I can.' He sighed heavily. 'I'm afraid we have a problem.'

'With my food?'

'Oh no, absolutely not. Your food is...' He bunched his fingers to his mouth in a chef's kiss. 'That beer-brined rotisserie cauliflower was delicious. In fact, Mr Feliz has requested it be a weekly special.'

'Terrific. So what's up?'

'It's about the other night when you threw out that customer.'

Cassidy frowned. 'The sleazebag who was hassling Mia?'

'I'm not sure if "sleazebag" is the right word.'

'He was old enough to be her grandfather and repeatedly made very inappropriate comments when she was serving his table. Mia came to me in tears, and seeing as our manager wasn't doing anything about it' – here, she pointedly eyeballed Mario – 'I went out and politely asked him to leave.'

'Politely?'

'Oh, believe me, I could have been a heck of a lot less polite.'

Mario grunted. 'Well, the gentleman's made an official complaint.'

Smarting at his use of the word 'gentleman', Cassidy snapped: 'I hope you told him where to get off, seeing as how he sexually harassed one of our team.'

'I'm afraid it's not that simple. It turns out he was a golfing friend of Mr Feliz and was dining at the Spring Street Smokehouse by our owner's invitation. He also has a prominent position in federal government. As I'm sure you can imagine, Mr Feliz was extremely embarrassed when he heard how his guest had been treated. Given the circumstances, I'm afraid we have no choice but to let you go.'

Cassidy's mouth fell open. Was this some sort of joke? She knew how happy the head chef, Manon – who also happened to be one of her closest friends – was with her cooking. So happy, in fact, that she'd been given a raise the other week. Surely they wouldn't get rid of her just because she'd stood up for a colleague?

'This isn't the first time I've had to speak to you about your manner,' said Mario, defensively. He clearly knew this was unjust. 'You're a very talented chef, Cassidy, but your volatility can be problematic.'

'Oh, come on, Mario, I'm hardly Gordon Ramsay! I just don't like bullies.'

'Well, I'm afraid the decision is out of my hands.'

'But you're the restaurant manager! Can't you fight my

corner with Mr Feliz?' Panic had started surging inside Cassidy; this couldn't be happening. 'Please, Mario, I love this job. I *need* it. And you said it yourself, my food is good.' Something occurred to her. 'Does Manon know you're letting me go?'

Mario shuffled some papers, ignoring the question. 'Please don't make this harder than it is for me already.'

'She doesn't, does she?'

'I've told you, it's out of my hands.'

There was a glass of Coke sitting on the desk in front of him and Cassidy fought the urge to throw it in his face.

'Well, this is just terrific.' She stood up. 'I guess I'll get my stuff then. Thanks for nothing.'

But as she headed for the door, Mario called her back. 'Cassidy, just one more thing?'

'What?'

He shrank under her furious glare. 'I, um, I trust this won't change anything between us? I do hope we're still on for dinner this Friday?'

She stared at him, wondering how she ever fell for his oily charm. 'No, Mario, we are definitely not on for dinner this Friday,' she said. 'And I can assure you this changes absolutely *everything* between us.'

And with that, she turned on her heel and strutted out as best she could in her kitchen Crocs.

It was only a ten-minute walk from the Spring Street Smokehouse back to her apartment – one of the many great things about this job (or rather *ex*-job) – but the afternoon was oppressively hot, and Cassidy was sweating within seconds. She kicked at a stone as she walked along, her lips pressed together to hold back the tears that were threatening to burst out of her again. She had only just managed to stop crying after being reduced to a sobbing wreck on telling her kitchen colleagues she'd been fired. Manon's eyes had flown wide on hearing the news, and then almost instantly narrowed in fury. "I'm going to tell that jerk Mario that if they won't keep you on then I'm gonna quit," she had fumed – and Cassidy knew she would have done so, if she hadn't begged her not to. Like her, Manon was a single mom, to the teenage Alexia and her six-year-old brother Ace, and deep down both women knew that supporting their kids had to take priority, even over loyalty to their closest friends. 'You and Nora are coming to my place for lunch on Sunday and we'll make a plan,' Manon had muttered, pulling Cassidy into a fierce hug.

Yet it wasn't just saying goodbye to her colleagues that made her want to howl. She'd been working at the Spring Street Smokehouse for nearly three years now and had started to get some of her own dishes on the menu, which made her feel like her career was finally progressing. Not only that, but because Manon understood the pressures of single parenthood, she had allowed her to work flexible hours – a rarity in an industry where punishing schedules and late nights were par for the course. For the first time in her fifteen-year career in fact, Cassidy had begun to think of this job as 'The One'. (Mario, not so much. He'd been a brief and unmemorable blip in her lengthy dating drought. Restaurant hours weren't exactly conducive to finding true love.)

As she trudged home, Cassidy thought back over the long, hard road it had taken her to get to this point. After graduating from Le Cordon Bleu College of Culinary Arts in Minneapolis, she had headed straight to New York with the blind confidence of the young and talked her way into a junior role at a prestigious Madison Square restaurant. Still in her early twenties, she had been steadily working her way up through the ranks, a glittering future seeming assured, when she had unexpectedly fallen pregnant with Nora. Cassidy had no doubt that she wanted to keep the baby, but with the father out of the picture (a drummer in a touring Colombian rock band, their romance had lasted for less time than it took to braise a shin of beef), she had no choice but to move back to Sacramento to live with her dad. Since then, she had worked at several different restaurants around the city, but it was tough finding a place that could offer the hours she required so she could spend time with Nora, while also giving her the creative freedom she craved. And now, after finally finding a job that ticked every box, she had been fired.

Cassidy gave up trying to hold back the tears. The thought of starting over – looking for another job in a city where she'd started over so many times before – made the knot of anger in her stomach unravel into a sprawling mess of anxiety. Surely her life should be sorted by now? Just last week she'd seen on Facebook that one of her Cordon Bleu classmates had been made head chef at one of the top bistros in Paris. Cassidy had been thrilled for him and had said as much in her congratulatory comment, although it had been a struggle to ignore the little voice in her head asking why it wasn't *her* name above the door of a Michelin-starred European restaurant. At least she had been able to reassure herself that while she may not have the glory, she had a job she loved that supported both her and her daughter. Now, though, she didn't even have that. The little voice went from whispering that she wasn't good enough to yelling that she was an out-and-out failure.

But as she turned onto her block, the voice fell silent when she spotted Nora sitting on the steps to their building, her face buried in her hands and her little shoulders shaking with sobs.

Cassidy broke into a run. 'Honey! What's happened?'

Nora slowly raised her head. Her cheeks were red and blotchy.

'Taylor doesn't want to be my friend anymore. She told me I'm boring and that I'll never get a boyfriend because I'm so weird.'

Cassidy bit down the urge to go straight round to Taylor's house and kick her nine-year-old butt. 'Oh, sweetie, I'm so sorry.' She sat next to her daughter on the stoop. 'That must have made you feel really bad.'

'Uh-huh. I had to eat my lunch on my own.' Nora wiped her eyes. 'Why doesn't anyone like me, Mom?'

Cassidy hugged her fiercely, desperately wishing she could find the words that would make everything right. She was her mother – shouldn't she just *know* these things instinctively? Nora had been struggling with friendship issues at school for months, but Cassidy still hadn't a clue how to help her. In her darkest moments, she even feared that she was to blame for her daughter's unhappiness. The circumstances of her birth couldn't be helped, and Cassidy's dad, Joe, had been the most terrific grandfather, but had the absence of a father affected Nora on some deeper level than she'd realised? The thought she was somehow responsible for her daughter's tears, even in part, made Cassidy's gut clench in pain.

Nora's voice was muffled by their hug. 'I try my hardest to fit in, Mom, but nobody gets me. I just wish there was a kid at school who liked the same stuff as me, like – I dunno... reading, and not being super loud. I don't need a ton of friends, I just want... someone.' Her voice broke on this last word.

Cassidy gently pushed her daughter out to arm's length to look at her directly. 'Nora Beeswhistle, you are brilliant, clever, kind and even funnier than Grandpa Joe. School just doesn't suit everyone. And often the popular kids at school are really terrible at being adults. Like... everyone assumed the homecoming queen in my year would become a movie star, but you know what she's doing now? Pumping gas. And it's not even her own gas station. And the quiet, bookish kid, Derek, who ate lunch on his own every day, is head of money at Amazon. What I'm trying to say is that you need to just hang in there. Never, ever change who you are, because who you are, my sweet girl, is awesome. You'll find your tribe, I promise you.'

Nora sighed. 'Not in Sacramento, I won't. I wish I could go to Hogwarts.'

'Dude, no way! I'd never see you. And those man-eating snakes and giant spiders would be kind of a bummer.'

This raised a small smile at least.

Cassidy put out her hands and helped Nora to her feet. 'How about a scoop of that mango gelato from the freezer? We could hang out, watch a movie, maybe order pizza?'

'Thanks, Mom, but I think I'll go to my room and read.'

'Sure.' Cassidy gave her another hug. 'But if you feel like talking, I'll be right here, okay?'

That night, Cassidy couldn't sleep. She tried meditation, yoga and weird breathing techniques she found on YouTube, but her mind felt like a tumble dryer with a full load of anxieties spinning endlessly inside. The job situation was worrying enough, but Nora's unhappiness – and her powerlessness to make it any better – felt so vast and unmanageable, it was as if Cassidy was drowning in it.

At about 2 a.m., she got out of bed, driven by a vague recollection of seeing something called 'Sleepy-time Tea' in the kitchen cabinet, but as she tiptoed down the corridor, she found herself coming to a stop outside her father's den. She always kept the door closed; partly in the hope that the room would retain its familiar smell, but also because it was too painful to keep looking inside. Six months on from his death and she still couldn't bring herself to touch anything in there. It felt as if the den was the last living part of Joe Beeswhistle.

Cassidy leant her forehead against the cool wall, waiting for the sting of sadness to fade. She'd given up expecting her dad to walk through the door at any moment, but every so often – like now – his loss would sneak up and skewer her in the guts all over again.

Joe had raised Cassidy alone after her mom, also called Nora, had died when she was too young to remember her, and then, after Cassidy had fallen pregnant, he had helped to bring up his granddaughter too. She conjured him in her mind now, revelling in the image of his blue eyes that were almost always crinkled into a smile, and that shock of bright white hair – so much of it, even in his seventies, that it stuck out from under his River Cats cap at unruly angles.

Joe had been one of those amazing dads who could fix a broken heart as well as he could a faulty plug. He had owned a successful plumbing company, yet still found time to play baseball with Cassidy at the park after school and take her fishing at the weekends. She remembered a road trip they'd taken back when Nora was very young: her dad at the wheel of his beloved Mustang GT, Cassidy in the back with her toddler daughter, the three of them singing along at top volume to 'Hotel California' while Joe drummed on the dashboard. As a teenager, Cassidy would listen to other friends moaning about their parents, and though she'd nod and roll her eyes along with them, she couldn't relate to a thing they were saying. Joe wasn't just mom and dad to her; he was her best friend.

In a way, she realised now, she'd never really had to grow up until he died. Whenever she was worried or stuck, Joe would pull her into a hug and tell her it would all be okay, that they would sort it out together and that he loved her. 'This too shall pass, honey,' he would say. 'It might pass like a kidney stone, but it'll pass.' She could still feel the reassuring solidity of his chest against her cheek and the soft rumble of his voice as he reminded her that she was strong and brilliant and could cope with 'every darn curveball life pitches at you'.

Now, though, whatever magic Joe spun to make Cassidy believe in herself had gone. She was the one who had to fix her family's problems – and her toolbox was glaringly empty. She had a sudden, visceral longing for a hug from Joe, so intense it made her insides crumple as if she'd been punched, and she bent double from the pain of it. Eventually, straightening up slowly, Cassidy reached for the door handle. Her dad might be gone, but his den could be the next best thing.

Joe had died after a sudden stroke, giving him no chance to get his affairs in order, so the room still looked like he'd just stepped out to get a coffee. Her heart aching, Cassidy scanned its familiar contents: the desk with its leather swivel chair, the sports trophies and books lining the shelves and his 'wall of fame' that featured photos of Joe meeting his baseball heroes and mementoes of a proud dad and grandpa, including Nora's paintings and a framed five-star review of the Spring Street Smokehouse. 'At this cosy spot,' it read, 'Californian cuisine meets southern BBQ with mouth-watering results, thanks to a top-flight team of talented young culinary creatives.'

Cassidy smiled, remembering how he'd tell anyone who'd listen about that one. 'Just you watch, my Cassie will open her own restaurant one day,' he'd boast to his buddies. 'Move over McDonald's, McBeeswhistle's is coming!'

She'd always thought her dad had been joking (as much as he enjoyed her more adventurous dishes, he was at his happiest with a burger), but after he'd died, she discovered just how serious he had been. As well as the apartment, Joe had left her a substantial amount of money, savings he'd been putting aside each month since his first job at eighteen, and in his will he had added this note: 'For my daughter, Cassidy, to set up McBeeswhistle's.'

She crossed over to the desk and sank into Joe's chair, swivelling round to gaze out at the darkened streets. After learning of her inheritance, she had looked into opening her own restaurant in Sacramento, but despite her father's generosity, she had still fallen short. After taking all the associated expenses into account, she would have had to sell the apartment to be able to afford it, and she obviously couldn't leave herself and Nora homeless.

In the distance, she heard the wail of a police siren. She

could sense the vastness of the city outside their apartment walls, the millions of people packed in around them. How many of them were awake now feeling as lost and lonely as she was? Not for the first time, Cassidy wondered if they should leave Sacramento and make a fresh start in a new town, a place where Nora could make friends and the perfect job could be waiting for her.

She leant back in Joe's chair and closed her eyes, letting a wave of sadness crash over her. No, it wasn't Sacramento that was the problem – it was her. Running away wasn't going to help.

What should I do, Dad? If you're listening, just give me a sign.

The room was silent.

Gradually, though, Cassidy became aware of a faint tick-tick-tick. She sat up and looked around, trying to find the source of the sound. It seemed to be coming from inside Joe's desk. Opening every drawer in turn, she eventually found the source of the noise: a travel clock, tucked behind a box file. Cassidy pocketed the clock – she reckoned Nora would like it for her bedroom – but it was only when she went to replace the file that Cassidy noticed the label on its spine. It read: 'Ancestry'.

Her eyebrows bunched together – her dad hadn't mentioned researching their family tree. They'd discussed their unusual surname in the past, but Joe had obviously done some further digging, and judging by the mass of papers contained in the file, he had struck gold. There were maps, photocopies of old documents and page after page of handwritten notes.

Her heart beating a little faster, Cassidy picked up the email printout on top of the pile and began to read.

FOUR

Dear Mr Beeswhistle,

What a wonderful surprise to hear from you! I admit to getting goose bumps when I saw who the email was from. It's such an unusual name and, as you will see, quite famous in our little corner of the Sussex countryside.

You sound like you've done a remarkable job with your own research, but I would be delighted to help fill in some of the blanks in your story. I have a keen interest in local history, and there are extensive community archives kept here at St Andrew's church.

As you have discovered, the Beeswhistle family built Dithercott Manor in the early 1700s (photo attached). They were wealthy farmers and landowners, well-liked by the villagers, who they treated with unusual care and respect for the time. This all changed, however, in 1836, when your great-great-grandfather, Albert Beeswhistle (known to all as Bertie) inherited the estate from his parents. He was still in his early twenties when he became lord of the manor, and, though *charming by all accounts, was overly fond of drinking and gambling.*

The story goes that one hot summer night in 1842 Bertie embarked on a game of Hazard (a gambling dice game) with a London acquaintance by the name of Henry Bamford-Bligh. The game went on for two days straight, accompanied by copious amounts of claret and punch, and by the end, Bertie had gambled away Dithercott Manor and his entire estate to Bamford-Bligh. The now destitute Beeswhistle fled England for America to escape his debts – and that is the end of the story as I know it. Quite a tale, isn't it!

But while the Beeswhistles are long gone from Dithercott, their presence is still very much felt here. There are family graves in the churchyard, and, of course, the Beeswhistle Inn, our cosy pub, which has been serving thirsty villagers since Tudor times.

I do hope you will be able to come and visit us sometime, as you suggest. I would be very happy to give you a tour of the village, and I'm sure you could also look round Dithercott Manor too – though I'm not sure how dear old Bertie would feel about the Bamford-Bligh family still being in possession of his ancestral home!

I very much look forward to hearing from you again.

Yours sincerely,

Revd James Keating
Vicar of St Andrew's, Dithercott

Cassidy stared blankly ahead of her. Their family was descended from English aristocrats? It was as if she'd just discovered that her father had been hiding an entire secret life from her. She vaguely remembered her grandparents, Mama Ellen and Pops, but their alfalfa farm in the Sacramento Valley was a world away from the enormous castle in the enclosed photo where their ancestors had apparently lived just a few generations before. She couldn't wait to tell Nora about this...

Cassidy noticed there was a sheet stapled to the back of the letter and turned it over to find another email.

Dear Joe,

Thank you so much for your latest missive. I attach photos of some of the Beeswhistle graves at St Andrew's as requested.

As to your enquiries about the so-called 'Lost Deed of Beeswhistle', I'm afraid I can't be of much help. The story (or perhaps legend??) is well-known in the village, but I've found no mention of it in the archives. If there ever was an actual deed, I fear that it has been lost to the mists of time, though my gut instinct is that it is little more than a very entertaining rumour!

Yours as ever,

James

The 'Lost Deed of Beeswhistle' had been underlined three times in red pen, and there were scribbled notes in the margin that Cassidy couldn't make out.

Goddammit, Dad, why couldn't you write more clearly?

Adrenaline pumping through her body, Cassidy gathered up Joe's papers and hurried back to her bedroom, where her laptop sat open on the desk. She navigated away from the 'Sacramento restaurant jobs' page and typed 'Dithercott' into the search engine. Instantly, the screen was filled with photos of the sort of idyllic English village that Cassidy thought only existed in Jane Austen novels: pretty little cottages, geese grazing on a green, a grey stone church that was twice as old as modern America herself. There was one image, though, that really jumped out at her. The building's white plaster facade was criss-crossed with beams, on which was mounted a carved wooden plaque that read '1593', but it was the sign hanging just below the thatched roof that really caught her eye – because it had her name written on it.

Cassidy gazed at the image of the Beeswhistle Inn, her heart pounding. It blew her mind to think that there was a little pocket of the English countryside where her family had so indelibly left its mark. As much as she liked Sacramento, she'd never been able to shake the feeling that it wasn't quite where she was meant to be. She'd always put it down to wanderlust, but now that unsettling niggle finally made sense. She wasn't meant to be baking under the Californian sun, she was born to be riding ponies in the rain and taking afternoon tea! No wonder she'd always enjoyed watching *Downton Abbey* so much.

Cassidy searched for more information about the inn, and the top result took her to the website of a sales agent. The Beeswhistle Inn was up for sale. Her heart racing, she read through the details, poring over every photo. In its earlier incarnation, the inn had offered bedrooms to guests and apparently had even once harboured King Charles II, but it was now run as a pub, with the owners occupying the original three guest bedrooms upstairs. At the back, there was an enormous garden surrounded by a brick wall where customers could sit and enjoy the sunshine, plus an area with a greenhouse and raised beds where the previous owners had grown fruit and vegetables.

Cassidy had a sudden vision of her and Nora digging for carrots, laughing and chatting as they worked. In her fantasy, her daughter's cheeks were rosy, her face shining with happiness. *Nora would love it here*, she thought, marvelling at the pictures of the surrounding countryside.

Intrigued, she searched for the village school and found the website of Dithercott Primary. Compared to Nora's current school, which housed hundreds of kids in a sprawl of anonymous concrete blocks, this place looked tailor-made for her dreamy, book-obsessed daughter. The pink-brick building was surrounded by woodland, where each class went for 'forest school' once a week, plus there was a herd of pygmy goats that the pupils helped to care for and an extensive library run by a smiley lady named Sheila.

With an ache in her chest, Cassidy forced herself to shut down the website. It was too painful knowing that Nora's perfect school existed thousands of miles from where they actually lived.

Cassidy wondered who would end up buying the Beeswhistle Inn and felt a stab of jealousy at the idea of someone else living in her inn. Because – crazy as it sounded – that was how she had already begun to think of it. She propped her chin on her hand, revelling in the agent's description of the 'charming, centuries-old hostelry' with its 'intriguing history as a tavern for soldiers and smugglers'. Joe had always wanted her to open her own restaurant: how amazing would it be to do so here, in the Beeswhistle Inn? She could cook with the produce she grew in the inn's garden, and judging by the surrounding countryside, there would be plenty of local suppliers in the vicinity.

Amazing... but impossible. Her and Nora's lives were in California; she couldn't just uproot them on a whim to move to a village she couldn't even place on a map. Cassidy chewed her bottom lip, her mind zipping back and forth. It wasn't an *entirely* crazy idea though, was it? Her ancestors had lived there. Her name was above the door, for God's sake! And she knew in her heart, as sure as night followed day, that Nora would be happy in this idyllic-looking village. She had asked Joe to give her a sign and he had delivered – and it couldn't be

clearer if it had been written in foot-high neon letters across the
wall.

Cassidy pressed her fingertips to her forehead, trying to
force her whirling thoughts into order. It was mad to even think
about relocating to England – a place that she'd never been and
didn't know a soul – just because she'd discovered a distant
family connection. But, allowing herself to indulge in that
fantasy for a moment, what would be the practicalities if they
did take the plunge? Money was the biggie, of course. Unlike
the restaurants she'd looked at buying in Sacramento, the
Beeswhistle offered the distinct advantage of combining both
living quarters and work premises, but the asking price quoted
on the website didn't mean anything to her as she was clueless
about the exchange rate.

Cassidy converted the price into dollars – and when she
saw the resulting figure, her eyes lit up...

Not so fast. She forced herself to bite down her excitement.
After all, it wasn't just the matter of buying the place, she
needed to factor in all the other expenses too. Judging by the
photos, the inn had been kept in immaculate condition and had
the added bonus of being sold semi-furnished, but she would
still need enough left over from the purchase price to cover
minor renovations and additional furnishings, plus have a pot of
money to support her and Nora while she got the business off
the ground. Surely that would be beyond her budget...?

Her exhaustion now forgotten, Cassidy opened a spreadsheet and got to work. She listed every possible cost she could
think of involved in a relocation and calculated what she might
get from the sale of the Sacramento apartment. It was a long
and arduous job, but as the sun started to rise, Cassidy finally
sat back and looked at the figures on the screen, and a smile
spread across her face. It would be tight, but she reckoned she
could just about cover it.

What had started a few hours earlier as just a lovely fantasy now felt like the logical – even sensible – next step for her and Nora. Perhaps she was delirious from lack of sleep, but at that moment, Cassidy was convinced that Joe had engineered the whole thing. If someone had suggested before last night that the solution to her problems would be buying a five-hundred-year-old English pub, she would have laughed, but now it seemed far from ridiculous. In fact, it felt like it was meant to be. After all, this wasn't just some random idea she'd dreamt up: Joe had somehow heard her plea for help and guided her to his ancestry research *at the exact same time* the Beeswhistle Inn had been put up for sale. This wasn't a coincidence, it was nothing less than paternal guidance.

Cassidy looked over at a photo of her dad on the wall. He was sitting in a bar, surrounded by his tight-knit group of friends, all of whom were raising their beer mugs towards the camera. Joe's eyes were scrunched up and his mouth half-open, as if he was on the verge of laughter, and as she gazed at his face, a warm glow began at Cassidy's core and then spread out, flooding her with a sense of well-being and peace. She wasn't particularly spiritual, but in that moment, she felt her father's presence in the room as strongly as if he was sitting right in front of her.

'Thank you so much, Dad,' she murmured, finally giving into tears. 'I just knew you'd make everything right.'

FIVE

Cassidy's eyes flew open. The darkness was so intense that for a moment she wondered if she was still dreaming, then she heard Nora's breathing next to her and the rustle of the sleeping bag, and she remembered where they were. The Beeswhistle Inn – or, rather, the ruins of what it had once been.

The combination of jet lag and a day of high-intensity cleaning had knocked her out like Valium, so Cassidy was pretty sure that something must have woken her up. She lay still, listening intently, her senses on high alert. If you'd asked her on a sunny afternoon if she believed in ghosts, she would have scoffed, but right then, entombed in blackness, in a five-hundred-year-old inn that creaked and moaned like it was alive, her imagination crawled with monsters. But all seemed quiet, apart from the constant shudder of the ancient plumbing. Cassidy's eyelids had started growing heavy again when a sudden crash downstairs made her jerk bolt upright.

Her heart thumping, Cassidy scrambled for her phone. It was just after 2 a.m., the absolute worst time for intruders, imaginary or otherwise. Ignoring the churning in her belly, she crept out of the room towards the top of the stairs, stepping on a squeaky floorboard that split the air like a pterodactyl's screech. She froze, and in the silence that followed, she heard the sound of something clattering to the floor.

She hadn't imagined it; there was somebody in the kitchen.

At once, Cassidy's mama bear instincts kicked in. Pausing to grab the nearest weapon (she wasn't sure how effective a dustpan would be against a determined assailant, but it would have to do), she tiptoed downstairs. She hesitated outside the kitchen, her heart pounding so violently she could feel it, and then slowly pushed open the door...

In a square of moonlight, a cat froze, staring back at her. It had been nosing through a half-spilled bag of rubbish that it must have tipped over in a search for food.

Cassidy's breath came out in a huge whoosh.

'You scared me, buddy,' she said, her hand outstretched towards the scrawny-looking animal.

It trotted over, tail bolt upright, and rubbed around her legs with a rumbling purr. It was very thin, but it seemed too friendly to be a stray.

'You hungry, little guy?'

The cat miaowed, so Cassidy fed it some milk and scraps left over from their supper, then made it a bed in the corner of the kitchen with her dad's baseball jacket.

'I'll deal with you tomorrow,' she said, closing the door behind her. 'Sleep tight.'

Back upstairs, Cassidy sank gratefully onto the bed and zipped up her sleeping bag. A moment later, there was a loud miaow and the cat jumped on the bed, snuggling up beside her with a purr like a motorbike's engine. She had no idea how it had escaped from the kitchen (perhaps it had slipped out as she'd closed the door, or maybe it was actually a Tudor ghost cat?), but she was too exhausted to put it outside now, so she let it stay put. Besides, there was a high probability they'd already caught fleas from the old mattress.

. . .

'Mom, look!'

Nora was sitting up in bed with the cat in her arms. Her daughter's face was radiant, while the cat looked pretty pleased with itself too.

Cassidy struggled up to her elbows. 'I found it in the kitchen raiding the garbage in the middle of the night. I guess it belongs to someone in the village.'

Nora's smile faded a little. 'Can't we keep her?'

'Let's find out if it's already got a home, and then we'll see. Are you hungry?'

'Starving,' she said, smooshing her face into the cat's tatty fur. 'And so is Hermione.'

For breakfast, Cassidy cut up the rest of Mrs Timothy's fruit buns and spread them with the butter she'd also brought over. It was like no butter she'd ever eaten, so golden and creamily delicious that Cassidy had been slicing off chunks and eating it on its own like a fine cheese. She made a note of the name on the wrapper: 'Apples & Eggs Farm Shop'.

Draping the sleeping bags over their shoulders for warmth, the three of them – Cassidy, Nora and Hermione the cat – sat under the back porch, watching the rain patter on the garden as they ate their buns. Here and there, Cassidy noticed green shoots bravely battling their way upwards through the piles of trash towards the sky. *Just like me*, she thought wryly.

Beyond the garden wall, she could see the tops of trees and beyond that the dark purple outline of distant hills. She took a snap of the view (taking care to crop out the mess of the garden) and sent it to Manon back in Sacramento, along with the caption: 'Our new hood'.

Cassidy's mind spiralled back to the moment she had told her friend about her plan to move to England. They had been on a hike along the Bay Area Ridge Trail, as Cassidy had decided she could then just run away if Manon took the news badly. Apart from Nora, who had jumped off the couch with excitement at the idea, her friend was the one person whose opinion she really cared about. But although Manon had plainly been shocked – freezing in the middle of the trail, her mouth forming a perfect 'o' – she had listened to Cassidy's rambling explanation of how she had come to discover the Beeswhistle Inn and then asked lots of sensible questions without judgement. She had stayed so scrupulously neutral, in fact, that in the end Cassidy had to ask outright if Manon thought she was being utterly mad.

'It could be a fantastic opportunity for you and Nora,' she had replied, clearly choosing her words with care, 'but I think it might be harder than you're expecting. So if you're going to do this, Cass, then you need to be all in and stick with it, even when things seem impossible...'

Cassidy's phone vibrated in her hand, nudging her back to reality. She glanced at the screen: Manon had already sent a reply. Sacramento was eight hours behind England, so she must just have finished her shift at the restaurant. Her throat tightening at the sight of her friend's name, Cassidy opened the message.

> Wow, that looks stunning!! Can't wait to come and visit. How's it going over there? Love to Nora xx

Cassidy quickly typed out a reply.

> Harder than expected but sticking with it ;)

Smiling to herself as she pocketed her phone, Cassidy took a deep breath, savouring the scent of the rain-soaked earth and sweet air, and the tightness in her chest began to ease a little. Perhaps this might work out after all.

Her optimism was short-lived, however, after she tried to run a bath. There was no shower in the bathroom, just a cast-iron tub designed to fit a small Victorian child, and when she turned on the taps, only a cough of dust wheezed out. In the end, she heated water in the kettle, running up and down the stairs to fill the tub, and she and Nora took turns washing in a couple of inches of tepid water. Cassidy wearily added 'replace plumbing system' to the list of jobs she'd started the previous day.

First things first, though. The morning's most pressing task was to find out who Hermione belonged to, a job which conveniently also took care of 'meet the neighbours'. Leaving the cat exploring the garden (Cassidy secretly hoped it might wander off while they were out; it was a nice animal, but she really had enough on her plate without taking on a pet), they started their enquiries at their nearest neighbour, Old Forge Cottage.

The cottage was obviously close in age to the inn, with the same weathered beams and diamond-paned windows, but that was where the similarities ended. With its glossy red door, window boxes of spring bulbs and rainbow windmills, it was the sort of house that had its own Instagram account. Next to the immaculate cottage, the Beeswhistle looked like an eccentric relative who kept ferrets and never went to the dentist.

Cassidy knocked on the sun-shaped brass knocker and moments later the door opened to reveal a woman of about Cassidy's age, her curly black hair swept up in a pink and orange headband.

'Can I help you?'

'Hi, I'm Cassidy, and this is my daughter, Nora. We've just moved into the inn next door.'

The woman's face lit up. 'Welcome! It's great to meet you, I'm Angeline.' She dropped her voice. 'Don't take this the wrong way, but I'm so glad you look normal.'

Cassidy smiled, touching her hair. 'I wasn't sure pink streaks would pass for normal round here.'

'Oh, believe me, after the last owners of the Beeswhistle, you could have rocked up in a rainbow wig and clown car and I'd have welcomed you with open arms. Besides, speaking as a hairdresser, I think the pink looks fab on you.' She stepped to the side, and Cassidy got a glimpse of buttercup-yellow sofas and a poster-sized painting of flowers in the room beyond. 'Would you like to come in? I've got some coffee on the stove. And, Nora, I think you're probably about the same age as my daughter, Tilly. She's nine.'

Cassidy gave her daughter a gentle nudge. 'Nora's nine as well, aren't you, honey?'

'Nearly ten,' Nora mumbled at her feet. She wasn't great with new people.

Inside, the cottage was light and airy despite the low ceilings, and the scent of coffee mingled with a spicy fragrance. It was a cheery and welcoming room, and Cassidy instantly felt at home.

Angeline shouted up the stairs: 'Tilly! Come and meet our new neighbours.'

Please like books, please like books. As they waited for Angeline's daughter to appear, Cassidy was repeating this in her head like a mantra.

They heard footsteps on the stairs and then a small, serious-looking girl appeared, regarding the newcomers warily from under her fringe. In manner at least, Tilly was the spitting image of Nora. Cassidy could have wept with relief.

'Hello,' said Tilly to the floor.

'Hey,' muttered Nora.

Angeline rested her hands on Tilly's shoulders. 'Will Nora be going to Dithercott Primary?'

'She's starting on Monday,' said Cassidy.

'Then you'll be in the same class! Tilly, why don't you take Nora upstairs and show her your hamster?'

The girl gave a half shrug, but didn't move.

After a moment, Nora asked: 'Is it a Syrian or a Russian hamster?'

'Chinese,' said Tilly. 'His name's Xiang. Like the panda.' She raised her head slightly, one eye just visible beneath her hair. 'Your accent's cool.'

'Thanks.'

They tailed off again into silence.

Angeline rolled her eyes at Cassidy and then shooed the girls towards the stairs. 'Up you go, ladies! I'll bring you some hot chocolate.'

Once the girls had disappeared upstairs, Cassidy followed Angeline through to the kitchen.

'Angeline, do you own a cat? Small, grey, kind of scrappy looking?'

'I've seen it, but it's not ours.'

Cassidy's stomach sank. 'I guess I'll ask the other neighbours, see if she belongs to anyone. She seems quite at home in the inn, though.'

'Perhaps she was abandoned by the Beeswhistle's previous owners? That's exactly the sort of low move they'd pull.'

'Yeah, I can't get over the state they left the pub in. I had no idea it was so bad.'

Angeline shot her a quizzical look. 'Didn't you see the place before you bought it? Over Zoom or something?'

'Well, there were loads of photos on the sales agent's website, and I suppose I just trusted they would provide an accurate picture...' Even to Cassidy's ears, she could tell how stupid she sounded. 'But now I realise they must have used the photos from before the Diaggios got hold of the place.'

'Honestly, they were the absolute worst.' Angeline poured out two mugs of coffee. 'I used to work at the inn when the old landlord was in charge, and it was the most perfect village pub you could imagine. The food was never that brilliant – Martin, the landlord, thought anything other than scampi and chips was "getting above" itself – but the atmosphere... You should have seen it at Christmas. The blazing fire, fairy lights criss-crossing the beams, the scent of mulled wine... And then the Diaggios arrived.' She sighed wearily. 'I handed in my notice after they'd been there a week. They had no interest in running a village pub, they just wanted somewhere to get drunk with their mates. Dave Diaggio would park his Mercedes out the front of the inn, music blaring so loudly it shook my front windows, and when I complained, he'd just laugh and turn it up. They kept the pub going for a few years, but nobody wanted to go there because you'd risk leaving with either a broken nose or food poisoning.' Angeline smiled. 'But now you're here! So what are your plans for the Beeswhistle?'

Cassidy felt a twinge of fear. It had all seemed so simple when she was back in California and this whole situation had been purely hypothetical. Of *course* she would be able to open a restaurant in a strange country where she didn't know a soul or understand the way anything worked. It would be *simple*! Now, however, after discovering the extent of the Beeswhistle's decrepitude, it felt as doable as getting to the moon with only a cardboard box and a Wi-Fi dongle.

'Well, I was planning to reopen the Beeswhistle as a pub, but with the emphasis on food,' she said.

'A gastropub?' Angeline beamed. 'Excellent.'

'Yeah. I was a chef back in California, you see. I had this idea, because of the inn's history, that I might offer a Tudor-inspired menu.'

'What, like turnips and gruel?'

Angeline's expression made Cassidy laugh. 'I was thinking more along the lines of game pies, pottage, baked custards – that sort of thing.'

Angeline took a sip of coffee, thinking this over. 'What did you cook back in the States?'

'Whatever was in season, really. Lots of fish and vegetable dishes. Mainly on a grill.'

'I don't know about pottage, but *that* sounds delicious. Why don't you do that here? We're desperate for a place that does good, seasonal food.'

'Well, I've got plenty of time to decide. It'll take months to get the inn ready to open. The renovations are going to cost a lot of money and I'm no expert in restoring Tudor buildings so...' The jitters started up in Cassidy's stomach again. She needed to change the subject. 'You said that you're a hairdresser, Angeline?'

'At the moment I am. I trained after leaving school, then, when I lost my job at the Beeswhistle, I picked it up again. I miss working in the pub, but at least I can see hairdressing clients at home during school hours, so it fits around being a single parent. My ex-husband lives in Brighton and sees Tilly at weekends. I'm trying to get together enough money to buy him out of his share in the house, but blow-dries and the occasional head of highlights aren't really cutting it. Excuse the pun.' She forced a grin, but her worry was clear. 'I'll get there in the end,' she finished.

'It's tough, isn't it? I'm a single mom too.'

'I knew I liked you.' Angeline smiled, leaning her elbows on the counter, her mug clasped in both hands. 'Is Nora's dad still on the scene?'

'No, and he never has been. My dad was the most amazing grandfather, though. He died last year.' The words still felt alien in her mouth.

'I'm so sorry, Cassidy.'

She flashed a smile of gratitude. 'I just wish he could have seen the inn. He's the reason Nora and I are here really. He was researching our family tree just before he died and uncovered our family's connection to Dithercott.'

'Yes, Mrs Timothy told me all about that. She grabbed me in the street yesterday afternoon and said that Bertie Beeswhistle's great-great-great-granddaughter had just moved in next door. You'd think it was Brad Pitt by the look on her face.' She grinned. 'Have you had a chance to see Dithercott Manor yet?'

'Just a glimpse. Have you ever been inside?'

'No, the Bamford-Blighs don't like to mix with us peasants.' She rolled her eyes good-naturedly. 'They won't be able to refuse you, though, seeing as your ancestors built the place.'

Not for the first time, Cassidy felt a pang of curiosity about the Bamford-Blighs, the family who now lived at Dithercott Manor simply because Bertie Beeswhistle had been bad at gambling. Though she knew absolutely nothing about them, she couldn't help but regard them with dislike. Bertie was undoubtedly an idiot to have wagered his house in a drunken dice game, but if she'd been Henry Bamford-Bligh, there's no way she'd have made him stick to the terms of the bet. Forcing a guy out of his home, even if he was the one who suggested it, seemed like kind of a dick move, and Angeline's 'peasant' comment hadn't done anything to ease her suspicions about Henry's snobbish descendants.

Just then, there was a thundering on the stairs and the girls burst into the kitchen.

'You won't believe this,' said Tilly, 'but Nora is a Hufflepuff like me! *And* she's read the whole of *The Lord of the Rings*!'

Nora was literally bouncing on the spot. 'You should see Tilly's room, Mom, she has so many books!' She held a stack aloft. 'She's let me borrow all these!'

And at that moment, Cassidy didn't care how many greasy surfaces she'd need to scrub or leaks she'd have to fix: it felt like she'd made exactly the right decision coming to Dithercott.

• • •

The rain had stopped by the time they left Angeline's cottage. Nora was so happy at having made a new friend that she skipped and twirled as they walked down the street, taking advantage of the fine weather to check out their new surroundings and see if any of their other neighbours would claim Hermione.

Cassidy had noticed that just like Old Forge Cottage, quite a few of the houses in Dithercott still bore the names of their original incarnations, such as the Old Saddlery, the Old Bakery (where Mrs Timothy lived) and, opposite the inn, the Old Post Office, although, confusingly, this was clearly still operating as a post office as well as being a home, so, in effect, was both the old *and* new post office. As they passed by, Cassidy noticed a woman staring at her from the window. She withdrew into the darkness of the shop as soon as she realised she'd been spotted, but the scowl on the woman's face lingered in Cassidy's mind. She knew that not everyone was going to be as welcoming as Angeline; Mrs Timothy had warned her as much. Still, it was unnerving to be confronted with the clear proof that certain people in the village didn't want her there.

SIX

As they approached the school gate, Nora's steps slowed and then ground to a halt. It was Monday morning and the playground ahead of them was full of children in navy Dithercott Primary sweatshirts, swarming over the play equipment while clusters of chatting parents stood watching. It was Nora's first day, but Cassidy felt the curious glances and the jitters in her belly as acutely as if she was the one starting Year Five.

'I can't do this, Mom,' muttered Nora, her voice quivering. 'Can't we just go home?'

Cassidy battled the bone-deep urge to scoop her up, march her back to the inn and home-school her until she was eighteen.

'It'll be okay, honey,' she said, as brightly as she could manage. 'Being the new girl is tough, but Tilly will be in your class, and we've already met Miss Poppy and she was super nice, wasn't she?'

They had spoken to Nora's smiley new teacher over Zoom while still in California, and by the end of the chat, Cassidy had wanted to go to Dithercott Primary herself.

Nora weakly raised a shoulder. 'I guess she was okay.'

'You said she was lovely. I just know you're going to have a fantastic day.'

'But what if...' Nora blinked, her eyes swimming with tears. 'What if nobody likes me, Mom?'

'We know that Tilly likes you, so that's a good start. Let's just take one day at a time, okay?'

So Nora allowed herself to be led into the playground, shrinking into herself like a tortoise withdrawing into its shell, while Cassidy plastered on an 'everything's fine!' grin and scanned the crowd for a friendly face, when, to her relief, Tilly ran up to Nora, closely followed by a smiling Angeline. Then, soon after, Miss Poppy appeared with a 'WELCOME, NORA!' sign that her new classmates had clearly made. When the head teacher appeared at the door and rang a handbell for the start of the school day, Nora glanced back to wave goodbye and managed a small, brave smile that just about floored the already fragile Cassidy.

After the children had gone inside, Angeline put an arm around her. 'You okay?'

'Yeah. Not sure how I'm going to survive the next seven hours though.'

'Stay busy,' Angeline advised.

That wasn't going to be hard, thought Cassidy, as she made her way back along the path through the woods that led to the inn. Her to-do list already filled two sheets of A4: a sprawling inventory of things to paint, buy, fix and renovate. Last night, she had looked up how much it would cost to re-thatch a roof and immediately wished she hadn't.

It was a sunny morning and the wood was alive with birdsong, the different calls harmonising like a well-rehearsed choir, while the stream running alongside the path chattered happily over its pebbly bed. Here and there, Cassidy spotted clumps of pale yellow flowers nestled in the tree roots that were embroidered into the banks.

She took a deep breath and blew out the stresses of the morning. The walk to Nora's school in Sacramento involved five city blocks, a fog of exhaust fumes and not a single tree; in terms of their daily commute, at least, this was a definite upgrade. Then, through the trees, Cassidy caught a glimpse of Dithercott Manor, its gothic towers soaring up towards the clouds. She stopped and stared, wondering what lay behind its stone walls. In her imagination, she saw vast rooms hung with tapestries and oil paintings of frowning old men, perhaps a sweeping staircase leading to a dining hall. Lost in her daydream, she had a vision of herself in a full-length gown and tiara, making her way down the wide stone stairs – before she tripped on her hem, tumbled down the last few steps and ended up in a heap at the bottom, knickers on show. *That was about right*, thought Cassidy, smiling to herself. Her ancestors may have been to the manor born, but she was straight outta Sacramento.

By the time she got home, Cassidy had decided to start her day with a visit to Apples & Eggs Farm Shop, purveyors of Mrs Timothy's divine butter. Strictly speaking, this wasn't on her to-do list, but she justified it as research. After all, if she was going to open a gastropub, she needed to acquaint herself with the local suppliers, plus it would be a darn sight easier and more enjoyable than investigating the workings of her septic tank.

Cassidy had been imagining a quaint roadside stall, but Apples & Eggs was to farm shops what Harrods was to fashion boutiques. It was located about a mile outside Dithercott on a main road that seemed to be the alternative route into the village if the other lane was blocked by a giant tractor. The store stood in a spacious plot in the midst of farmland, next to what appeared to be a restaurant. Both establishments shared the same faux-rustic aesthetic, with distressed brickwork and weathered wood cladding, and their mutual car park was crowded with SUVs that had clearly never been off-road in their life.

There was a sign out the front of the restaurant depicting a gold feather against a glossy black background and with a start Cassidy realised this must be the Quill, the gastropub Mrs Timothy had mentioned. Curious, she wandered over to look at the menu on the board outside. It was a mishmash of culinary greatest hits from around the world, including pad thai, lobster spaghetti, steak and ale pie and paella. Cassidy's chef's instincts smarted at the missed opportunity. The pub was surrounded by farms producing beautiful food, yet here they were probably importing sugar snaps from Kenya! She made a mental note to dine here at some point soon, to check out the competition.

The entrance to Apples & Eggs was decorated with a display of gourds in fetching Farrow and Ball tones and dinky pots of herbs that probably cost more than it would to buy, well, a new pump for the septic tank. At the door, Cassidy picked up one of the antique wicker baskets that were intended for customers' use. They were impractically tiny, but this wasn't a place for bulk-buying groceries. Here, you were meant to purchase one apple, a single glossy leaf still attached, or a tiny handful of new potatoes dusted with the finest golden soil.

Cassidy wandered up and down the aisles, gorging herself on the sights and smells. The meat was local and the cakes came from a village bakery. She wanted to try everything, but even with the additional challenge of converting pounds to dollars, it was obvious she was in millionaire territory. In the end, she decided on a tray of parkin (a sticky, gingery flapjack), some charmingly misshapen vegetables and a bar of goat's milk soap, as a 'thank you' to Mrs Timothy for the warm welcome. The estate agent had promised that the oven would be fixed today (though had been infuriatingly unwilling to admit responsibility for any of the other myriad of issues at the inn) so she also bought some new-season lamb, excited at the thought of cooking the first hot meal for Nora in their new home.

At the cash desk, a young woman rang up her purchases.

'Would it be possible to speak to the manager?' asked Cassidy, as the cashier placed the parkin in a branded paper bag as carefully as if she was laying a new-born baby into a cradle. 'I've just moved to the area and I was hoping to find out more about local suppliers.'

'I'm afraid she's not here right now, but if you'd like to leave your number, I can ask her to give you a call?'

'That would be great, thank you.'

Cassidy gave the cashier her details and was heading for the exit when she heard someone calling behind her.

'Hello! Excuse me!'

She turned to see a thirty-something woman striding towards her. She had long blonde hair twisted into mermaid waves and was clad in Kate Middleton-style country casuals with skinny jeans.

'I couldn't help overhearing your conversation,' said the woman, her eyes sparkling like the diamonds at her ears and wrists. 'You're really Cassidy Beeswhistle?'

'I am, yes.'

'Well then, I believe our families have history.' The woman offered a hand, holding it in a way that suggested it should be kissed rather than shaken. 'Sophia Bamford-Bligh.'

As she took her hand, the name hit Cassidy like a speeding truck. 'Of Dithercott Manor?'

'The very same. No hard feelings, I hope, for what happened between Henry and Bertie all those years ago!'

'Of course not! In fact, I was hoping I might bump into you, I've admired the manor from a distance and I've gotta say, just – wow.'

'It *is* magnificent, isn't it? Quite the money pit though, as you can imagine.'

'Yeah, that's a heck of a lot of windows to clean.'

Sophia laughed, which encouraged Cassidy to grab the bull by the horns.

'Actually, Sophia, I was hoping that I might be able to come and take a quick look around some time? You know, because of my family's history with the place.'

'Gosh, but that was so long ago now, wasn't it? To be honest, it feels as if the Bamford-Blighs have always been at Dithercott. The manor has certainly changed beyond all recognition since the dark days of the Beeswhistles. Dear old Bertie left the place in the most horrendous state!'

Cassidy blinked, confused by the juxtaposition of Sophia's dazzling smile with what she'd just said. Or had something had got lost in translation from upper-class British to west-coast American?

'Oh, it's *so* lovely to meet you!' Sophia went on, as if she hadn't just told Cassidy she wasn't welcome at the manor and that her great-great-great-grandfather was basically a pig. 'How are you finding the village?'

Cassidy had no choice but to put the weirdness of a moment ago behind her. 'I do love Dithercott, but the inn needs a lot of work.'

'So I've heard. Such a dreadful shame what happened. The Beeswhistle Inn used to be the sweetest little spot, although the food was always dire. Stuck with both feet firmly in the 1980s.' She grimaced. 'Chips *avec tout les plats*.'

'Well, I'm a chef, so I'm hoping to improve things in that department at least.'

'Oh really? So the Beeswhistle's new menu is going to be all cheeseburgers and apple pie?' She put on a terrible American accent. 'Extra pickles, hold the mayo!'

'I'm actually Cordon Bleu trained, so...'

But Sophia ignored her. 'My husband, Xavier, and I are in the catering business as well. We own the Quill next door.'

'Oh yes? I've heard good things.'

'You're too sweet!' Sophia simpered. 'Our goal was to bring a city sensibility to a rural setting, and it's actually been the most tremendous success. It's our attention to detail that gives us the edge. Our team has a professionalism that can sometimes be lacking in other local establishments. You must come along and sample our wares! Just let me know when you're coming and I'll make sure I'm there. I tend to be at our London residence during the week.'

Cassidy gaped at her. 'You have a house in London as well?'

'Of course! In Notting Hill.' Sophia seemed to think this was completely normal. 'So when's the Beeswhistle's grand reopening?'

'Not for a quite a while, I'm afraid. As I said, it's a bomb site right now.'

Sophia waved a hand airily. 'Oh, I'm sure you'll sort that out, you seem like a resourceful girl. Just try not to gamble the place away in the meantime – I know what you Beeswhistles are like!' Her laugh was like the tinkling of fairy bells, but her stare was granite-hard. 'Anyway, I must dash, such a delight to meet you, Cassidy. I look forward to our paths crossing again soon.'

Then, with a toss of her princess hair, Sophia was gone, and moments later the biggest and shiniest SUV rolled out of the parking lot, leaving Cassidy with two distinct impressions. Firstly, that if Sophia was in charge of the keys, it was going to be harder to get inside Dithercott Manor than she first thought. And, secondly, that Cassidy's misgivings about the Bamford-Bligh family appeared to have been entirely correct.

SEVEN

'Do you want to keep this, love?'

Cassidy looked up from where she was scrubbing the path to see Mike, the contractor from Hump 'n' Dump Garden Clearance, waving a broken gnome at her.

'No thanks,' she said, 'unless you've seen its head anywhere.'

He grunted and chucked the decapitated statue on top of the growing pile of rubbish in the skip. They were making progress, albeit slowly.

Mike had arrived earlier that morning while Cassidy was taking Nora to school, and by the time she'd got back, he had already cleared an old wire bed frame, a pile of brick rubble and seven dismembered chairs from the raised beds. She could now almost envisage the rows of carrots, beans and chard she hoped to grow there.

As Cassidy worked, positivity bubbled up inside her, giving her the sort of boost she usually only got from her first coffee of the day. It was Friday, the end of their first week in Dithercott – a week which had started out so bleakly. But now they had a working oven, a clean-ish kitchen and the beginnings of what could potentially be a charming garden. Of course, they also still had no water in the bathroom, a hole in the bedroom ceiling, zero furniture, a leaky roof and the lingering smell of sour beer, damp and drains (which no amount of airing seemed to shift, despite keeping so many windows open that they had to wear woolly hats inside).

Focus on the positive, focus on the positive. Cassidy had taken to repeating it like a mantra.

The best thing to happen this week, though, was that Nora had fallen head over heels in love with Dithercott Primary. She had already been Star of the Day twice, had given a presentation to her class on life in Sacramento (quite a feat for a girl who hated public speaking) and had been selected for the netball team, despite never having played in her life. And she had friends! Not just Tilly, but Kira, Rose, Olive, Harry – Nora had mentioned so many different names that Cassidy had lost track of them. She had taken to walking home after school with her new friends, climbing trees and playing games as they went, and she had already invited the entire class to the inn to celebrate her tenth birthday next month, a first for Nora who had never asked for a birthday party before, let alone one with schoolfriends. For Cassidy, it was yet another incentive to get the inn ship-shape in time for her daughter's special day.

As Cassidy scrubbed at a black stain on the garden path, a furry face bumped up against hers.

'Hey, Hermione,' she said, smiling as the cat nudged at her cheek.

They had now discovered that Hermione was a 'him' rather than 'her', but the name had stuck, as had the cat. Cassidy had asked around in the neighbourhood, and the general consensus seemed to be that he had been abandoned by the Diaggios. And despite her wariness, he was such an affectionate animal, and made Nora so happy, that even Cassidy had to admit that she enjoyed having him around.

'Cooee! Cassidy? Are you there, love?'

Mrs Timothy appeared around the side of the inn, dressed head-to-toe in mauve velour.

'Well, this is looking better!' She surveyed the garden, hands on hips. 'I can almost remember how nice it used to look when Martin was here.' She bent down and swiftly plucked a weed from the paving. 'I'll bring you some cuttings. I've got a Japonica that would look lovely against that wall.'

Cassidy leant back on her heels. 'What are you up to this morning, Mrs T?'

'I was actually just on my way to the church hall for Zumba and I thought, "I bet Cassidy would enjoy that," so I made a detour to come here. I imagine you have quite a nimble pelvis.'

'Um – thank you?' Cassidy smirked at the unconventional compliment. 'It's kind of you to think of me, but I've never done Zumba before, so...'

'We've all got to start somewhere. You'll be fine in what you're wearing, dear, Jasha isn't fussy when it's your first time.' Mrs Timothy waited, smiling expectantly. 'Well, come on then, look lively. We best not be late or we'll end up in the front row, and, believe me, you don't want that sort of scrutiny on your first merengue!'

Cassidy hesitated. There was still so much to do in the garden, and taking an hour off to test the nimbleness of her pelvis seemed an unnecessary waste of time, but judging by the determined set of Mrs Timothy's jaw she wasn't going to take no for an answer. Besides, it could turn out to be a good opportunity to meet some more of the villagers.

Cassidy called over to the contractor. 'Can you cope on your own for a bit, Mike?'

He held up an arm to signal this was fine with him.

'Okay then.' She jumped up, brushing the dirt off her trousers. 'Lead the way, Mrs T.'

· · ·

The church hall was a compact brick building at the far end of the high street that was set back from the street with a stretch of grass out front. Inside, the hall was packed with women, mostly around Mrs Timothy's age, but Cassidy recognised a few mums from the school gate as well. And at the front, standing head and shoulders above everyone else, was the only man in the room. He was bald and heavily muscled, with a neck that somehow appeared wider than his head, and was dressed for competitive weightlifting, but with a scarlet scarf trimmed with jingles about his hips.

'Jasha's from Slovakia,' explained Mrs Timothy. 'He's a builder by trade, but he started running Zumba classes to help him to learn English and, well, we all just *love* him. His classes have given me a new lease of life.' As they approached, her voice became louder and slower. 'Good morning, Jasha! How are you today?'

'I am well, Mrs Timothy, thank you.' He replied in smooth English, with only the hint of an accent.

'This is Cassidy, she's just moved here from America. She's a Zumba virgin.'

Jasha raised an eyebrow. 'A virgin, you say?'

'At Zumba, yes,' said Cassidy quickly. 'Not at, you know... other activities.'

'Don't worry, I will be gentle with you,' he said with a wink.

Mrs Timothy clasped her hands at her chest. 'Ooh, Jasha, you made a joke! Your English is coming on a treat!' She turned back to Cassidy. 'You should talk to Jasha about the work that needs doing at the inn. He's very handy. Plumbing, carpentry, plastering – the lot.'

'You need a builder?' He produced a card from somewhere in the region of his groin and pressed it into her hands. 'Special rate for my Zumba ladies.' He flashed his teeth, then bounded onto the low stage at the front of the room and boomed: 'Okay, let's get this show on the highway!'

'Bidi Bidi Bom Bom' burst out of the speakers and, like a
well-drilled flash mob, the room instantly broke into a complicated routine. Cassidy tried her best to keep up, but after
colliding with a table of Sunday School crafts during her
attempt at a travelling salsa – sending a toilet roll Jesus and all
his disciples tumbling like skittles – she gave up and jiggled on
the spot like the only sober person at a wedding.

'Hey, new girl!' barked Jasha. 'You gotta move your hips!'

Cassidy fired him a salute and was doing her best to copy
the woman in front (who must have been twice her age, yet
moved with the sinuousness of a Latina teenager) when across
the hall she spotted a vaguely familiar face. It took Cassidy a
moment to place her. It was the woman she'd seen scowling at
her from the post office window. Her bleached-blonde hair was
teased into a rigid helmet, and she was executing the dance
moves with the grim laser focus of a chess grandmaster. So
intent was she on perfecting the moves that the woman seemed
not to have noticed Cassidy's presence, which was a relief as she
was struggling to get the hang of even the most basic of steps.

At the end of the hour, Cassidy was whimperingly grateful
for the tea urn and biscuits that had been laid out in the kitchen,
where she was reunited with a tomato-faced Mrs Timothy.

'I'm exhausted,' said Cassidy. 'I have no idea how y'all
kept up.'

'To be honest, I'm quite surprised you were so bad at it,
Cassidy love,' said Mrs Timothy, although her voice was warm
as she bit into a Custard Cream. 'I'm sure you'll get the knack
after a few sessions.'

'Let's hope so.' Cassidy pointed in the direction of the dour
woman she'd noticed earlier, who was now standing on her
own, sipping a cup of tea. 'Who's that over there?'

'Bettina Flint. She runs the post office with her husband,
Ian. Come on, I'll introduce you.'

Judging by the way she had been scowling at her from the

post office window, Cassidy wasn't sure she wanted to be introduced; nevertheless, she followed Mrs Timothy through the crowd of chatting women towards her.

'Morning, Bettina! Sweaty one today.'

The woman inclined her head. 'Mrs Timothy.'

'Bettina, I'd like you to meet Cassidy. She's just moved into the inn, which makes you neighbours.' She raised her white brows. 'So let's be neighbourly, shall we?'

'Pleasure to meet you,' she said after a beat, looking as if it was anything but.

'Bettina and Ian don't approve of an American taking over the Beeswhistle,' Mrs Timothy told Cassidy. Her tone was teasing, but dots of colour appeared high on the woman's narrow cheeks in response.

'That's not the case at all,' said Bettina. 'We had just hoped, after the frankly appalling experience with the last people, that the new owners of the inn might be someone from around here. Someone *local*.'

'Well, I guess I am kind of a local,' said Cassidy, 'just a few hundred years back.'

'Indeed.' The tendons in Bettina's neck stood out like ropes. 'If you'll excuse me, I must get back to the post office. We're expecting a delivery of communion cards and Ian has a golfing tournament.'

As she made a beeline for the exit, Mrs Timothy watched her go. 'Dear oh dear,' she muttered. 'I'd hoped she might give you a chance because you're a Beeswhistle, but it looks like she's already made up her mind.'

'Why does she have a problem with Americans?'

'Oh, it's not just Americans. Bettina would have a problem with you taking over the inn whether you were from Brazil, Italy or even London.'

'Isn't that a bit small-minded?'

Mrs Timothy rubbed her cheek. 'You have to understand

that the Flints bore the brunt of the Diaggios' hooliganism, partly because the inn is opposite the Post Office, but also because that thug Dave Diaggio had a grudge against them. At one point, the Flints were on the verge of selling the post office and leaving the village. Bettina is Dithercott born and bred, so you can imagine how bad things had got.'

'Why did the Diaggios have a grudge against them?'

'It started because their kids were stealing sweets from the post office and Ian went to speak to them about it. Mrs Diaggio basically told him to eff off, and then, that night, a tin of red paint was thrown over the post office window. It caused terrible damage. I can still see Bettina's tearful face now...' She sighed. 'Anyway, they reported it to the police, and from then on it was out-and-out warfare. Not a week went by without some trouble at the post office. The police did get involved, but the Diaggios were a wily bunch and none of it could ever be pinned on them. There's a bench on the green that's a memorial to Bettina's late mother, and the final straw for her was when someone – I think you can guess who – covered it in graffiti.'

'Oh my gosh, that's terrible... But surely Bettina realises that the fact that I'm not from Dithercott doesn't automatically mean I'm out to destroy her? That doesn't make any sense.'

'You'd think so, but you've got to understand that her fears aren't rational. As far as she's concerned, you're an outsider, like the Diaggios, so just you being here is a threat to her happiness – to her whole way of life, in fact. It's nothing personal, but she was so scarred by the previous ordeal, she's just terrified it's going to happen again.' Mrs Timothy dropped her voice. 'Plus, of course, our Bettina is a terrible snob. She's worried you'll corrupt the entire village with your dodgy vowels and pink hair. Which I *love* by the way. Anyway, try not to worry about it, I'm sure the Flints will come round in time.' She didn't sound convinced, though. 'I'd best be getting on, lovey, it's my gardening group in an hour and we've got a guest speaker who's a bigwig in the hydrangea world. See you soon!'

After Mrs Timothy had gone, Cassidy said goodbye to Jasha, promising to return next week and apologising for her lack of coordination – 'Yes, you were very bad,' he agreed, though his voice was kind – and she was making her way down the path, thinking over what Mrs Timothy had just told her about the Flints, when she heard the tinkling of a bicycle bell.

'Hello there!'

It was Reverend Keating. He swerved to a stop and jumped off his bike in an impressively athletic fashion. He really did look more like a movie star playing the part of a vicar, than an actual vicar. Cassidy was suddenly conscious of her flushed face and sweaty everything, and she swiped away a clump of hair that had been clinging to her damp cheek.

'How are you this morning, Miss Beeswhistle?'

'I'm great, thank you, Reverend. And please, call me Cassidy.'

He smiled delightedly. 'Then you must call me James. Were you just at Zumba?'

'Yup. It very nearly destroyed me.'

James chuckled. 'Ah yes, I've heard Jasha's quite the taskmaster.' He glanced down the street in the direction of the inn. 'Are you walking home?'

She nodded.

'Would you mind if I accompanied you?'

Cassidy felt a pleasant twinge of surprise. 'Sure, that would be nice.'

They started along the high street together, with James wheeling his bike alongside, although not before he had exchanged positions with her so that he was closer to the oncoming traffic. Perhaps it was his gentlemanly manners, but something about James reminded Cassidy of her father. His presence generated in her the same sense of security and comfort that Joe had always given her, although on a far lesser scale. She barely knew him, but she could feel in her bones that he was one of the good guys – and not just because of what the clerical collar represented.

'So, how are you settling in?' he asked. 'It must be quite a change from California.'

'It is, but I think we're doing pretty well. Nora loves school, which I'm just thrilled about.'

'Oh yes, Dithercott Primary is a very special place. Your daughter has Miss Poppy as a teacher, I think? I always like to say she should be called Miss Poppins – practically perfect in every way!'

Noting the warmth in his voice, it suddenly occurred to Cassidy that perhaps James was dating the teacher. They would certainly make a wholesome couple, and she doubted the reverend's dazzling good looks had gone unnoticed by his other parishioners. Well, if that was the case, then lucky old Miss Poppy.

Just then, an elderly man walking an equally doddery dog waved from the other side of the street. 'Morning, Reverend! Lovely day for it.'

'Hello, William!' He gestured towards the dog. 'How's Belle's leg?'

'A little stiff, but on the mend. She'll be back terrorising the local squirrels before we know it!'

After the man had gone, James asked: 'Have you got to know many people in the village yet?'

'A few. I ran into Sophia Bamford-Bligh the other day.'

He frowned. 'Oh, you mean Sophia Quill? She generally goes by her husband Xavier's name. Perhaps she used her maiden name so you'd know exactly who you were dealing with.'

Surprised by the edge to his voice, Cassidy looked at him as he continued.

'The Bamford-Bligh family has always been very supportive of St Andrew's and have contributed a great deal to the village, but the Quills...' James stopped himself. 'I could be speaking out of turn, but I fear Sophia may be a little unnerved by your arrival here in Dithercott.'

'Why would she have a problem with me being here?' Cassidy hadn't meant it to come out quite so forcefully, but she was feeling a little raw from the run-in with Bettina Flint.

Thankfully, James didn't seem fazed. 'It could be that she fears that the newly renovated Beeswhistle Inn will be a threat to her own gastropub, the Quill. There aren't many other good restaurants in the area.' James's forehead puckered. 'Or I suppose it's possible she's worried about the Lost Deed of Beeswhistle, although that does seem a little far-fetched.'

Cassidy looked up sharply. 'Is that the document my dad asked you about in his emails?'

'It is, yes. Although, as I said to him, it's assumed to be a myth. I'm sure there would be some sort of record if such an important document ever existed.'

'But what is it exactly? I mean, what was the deed rumoured to be?'

James slowed to a halt. Cassidy noticed they were right outside a cafe called the Buttered Crumpet that had been on her list of places to visit in the village. It had the look of a traditional English tearoom, and every time she had walked past, the scent of warm sugar and burnished dough had wafted out to greet her, as comforting as a hug.

'How about I tell you about it over a cup of tea and a cake?' said James.

Cassidy couldn't think of a nicer way to recover after Zumba. 'I'd like that, thank you.'

'After you,' he said, flashing his Hollywood smile.

EIGHT

Cassidy took a step inside the Buttered Crumpet and then froze on the 'HELLO, GORGEOUS' doormat. The place looked like it had been decorated by a fourteen-year-old girl with too much pocket money and a car-boot-sale addiction. Every surface, every shelf – even the space along the skirting boards – was crowded with knick-knacks: Chinese waving cats, garlands of paper flowers, snow globes, Day of the Dead skulls, glow-in-the-dark Virgin Mary statuettes. The green wallpaper was covered in a cacti design, while rugs in a rainbow of colours were scattered over the floorboards. It was a room that sneered at the word 'beige'.

'Quite a place, isn't it?' said James, smiling at her open mouth.

'It's... incredible. Like the Sistine Chapel of kitsch.'

He chuckled. 'Dale would enjoy that. He's the Buttered Crumpet's owner.' He signalled to one of the few empty tables. 'Let's sit in the window.'

Cassidy found herself trying to identify the notes in the baking scents coming from the kitchen. There was cinnamon and vanilla – those were easy enough – but was that cardamon too? And something sharper, perhaps lemon syrup... She had never worked as a professional pastry chef but had covered the basics in her training and always enjoyed her Sunday baking sessions with Nora.

They settled at the table in the bay window, its carved legs and lacy tablecloth clashing with the modern plastic chairs, and Cassidy found herself face-to-face with a gigantic painting of Elvis Presley on the opposite wall.

'One of Dale's portraits,' said James, noting her interest. 'He's a keen amateur artist as well as being a terrific baker.'

'And an Elvis fan, clearly.' Cassidy peered at it more closely. 'Although, *is* that meant to be Elvis? It looks more like Donald Trump in a wig.'

'Actually, it's Ron Dunphy in a wig,' came a voice behind them. 'Though now you come to mention it, I suppose he does have a Trump-esque quality.'

Cassidy jumped and turned to find a trim man of middle years, his trendy tortoiseshell glasses incongruous with the frilly apron around his waist. Her face went hot at being overheard, but at least the man looked amused.

'Morning, Your Rev-ness,' he said. 'Who's the art critic?'

'Dale, I'd like to introduce you to Cassidy Beeswhistle. She's just moved into the inn.'

'Ooh, the long-lost Beeswhistle! I've heard all about you from Mrs Timothy, though she didn't mention how pretty you are. Quite the stunner, isn't she, James?'

The reverend's cheeks went pink, and he suddenly found his hands fascinating.

Dale giggled – 'Just teasing, Rev' – then turned back to Cassidy. 'I said to Ron just this morning, "Won't it be nice to have the Beeswhistle open again?" We're not at all keen on the Quill. It's like having your tea in an airport departure lounge.' He paused. 'Ron's my husband, by the way. And an Elvis tribute act,' he added, gesturing to the painting.

'Ah, that makes sense,' said Cassidy. 'It's great to meet you, Dale. I love your cafe. It's so joyful.'

'Thank you! It's not to everyone's taste, but, as I always say, you can't please everyone so you might as well just please yourself.' He produced a notepad. 'What can I get you, Cassidy?'

'I'll have a flat white please, with oat milk if you have it.'

'So that'll be an English breakfast tea with semi-skimmed.' Dale chuckled. 'I'm afraid we're a coffee-free zone. As far as I'm concerned, it's the devil's drink. Oops, sorry, Rev.'

James waved it off with a smile. 'I'll have an English breakfast too, thank you, Dale. And perhaps some crumpets with jam too – if you'd like, Cassidy?'

'Absolutely. I've never had a crumpet.'

Dale gasped theatrically. 'Never had a crumpet! These Americans, *so* uncivilised... Be right back, folks.'

When Dale had disappeared back into the kitchen, James folded his hands on the table, as if bringing a meeting to order. 'So, the Lost Deed of Beeswhistle.'

'I found some notes about it in my father's file, but I can't make sense of them. His writing was always illegible.'

'I can tell you what I know. You're familiar with the account of how Bertie Beeswhistle lost Dithercott Manor to Henry Bamford-Bligh in a game of dice?'

Cassidy nodded.

'So Bertie ran off to America to avoid his debtors and the estate has been in the hands of the Bamford-Bligh family ever since, in accordance with the terms of the duo's original bet. Except...' James paused for dramatic effect. '...if you believe in the existence of the Lost Deed of Beeswhistle, this shouldn't actually be the case.'

Cassidy leant forward, hanging on his every word. His voice was rich and melodic, designed for storytelling.

'According to the rumours, Bertie and Henry never agreed that Dithercott Manor would remain in the hands of the

Bamford-Bligh family in perpetuity. Rather than gamble away his home forever, what Bertie *actually* proposed was that the manor should be occupied by the Bamford-Blighs for two generations and when it came time for the next heir to inherit the estate, it would revert back to the ownership of the Beeswhistle family. The story goes that before Bertie fled England, a deed was drawn up and signed by both men confirming this unusual arrangement, although, as you know, such a document has never been found and it's now widely assumed that no such agreement ever took place.' James dropped his voice. 'My feeling is, though, that the story had to originate from somewhere. It's not the sort of thing that grows out of nothing. And if it were true...'

Cassidy's eyes had become saucer-like. 'Then it would make *me* the rightful owner of Dithercott Manor,' she finished in a whisper.

'Indeed.' James sat back with a satisfied grin. 'So now you see why Sophia Quill might have been a little less than thrilled to have a Beeswhistle back in Dithercott.'

Just then, Dale arrived with their order. 'Right, that's a pot of English breakfast and crumpets for two.' He took in Cassidy's dazed expression. 'Is she all right, Rev?'

'I've just been telling Cassidy about the Lost Deed of Beeswhistle.'

'Ah, no wonder. Just imagine Sophia Quill's face if the deed *did* turn up. I'd pay good money to see Her Snootyship booted out of the manor!'

He left, chuckling to himself, but Cassidy was still trying to process what she'd just heard.

'So, you see,' James went on, 'the reason your father was so interested was because if the deed were found, it could mean that your family might have a legitimate claim to the estate. Though, as I said to Joe, there's little hope of finding it after two hundred years. If it's anywhere, it's probably somewhere in

Dithercott Manor – and if that's the case, the Quills will make absolutely sure it never sees the light of day.'

'I understand,' Cassidy said. The idea that she might inherit Dithercott Manor after all these years: it was the stuff of fairy tales! And even if the deed did miraculously turn out to exist, Cassidy would never in a million years attempt to action it: she couldn't have lived with herself after forcing a family out of their home, however dubiously the Bamford-Blighs might have come into possession of it. Besides, what would she do with a ginormous stately home? She had more than enough on her plate trying to fix up a very small inn. But for one brief, wonderful moment, Cassidy had let herself imagine what it would be like to live in such a beautiful place, and it was a feeling she would savour for some time. She smiled at James. 'It's a fantastic story, and you told it beautifully. You should have been an actor.'

James laughed. 'Stage, pulpit – not much difference really! Though I do have more of a face for church rather than television, I think.'

Taking in his perfectly symmetrical features, Cassidy wasn't entirely sure she agreed.

Later that afternoon, Cassidy was out in the garden sweeping up the remaining dust and debris. Mike had driven off about an hour ago with a skipful of rubbish and even he had been impressed by the transformation. 'I can just imagine sitting out here in the summer with a nice cold pint,' he'd said, surveying the space.

Now that it had been cleared, Cassidy could see exactly what she could do with the garden. There was room for at least eight tables for customers, a paved area that would accommodate a large grill for summer barbecues and a huge expanse of lawn, which would easily fit swings and a climbing frame and still have plenty of room for games.

Cassidy grinned to herself, leaning on the handle of the broom to survey her little kingdom. She was on her way to making a wonderful new life for her and Nora.

'Mom?'

At the sound of her daughter's voice, Cassidy looked up to see her rushing around the side of the inn, but her happiness at seeing her home was short-lived. Her daughter's cheeks were blotchy and wet from crying, and she had muddy streaks all over her legs. She flew straight into Cassidy's arms and clung to her like a life raft.

'Honey? Have you hurt yourself?' Cassidy struggled to sound calm as all sorts of horrific scenarios flashed through her mind. 'Can you tell me what's happened?'

Nora's voice was choked with tears. 'I was playing hide-and-seek in the woods on the walk home from school with Tilly and some other kids, and I wandered away from the path trying to find a good place to hide. I jumped over the other side of the stream and then suddenly I heard this really loud barking and these dogs ran up to me. I was so scared, I thought they might attack me! And then...' She seemed to struggle to get the next words out, and when she did her voice was barely audible. 'Then this man appeared.'

Cassidy's throat felt so tight she could barely get the words out. 'It's okay, just tell me what happened, sweetie.'

Nora bit her lip, trying to calm her sobs. 'He called the dogs back to him, but he was so *cross* with me, Mom! He was going on about me being on the manor's land, and that I wasn't allowed to be there or something. I tried to tell him that I was just playing a game, but he wouldn't listen. He was really tall and scary. And he was carrying a gun.' Her voice broke on the final word.

Fury burned inside Cassidy at the thought of this man terrifying her daughter. And how utterly predictable that it was someone from Dithercott Manor! Perhaps it was even Sophia's husband? As she pulled Nora into a fierce hug, she was already acting out a terrible and bloody revenge on the entire Bamford-Bligh family inside her head.

'You did absolutely nothing wrong, honey,' she said, through clenched teeth. 'I'm going to take you to Angeline's, then I'm going up to the manor to have a word with this man myself.'

It certainly wasn't the ideal circumstances for her first visit to the Beeswhistle ancestral home, but right now Cassidy's only concern was finding the bully who scared Nora and making him regret ever raising his voice to her daughter.

NINE

Angeline had given Cassidy directions to Dithercott Manor, but even without her help, the driveway would have been impossible to miss. After following the estate's boundary wall that ran alongside the lane for a half mile, she had abruptly come to a gap, flanked on either side by a pair of imposing stone pillars, one topped with an eagle, its wings spread wide as if about to take flight, and the other a stag, mirroring the Beeswhistle crest on the inn's sign. Cassidy was surprised the Bamford-Blighs hadn't removed this reminder of the former owners, but they did look very impressive. Surprisingly, there was no gate, but there was a grid across the road at the entrance, which Cassidy assumed was intended to keep the deer in. *Or the peasants out*, she thought grimly, as she picked her way across the bars.

She looked up the hill to the place where the manor should be, but it was already getting dark and a thick mist had settled in, giving the impression that the road ahead of her wound into nothingness. There were no lights along the drive, just the black skeletons of trees standing on either side, which gave the landscape an eerie slasher-movie vibe that entirely suited Cassidy's mood. A gust of wind rattled their bare branches, and the ghostly whisper seemed to be warning her not to go any further.

'Just you try to stop me,' she muttered, storming up the drive, the thought of Nora's tears spurring her on.

The hill was steep and the driveway long, and pretty soon Cassidy's furious march had morphed into a weary slog. The fog muffled the familiar countryside sounds and with nothing but a sea of grey surrounding her, she could well have believed she was the only person left on earth. Gradually, however, the dark shape of the manor began to reveal itself, the lights in the windows shimmering dully as if the whole scene was being viewed underwater. As she got closer, she felt a tingling on the back of her neck: the same sensation as she'd had before, as if the house was watching her – or at least someone hidden behind its endless rows of windows.

The driveway ended in a broad circle in front of the house, in the centre of which was an elaborate marble statue that might have been plucked from a fountain in Rome. Cassidy's footsteps crunched on the gravel as she approached the front door, passing Sophia Quill's SUV and a battered Land Rover, plus a couple of small cars that probably belonged to the manor's employees. She imagined it would take a whole army of people to run this place.

The knocker was so heavy, it took both hands and all her strength to lift it, and when Cassidy dropped it, the giant front door that had clearly been built to withstand battering rams rattled on its hinges. It was only then that she noticed the video doorbell on the wall nearby. Not in the mood for waiting, she jabbed at that too.

The woman who answered the door had steel-grey hair and was wearing a navy trouser suit. Cassidy was no expert on English country houses, but she'd watched enough period dramas to guess this was the housekeeper.

'Can I help you?'

The woman's eyes flicked over her, and Cassidy wished she'd changed out of the sweatpants she was still wearing from Zumba, or maybe brushed her hair. And – *jeez* – was that a whiff of BO?

She held her head up a little higher, reminding herself she had every right to be here. 'Good afternoon to you,' said Cassidy, trying to match the woman's tone. 'I wish to speak to Mrs Quill.'

'And you are?'

'Cassidy Beeswhistle.'

A flicker of surprise ruffled the woman's professionally neutral features. 'I'll see if Mrs Quill is available. Just one moment please.'

She disappeared inside, leaving the door ajar. Warmth and light poured out from the hallway, and Cassidy got a glimpse of Turkish rugs, polished wood furniture and a sweeping staircase – exactly the sort of decor she had been expecting. Although what she hadn't anticipated was how warm and inviting it would feel. It was a long way from the chilly Dracula's castle she'd built in her mind.

From inside the house, she heard a child shouting and then another join in, followed by the air-raid siren wail of a cry. Moments later, there was the clacking of heels across the floor and Sophia Quill appeared at the door.

'Cassidy, this is a surprise.'

She wrapped her cardigan around her and stepped out onto the doormat, pulling the door behind her, as if she was worried Cassidy might bolt past her into the house. 'What brings you all the way out here?'

'I'm sorry to bother you, but I've got a very upset kid at home. She was playing in the woods when a man from your estate yelled at her and made her cry.'

'Oh gosh, I'm terribly sorry! What happened?'

'His dogs barked at her, then apparently he got really angry and accused her of trespassing. She's only nine, and she was terrified because he had a gun. Might it have been your husband?'

'Gracious no, Xav wouldn't be caught dead wandering around the woods. That would be Ned.' Sophia's mouth twitched, as if the name caused her discomfort. 'I think he's round the back of the house, you're welcome to go and speak to him about this yourself. As you can probably hear, I'm a little tied up right now.' She gave another tight smile, as more cries came from inside. 'Mummy duty calls, I'm sure you understand.'

'Of course. And thank you,' said Cassidy, but Sophia had already shut the door behind her.

If she was annoyed that Sophia wouldn't deal with her staff herself, Cassidy's curiosity at getting a closer look at the manor overrode that. She slowly made her way around its exterior, the windows casting golden squares on the dark lawn to light her way. Cassidy ran her hand over the walls, as if to absorb the memories they held, admiring how the centuries-old stone had been weathered to a velvet-smooth finish. The manor had stood here for so long that it seemed part of the landscape – and nature had certainly done her bit to reclaim it, scattering the stone with lichens and sending vines snaking up its high walls.

The mist had now lifted a little and in the distance Cassidy could make out the black silhouettes of trees and hills. She was passing a clock tower, its hands stuck at midday (or, more appropriately for the eeriness of the atmosphere, at midnight), when suddenly there was a flash of movement and she swung round to catch a white owl flying past, glowing ghost-like in the light from the house. Barely breathing, Cassidy watched it until it was swallowed up in the darkness. Then, through the gloom, she became aware of a faint thumping noise and without a second thought, she struck out across the lawn towards its source, assuming it would be where she'd find this Ned character.

As it got louder, she realised it was leading her towards a cluster of outbuildings at the end of the driveway that had curved around the side of the house. In the centre of the buildings was a well-lit courtyard and, as she approached, she was greeted by a volley of barking.

The dogs – two spaniels and a Labrador – instantly fell silent at one word from the man who was swinging an axe at a stump of wood. Cassidy knew that she'd found her guy. He was dressed like a groundsman – in trousers and a work shirt with the sleeves rolled up despite the chill – and he was tall, just as Nora had said, with the wiry, wind-beaten look of someone who spend their life working outside. He didn't look English, however. His hair was jet-black (and, in her opinion, in serious need of a cut) and he had the sort of skin that looked like it would turn a deep golden-brown from just the briefest glimpse of sun.

He didn't look up as she stalked across the gravel towards him.

'Excuse me?' she said, raising her voice to be heard above the chopping.

He swung the axe down, the muscles and tendons in his forearms moving beneath his skin.

'Are you Ned?'

'I am.'

Cassidy waited, but he still didn't stop or make eye contact, and she bristled at his rudeness.

'My daughter was playing in the woods this afternoon and apparently you got mad at her for being on the estate's land. You really scared her.'

'Well, perhaps you should teach your daughter to stay off other people's land.'

Cassidy's mouth fell open. 'Is that all you've got to say? She's really upset. What sort of person yells at a nine-year-old?'

'I'm afraid I'm not in the habit of asking trespassers how old they are.'

He hurled the logs he'd just chopped onto a pile.

'She was terrified,' Cassidy persisted. 'She thought your dogs were going to attack her.'

'Do these dogs look capable of hurting anyone?'

He had a point; one glance in their direction and they all started wagging their tails. Cassidy had an urge to pet them, but there was no way she'd give this rude man the satisfaction.

'How was my daughter meant to know that? They ran at her, barking like crazy, and then you appeared like some crazed gunman and started yelling at her. What was she supposed to think?'

He launched the axe up into the air again. 'Like I said, it's not my fault that your child was trespassing.'

But Cassidy wasn't going to give up. 'I've walked that path and there are no signs to tell people that it's private property. No fence or boundary marking. How the hell was my daughter supposed to know where the public land ends and the estate begins?'

He finally stopped and turned to look at her, resting his hands on the head of the axe. His eyes were set wide apart and his cheekbones were high and angular, giving him a haughty look. It seemed the Bamford-Bligh family's sense of entitlement even extended to their staff. Cassidy jutted out her chin, refusing to be cowed.

'You're not from round here, are you? The land on one side of the stream is for public access, and the other side belongs to the manor. Everyone in the village knows that. It's not my duty to inform every American tourist who blunders blindly around the woods of that fact.'

Cassidy's hands clenched into fists. 'I'm not a tourist, my

daughter and I have just moved here. And I'm afraid my Dithercott welcome pack was missing the section on the exact by-laws and details of land ownership in the area.'

He ignored her sarcasm and was now regarding her with interest. 'You've moved here? I didn't catch your name.'

'Cassidy Beeswhistle.'

The man's lips curved upwards and his eyes flew wide. 'Well, I never...'

'Maybe you enjoy scaring kids, but...'

He was looking at her intently, as if she was some rare artefact he'd just dug up. She felt exposed, her insides flinching strangely in response.

'What the hell are you staring at?' she snapped.

'I'm sorry, I'm just – you really don't look much like Bertie.'

'I beg your pardon?'

'There's a portrait of him in one of the guest rooms. Ugly sod, he was.'

Cassidy glared at him. 'So you terrify my daughter and now you're insulting my ancestors. You really are unbelievable!'

With a shrug, he picked up the axe and returned his attention to the logs.

'Are you not even going to apologise?'

'I'm sorry that your daughter is irrationally afraid of dogs.'

'That's not what I...' Cassidy bit back the rest of her words; she clearly wasn't going to get any more out of him. 'Well, thank you *so* much for your valuable time. This has really been quite the pleasure. And if you ever upset my kid again, I'll be making a formal complaint to Mrs Quill – and I'm sure she'll have plenty to say about it.'

The man gave a derisive snort. 'I'm sure she will.'

With a grunt of frustration, Cassidy turned on her heel and started back the way she had come. It was properly dark now and she wasn't entirely sure she was even going in the right direction, but she was so angry, she didn't care.

She hadn't taken many steps when, behind her, the sound of chopping fell silent. Glancing back, she saw that the man was standing still, watching her go.

'Asshole,' she muttered savagely, storming blindly on into the blackness.

TEN

'You're not gonna believe this,' Nora said to Cassidy, as they stepped out of the inn's back door into the spring sunshine, 'but a Milky Way in England is the same as a Three Musketeers in America, and a Milky Way in America is called a Mars Bar over here!'

They were on their way to buy sweets to celebrate Nora's first week at Dithercott Primary, which meant a visit to the Old Post Office – and, most likely, another encounter with Bettina Flint. Cassidy didn't much care if the woman liked her or not, but she better not be rude to Nora, or God help her. She was still fired up after her encounter at the manor the previous night.

'Mom? Did you hear me?'

'Sorry, honey, I was miles away. So which are you gonna get? Mars Bar or Milky Way?'

Nora thought about this for a moment. 'Probably both. For research purposes.'

'Very wise.'

Cassidy looked up at the cloudless sky. She couldn't believe how erratic the weather was in this country. Last night, she could barely see her feet through the fog; this morning, it was so bright she could almost believe they were back in Sacramento (though it was thirty degrees colder than in California).

Nora bent down to pet Hermione, who was winding himself around her legs. 'And get this, Mom, they don't have Hershey's in England. Not even the Kisses!'

'No way! Though perhaps they have something even better.'

'That's exactly what I was thinking,' said Nora, as she hopscotched her way down the path.

It was a huge relief to see that Nora seemed unaffected by her scare in the woods – she hadn't even mentioned it again – but Cassidy was still angry about it. The rudeness of that groundsman! She kept thinking about the way he had stared at her, his dark eyes devouring her like prey, and her insides tensed at the memory.

'Tilly says I should get a mint Aero, but I literally have no idea what that is,' Nora went on.

'Let's get one of those too,' said Cassidy, the scrunched-up feeling inside her already starting to ease. She refused to let that idiot from the manor ruin another moment of her precious weekend with Nora.

The Old Post Office was another Tudor gem, and Cassidy had to grudgingly admit that the Flints had done a wonderful job of maintaining it. Even the rack of postcards by the door was tasteful: wood rather than plastic, and stocked with photos of pretty wildflowers and airbrushed cows. Inside, there was the scent of lavender and the strong impression that the shelves had been dusted and tidied that very second.

The Flints clearly ran a tight ship: everywhere you looked were handwritten signs seemingly designed to make the shopping experience as stressful as possible. 'Any melting of confectionery due to excessive handling during browsing MUST be paid for,' read one. 'THIS IS NOT A LIBRARY!!!' said another next to the newspapers.

The counter at the back of the shop was divided in half, with one side for post office services and the other for general purchases. Bettina Flint was standing on the non-post-office side, while next to her was a man who Cassidy assumed was Ian Flint.

As Cassidy herded Nora towards the shelves of sweets, she heard Bettina hiss: 'That's her. The *American*.'

'I see what you mean,' replied Ian. 'You didn't mention a child, though, Bettina.'

'I had no idea! There's no husband, as far as I've been told.'

In the barrage of muffled tutting that ensued, Cassidy resisted the urge to excessively handle *all* the confectionery, and instead focused on helping Nora work out whether wine gums were actually alcoholic.

Once Nora had made her selection, Cassidy herded her towards the door.

'Why don't you go and wait for me on the bench outside? I'll be straight out once I've paid, okay, sweetie?'

As she approached the counter, both Flints suddenly found something urgent to busy themselves with, Bettina rearranging the porcelain figurines on the shelf behind her, while Ian held up a newspaper in front of his face.

'Good morning, Bettina.'

The woman turned around very slowly, a porcelain bunny clutched to her chest.

'We met at Zumba? I'm Cassidy.'

'Yes, I remember you. Good morning.'

'Hi.' Cassidy smiled, then looked in Ian's direction. He was still hiding behind the newspaper, which she was amused to see he was holding upside down.

Bettina cleared her throat. 'This is my husband, Ian Flint.'

He slowly lowered his hands. 'Hello,' he said.

'Great to meet you, Ian.'

'Likewise. If you'll excuse me...' He ducked beneath the counter and didn't reappear again.

The rest of their business was conducted in silence, and Cassidy had turned to leave when she hesitated. She knew she was probably going to make the situation worse, but the Flints' muttered comments about Nora's parenthood were still ringing in her ears.

'Oh, just for your records, Bettina – there is no husband. Never has been. Just a fabulous one-night stand with a Colombian rock star.' With a grin and a wave, she skipped towards the door. 'See ya!'

Back at the inn, they were greeted by the scent of roasting chicken, which made a nice change from the usual notes of stale beer and rising damp. Angeline and Tilly would be arriving for lunch in an hour, so Cassidy went straight to the kitchen to check on the food. She threw in some shallots and garlic to cook in the chicken's juices, before starting work on a kale and avocado salad. Cassidy usually found cooking at home as relaxing as yoga, although today she felt as jittery as if she had an army of restaurant critics to impress. She had an idea she wanted to put to Angeline – an idea that could potentially make or break her ownership of the Beeswhistle Inn – and its success was largely dependent on her neighbour believing in her as a chef.

This had been her motivation for staying up until 2 a.m. to make a Japanese mille-crepe cake. You don't attempt a pudding that calls for 'a thousand pancakes' unless you're serious about impressing someone. Cassidy just hoped that Angeline would forgive the less than elegant surroundings. The building work hadn't started yet, and they were still making do with just the one table and camping chairs, as Cassidy hadn't had a chance to go furniture shopping, and though the interior was now at least clean (the raw patches on her hands testament to the hours of scrubbing that had been required), it still felt as though they were living in a squat. Strategically placed candles and vases of tulips could only do so much to banish the air of neglect.

Thankfully, Angeline was too distracted by the food to be worried about the scuffed walls, clanking pipes and lingering smell of drains.

'How do you even make chicken taste like this?' Her face was in raptures. 'It's like the megastar of chickens. It's... it's Hen-ifer Lopez. Or Meryl Cheep.'

'This salad is actually kind of nice too,' added Tilly.

Angeline gasped theatrically. 'I better get my scissors,' she said, having promised Cassidy a free haircut if she could get Tilly to eat kale.

'I'm so glad you're enjoying it,' said Cassidy. It had been a while since she'd cooked for anyone other than Nora, and she'd forgotten what a kick she got from people appreciating her food. Also, it would make what was coming next a whole lot easier.

'I had no idea you were such a talented chef,' Angeline went on. 'I reckon you'll clean up round here.'

'On that subject...' Cassidy put down her knife and fork. 'I know it's still a long way off, but I was thinking about staffing the inn when we reopen, and I wondered if, in theory, you might be interested in coming back to work here as manager.'

Angeline's fork froze in mid-air. 'Manager? I—'

'You know way more about running a pub than I do,' Cassidy cut in, 'and I reckon we'd be a good team. I mean, obviously we'd have to work out the details, as you have Tilly to think about, and I appreciate that the place is still a total wreck, so it's a leap of faith on your part, but I've got Jasha, the Zumba builder, coming to start work on the renovations next week, and I think that with my cooking and your expertise, we could make a real success of the place.'

Cassidy couldn't work out the expression on Angeline's face. Was that shock? Excitement? Horror? She really shouldn't have sprung this on her over lunch. Perhaps her neighbour actually hated the idea but was too embarrassed to say so. Well, too late now.

She ploughed on: 'I know you're trying to save up, so I thought this might give you a more reliable source of income than hairdressing, and you did say you missed working at the Beeswhistle, so...'

'Cassidy, I'm—'

'No need to give me an answer now! It's just something to think about. Food for thought.'

Angeline started to smile. 'If I could get a word in?'

'Sorry.' Cassidy grimaced. 'Go ahead.'

'Thank you. So, what I was *trying* to say is that I would absolutely love the job.'

'Really? I mean obviously we'd need to discuss all the details before making it official...'

'Of course, but in theory I'm one hundred per cent on board.' Angeline reached out to give her hand a squeeze. 'I'm thrilled you asked me, Cassidy, thank you. Like you said, I think we'd make a really good team.'

'I can't tell you how pleased I am to hear that!' Cassidy held up her wine glass. 'To us – and the new Beeswhistle.'

'The new Beeswhistle!'

They clinked glasses and the girls joined in too with their orange squash, the four of them toasting their future.

'Just one thing: no pigeon pies or turnip soup, okay?' Angeline gestured to her plate. 'And Khicken Kardashian here *must* be on the menu.'

Cassidy beamed at her. 'Deal.'

After they had finished lunch, Cassidy and Angeline took their espressos outside while the girls played upstairs.

'I think the guy was a groundsman, or perhaps a gardener,'

Cassidy was saying. She hadn't had the chance to tell Angeline about her run-in with Ned when she'd collected Nora last night, so she was now filling her in on all the details. 'Man, he was so arrogant!'

'This bloke, was he very tall? Black hair, olive skin?'

'Yeah, that's him. Have you had a problem with him too?'

'He's not a gardener, Cassidy. He owns the place.'

'No, it wasn't Sophia's husband, this dude's name was Ned.'

Angeline was nodding. 'Edward Bamford-Bligh. Lord of Dithercott Manor. Otherwise known as Ned.'

'But... I thought Sophia was in charge of the manor?'

'She'd certainly like to be. No, the entire estate passed to Ned a couple of years ago when his father, Humphrey Bamford-Bligh, passed away. Sophia is Ned's younger sister.'

It took a few moments for this to sink in. 'I don't believe it,' muttered Cassidy, running through their conversation in her head. 'He mentioned something about portraits in the guest wing, which I thought at the time was a weird thing for a groundsman to say, but if it's actually his home... Makes sense though – he was so thoroughly unlikeable, he had to be a Bamford-Bligh.' Her eyes bulged. 'Oh God, I basically threatened to get him fired! Why didn't he tell me who he was?'

'Ned's had a tough few years. Honestly, Cass, if you'd met him in better circumstances, I think you'd really like him. He used to be wildly popular round here. He always held the Dithercott fête up at the manor and he was always helping out at community events. He couldn't do enough for the village.'

'At the risk of feeling a modicum of sympathy for the guy, what happened?'

'He was engaged to this society heiress, Tamara something-something, I don't remember her name, but she was as blue-blooded as they come. Very pretty, extremely posh, but totally lacking in Ned's charm. More of a Sophia type, if you get my drift... Anyway, three years ago, just a few months before their big society wedding, she was killed in a car accident.'

Cassidy gasped. 'That's terrible...'

'Yeah, apparently she was driving too fast down the lane and crashed with a lorry. She was killed instantly, although her black Labrador, Mungo, survived. Since then, Ned won't let the dog out of his sight.'

Cassidy remembered the Labrador she'd seen at his side yesterday.

'Anyway, after Tamara's death Ned just seemed to shut down – heartbroken, I suppose, poor bloke. It's been three years now and we rarely see him in the village anymore. Ned and Sophia were never close, but she came to stay at the manor after the accident and just never seemed to leave. It's so obvious that she's angling to take over the estate...' Angeline pulled a face. 'But I guess Ned's been too distraught to worry about all that. In fact, I've heard a rumour he's planning to leave Dithercott for good. How did he seem to you?'

'I told you: cold, arrogant and unfriendly. Though, from what you just said, I guess he gets a pass.' She thought for a moment. 'I can't believe he and Sophia are related, they look totally different.'

'Half-siblings. They share a father, but Ned's mother was a Spanish countess and Sophia's mum was your classic decades-younger second wife. The word "gold-digger" has been mentioned, though not by me, obviously,' said Angeline, tweaking an eyebrow. 'Sophia and Xavier live in London during the week, where their kids go to school, then they're up here at weekends, throwing parties for their friends and having photo shoots for society magazines. Sophia absolutely loves the whole "lady of the manor" shtick. You'd never guess at Ned's background if you met him, but Sophia really likes to rub it in everyone's face.' Angeline tutted. 'Poor Ned. He was always the village's golden boy, you know? Incredibly well-to-do and obviously loaded, but just a really sweet guy.'

Cassidy obviously looked sceptical, because Angeline went on: 'I remember once I was on a walk with Tilly and she'd twisted her ankle down a rabbit hole. We were trying to walk home – me supporting a sobbing, limping Til – when Ned drove past. As soon as he saw us, he pulled over, then took us straight to the minor injuries unit twenty miles away, waited until Tilly had been seen and then drove us home again. *And* he sent her a get-well teddy the next day. You tell me those aren't the actions of a kind and decent man.'

'The guy I met last night would have driven straight past both of you, making sure he swerved through a puddle as he went so you were both soaked in dirty water.'

'No way.' Angeline shook her head decisively. 'Ned's genuinely nice – plus, of course, extremely handsome.'

Cassidy wrinkled her nose. 'You think?'

'Oh God, absolutely! You don't agree?'

'I didn't even notice, I was too busy trying not to completely lose my shit.'

'Well, take a closer look when you run into him again. Honestly, Cass, he's a stone-cold fox.'

'I think we'll probably have to agree to disagree on that one.'

Besides, if she could help it, Cassidy planned never to run into Ned Bamford-Bligh again – bad-behaviour pass or not.

ELEVEN

It was a long time since she'd had a man in her bedroom in such a compromising position, thought Cassidy, on finding herself cheek-to-cheek with Jasha's impressively toned glutes.

She was standing at the foot of a stepladder, holding it steady while he climbed up to plaster the crack in the spare-room ceiling, which would soon be Nora's bedroom. It had been raining on and off for days, turning the leak in the ceiling to a torrent, and having fixed the source of the problem, Jasha was now making good the water damage.

The Zumba-teacher/builder was proving to be a godsend. He had been working at the inn for two weeks now, speeding through Cassidy's to-do list with the same proficiency that he knocked out a salsa box step on a Friday morning. Occasionally, his apprentice, Lance, a local teenager with a non-existent work ethic, would bother to turn up as well. Cassidy had been working alongside the two of them as a way of keeping costs down and now knew more about dry rot and damp-proof coursing than she ever thought possible or, indeed, desirable.

They had been in Dithercott for a month now. Sometimes, Cassidy wished she was back in California – she missed

Manon, and had forgotten what it felt like to be warm – but as she walked the country lanes, her pulse would slow and her mind would calm in a way that never happened in Sacramento. Maybe she was imagining it, but there was a familiarity to the surroundings that might have come from her family's roots in the area. Besides, Nora's love for England was proving more than enough for both of them. Even the grey skies and drizzle were objects of adoration for her daughter, who relished standing in the rain the way most people felt about sunbathing. And she was picking up English-isms at lightning speed. Just that morning, she had reacted to Cassidy's irritation over a wet towel on the dusty floor with, 'Don't get your knickers in a twist, Mom!' which had made Cassidy almost teary with pride. It was wonderful to see Nora so at home here.

As he skimmed plaster onto the ceiling, Jasha was telling Cassidy about what he'd got up to at the weekend.

'... and then Suki waited in the emergency room for five hours so that Jasha Junior could have the Pokémon removed from his nose, while I stay at home with all the others. We watched *Fast and Furious* movies three, four, five and nine.'

'Aren't your kids a little too young to watch those movies?'

Jasha gave an offhand shrug. 'Most of the time they are fighting or sleeping.'

'I don't know how you and Suki do it. Four kids under six! Incredible...'

'My wife is a very strong woman.' He was silent for a moment, then asked: 'Why do you not have a family, Cassidy?'

'I do have a family. Nora.'

'No, I mean a proper family. With a man.'

Cassidy's entire body instantly tensed, and she forced herself to swallow down a four-lettered retort. It wasn't Jasha's fault that he'd accidentally landed a sharp kick to her Achilles heel, which was her deep-seated fear that she had failed Nora by not giving her a father. In her saner moments, she knew this was ridiculous; after all, she hadn't planned to get pregnant from a one-night stand with a rock star. It had been an accident – the best of all possible accidents, but an accident nonetheless. And it wasn't as though she hadn't given Nora's father ample chance to be involved in their child's life. When she had found out she was pregnant (after initially dismissing her weird symptoms as irritable bowel syndrome), Cassidy had immediately got in touch with the band's record company and told them she needed to contact the drummer about an 'urgent personal issue'. She knew they weren't just going to hand out his number; still, she had no idea just how hard it would be to get a message to him. In the end, after endless polite emails and letters had gone unanswered – the recipients probably writing her off as some desperate groupie – she had called up the band's manager in Colombia and had no option but to explain to the switchboard operator as best she could in her elementary-school Spanish that she was pregnant by the band's drummer and that she *honestly* wasn't after any money, but wanted to let him to know. (Trying to come up with the Spanish word for 'gold-digger' had been a particular challenge.)

A week later, she had finally heard back, but not from the drummer. It had been a polite email from a member of the band's management wishing her the best but stating that the drummer 'has no interest in being part of your child's life'. It went on to say that if Cassidy wished to pursue her paternity 'allegation', then the matter would be handed over to the company's lawyers to arrange the relevant DNA testing. Even more depressingly, the email had the feel of a standardised response that had been sent out many times before.

Cassidy had read the email with a creeping flush of shame and sadness. Despite the brevity of their relationship, she had felt an instant and intense connection with the drummer. He had been funny, charming and wildly sexy, with his long black hair and Jagger-like energy, and when after two hours of intense conversation in the club where they'd met he had suddenly looked her in the eye and said he would spend the rest of his life regretting it if he didn't ask her back to his hotel, she'd happily made an exception to her rule against one-night stands. And though she knew it was just a line when he'd murmured (in Spanish) that she was the most beautiful woman he had ever seen, and that he'd never forget this night as long as he lived, she had lapped it up nonetheless.

So, deep down, Cassidy had been hoping that when he found out about her pregnancy, he would want to play some part in their baby's life (and, if she was being brutally honest, in *her* life too) and the fact that he couldn't even be bothered to send a personal response felt like a door being slammed in her face. Worse still, her wonderful secret that she'd been cherishing and protecting like a jewel had been cheapened, and made to feel almost tawdry. It had been a wake-up call for Cassidy. Cradling her belly, in which she could already feel the first flutters of life, she had made a solemn promise to her baby that she would be the best single parent she could possibly be, then had promptly deleted the email.

Rather than explaining any of this, though, Cassidy just rolled her eyes. 'Come on, Jasha, it's a little old-fashioned saying I need to be with a man to be a proper family.'

'Okay then, with a woman. Whatever floats your ship.'

'I meant... Oh, never mind. I don't want a man, Jasha, I manage just fine by myself.'

'You are very capable for a female, I agree, but I think you must get lonely.'

'I really don't. Not at all.'

Jasha looked down at Cassidy, appraising her as if she were a freshly painted wall. 'It can't be because no man wants you. Lance says you are as hot as all hell.'

She snorted with laughter. 'Well, that's nice to hear. I think he's a little young for me though.'

Jasha pointed to the bucket of plaster, and she held it up
to him.

'Honestly, Jasha, a relationship is the last thing I'm looking
for right now.'

'Fine, I won't mention it again. But I think you would make
a good wife, even if you dance like a very tired old man.'

That night, after Nora was asleep and the inn was dark and
silent, Cassidy lay in bed, staring at the ceiling, thinking back
over their conversation. It was true that she was fine with being
single, just as she had told Jasha. In fact, it was a struggle to
remember the last time she'd been genuinely happy with a man.
Not fleetingly happy (as she had been during that night with
the Colombian drummer) but properly, long-term happy. The
sort of happiness that comes from snuggling together on the
couch to watch movies on a Sunday afternoon. Contentment,
she supposed you'd call it.

In her late teenage years, she'd had a few brief relationships
with the type of guys that now, as a mother herself, she would
be horrified if her daughter brought home. Boys with motor-
bikes, all-leather outfits and armfuls of tattoos (and in one
memorable instance, a faceful) who fancied themselves the next
Travis Barkers. Those relationships had been low on couch-
snuggling and high on tequila-fuelled drama, and it wasn't until
Cassidy went to college that she discovered that love was actually a very different thing to crazed lust. She had been as
surprised as anyone when she fell for Scott, a clean-cut
Midwesterner with a sensible haircut and unpierced nipples in
the year above, yet the pair of them had bonded over a shared
interest in molecular gastronomy, and within a month they had
moved in together. There followed eighteen months of contentment, until Scott was offered a job at a restaurant in Madrid
that specialised in the sort of food-science geekery that had

become his passion. They had spent hours agonising over what they should do, but Cassidy had another year of study to go and this was Scott's dream job, so in the end she had insisted he take it, even though she knew it would end their relationship. Sure enough, within a few months of him moving to Spain, the romance had fizzled out, leaving her with a broken heart and a lifelong aversion to 'frozen parmesan air' and 'spherical melon caviar'.

After moving to New York, Cassidy was too absorbed by her fabulous job to go on more than the occasional date, and when Nora was a baby, the only thing she wanted to do with her infinitesimal amount of spare time was sleep. Over the past few years, she'd dipped her toe into the world of online dating, but she'd never managed to get beyond a third date with men she met on Tinder. She'd actually begun to wonder if her profile was somehow tailored to be irresistible to guys with narcissistic personality disorder. Her most recent relationship, of course, had been with Mario, the manager of the Spring Street Smokehouse, but if she was being honest with herself, the only reason she had agreed to go out with him was because she missed being taken out for dinner, and, although Mario was several inches shorter than her, flirted openly with other women and talked about himself the entire time they were together, he did eat at nice places.

Yet despite her patchy history, Cassidy wasn't against the idea of a relationship – in fact, she sometimes felt a longing for a heart-lurching shot of desire as viscerally as hunger. And if she was being honest, she did occasionally get lonely. But when it came to seriously thinking about finding a partner, her list of requirements was off-puttingly long. It would have to be someone who gave her butterflies every time she saw them; someone who made her laugh, but also challenged and inspired her. Own job, own hair, own teeth – naturally. Most importantly, they would have to treat Nora like a princess. And this magical person (if he even existed) would have to make her life many times better and happier than it would have been without them, because otherwise what was the point? Besides, Cassidy had more than enough on her plate making the most of this fresh start for her and Nora. There certainly wasn't time to seek out romance when she had a half-derelict gastropub to get off the ground.

TWELVE

On the first Sunday in March, after they had been in Dithercott for just over a month, Cassidy decided they should put in an appearance at church.

Cassidy and Nora stepped outside mid-morning to be greeted by spring sunshine. The long days of rain had served their purpose: as they crossed the village green, plants and trees that had looked like sticks just days before had magically come to life. Nora stopped every now and then to pick a wildflower, and by the time they reached the churchyard, she had gathered a glorious posy of pink, blue and yellow that you could have tied up with raffia and sold for fifty bucks in a Sacramento florist.

St Andrew's church crouched amongst trees on the top of a small hill, surrounded by ancient gravestones that stuck up at rakish angles through the grass. Cassidy kept an eye out for the Beeswhistle name amongst the gravestones, but most of the writing was too weathered to be able to read without taking a closer look.

Inside, the church was dimly lit and stuffy with the smell of dusty radiators. Although the pews were surprisingly full, the interior was almost silent, apart from a low dirge from the organ, which was being played by someone unfamiliar with the basic concept of music. Above the altar there was a panel of stained glass depicting stern-looking disciples and an extremely disappointed-looking Jesus, under whose gaze Cassidy automatically felt guilty, despite having no particular sins to repent for (unless you included occasional impure thoughts about the vicar of St Andrew's). She couldn't help feeling it would have been more appropriate to be worshipping outside in the glorious spring air, rather than in this solemn place that wore every one of its eight hundred years with weary resignation.

Nora tugged her hand. 'There's Mrs Timothy,' she whispered.

'Let's go sit with her,' replied Cassidy.

They slid into the wooden pews, which clearly dated from a time when people were about a foot smaller than the modern day and less accustomed to the concept of comfort. The lack of legroom wasn't helped by the bulky leather kneeling cushions hanging from the back of the seat in front.

Mrs Timothy beamed at them. 'Hello, my dears, what a nice surprise seeing you here. Have you come to celebrate the Feast of Annunciation?'

'I'm afraid not, Mrs T,' said Cassidy. 'Just the Feast of digestive biscuits and orange squash.'

'Godless heathen,' Mrs Timothy replied, though this was accompanied by a smile.

A moment later, they heard loud talking – clearly, *someone* didn't feel the need to speak in hushed tones in here – and Cassidy turned to see Sophia Quill strutting up the aisle, bestowing gracious smiles on the congregation as she went. She was with a man who was a decade or so older than her, with a quiff of reddish-blonde hair – presumably the elusive Xavier – plus two children, a girl and boy, who had similar colouring to their father. The whole family was immaculately turned out in matching shades of navy, white and beige.

When Sophia spotted Cassidy, her eyes briefly narrowed before she plastered on a quick smile.

'Why, Cassidy, hello! Goodness, there hasn't been a Beeswhistle in St Andrew's since... well, since forever probably! How are you getting on at the inn?'

'Hi, Sophia. We're making good progress, thanks. We hope to be open in a month or two.'

This was an extremely ambitious estimate, judging by the current state of the inn, but Cassidy had no desire to admit to Sophia that she was struggling.

'Wonderful!' Sophia clasped her hands under her chin. 'I don't think you've met my husband, Xavier?'

He glanced at Cassidy, decided she was irrelevant, then muttered an offhand, 'Super to meet you,' while looking around for someone more important to speak to.

Just then, there was a disturbance between the Quill children and the girl began to howl, the noise echoing around the ancient walls.

'Cosmo!' shrieked Sophia. 'Leave your sister alone.'

'Mimi pinched me!'

'I did not!'

Sophia flashed Cassidy another tight smile and then herded the children towards the front row, followed by Xavier. It was only then Cassidy noticed that sitting in the pew behind them were Ian and Bettina Flint, who greeted the Quills with an enthusiasm she wouldn't have imagined the couple to be capable of. She watched as Sophia turned to speak to them, dipping her head in a conspiratorial fashion, and Cassidy couldn't help but wonder what they were discussing so animatedly. At one point, the three of them turned in unison to look back at her, then immediately looked away when they realised she was watching them.

Meanwhile, Nora was chatting away to one of her school friends who was sitting in front of them, and Mrs Timothy was exchanging gossip with a grey-haired woman in the pew behind. She'd introduced the woman to Cassidy as 'Mrs Seymour from over the way'. Cassidy overheard snippets of their conversation: 'Of course everyone knows he's having an affair with her from the garden centre... No, the one with the squint... Well, she might claim not to have a drinking problem, but her recycling bin on a Monday says otherwise...'

Cassidy had started to tune out, her eyelids growing heavy, when Mrs Timothy suddenly gasped: 'Heavens, it's Ned Bamford-Bligh! What on earth is *he* doing here?'

As one, the entire congregation turned in their seats, a Mexican wave of whispers and swivelled heads. Cassidy looked round too, to see Ned slipping into the empty back row, accompanied by the dog she'd seen with him at the manor. He was dressed far more smartly than when she'd last seen him, though the jacket seemed too big for his lean frame, and his hair was still in dire need of styling. Judging by his hunched posture, he wasn't comfortable at finding himself the centre of attention. His hand was resting on the Labrador as if it was an emotional support dog.

'Goodness, I've not seen him in church for years,' said Mrs Timothy. 'Certainly not since that terrible business with his fiancée.'

Cassidy was still scrutinising Ned. How did Angeline describe him the other day? That was it: 'a stone-cold fox'. Cassidy almost snorted. True, he cut an imposing figure – tall, and with those cheekbones that put her in mind of a Disney prince (one of the villainous ones). Sitting in that shaft of sunlight, his skin did have a sort of honeyed glow to it, but he certainly wasn't what she'd describe as attractive. No way! Not unless you had a thing for stuck-up Englishmen with bad hair-cuts and worse attitudes.

The couple sitting in front of Ned turned to greet him and as he replied (smiling politely, she noticed; he did have *some* manners then), his eyes found hers. She expected him to look away – after all, their meeting had been brief and hardly cordial – but he held her gaze. Cassidy felt a stab of irritation. Why was he staring at her? Well, if he thought he could intimidate her, he had another thing coming; she was damned if she was going to look away first. And then, to her horror, he opened his mouth as if he was about to say something to her.

Her cheeks burning, Cassidy swung back to face the front of the church, cursing herself for even looking at him in the first place. The last thing she wanted was for Ned Bamford-Bligh to think she had even an iota of interest in him.

Nora had noticed him too. 'Mom, it's that scary man from the woods,' she whispered.

Cassidy shushed her. 'Don't worry, honey, he's not scary, just a bit grumpy. I told you I'd spoken to him, and he said that he was very sorry and didn't mean to frighten you.' (A small lie had seemed sensible here.)

Mrs Timothy turned to Cassidy with surprise. 'You didn't say you've met Ned Bamford-Bligh?'

'Our paths crossed.'

'Well, I never! You were lucky there, he's rarely outside the estate these days. Isn't he the most charming young man?'

Cassidy gave a non-committal grunt.

Just then, the organ music, which had been droning on discordantly in the background, suddenly changed into something that at least vaguely resembled a tune, prompting the entire congregation to stand up.

As Cassidy rose, a choirboy processed up the aisle carrying a large cross, followed by James in his Sunday robes. With his golden good looks and aura of perfect calm, the vicar was like Prince Charming compared to the dastardly Ned Bamford-Bligh. As he passed by her pew, James spotted Cassidy, and he looked so pleased to see her that it banished all her irritation and uneasiness from a moment ago. She automatically returned his smile, their eyes briefly locking, as if they were the only two people in the room.

THIRTEEN

An hour later, Cassidy joined the throng moving at a glacial pace down the aisle towards the church door. Nora had disappeared with her school friends, while Mrs Timothy was holding court by the tea urn. To Cassidy's relief, she couldn't see Ned Bamford-Bligh anywhere; he must have slipped out as soon as the service had finished. Angeline was clearly right about the Bamford-Blighs not wanting to mix with the peasants.

As she neared the door, she could see James standing just outside the porch, his hair shining halo-like in the sun, greeting the long stream of parishioners, most of whom seemed to have an awful lot to say to him. Not that James seemed to mind. He was kind and patient with the older parishioners and stooped to high-five the little ones, and Cassidy marvelled at his ability to make every person feel special.

Eventually, she made it to the front of the queue.

'Cassidy, how lovely to see you,' he said warmly.

'You too.' She smiled. 'Great sermon – though, between you and me, I do feel bad for Mary. Being pregnant is stressful enough without the pressure of being told you're carrying the actual Son of God.'

James's laugh was genuine. 'I hadn't thought about it that way, but you're absolutely right.' He glanced at the queue behind her. 'Cassidy, would you mind waiting behind for a moment? There's something I was hoping to speak to you about.'

'Sure,' she said, happy at the thought of spending more time with him. 'I'll take a look at the graves while I wait, see if I can track down some dead Beeswhistles.'

James gestured to the far corner of the churchyard. 'You'll find them in the oldest part, just over there. I won't be long.'

Heading in the opposite direction to the flow of people strolling back down the hill to the village, Cassidy wandered around the side of the church. It was peaceful here, the sunlight falling through the leaves overhead in a shower of gold on the grass.

She was just bending down to try to make out the writing on one of the gravestones, when she heard a rustling and spotted a dog sniffing in the grass nearby. It was a black Labrador. Her stomach plummeting, she straightened up just in time to see Ned Bamford-Bligh walking towards her.

'Hello. Cassidy, isn't it?'

He didn't look particularly unhappy to see her; then again, he certainly didn't look that pleased, either.

She flashed a tight smile, not wanting to be rude, although she had no desire to have a conversation with the man.

Ned glanced towards the graves. 'Found any relatives?'

'Not yet.'

'There are a few Bamford-Blighs here, but they're mainly over there in the newer section. We're the Johnny-come-latelys of the parish, you see.' The corners of his mouth twitched up, then fell again when Cassidy showed no sign of returning his smile. Judging by his body language, this encounter was just as uncomfortable for him as it was for her, but he seemed to feel obliged to continue the conversation out of misplaced politeness. He went on: 'I imagine it must be fascinating, moving to a place where one's family has so much history. In fact, I was wondering if perhaps—'

'Why, Ned, hello!' James had appeared around the side of the church. 'I was hoping I might catch you before you left. Wonderful to see you today, and of course dear old Mungo too.' He bent down to pat Tamara's dog.

'Thank you, Reverend, it's good to see you too.'

Ned glanced again at Cassidy, and now she could see it: his eyes looked haunted. Her heart softened a little towards him. He must be suffering terribly from the loss of his fiancée. She briefly wondered what he had been about to say to her when James had come to the rescue, but the only thing she wanted to hear from him was an apology for the way he had behaved to Nora, and he'd already made it clear that wasn't going to happen.

'Well, I must be getting on. Goodbye, Cassidy.' Ned turned to James. 'Reverend.'

He strode off briskly in the direction of the wood, tapping his leg to call Mungo to heel. He lifted the elderly dog over the stone wall that bordered the churchyard, before hurdling over it himself and quickly disappearing out of sight between the trees.

When he had gone, Cassidy let out her breath. There was something about the man that unnerved her. Perhaps it was simply because he was a Bamford-Bligh.

'I'm so glad you got to meet Ned,' said James. 'You were lucky, he doesn't come to the village much these days, but hopefully this is a sign we'll be seeing more of him. Did you talk to him about the manor?'

'Only briefly.' She didn't want to get into the details of their previous unpleasant encounter.

'He's a wonderful chap, despite a tough few years,' added James. 'I'm sure he'd be very happy to show you round the estate.'

'Maybe,' replied Cassidy, although it seemed unlikely she'd ever get to look inside her ancestral home after alienating the entire Bamford-Bligh family. She would have to find some other way to get in.

'Shall we go through to the vestry? Nora is playing Connect Four with Mrs Timothy in the Sunday School room. It looked extremely competitive.'

'I'm afraid Nora has a killer instinct when it comes to board games.'

'Oh, she'll need it. Mrs Timothy once got herself banned from the Ladies' Gin Rummy evening due to what was described as "underhand tactics and heckling".' James chuckled. 'An inspiration for us all in our later years, I think.'

They walked back inside the church together and headed up the aisle towards a small door set in the left-hand wall of the church. James stood aside to let Cassidy in first.

'After you,' he said with a smile.

The vestry was small and tidy with a bright blue carpet, wood-panelled walls and a single leaded window that was too small to give much of a view. The only furniture was a desk and a couple of comfy chairs, which was where James gestured for Cassidy to take a seat.

While he sifted through some papers on his desk, she looked around the room, her gaze falling on a framed photo of a sports team.

'Do you play soccer?' she asked, spotting him amongst the players.

'Oh yes! Before finding God, I found football. As a boy, I was desperate to play professionally, but, sadly, enthusiasm isn't a substitute for talent. I do love being a part of the village team though.'

She peered a little closer at the photo. 'And is that...?'

'Ned Bamford-Bligh? Yes, he was our captain. A brilliant footballer, and just as good at keeping up the team's morale –

though he doesn't play for us anymore.' He sighed. 'Anyway, on to happier things. I was looking through some documents in the village archives, hoping to put together some items you might find of interest, when I came across this.' He brandished a folder. 'It's a letter from Bertie Beeswhistle to one Elizabeth Heggarty, a local girl who he had been courting in secret before he left England. Not the only one, if the rumours are to be believed...'

He handed the folder to Cassidy and took the seat opposite her. Inside, there was a single piece of paper, yellowed and flimsy with age, covered in elegant, slanted handwriting. Entranced, she bent closer to examine the swoops and swirls of ink and caught a trace of the letter's faint musty scent.

'This was really written by Bertie?' she asked, eyes wide.

James nodded, and Cassidy started to read.

New York, Sunday 2 July 1843.

My beloved Lizzie,

I am staying with friends in New York. It is a truly magnificent city, though I admit to missing my dear Dithercott.

Cassidy looked up. 'This is incredible – it's like hearing Bertie speak!'

'Isn't it just? We're so lucky to have such well-maintained archives.' James leant over to look at the letter. 'This is the part that I particularly wanted you to see,' he said, pointing to the last passage.

She held the letter closer to her face. 'Gosh, I can barely make out this writing...'

'May I?' He held out his hands, but as she passed the letter to him, their fingers touched, and he jerked his hand away as if he had been stung.

She glanced up at him, surprised, to discover that James was staring directly at her. He immediately returned his gaze to the letter, but not before she had registered the strange way he had been looking at her. Gone was his usual vicarly twinkle; he had looked unsettled, as if she had just asked him a deeply personal question that he didn't have a clue how to answer.

He cleared his throat. 'Anyway, this is the part I wanted you to hear,' he said, glossing over the weirdness of the previous moment. 'Here we go: "Know that I am deeply ashamed of my actions and the covert and abrupt manner of my departure, but please be assured that despite my foolish actions, I have taken steps to protect the Beeswhistle name and my family's legacy for future generations."'

James looked up at her triumphantly, clearly anticipating a big response.

Cassidy rubbed her cheek. 'I'm not sure I...?'

'The deed!' He tapped the page. 'Bertie says he's taken steps to "preserve his family's legacy". Surely that's a reference to the lost deed! This could be the proof that it actually exists!'

'Or maybe he was just trying to persuade this Lizzie chick to shack up with him in New York and make her think he's not such a loser after all?'

'Ah.' His face fell. 'Yes, that would certainly make sense.'

'So, did she? Join Bertie in America, I mean?'

'No, it seems Lizzie had a sensible head on her shoulders and decided to stay in England. According to your father's research, Bertie married the daughter of a New York tobacco merchant and started a surprisingly successful business exporting turpentine, until, in the 1850s, the couple upped sticks and moved to California. It was the time of the gold rush, so I imagine that might have been the reason.'

Cassidy gave an amused snort. 'The old Beeswhistle impulsiveness.'

'I'm sorry?'

'Oh, it's just something my dad used to say about me when I was younger. I get the impression that recklessness runs in our family. Not that I was super wild,' she added quickly, worried James might think she'd been some sort of crack addict. 'I just went through a phase of staying out late, going to gigs and drinking too much. I'm sure you remember what it's like to be a teenager.'

'Well, actually, I was quite a serious chap in my youth. I had the Church, of course, and I was very keen on football and playing the cello, so that took up a lot of my spare time.'

'So, no sex, drugs or rock 'n' roll?' she asked, teasingly.

'Goodness, no! More like praying, porridge and chamber music.'

Cassidy laughed. 'I hope Nora follows in your footsteps when she's a teenager. I don't think I could cope with the stress I put my poor dad through.'

'I don't think you need to worry about Nora, she's a lovely child. You must be very proud of her.'

'Oh, I am, she's the best thing in my life by a long shot. I still can't believe I played a part in creating such an incredible human.' Cassidy hesitated, wondering whether to say more, but there was something about James that invited confidences. 'I do sometimes worry, though, that I haven't given Nora a more stable family life.'

What she actually meant, but couldn't bring herself to say, was 'given Nora a father'. Cassidy knew she had tried her best to be both parents to her daughter, but her relationship with Joe had been so special that it saddened her that Nora would never have a chance to enjoy the same closeness with her own dad.

James looked at her with a sincere expression. 'Families come in all shapes and sizes, Cassidy, and from what I've seen, you're a wonderful mother to a very happy child.'

'Thank you, that means a lot. She's certainly very glad we moved to Dithercott.'

'As am I,' said James. There it was again, that same intense look – sort of hopeful and hopeless all at once – but this time he held onto her gaze. 'I'm really enjoying spending time with you, Cassidy.' He hesitated for a moment. 'Investigating the Beeswhistle family history, I mean.'

But that pause had spoken volumes, and it occurred to Cassidy, with a jolt of surprise, that it might not be just her family tree that James was interested in.

'Do you think you'll ever get married, Mom?'

Cassidy and Nora were walking home through the woods, sharing a packet of Bourbon biscuits that Mrs Timothy had given them.

Cassidy looked at her daughter, eyebrows raised. 'Why do you ask, honey?'

'It's just something Kira said to me at school the other day. Not in a mean way, but she wondered why it was just you and me and no dad.'

'I see.' Cassidy was momentarily flustered; it wasn't a subject Nora had ever really raised before. 'Well, would *you* like me to get married?'

Nora stopped to pick up a pebble, then threw it in the stream.

'Sometimes I think I'd like to have a dad,' she said, still looking at the water.

Cassidy felt like her heart was being squeezed in a vice. 'And why's that?'

She shrugged. 'It might be fun. And I'd like to have someone who could look after you, because you work so hard at looking after me.'

Cassidy dropped to her haunches and reached for Nora's hands. 'You do know that looking after you is my favourite thing to do in the whole world, right?'

Nora smiled down at her. 'Sure, Mom.'

They hugged, then started walking again.

'Maybe one day I *will* get married,' said Cassidy. 'But he'd have to be extra-special, right?'

'Absolutely. The best of the best of the best.'

Ridiculous as it was, Cassidy's thoughts instantly returned to James, their conversation in the vestry still fresh in her mind. Had she imagined that spark between them? They barely knew each other, of course, and she was out of flirting practice so may have misread the signs, but it had been a very long time since she'd felt such an easy rapport with a man. And he would certainly make a wonderful stepfather to Nora...

Cassidy shook her head, smirking at her ludicrousness. *You can't marry yourself off to the first nice guy who comes along – even if he does have a good job and teeth.*

She took her daughter's hand in hers. 'How about we go home and make chocolate cupcakes? The ones with the extra-gooey fudge frosting?'

'Cool!' Nora squeezed her hand. 'I love you, Mom.'

'You too, sweetie. More than anything in the whole world.'

FOURTEEN

'Why does your house smell so bad?'

The boy – Rufus, Cassidy thought his name was – had Nora backed against the wall, screwing up his nose as if she was the source of the pong.

Cassidy watched in horror as her daughter's face crumpled. 'It's just a very old building, but we're going to make it nice again,' Nora said in a small voice. 'My mom's working really hard, and I'm helping too...'

Nora had invited everyone in her class to her tenth birthday party, which wasn't a problem as there were only twelve kids in the year, but it meant that Rufus, the class tyrant, had to come too.

He took a step closer to Nora, looming over her. 'Well, it stinks. And it's creepy. Just like you.'

Cassidy had heard enough. She swooped over to intervene.

'You'd probably smell a bit too if you were five hundred years old,' she said to Rufus, smiling through gritted teeth. 'Come on, birthday girl, let's join the others outside, it's nearly time for your cake...' She steered her daughter towards the back door and then, as soon as Nora was out of earshot, turned back and hissed at Rufus: 'And it's creepy because it's haunted by the ghost of a murderer, so you better watch your mouth or I'll send him over to your house.'

As his mouth fell open, Cassidy headed out to the garden. She knew she shouldn't have said that, but Rufus had upset Nora once already today by loudly declaring her party was 'lame' and asking why it wasn't at Laserzone. 'Is it because you're poor?' he had sneered.

Outside in the garden, the kids were playing limbo. Mrs Timothy and Angeline were holding either end of the pole, and Nora's friends were cheering and clapping as the birthday girl shimmed underneath it. Her daughter was laughing and the rain had thankfully held off, yet Cassidy still felt wretched. As much as it pained her to admit it, the odious Rufus had a point: the inn *did* smell, and they *were* poor. The stench had grown so bad, in fact, that Cassidy wondered if some large animal – *please, not a rat* – had died somewhere inside the inn, and she'd taken to wrenching up floorboards at random to find its source. Yet another job she would have to pay Jasha to fix. No doubt the fact that the downstairs gents' toilet had yet to be unblocked wasn't helping the situation, and even with all the windows open and cheap scented candles dotted about the bar, there was still the lurking whiff of decay – which was why Nora's party was taking place in the garden, despite the fact that the guests had to wear gloves and coats against the chill.

As for being poor, last week Cassidy had been horrified to discover that the money she'd set aside to support them for six months while she wasn't earning a salary was nearly a third gone after just one month. This scare had arguably been a good thing, as it had forced Cassidy to take a far more meticulous approach to budgeting, but the timing couldn't have been worse, coming as it did just before Nora's birthday.

Determined to make her daughter's big day perfect despite the enforced belt-tightening, Cassidy had made the party decorations herself out of newspaper and glitter, baked Nora's favourite red velvet cake and, best of all, had found a lovely second-hand bike for sale on a community webpage. Cassidy had been thrilled: Nora had wanted a bike for ages – it was the sole present she had asked for – and this one was nearly new, just within her budget and was a cherry-red colour, which Nora would adore. When she had gone to collect it yesterday, however, the vendor had looked surprised. 'Oh, I didn't think you wanted it anymore,' she said. 'I sold it to someone else a few days ago.'

Cassidy had forced a smile and walked away before she said something she would regret. There was no point reminding the woman that she had actually emailed her – *twice!* – to confirm that, yes, she did indeed want it. She had to find Nora another present. After some quick googling, Cassidy had taken two buses and then a train to the nearest town with a bike shop, but even the cheapest model was way out of her budget. In the end, she had bought some books and sweets and had headed home, feeling like the worst mother in the world.

The next morning, even though Nora had tried her best to hide it, Cassidy had noticed how her daughter's face had briefly fallen when she'd realised there wasn't a bicycle-shaped present amongst her gifts.

'I promise I'll get you a bike as soon as I can,' Cassidy had told her. 'I'm keeping a look out and we'll find something perfect for you.'

'That's okay, Mom, I know we need to spend all our money on the inn right now.'

But Nora's wise-beyond-her years thoughtfulness had made Cassidy feel even worse. Her girl shouldn't be worrying about things like this at her age; she should be happily riding around on her cherry-red bike and not giving the state of their finances a single thought.

. . .

That night, Cassidy lay awake in bed staring at the darkened ceiling, listening to the plink-plink of the new leak that had just appeared in their bedroom, as if in retaliation for the fact that Jasha had fixed the one in the other room. Her shoulders and backed ached from being hunched over retiling the bathroom the other day, and there was a cut on her hand from a rusty nail that had started to throb. Cassidy wondered if her tetanus shots were up to date, then immediately forced it from her mind. If they were to open in six weeks as planned, she didn't have time to fit in a trip to hospital on top of everything else. She had tried to register them with the local GP when they had first arrived, but when she had phoned the surgery, she'd been informed that she would need to do so in person, plus bring in various pieces of paperwork that Cassidy didn't have, so she had put it to the back of her mind.

She shifted uncomfortably on the bed: the dust that had covered everything since the renovations began must have now worked its way inside her sleeping bag. Nora seemed to have had a permanent cold since they got here, and the other day she had blown her nose and given a yelp of disgust. 'Ew, gross! Look, Mom,' she had said, showing Cassidy the blackened contents of her tissue.

A horrible thought suddenly occurred to her: could it be harming Nora's health living in these conditions? Another flurry of guilt settled on top of the avalanche that was already smothering her.

You shouldn't have bought this place.

Cassidy squeezed her eyes closed, her breath coming out in a shuddering rush. Looking back, she couldn't believe how reckless she'd been in moving them here. She was no better than Bertie Beeswhistle, gambling her and Nora's entire lives on a stupid whim. She'd been convinced that her father's hand had been guiding her when she'd discovered the Beeswhistle was up for sale, but just a moment's rational thought would have made her realise what a ridiculous notion that was. Joe had always been as cautious as she was reckless; he would never in a million years have suggested that she pour all her money into a property that she hadn't even seen in person.

What a mess this all was... But here they were, and Cassidy had no choice but to make the best of it. She turned her head to look at her sleeping daughter, cuddled up with the teddy she'd had since she was a baby, and the sight melted her heart at the same time as it hardened her resolve. Even if she had to toil around the clock, she would make this work. For Nora's sake, if nothing else.

FIFTEEN

Cassidy was working up in the loft, sweeping up the dust and wisps of stray thatch that had gathered in drifts beneath the roof, when she heard Jasha calling.

'Cassidy? There is a man at the door asking for you. You are in trouble with the police, I think.'

She poked her head through the hatch. *'What?'*

'You must come downstairs right away,' said Jasha, his face grave. 'He looks very angry.'

Cassidy half climbed, half slid down the loft ladder, her heart hammering in her chest. She caught sight of herself in the mirror behind the bar as she hurried past: her hair and clothes were covered in centuries-old dust. Well, there was nothing she could do about that now. Besides, if she was in trouble with the police and bit of dirt was the least of her worries.

The man standing at the front door didn't look much like a policeman, though Cassidy supposed he could be plain-clothes, and despite what Jasha had said, he didn't look so much angry as officious. Like everyone's least favourite maths teacher, complete with clipboard.

'Cassidy Beeswhistle?' He barked at her like a sergeant major.

'Yes?'

'You're the owner of this establishment?'

'I am. What's this about?'

'My name is Brian Pinson. I'm from the local authority planning department.'

'Not the police?'

He frowned. 'No.'

'Phew,' she said, drawing her hand across her brow in theatrical relief.

The man's frown grew even frownier. 'I understand you're currently undertaking some renovations to this building?'

'Yeah, just fixin' up the old girl before we reopen.' Cassidy patted the door frame fondly. 'Giving her a bit of a face lift, a little Botox, you know.'

He pursed his lips, then cleared his throat, glancing at the clipboard. 'You are, of course, aware of the restrictions in place concerning Grade II listed buildings such as this. And that any work beyond minor repairs is subject to listed building consent.'

Cassidy stared at him for a moment. She had no idea what he was talking about, though she figured it would be wiser not to admit that. 'Of course I am! Fully aware, and right across all of those restrictions. Yes, sir.'

'Then you'll know that failure to obtain an assessment of the impact of any proposed works by a planning officer prior to the commencement of said works is a criminal offence and could lead to prosecution.'

'Yes, that is something that I do know, and have paid full attention to. Absolutely.'

The man was staring at her as if he would find direct evidence of contraventions written on her face. 'It's just we've had a complaint about unauthorised works taking place at this property.'

'What? Wow, no, we're certainly not doing anything that dramatic. Just a lick of paint and a little light plumbing. Barely anything, really.'

At that moment, Jasha started hammering upstairs. It sounded as if he was knocking down an entire wall.

Cassidy discreetly pulled the front door closed behind her. 'Is that everything?'

He narrowed his eyes. 'For now. I'll make an official note of your assurances, but if I receive further complaints, I will be forced to investigate the works under the powers of Section 88 of the 1990 Planning Act.'

'Absolutely, I totally understand. I mean, it would be remiss of you not to.'

He gave a curt nod and turned to go.

'Sorry, Mr Pinson, is it? Can I just ask who it was that made the complaint?'

'It was a concerned citizen who appreciates the importance of protecting Dithercott's heritage, but that's all I'm at liberty to say.'

She bristled at his tone. 'I may not be from round here, but, believe me, I appreciate that too.'

Cassidy closed the door, resisting the urge to slam it in the planning officer's face. Fury rising inside her like lava, she looked around for something to throw. There was a wet cloth nearby with which she'd been wiping down the bar; she chucked it at the wall, where it made an unsatisfying plop. Cassidy clenched her teeth. It didn't really matter that Mr Pinson wouldn't tell her who had made the complaint, because she was already sure she knew who it was.

'Jasha! I'm going out.'

He appeared at the top of the stairs. 'You have been arrested?'

'No, but give me a few minutes and I might well be.'

Cassidy bashed her head on the door frame on the way out, too angry to remember to duck.

This had the Flints' fingerprints all over it, she was sure of it. After all, they had made it crystal-clear that she wasn't welcome in Dithercott, and hadn't Mrs Timothy warned her she should watch out for them? Cassidy had tried being nice, but, as her dad liked to say, you don't bring a knife to a gunfight.

She threw open the door to the Post Office, gratified to note that she was in direct contravention of the 'NO DIRTY BOOTS OR CLOTHING' sign, and marched up to the counter, leaving a trail of debris in her wake.

To Cassidy's immense disappointment, neither Ian nor Bettina Flint were at the counter to witness her entrance in a cloud of dirt. Instead, there was a girl, probably in her late teens, who was too busy painting her fingernails to worry about whether Cassidy's clothes were clean.

'I need to speak to Mr or Mrs Flint. Preferably both of them.'

'They're out,' she said, fully focused on her nails. Cassidy noticed she was painting each one a different colour.

'When will they be back?'

'Later, I guess.'

She gritted her teeth. 'Could you possibly be any more specific?'

At this, the girl looked up. 'Hey, are you the American who's bought the Beeswhistle?'

'Yes, Cassidy. Hi.'

'Cool! I was hoping I might run into you. I'm Natasha Flint. Tash.'

'Are you related to...?'

'Mum and Dad.' This was accompanied by a very teenage eye roll.

Cassidy smiled at her expression. 'I'm afraid your parents don't like me very much.'

Tash airily waved a hand. 'Oh, it's nothing personal, just your usual middle-aged small-mindedness. My parents aren't bad people, but they're not exactly woke. You should have heard the row we had over trans rights. Actually, you probably *did* hear it, over in America... Anyway, the fact that you're an "outsider"' – she made heavy air quotes with her fingers – 'and your plans for opening a burger joint have sent both of them into pearl-clutching mode. They're massive food snobs, you see. That's why they're not here today, they've gone to some culinary thing in London. Something to do with oysters maybe? I wasn't listening.'

'Hold up – your parents think I'm opening a burger joint?'

'That's what they told me.' Tash took in Cassidy's expression. 'Listen, I've got no issue with that at all, I'm a big fan of burgers.'

'Me too, but it's totally untrue. The Beeswhistle's going to be a gastropub focusing on local, seasonal ingredients, basically about as far from fast food as you can get.'

'Really? I wonder where they got the idea about burgers?'

'I can't imagine.'

Then Cassidy suddenly remembered Sophia Quill's clumsy attempt to imitate her American accent and the comment she'd made about cheeseburgers, and she *had* seemed suspiciously chummy with the Flints in church. Could Sophia feel so threatened that she would spread fake rumours to jeopardise her business? Cassidy's mouth set in a grim line. From what she'd seen of the woman's character that seemed entirely feasible.

Tash leant on the counter and looked at Cassidy, her head tipped to the side. 'Hey, you wouldn't need any help at the Beeswhistle, would you? I'll do anything: waitress, pot-washer, potato peeler. I'm on my gap year right now, but I'm going to be taking a degree in hospitality and it would be great to get some experience. Mum tried to get me to work at the Quill, but I'd rather stick pins in my eyes.'

An idea began to take shape in Cassidy's mind. It was true she was going to need all the help she could get at the inn, and she liked what she'd seen of Tash. The girl seemed level-headed, plus she obviously had an interest in the industry. Yet Cassidy was also a big fan of karma, and offering Ian and Bettina's daughter a job felt like the perfect way to repay them for reporting her to the planning officer.

'I think that's a very interesting idea, Tash. I'll be in touch.'

'Cool, thank you so much!'

They swapped numbers, then Tash went back to her nails.

'Oh, did you want me to pass on a message to my parents?'

'No need, thank you,' said Cassidy with a little smile.

Instead, she would leave this little time bomb here – Tash's potential new job at the Beeswhistle burger joint – and then wait for it to explode. No doubt she would be hearing from Ian and Bettina when it did.

SIXTEEN

Cassidy's chest tightened, emotion choking at her throat. *Goddammit, don't cry!* She rubbed her fists in her eyes, as if she could physically push back the tears.

'Well?' Jasha called down from the top of the ladder. 'Is it hanging straight?'

Cassidy nodded, her lips pressed together against the storm of emotion whipping up her insides. 'It's perfect,' she managed.

The Beeswhistle Inn's newly restored sign was back in the spot it had hung for centuries, its lettering picked out in gold paint and the crest with its eagle and stag skilfully brought back to life by an artist friend of Mrs Timothy's. To Cassidy, the sign felt like a symbol of all they had managed to achieve in the two months since she and Nora had arrived in Dithercott. It had been a mad gamble moving here, but for the first time, it looked as if all that hard work was finally paying off. She only wished that Joe was here to see it. She could imagine him standing beside her, looking up at the sign – tipping the peak of his baseball cap back to get a better view – and then turning to her with that big, easy grin. His voice was as clear to her as if he was actually there. 'I'm proud of you, kiddo. Your mom would be too.'

It wasn't just the new sign, though. The whole inn was now looking – in the words of an admiring Mrs Timothy – 'ship-shape and tickety-boo'. The broken windowpanes had been replaced, the plaster on the facade sanded and repainted and the timbers carefully renovated, all in accordance with the planning rules that Cassidy had belatedly tracked down after Mr Pinson's visit. The window boxes were bursting with marigolds and petunias, while the vines creeping over the flint walls that Cassidy had been intending to rip out had suddenly revealed themselves to be wisteria, their flowers exploding like purple waterfalls. And it might be her imagination, but since it had come into bloom, its fragrance seemed to have driven out the terrible smell inside the inn, although this may have been down to the fact that Cassidy had finally got round to unblocking the gents' toilet (thirty minutes of her life she was trying her hardest to forget).

In fact, the only remaining evidence of the five years of neglect the Beeswhistle had suffered at the hands of the Diaggios was its roof, which was still tragically bald. Cassidy was clean out of funds, and besides, even if she wasn't, it would cost tens of thousands for a full re-thatch. As always, though, Jasha had come to the rescue. He had tracked down a lovely retired thatcher called Fred Smith, who had agreed to replace the roof's ornamental ridge for little more than a love of the job and frequent cups of strong tea. It would at least make it look smarter until she could afford to replace it entirely. Cassidy was so grateful for Fred's help that she was more than happy to overlook his fondness for smoking a pipe while sitting on top of the pile of highly flammable thatch. *Just another one of those charmingly eccentric English habits*, she had reassured herself.

Cassidy called back up to Jasha. 'Before you come down, could you take a photo of the sign for Instagram?'

With the reopening date now just a month away, she had set up an account to promote the pub and already had several hundred followers and a number of messages from people excited about the relaunch.

He saluted in acknowledgement and Cassidy headed back inside, excitement fizzing inside her. Moments later, her phone pinged with a message. It was mostly a selfie of Jasha's huge face, a beefy thumb raised aloft, with the pub's sign barely visible in the background. Cassidy grinned: it wasn't exactly what she had intended, but it was perfect. She put it straight on Instagram and captioned it: 'One month to go!'

Almost instantly a text appeared from Manon back in Sacramento.

> Who's the hunk?! Congratulations, honey, I'm
> so impressed xx

Just before 5.15 a.m. the following morning, Cassidy slipped out of the back door for a run. She had checked on Nora, now in a bedroom of her own, but she was still fast asleep, Hermione curled up in the crook of her body.

There was still an hour to go before sunrise and the sky was dark. Cassidy loved this time of the day, the stillness and sense of anticipation for a new day ahead when absolutely anything could happen. Okay, so it would probably just be more of the same as yesterday and the day before, but that didn't matter. It was the feeling of *potential* – that life wasn't set in stone and adventure could always be round the corner – that Cassidy loved. Plus there was a sense of peace here that would have been impossible to find in Sacramento, whatever the time of day or night.

Pausing for a moment to knot her long hair on top of her head, her pink ends now washed out to dull blonde, she took a deep inhale, wishing that she could bottle the air in this place. She would make a fortune flogging it to smog-bound city dwellers back in Sacramento. Then she set off down the high street, past closed curtains and shuttered windows, smug to be up and at 'em while the rest of the world was still in bed.

Cassidy had always enjoyed running, but since arriving in England, it had become a vital part of her daily routine. It felt good for her soul to be out amongst the ancient trees, giving her an inner peace others found in meditation, plus it was the only time her feet ever really felt warm these days.

After some experimentation (and a few disasters involving irate cows and impenetrable bogs), she had perfected a roughly five-kilometre loop that took her across the fields and down by the river and then back along the woodland path that passed by school.

She turned off the main road and hurdled a stile that led to a public footpath across farmland. The path began to climb alongside a field of bright green shoots and Cassidy kicked up a gear, her breath fogging like a steam engine in the chilled air. On the crest of the hill ahead of her, a family of rabbits froze, then, at some invisible signal, all scampered towards the hedgerow. Watching their white tails bobbing away, Cassidy became aware of a lightness inside her, a softening of jagged edges, and with this came a sudden appreciation for the world around her. See the green of those leaves! Smell the sweetness of the wet grass! Life was... *good*. The pub finally felt like their home. Nora was happy. She had made good friends and was working on a project she felt passionate about, with the help of some wonderful local suppliers who were excited at the prospect of working with the Beeswhistle.

As a flock of crows took off in front of her, Cassidy broke into a grin, revelling in the unfamiliar sensation of feeling perfectly relaxed and happy. It made her realise just how much of her life had been lived flying by the seat of her pants.

She was now into the favourite part of her run, partly because it was the only flat stretch, but also because it followed the course of the river along the valley bottom and there was something very soothing about being near the water. She often saw a grey heron here, watching her from the willow-shaded shallows, and the other day she had spotted the electric-blue flash of a kingfisher dart to the opposite bank.

Cassidy was now approaching a bend in the river where the bank widened into a shingle beach that was wildly popular with cold-water swimmers, or crazy people, as Cassidy liked to call them. This spot also offered the best view of Dithercott Manor, which was currently cloaked in darkness at the top of its hill. She slowed her pace and then, in an abrupt change of plan, turned off the path and picked her way through the bracken that bordered the shore, feeling a sudden need to get closer to the river.

The water looked black in the faint pre-dawn light, tendrils of mist unfurling across its surface, and she could imagine huge fish with needle-like teeth lurking in its depths. Why anyone would want to swim in this was beyond her, although perhaps it wasn't as cold as it looked? She bent down to dabble her hand and immediately yanked it out again. Nope, that was frostbite waiting to happen.

Then, in the stillness, she became aware of a rhythmic lapping sound and turned to see a man swimming towards her. The first thing she noticed was his hat, which looked like a badly knitted orange tea cosy, and the second was that it was Ned Bamford-Bligh.

'Terrific,' muttered Cassidy under her breath. For a man who was supposed to be a recluse, he seemed to be crossing her path with disturbing regularity.

He raised a hand in greeting as he swam, and she responded with a half-hearted wave. Now that he'd seen her, she couldn't very well just run off again without saying hello. She glanced down at her outfit: one of Joe's cast-off hoodies and a pair of fraying running tights that were older than Nora. No doubt Ned Bamford-Bligh would now be judging her for looking like a hobo on top of everything else.

'Morning,' he called out, as he breast-stroked to shore.

'Hey,' she said. 'I gotta get going, nice to see you and all...'

'Hold on, might I have a quick word?'

With great reluctance, she stayed put.

Way to ruin my morning, she thought sulkily, kicking at a stone.

Ned's feet found the riverbed and he rose up out of the water. His chest was bare, his skin glowing from the shock of the cold water. Cassidy looked away, but not before she had responded to the sight of his broad shoulders and muscled torso with an electric jolt of some long-forgotten feeling. She stared at the ground, mad at her body for betraying her, although, as she firmly reminded herself, you could dislike a man's character while still acknowledging his superior muscle tone. It was the same as admiring a marble statue of some brutal Roman emperor: the baby-killing and slave-trading were totally separate issues from his shapely thighs.

Ned began to towel himself dry. 'You're up early.'

'I'm going for a run.'

He grunted. 'Never seen the point in jogging myself.'

'I could say the same about swimming in this. Not exactly Malibu, is it?'

'True. But the cold helps me deal with...' Ned stopped himself. '...to deal with life.'

He pulled on a jumper, then wrapped a towel around his waist so he could remove his trunks. Cassidy faced the opposite direction to spare both their blushes. Neither spoke for a while, and she was relieved to lose herself in the soothing lapping of the water. A small brown duck with an orange beak swam into view, followed by a line of ducklings. Before she could stop herself, Cassidy glanced round at Ned to share her delight, and she found him watching the family with a smile that was so full of childlike wonder that she started in surprise. She'd half expected to find him reaching for a shotgun.

'They're gadwalls,' he said softly. 'The babies are just a few days old. The nest is on the bank over there, I saw it last week.' He playfully raised his brows. 'I doubt you'd get *that* in Malibu.'

Cassidy's lips twitched upwards. 'Look, I really should get back to the inn before my daughter wakes. What was it you wanted to speak to me about?'

'Right. Well, I was thinking what I said to you about the portrait of Bertie Beeswhistle a few weeks ago. I fear I may have been a little harsh in calling him ugly.'

'You think?'

'Well, you see, he *is* ugly. But I was unnecessarily blunt. So I was wondering if you'd like to come and assess his attractiveness for yourself? I could sweeten the offer with a full tour of the estate and grounds, and a jar of our housekeeper's famous marmalade?'

She replied instantly. 'No, thank you.'

'Really? If I was you, I'd be desperate to have a nose around. You're not curious about the place?'

Duh. Of course she was curious. Every time she caught a glimpse of Dithercott Manor, there was a quickening inside her, a feeling that the pair of them had unfinished business. Cassidy could clearly remember how its stone walls had felt beneath her fingers, the way the house had seemed so strange, yet at the same time weirdly familiar. So, yes, she was desperate to take a look inside, just not under the unsettling gaze of Ned Bamford-Bligh. More importantly, she hadn't forgiven him for scaring Nora. The thought of her daughter's tear-streaked face came to mind, triggering her to lash out.

'Perhaps if you'd been less unpleasant to my daughter, I might have considered the offer.'

Ned frowned. 'I thought we'd been over this already.'

'We have. You made it clear that you felt you'd acted reasonably, whereas I believe you were rude and intimidating.'

'Is it an apology you're after? Because if that's the issue, then I apologise. I still believe I reacted in an entirely proportionate manner to someone trespassing on my land, but I am sorry that your daughter was upset.'

'Jeez, would it kill you to say "I'm sorry I made your daughter cry"?'

Ned's mouth tightened. 'If you'd grown up in the English countryside, I think you'd have an entirely different perspective on this whole episode.'

Cassidy balled her fists. How anyone could consider this man to be charming, she had absolutely no idea. 'A different perspective on rudeness? I very much doubt it.'

Ned reached down to gather up his things, moving infuriatingly slowly, as if he owned the place. Which, considering the proximity of the manor, he probably did. Goddammit, she would have to find a different route for her run.

'Well, if you change your mind, the invitation stands.'

'Thank you, but the phrase "when hell freezes over" comes to mind.'

He flinched. 'I see. Then I won't waste your time by asking again.' He inclined his head. 'Goodbye.'

He set off, crunching up the shingle in the exact direction she'd been planning to continue her run. Cassidy watched him go, livid at both Ned and herself. Why on earth did she say that to him? Not only had she been unnecessarily rude, she'd blown any chance of seeing the manor. She just found the man so *infuriating*.

Cassidy had no choice to return home the way she had just

come to avoid another encounter with Ned. She ran the rest of the way with her face in a scowl, every trace of her previous contentment destroyed in a toxic cloud of murderous thoughts about Ned Bamford-bloody-Bligh.

SEVENTEEN

Cassidy was cooking on gas – quite literally. She was wearing her favourite apron (a stripy canvas one from the Spring Street Smokehouse) and had set aside the day for testing recipes for the Beeswhistle Inn's new menu. If she still hadn't quite got her head around the fact that she would soon be opening her very own gastropub, at least the prospect no longer filled her with crushing terror and a desperate urge to run away. Nora was at school and Jasha was busy at another job; it was just her, a kitchen full of ingredients and a carefully curated playlist of heavy metal, turned up loud.

Since arriving in Dithercott two months ago, Cassidy's life had been mostly about fixing leaks rather than chopping them, and like a racehorse set loose after weeks cooped up in a stable, she was overjoyed to be testing recipes again. She scuttled between the worktop, stove and fridge, pausing only to make the occasional note. She was so focused, in fact, pounding a promising-looking watercress pesto in her pestle and mortar to the rhythm of AC/DC's 'Thunderstruck', that when there was a knock at the inn's front door, she didn't even notice it.

Moments later, the knocking came again and this time

Cassidy heard it. She paused, looking towards the door, then got back to the pesto. Whoever it was would come back. Would Beethoven have interrupted composing his Fifth Symphony to sign for an Amazon parcel? No, he would not. She reached for a hugely expensive bottle of olive oil that was so extra virgin it was virtually a nun.

It was only when the knocking came for a third time, and with an urgency that was impossible to ignore, that Cassidy reluctantly tore herself away from her pestle and went to answer it.

As usual, the front door stubbornly refused to do its one job: being able to open.

'Darn it,' she muttered, pulling with all her strength. 'Sorry, give me a moment!'

When she managed to force it open a crack, she peered through to discover Ian and Bettina Flint, standing on the doorstep in matching red gilets. Bettina looked furious.

'We need to speak to you about a matter of extreme importance,' she said, pushing her face towards the crack.

It looked like Tash must have broken the news about taking a job at the Beeswhistle. Cassidy's bomb had exploded.

'Sorry, I can't get this door open,' said Cassidy, giving it another yank.

'You might want to try a squirt of WD-40 on the hinges,' suggested Ian.

'*Ian,*' hissed Bettina.

'Sorry, dear.'

Cassidy sighed. 'Why don't you come round the back so we don't have to shout at each other through the gap?'

Bettina huffed, as if this was the most tremendous inconvenience, but headed towards the side passage, with Ian following at her heels. Cassidy wrenched the door closed, then made her way through the bar to the back door. As the Flints approached, she heard Ian say, 'Don't the beds look lovely?' and Bettina mutter something angrily in response. She had clearly made up her mind to hate everything to do with the Beeswhistle, even the petunias.

'So what's this about?' asked Cassidy, once they had reached the back door.

'Our daughter, Natasha,' said Ian.

'Tash? How is she?'

'Oh – yes, very well indeed, thank you,' he replied.

Bettina scowled at Ian. 'We're extremely concerned to hear that you've persuaded her to come and work for you.'

'To be fair, Tash asked me if I had any jobs available. I need the help, and I understand she needs a job before starting college, so it seemed like a perfect match. Is there a problem?'

'The problem,' said Bettina, 'is that washing dishes in your *burger bar* is hardly going to help Natasha advance her career.'

'Bettina, I don't know where you got the idea that I'm setting up a branch of McDonald's, but it's simply not true. I'm a qualified Cordon Bleu chef with years of experience working in fine-dining restaurants. Food is my passion. I think we have that in common at least?'

'I can't imagine we have anything in common, and certainly not when it comes to the appreciation of *haute cuisine*.' This was pronounced in an ostentatious French accent. *Oat kwizeen.* 'Natasha won't be working for you and that's final. Isn't that right, Ian?'

Silence.

Cassidy glanced at Ian to find him craning his head towards the direction of the kitchen window, out of which was wafting the scent of roasting pork.

'Ian!'

He jumped to attention. 'Yes, dear, absolutely.'

'Well, that's a shame, but I understand. Before you head off, though, why don't you at least try my food? I'm testing recipes and would appreciate a second opinion. Especially from people with such obviously sophisticated palettes.'

'No, thank you,' Bettina replied tartly.

Ian glanced at her. 'I don't see the harm in it, my love...'

'If you hate it after one bite, you're free to go. I promise not to lock you in the cellar along with the other people who've criticised my food. I'm joking,' she added quickly.

She could see Bettina wrestling with this, her curiosity pitched against her determined dislike of Cassidy. In the end, however, her foodie side – or perhaps her nosy side – won out.

'Fine. But don't think it's going to change our minds about Natasha working here.'

'You're welcome,' muttered Cassidy, as she stood aside to let them in.

She noticed Bettina's eyes darting about, as if searching for further evidence of her poor character, but Cassidy knew that she would struggle to find anything: the bar was looking beautiful. The walls had been whitewashed and the flagstones scrubbed clean of old stains. There were bunches of dried hops hanging over the bar, which she'd garlanded with fairy lights, and the scent of woodsmoke lingered from the fire that she and Nora had enjoyed last night, telling each other ghost stories and toasting marshmallows.

'Here we go,' said Cassidy, pulling out a chair. 'The best table in the house.'

Also, one of the only tables in the house. She was still desperately short of furniture, although Dale at the Buttered Crumpet had promised to give her a few bits, Jasha had found some chairs in a skip and James had kindly loaned her a couple of tables from the vicarage.

Now that the Flints were seated, it was easy to imagine they were just any other awkward customers, and Cassidy had had plenty of experience with those over the years. She gathered up the dishes from the kitchen and, after a moment's consideration, took out a very nice bottle of Sancerre from the fridge. On the one hand, she didn't want to waste her best wine on the Flints, but on the other, it would bring her immense satisfaction to prove Bettina wrong.

She showed the Flints the bottle to appreciative murmurs from Ian and then eased out the cork and poured it into the elegant wine glasses she had bought for the pub that had cost far too much money but made her heart sing.

Ian swirled the glass, then brought it to his nose and gave it a flamboyant sniff.

'Notes of menthol, redcurrant and apricot,' he said.

'You know your wine, Ian?'

'I do. In fact, I've just signed up for sommelier evening classes.' At this he puffed up with pride.

'Then perhaps I could pick your brain when I'm putting together a wine list for the pub?'

'Oh yes, I'd be very happy to help!'

Bettina turned her Medusa stare on him, and he visibly wilted.

'Okay,' said Cassidy, 'so we've got lemon roasted asparagus with jersey royals and peas, purple sprouting broccoli and chorizo on sourdough, grilled mackerel with beetroot and fennel, pork tenderloin with rhubarb, onions and tarragon, and a nettle, sorrel and wild garlic soup.' She stood back, hands on hips. 'See? Not a chicken nugget in sight!'

'This all looks quite delicious,' said Ian, rubbing his hands together. 'Bon appétit!'

'We'll see about that,' grumbled Bettina.

Cassidy watched as she helped herself to a small portion of the mackerel, sniffed it, then took the tiniest nibble. The scowl on her face flickered like a faulty circuit. After a pause, she had a bigger mouthful, her eyes drifting closed as she chewed. She then helped herself to large amounts of all the other dishes on the table, monopolising the whole soup bowl before Ian could even get a taste, and got stuck in.

'So what do you think?' asked Cassidy after a few moments.

Bettina started, as if she'd forgotten she was supposed to be hating everything. 'Quite nice, I suppose,' she muttered.

Ian looked shocked. 'Bettina!'

'Fine.' She put down her cutlery. 'It's delicious. All of it. I'm...' Her mouth worked, as if she was struggling to get the words out. '...extremely impressed.'

'Thank you, that means a lot.' Cassidy smiled. 'Look, I understand why you're worried about me being here. Mrs Timothy told me what you went through with the Diaggios. It must have been horrendous.'

'It was,' said Ian, reaching out to take his wife's hand.

Bettina clutched her throat, her lip trembling, and Cassidy felt her anger start to ease.

'I'm so sorry you had to deal with that, but you have to believe me, even though I'm not from around here, I do have Dithercott's best interests at heart.'

The Flints looked at each other.

'The thing is,' began Ian, hesitantly, 'we've heard that you applied to the council to extend the pub's opening hours, and for an entertainment licence to put on musical gigs and the like. After the disruption of the past few years, you'll understand why we're a little worried.'

'Did you hear this from the same person who claimed I was opening a burger joint?'

Bettina's gaze flicked to her husband again.

'It came from a well-respected member of the community,' he said.

'Well, again, it's untrue. You can check with the council.'

Bettina twisted her necklace. 'It's just... I'm not sure why this person would lie to us.'

'I have no idea, but I can assure you that all I'm trying to do is restore the Beeswhistle to its former glory as Dithercott's much-loved village pub. And as such, it would be great if you'd allow Tash to come and work here.'

The Flints exchanged another meaningful look, and Bettina gave Ian the ghost of a nod.

'We'd need to discuss it,' said Ian. 'But, taking into account your obvious talent as a chef, I think it could be a wonderful opportunity for Natasha.'

Cassidy beamed at him.

'And I love what you've done with the place,' he went on, waving his hand in the air. 'The hops above the bar remind me of that little place we went to in Valencia – do you remember, Bettina?'

Her face instantly lit up. 'Ooh yes! We had that amazing seafood fideua, and the owner brought over a bottle of some very potent thyme liqueur and we got really rather tipsy.'

She broke into giggles, which made her look ten years younger. This was a very different Bettina from the one Cassidy had met before; one she could almost imagine being friends with.

'I'm so glad we could sort this out,' said Cassidy. 'It's been a heck of a lot of work to get here, and it very nearly ended in disaster after I had a visit from a council planning officer the other day. Apparently he'd had some local complaints.'

'I'm sure he was just doing his job,' said Bettina quickly. 'You can't be too careful after the palaver we had with the Diaggios. But I suspect you won't have any further problems.'

After school, Cassidy took Nora for tea at the Buttered Crumpet. There were still plenty of leftovers from her day of recipe testing, but though Nora was an adventurous eater for a nine-year-old, wild garlic soup couldn't compete with Dale's ham and cheese toasties and a Biscoff milkshake.

The pair of them took the seat in the window, Nora chattering away about the school's Easter parade, and her ambitious plans for a Taylor Swift–themed bonnet.

Dale stopped by their table. 'Everything okay, my angels?'

'Delicious, as always,' said Cassidy, through a mouthful of sourdough.

'You make the best milkshakes *ever*,' gushed Nora. 'Even better than our old ice-cream parlour back in Sacramento.'

Dale mimed a swoon. 'Better than American milkshakes? That is praise indeed.'

Something caught his attention out of the window, and he craned his head to look down the street.

'Do you hear that, Cassidy?' Dale knitted his brows. 'Sounds like a bit of a to-do down the street.'

She paused, listening. Yes, she could hear the sound of raised voices. As she tried to make out what the shouting was about, she heard the distant wail of an emergency siren. A few people hurried past the window, some running, their faces etched with concern.

Dale crossed over to look out of the door. 'Goodness, I can see smoke! I can't see where it's coming from, though...'

Cassidy realised he was looking in the direction of the inn and her chest tightened.

He called out to a passer-by. 'What's going on down there?'

Their answer was mostly drowned out by the now blaring siren, but when Cassidy caught the words 'fire' and 'Beeswhistle', she was on her feet in an instant.

'Just wait here with Dale, okay?' she told Nora, cursing the tremor in her voice. She plastered on a reassuring smile. 'I'll be right back, sweetie, I promise.'

Cassidy flew down the street at full pelt, her stomach roiling, as the shouts gradually got louder and mingled with the hiss of jets of water. Perhaps they'd caught the fire before much damage was done? But as she turned the corner, a moan escaped from her lips. Two fire engines were jack-knifed across the narrow street, jets of water arching towards the inn's smoking roof, smog choking the air. Firefighters were keeping people from getting too close, but the extent of the damage was evident in the onlookers' horrified expressions. The smouldering roof – or what was left of it – looked like a burnt cornfield, revealing the skeleton of charred beams beneath, and the white plaster facade that she'd so recently finished painting was smudged and blackened with soot, while all that was left of her beautiful new hand-painted pub sign was the metal fittings.

Cassidy stared at the scene in open-mouthed horror, her hands clamped on either side of her head. How on earth had this happened? She'd only been here half an hour ago, and everything had been fine. As she'd left, she remembered waving to Fred, who had been up on the roof, finishing off the thatched ornamental ridge, and...

Fred.

Cassidy froze. Where was the sweet old thatcher?

EIGHTEEN

Cassidy ran towards the melee of people around the fire engines. Perhaps it was shock, but her senses seemed cranked up to superhero level. As she made her way through the crowd, she caught flashes of concerned faces, as vivid as Munch's *Scream*, and the rush of water and whirr of machinery was so loud, it hurt her ears. Cassidy was taking everything in, yet at the same time could make no sense of any of it at all.

And then – thank God! – she spotted Fred, sitting on a wall on the other side of the street. He was hunched over, his head cradled in his hands, but at least he was safe.

When he saw her running towards him, his face crumpled. He took out his pipe, which had been clenched between his teeth.

'Oh, Cassidy, love, I'm sorry! I can't believe it.'

'I'm just so relieved you're safe.' She sat down beside him. 'Can you tell me what happened?'

'It... it all happened so quick. I went inside to make some tea – I was a little while, you know how I like it properly brewed. And when I came out again, the roof was...whoosh! All of it up in flames. I called nine-nine-nine from my portable telephone and... well, here we are. I'm so sorry, Cassidy, I really am. Your beautiful home... And you've only just got it looking lovely again after all that work...'

He started to cry, and Cassidy put her arm around his bony shoulders. She had a vivid flashback to the last time she had hugged her dad, and her throat tightened with emotion. If only Joe was here now. Her dad would know what to do.

A firefighter, helmet visor pushed up, was walking towards them.

'I understand you're the landlady?' said the woman.

'Yes. Cassidy Beeswhistle.' She stood up, her legs wobbly beneath her.

'I'm Sal Gray, Watch Manager. You're lucky we caught it when we did. It always looks more dramatic when it's thatch, but the roof's taken the worst of it. It looks like you've escaped anything too serious inside, probably just soot and smoke damage, and we've done what we can to divert the water from any household items, though you won't be able to move back in for a while. It'll need a safety inspection and a professional clean.'

'It's okay, I can clean it myself,' said Cassidy, her mind going straight to the cost.

'Best to get a fire damage specialist on the case, just to make sure everything's safe,' Sal informed. 'We can sheet up the roof to protect the exposed areas in the short term, but I'm afraid the whole thing is going to need replacing.'

As the seriousness of the situation sank in, Cassidy looked again at the charred wreck of the Beeswhistle. All that time and money spent restoring it to its former glory, and now it was in a far worse state than even when the Diaggios had finished with it! She bent over, planting her hands on her knees, forcing herself to take deep breaths. 'We were meant to be reopening in a couple of weeks,' she muttered. 'I had it all planned out.' She glanced up at the firefighter. 'I don't have any money left.'

Sal Gray's face was kind; no doubt she was used to dealing with people who were in shock. 'Just make sure you contact your insurance company as soon as possible.'

Cassidy couldn't think straight. Did she even have insurance? There had been so many things to sort out when she had first moved here, and the systems were all so different than in the States. She had a vague recollection of paying for some sort of insurance, but for all she knew that may well have been the travel insurance. And what if her documents had been destroyed by the fire?

Cassidy swallowed down another wave of nausea. 'Do you know what caused the fire?'

'Not with any certainty. By its nature, a fire scene is one in which evidence can easily and quickly be lost to the effects of the fire or firefighting operations. But it's sometimes possible to identify a limited number of possible causes. I understand your thatcher, Fred Smith, had been working up there at the time?'

They both looked at Fred. He was taking a long draw on his pipe, the cloud of smoke matching the steam billowing from the hot, sodden roof.

Sal gave Cassidy a meaningful look. 'As I said, we can't say what started it for sure,' she commented, clearly choosing her words with care. 'But we'll be having a chat with Mr Smith to remind him about the dangers of smoking while working with thatch.'

Cassidy was grateful for her discretion; even if Fred had been to blame, she certainly didn't want him getting in any trouble.

'Well, thank you for getting here so quickly and putting it out,' said Cassidy.

Another firefighter appeared, this one holding a scrabbling, bedraggled Hermione.

Cassidy cried out, relieved to see the cat safe. Amidst the panic and chaos, she hadn't even thought about him.

'Is this yours?'

She held out her arms. 'Yes! Yes he is.' Cassidy cuddled Hermione to her, dropping relieved kisses on his head, and he instantly began to purr.

'Guv, you're needed over here,' said the firefighter.

'Right you are.' Sal Gray turned back to Cassidy. 'We'll get you inside when it's safe, so you can pack up some essentials.'

'Thank you, I—'

'Cassidy!'

She turned to see Angeline running towards her, her face etched with worry. 'Thank God! Are you and Nora okay?'

'Yes, we were out when it started. God, your cottage hasn't been damaged, has it?'

'No, it's absolutely fine.'

Cassidy let out a heavy breath. That was something at least.

'Angeline, I left Nora at the Buttered Crumpet with Dale. Would you mind taking her back to your place? I'll be round to get her as soon as I've sorted out the formalities.'

'Of course. Here, let me take Hermione too.' Angeline started to leave, but then turned back. 'Just take everything one step at a time, okay? Remember, we all want to help.'

After she had gone, Cassidy glanced back at Fred, but he was now talking to one of the firefighters. Standing alone amidst the smoke and noise, the momentousness of Cassidy's situation began to sink in, bringing with it an uncontrollable urge to run away. She even started to walk off – going where, she had absolutely no idea – before forcing herself to turn back after just a few steps.

She looked at the inn again, her face twisting in anguish. There was nothing for it: she would have to sell the Beeswhistle. The thought of starting again on the renovations, after it taking so much time and effort (not to mention money) to get to this stage, was just too much to face. As far as Cassidy was concerned, when life gave you lemons, why go through the faff of trying to make lemonade? Far easier to say 'no, thank you' to the lemons and go off in search of strawberries instead. And, right now, every fibre of her being wanted to wash her hands of this place: flog it for whatever she could get, leave Dithercott and go in search of strawberries elsewhere.

And she *would* have, if she had anywhere else she could go – but Joe was gone and the apartment in Sacramento had been sold. The realisation hit her in the gut so hard it was like she'd been punched. Cassidy had nobody to rely on but herself.

Then through the crowds she spotted James Keating. It seemed to Cassidy as if he was moving in slow motion: a super-hero striding through the rubble and smoke of a ruined city, his square jaw set in determination.

At the sight of him, Cassidy finally gave into her tears.

'Thank goodness you're safe,' said the vicar, putting his arm round her shoulder and pulling her towards him. The warmth and solidity of his body felt like a refuge from the chaos. 'Do you know what happened?'

She told him everything she knew, careful to avoid putting even a hint of blame on Fred. After all, as Sal Gray had explained, it was impossible to know for sure how the fire had started. It could well have been a build-up of hot gases in her chimney or a spark from another cottage's fire, rather than Fred's pipe.

James still had his arm around her. 'I hope I'm not speaking out of turn, but I think you and Nora should come and stay at the vicarage until it's safe to move back to the inn.'

'That's so kind of you, but—'

'You won't even have to see me if you don't want. There are six bedrooms and my housekeeper, Mrs Arbuckle, lives there too, so she can act as a chaperone. Besides, being a local vicar is a twenty-four-hour job, so I'm hardly ever there. Please, Cassidy? I would really love to help.'

It felt like an imposition, but where else were they going to stay? She knew that Angeline would welcome them in an instant, but Old Forge Cottage didn't have any spare bedrooms, and they couldn't very well camp out in the living room indefinitely. Who knew how many weeks it would take for the inn to be safe to live in again?

'Could I bring the cat, too?'

'Absolutely.'

She managed a smile. 'Thank you so much, James, you're a lifesaver.'

'Honestly, it will be my pleasure.'

She tilted her head to look at him. 'Why are you being so nice to me?'

'Well, it's my job, but even if it wasn't, then I'd want to help. Besides,' he added, 'I'll enjoy having you and Nora around.'

NINETEEN

When it came to emergency housing, there were definitely worse places to have ended up. In fact, thought Cassidy, as she settled into a sunlit spot in the gardens of the New Vicarage, this was probably about as good as it got.

She was wearing a woolly jumper, hat and scarf, but was stretched out on the wooden lounger in a pair of sunglasses as if it was summer. Next to her, on a wrought-iron table, was a large slice of Victoria sponge. (Practically a quarter of the entire cake, in fact, but she hadn't had breakfast and there was nobody around to pass judgement.) If she turned her head very slightly – although right now even *that* felt like a bit too much effort – she could see the peach-coloured brick of the elegant Georgian vicarage, a perfectly symmetrical house with rows of white-framed windows and a sage-green front door. Vicars in the Georgian era clearly knew how to live.

Cassidy closed her eyes, enjoying the sun on her face, the hum of a distant lawnmower and the rich scent of lilac. Right at that moment, she was almost – *almost* – glad that the inn had caught fire.

The New Vicarage was new in the same way that New

York was, in that it was a few hundred years old. It was built fifty years after Bertie Beeswhistle had left for America, and, just like the city he ended up in, it was a triumph of bricks and mortar, though that was where any similarity between the two ended. The city that never sleeps would have been bored rigid at the New Vicarage, which was a place of homemade jam, afternoon naps in front of the fire and the murmur of muted conversation on the kitchen radio.

Cassidy and Nora had moved in on the evening of the fire. Earlier that afternoon, Cassidy had ventured back inside the inn with one of the firefighters to pack up some clothes and rescue their valuables. Downstairs didn't actually look too terrible, if you ignored the inches of water on the floor, but the entire upstairs was so lavishly coated in soot, it looked as if someone had spray-painted it from floor to ceiling in black paint. And this stuff was evil: Cassidy had only briefly touched a door handle, but the oily stain on her skin had still lingered after three lots of scrubbing. As she had stood in her bedroom and surveyed the mess, her heart plummeting, she had found herself wishing the inn had been entirely destroyed; at least then she would have had no alternative but to throw in the towel. As much as she loved this place, she had no fight left in her to stay and fix the latest in what felt like a never-ending succession of disasters.

Later that evening, however, sitting at the kitchen table of the New Vicarage with a bowl of minestrone soup in front of her and Nora sleeping upstairs, Cassidy's tight chest had begun to ease. It was impossible to feel like your world had imploded when your feet were being warmed by an Aga the colour of double cream, and the gentle ticking of a grandfather clock was soothing your tattered nerves. The vicarage felt like a place where only good things happened, and if bad things *did* happen, well, it would do its best to help you cope, while bringing you cups of tea and slices of cake.

James hadn't been exaggerating when he'd told Cassidy she would barely see him. He was so busy with church business and needy parishioners that in the three days since she and Nora had arrived, Cassidy had seen him a grand total of once, and that was just a brief 'hello' as they had passed in the hallway. Embarrassing night-time encounters were off the table too, as his bedroom was at the far end of the house and between them, like a guard tower at a prison camp, was the room occupied by the live-in housekeeper Sally Arbuckle.

Stout and no-nonsense, the fifty-something widow had worked for James since he had first arrived at St Andrew's Church and, judging by her offhand manner, Cassidy got the impression she wasn't overly keen on an interloper messing up their cosy domestic situation. She doted on the reverend like a son, and in this scenario, Cassidy was a new girlfriend who'd just arrived on the scene and clearly wasn't good enough for her boy. It didn't help that Hermione kept catching birds and leaving the poor creatures on the kitchen floor. Mrs Arbuckle was as fond of the garden's sparrows and tits as she was proud of her spotless kitchen, so it was black marks all round.

At least the housekeeper had taken to Nora, calling her 'poppet' and roping her into whatever she was doing, whether that was sewing on buttons or overseeing the church flowers. They quickly fell into a surrogate grandmother-granddaughter arrangement which suited them both. Mrs Arbuckle was also an incredible cook, though she never followed recipes or, frustratingly, even seemed to remember what ingredients she'd used in a dish. When Cassidy asked for details of exactly how she made her porridge, which tasted as though angels had been involved, Mrs Arbuckle had looked at her as if she was daft and said, 'I just whack it in the Aga.'

All this domestic support and childcare left Cassidy with little to do but wallow in her misfortune and spend hours on the phone, ping-ponging between departments at her insurance

company, who were clinging onto their purse strings with the
desperation of the drowning, although at least it had turned out
she did have the appropriate policy. In the meantime, with no
way of earning, the pit that was Cassidy's finances was getting
deeper and blacker and scarier by the minute. Her only option
was to find a job as soon as possible, but none of the vacancies at
local restaurants offered hours that would suit a single mother
with a major pub renovation on her hands. Day and night, her
stresses nibbled away at Cassidy like hungry rats, so when she
had seen the sunshine through the window that morning, she
had immediately cut herself a slice of cake and plonked herself
on the lounger. She knew this moment would provide a brief
break from the chaos and she was determined to make the most
of it.

Cassidy was just messaging Manon back in Sacramento
with an account of everything that had happened over the past
few days when she heard the rumble of tyres on gravel and
looked up, hoping to see James's Ford Fiesta, but instead it was a
large silver estate car. She watched as the driver parked, inching
back and forward until the car was perfectly aligned with the
herbaceous border, then the doors opened and Ian and Bettina
Flint got out. They waved, then headed in her direction, Bettina
gingerly making her way over the lawn in her wedge sandals. It
was so nice to see them smiling. Since that day at the Beeswhistle, the Flints' attitude towards Cassidy had done a complete
360.

'Hey, guys, I'm afraid James isn't here right now,' she said,
sitting up to greet them.

'It's actually you we've come to see,' said Bettina.

'We've got a proposition,' added Ian.

'That sounds intriguing. Would you like some tea?'

She had finally got used to the English habit of offering tea
at every opportunity, whatever the occasion or time of day. Lull

in the conversation? Cup of tea. Won the lottery? Cup of tea. Severed limb? I'll go and pop the kettle on...

'No, we're fine, thank you.' Bettina glanced at her husband. She looked like she had a secret she was bursting to share. 'Will you tell her, Ian, or shall I?'

'We've had an idea,' he said. 'To help you get the pub back up and running.'

'That's really kind of you, but I'm not sure you can help. I can't get started on repairs until the insurance company pay out and God knows how long that will take.'

'But that's just it,' said Bettina. 'Our idea will raise the money you need to get started on the renovations yourself.'

'And at the same time, it will be a way to let everyone in the village taste your food,' added Ian. 'We need to spread the word, let people know what an amazing chef you are!'

Having just put together a spreadsheet of the repairs that were needed, Cassidy suspected that the Flints' fundraising idea would barely be a drop in the ocean, but the couple looked so excited, she didn't want to be downbeat.

'We'll have a special fundraising fête,' said Bettina. 'In the inn's garden.'

'A fête?' The word felt unfamiliar, though Cassidy vaguely remembered Mrs Timothy mentioning it in passing.

'Yes, you know, a traditional parish fête. Hoopla, Pimm's, a dog show, raffle, Morris dancing – that sort of thing.'

'I suppose it might be a bit early in the season for "guess the weight of the marrow", but Bettina and I will be happy to take charge of the tombola.'

Cassidy was staring at them blankly. They might as well have been speaking French.

'Don't you have fêtes in America?' asked Ian.

'Not that I'm aware of.'

'Well, it's a sort of village party, with jolly games and family entertainment,' said Bettina. 'And, of course, lots of delicious food. Which is where you'll come in, Cassidy.'

'The village used to have a fête in the grounds of the manor every year,' continued Ian, 'but that hasn't happened for some time now. Since... well, you know. Poor old Ned. Anyway, I'm sure everyone in the village would get behind it, especially for such a good cause. Goodness knows we all want our pub back again.'

Cassidy was touched they had clearly put so much thought into the idea. 'It's so lovely of you to try to help, but I'm afraid I wouldn't know where to start organising something like that.'

'But that's just it, you wouldn't need to,' said Bettina, triumphantly. 'We'll just get the Dithercott fête committee back together again.'

Ian glanced at his wife, chuckling. 'I suspect old Nigel will jump at the chance...'

'I think everyone in the village will,' added Bettina.

For the first time since the fire, Cassidy felt a flicker of hope. She might not have a clue about village fêtes, but Ian and Bettina clearly knew what they were doing, and it sounded as if there were others in the village who would help too. She didn't want to get too excited, but perhaps this *could* be a way to ease her financial worries.

Also: giant marrows? Morris dancing? Pimm's? Whatever it all was, it sounded like it could be fun.

TWENTY

The grandfather clock in the hallway of the New Vicarage chimed six times as Cassidy padded to the kitchen. She had just showered after her morning run and now needed coffee. As much as she had grown to appreciate a cup of English tea, it didn't give her the defibrillator jolt needed to kick-start her day.

Clad only in a towel and with her hair still wet, Cassidy let out an 'aaah' as her feet touched the flagstones, which had been warmed by the underfloor heating to the temperature of a Californian beach at sunset. Through the window, the garden shone in the clear morning light, holding the promise of a beautiful day ahead.

Cassidy paused, looking at the yellow laburnum blossoms that had seemed to appear overnight. Just when she thought the garden was looking its best, another plant would magically explode into bloom. Pow! Here are some ballerina-pink peonies. Zap! Check out these plumes of lilac! It still astounded her that the grey wasteland that Dithercott had been when they'd arrived was now as lush and gaudy as a rainforest.

As she waited for the water to boil, she leant against the Aga and thought about the morning ahead. Things had moved fast

in the two days since the Flints had told her of their idea for
holding a fête at the inn. She had done some research to bring
herself up to speed, and now at least had a basic understanding
of how they worked, even if she still found the concept of
Morris dancing baffling (though Bettina assured her that it was
baffling to most English people as well).

The fête's committee had already convened, consisting of
Ian, Bettina and Angeline, plus the local butcher, the aptly
named Nigel Lamb, who had been chair of the preceding
fêtes before they came to an abrupt halt a few years back.
Cassidy hadn't met him yet, but she was aware of his reputation as the village fixer. The committee's first meeting was
taking place that afternoon at the Quill. Nigel had suggested
the venue, despite some unspecified feud with Sophia and
Xavier, because he was fond of their Ploughman's sharing
platter. In any case, it was a weekday, which meant Sophia
would be in London and there was no danger of her crashing
the party.

Cassidy was just reading a long reply from Manon to her
message about the fire (which began 'WTF OMG...') when
James came in through the back door. He didn't notice her for a
moment, giving her time to take in his dishevelled hair and
weary manner, and he jumped like a cartoon character when he
realised she was there.

'Oh! I'm sorry, I didn't want to wake the house, so I thought
I'd come in the back.'

Having registered her semi-naked state, he immediately
looked away, clearly embarrassed. Cassidy glanced down to
discover that her towel was barely covering the bits of her it
should have been, and she scrabbled to make herself decent, her
cheeks burning. In the silence, the ticking of the grandfather
clock just served to underline their mutual awkwardness.

'Sorry,' James blurted again, his gaze drilling into the wall.

Cassidy scrabbled around for something to talk about.

'Have you been out all night? I bet you're exhausted. Would you like some coffee?'

'Oh, yes please, if that's not too much trouble.'

'Coming right up!' Grateful for the distraction, she went to retrieve the mugs, one hand firmly clutching onto her towel. 'So, what have you been up to?'

James took a seat at the table. He sat down heavily, in a way that suggested he'd never get up again. 'I was called out yesterday evening by Maggie Turnbull. Do you know the family?'

Cassidy shook her head.

'They farm the land just past the village hall. Maggie's husband, Bill, was dying, and they wanted me at his bedside.'

'I'm sorry, that must have been tough.'

James smiled briefly and Cassidy noticed the dark shadows beneath his eyes. 'Bill was ninety-six, and it was a peaceful passing. In those circumstances, it's easier to celebrate a life as well as to mourn it. He knew it was his time, and he'd made peace with that. He died in the early hours of this morning, and then Maggie and I sat at his bedside, talking and sharing memories. It was actually rather beautiful.'

Cassidy had stopped what she was doing and was looking at James, swept up by his words. He was such a sweet, thoughtful man – she'd never met anyone like him before.

James had been looking down at his hands while he spoke, but he tipped his head up to look at her. As he gazed at Cassidy, his brows bunched together, like an actor who has forgotten his next line. Then he took a breath and said: 'Cassidy, I—'

The creak of floorboards upstairs abruptly cut him off. Both of them looked at the ceiling; moments later, there was the sound of footsteps on the stairs.

'What were you going to say?' Cassidy asked, conscious that they were about to be interrupted.

James opened his mouth to speak, but it was too late. Mrs

Arbuckle appeared in the doorway, already dressed in her unofficial uniform of an apron decorated with a splashy fruit design.

'Good morning, Reverend. How was your night? Did Bill Turnbull pass?'

'Morning, Mrs A. And yes, I'm afraid so.'

'Ah, that's a shame. But it was his time, I think. I mean – ninety-six! It's a grand old age. He was close to outstaying his welcome!' She was smiling as she said this, but as she turned away, Cassidy heard her mutter, 'Maggie Turnbull certainly thought as much...'

Mrs Arbuckle only now noticed Cassidy by the Aga and her eyebrows shot upwards with comedic exaggeration. Judging by the housekeeper's expression, Cassidy might as well not even be wearing the towel.

Mrs Arbuckle hurried towards her, her hands outstretched as if to cover her shamelessness. 'Gracious, you must be freezing! Off you go, missy, and put on some clothes.'

As she shooed her out of the kitchen – barely giving her time to grab her coffee – Cassidy glanced back at James. He was watching her go, and the look in his eyes made her catch her breath. She had seen that look on a man's face before, and it almost always led to trouble.

TWENTY-ONE

The reception area at the Quill was dominated by a large photograph of the Quill family posed outside Dithercott Manor's enormous front door. A beaming Sophia was giving lady-of-the-manor vibes in wellies and a waxed jacket, a trug full of freshly dug vegetables over her arm. Xavier was dressed in tweed, as if he had just popped back from shooting some pheasants (though while the outfit would have suited Ned Bamford-Bligh, he looked as if he was trussed up in fancy dress), while the Quill children posed stiffly in miniature versions of their parents' outfits. The only member of the party who looked remotely natural and relaxed was the spaniel sprawled at their feet.

Beneath the photo there was a plaque that read: 'From our family to yours, a warm and heartfelt welcome to the Quill', below which there was a quotation: 'There are no strangers here; only friends you haven't met yet.'

Angeline, who was waiting with Cassidy, was looking at the photo too.

'Surely that should read: "There are no strangers here, only

friends you haven't reported to the council for planning viola-
tions yet.'"

Cassidy snorted with laughter. 'We don't know for sure that
Sophia was the one spreading rumours about me.'

'True, but it seems exactly the sort of shitty thing she'd do.
Plus we know she feels weirdly threatened by you.' Angeline
thought for a moment. 'In fact, it was probably Sophia who set
fire to the inn. Climbed onto the roof when nobody was looking
and started the blaze with a scented diptyque candle.'

Cassidy gave her a jokey shove, just as the waitress returned
to seat them.

'Right this way, ladies. You're the first of your party to
arrive.'

'Excellent, we can have a catch-up before the rest get here,'
said Angeline, looping her arm through Cassidy's.

The dining room was vast and open, with none of the
Beeswhistle's cosy nooks and corners, its windows soaring from
floor to ceiling. It was a chilly day, but air conditioning vents
were blasting cold air, which meant most of the customers were
still wearing coats. Cassidy now understood why Dale had
compared the Quill to an airport departure lounge.

The waitress showed them to a round table by the window
and distributed poster-sized menus. No seasonal specials,
Cassidy noted with disapproval. She was trying to be open-
minded and not let her personal opinion of the Quills colour
her judgement of their pub, but with all the money that had
obviously been lavished on the decor, it seemed a shame they
weren't taking such care over the food.

'Can I get you a drink while you wait?' asked the waitress.

Angeline was already scanning the menu. 'What's a Sophia
Sour?'

'Our house cocktail. Amaretto, cherries and lemon.'

Angeline grimaced at Cassidy. 'We'll take a bottle of Pros-
ecco, thank you,' handing back the menu.

'Woah – aren't we here to work?'

'I don't know about you, but I find I'm at my most creative when I'm a bit drunk.'

After the waitress had gone, Angeline leant her forearms on the table.

'So, how's life at the New Vicarage?'

'Idyllic. Like living in a Jane Austen novel, but with under-floor heating and Wi-Fi. Nora absolutely loves the place – *and* Mrs Arbuckle. I love it too, but...' She tailed off with a shrug.

'Mrs Arbuckle not so much?'

'I think it's more that she doesn't love me. I do get it, though, she's had James to herself for years, and now there's this other woman sharing the bathroom.'

'She's always been very protective of the reverend. Imagine what she'd be like if James ever got married!'

Cassidy hesitated. 'Has he ever been in a relationship while he's been at St Andrew's?'

'There was a rumour about him and a woman who lived in another village, I think she was an artist. But that was ages ago. Why do you ask?'

'I just wondered. He's a good-looking guy, and so kind. He can't do enough for us. Plus that vicarage is one heck of a crib. All things considered, I'm surprised he hasn't been snapped up.'

Angeline was looking at her beadily. 'Is this just hypothetical interest, or are you "asking for a friend"?'

Thankfully, at that moment, the waitress arrived at their table with a carafe of water, which gave Cassidy a chance to consider how much she should reveal to Angeline of her feelings about James. By the time their glasses had been filled, she decided Angeline was a good enough friend for her to be honest. Besides, she needed advice.

'So?' Angeline raised her eyebrows. 'What's going on?'

'Nothing. Honestly! But... I do like James. I enjoy spending time with him. And I might be totally off the mark, but I get the impression he feels the same about me.'

'Well, this *is* big news. How exciting!' Angeline's expression turned thoughtful. 'Don't take this the wrong way, but I didn't think James would be your type.'

'Why's that?'

'Well, he's a lovely guy – I mean he's a vicar, so being a lovely guy plus some praying is basically the job description – but I guess I had you down for someone a bit more... well, dangerous. I can't imagine James ever dancing on tables after too much tequila, but I can bet my entire bank balance that you have.'

'But perhaps that's where I've been going wrong in the past? James is just so... so steady. And reliable. He's a breath of fresh air after the freaks and commitment-phobes I've encountered on Tinder over the past few years.'

'I know what you mean, and you're right, steady and reliable *are* important qualities – I certainly wish I'd realised as much when I married Tilly's dad – but you're not buying a family car here. There has to be chemistry too. Do you fancy him?'

'Oh, come on, you must agree he's handsome.'

'True, but that's not what I was asking. Does the dude give you flutters?'

Cassidy giggled; it felt wrong to be talking about a vicar like this. 'I'm not sure. Maybe. I guess I—'

But just then, the Flints arrived at the table, accompanied by a red-faced man with a fuzz of ginger hair encircling his otherwise bald head. He pounced on Cassidy.

'So you're the Beeswhistle, are you? Delighted to meet you. Nigel Lamb.'

'Hi, Nigel, thank you so much for helping out with this.' Cassidy looked around at the whole party. 'In fact, thank you all. I'm so grateful for your support.'

'Tsk, not at all,' said Nigel, plonking himself down next to her. 'What's good for the inn is good for the whole village. You probably heard about the trouble we had with the previous occupants?'

Bettina clutched at her necklace.

'Yobbos,' barked Nigel. 'Absolute ruffians. So you, my dear, are a bloody breath of fresh air, and a very pretty one at that! I hear you're a chef?'

'Honestly, Nigel, Cassidy's food is exquisite,' said Ian.

'I can vouch for that too,' added Angeline. 'The village is lucky to have her.'

'I look forward to trying it for myself,' said Nigel. 'And if you need help sourcing meat, I'd be very happy to point you in the right direction. I presume you'll be using local suppliers?'

'Of course,' said Cassidy.

'Glad to hear it. Because certain local establishments prefer to get their lamb flown in from New Zealand. Apparently, meat needs to have its own passport before its considered good enough for *some* people.' He glanced furtively around the room. 'She's not here today, is she? The Duchess of La-di-da?'

'We've not seen her,' said Angeline.

'Praise the lord,' bellowed Nigel. He rubbed his hands together. 'Right, let's get started. Welcome all to the inaugural planning meeting for this year's Beeswhistle fête. What a joy to be saying those words again after so many years! Now, all of us around the table – apart from our lovely American friend here – have plenty of experience in this field, so this should be a piece of cake. I've put together an agenda.' He produced a sheaf of papers, which he passed around. 'Any objections to me being Chair.'

This wasn't a question.

'I'll take the minutes, Nigel.'

'Thank you, Bettina, we couldn't do it without your fault-less secretarial skills.'

She glowed at the compliment.

'First item on the agenda. As this is not, strictly speaking, a village fête of the sort we used to have up at the manor before that awful business with poor old Ned, I propose we come up with a different name for the event. Something fun and trendy, befitting our lovely new landlady here.'

'How about the Beeswhistle Festival?' suggested Angeline. 'Cassidy's going to do barbecue food, so that somehow feels more appropriate than fête, anyway.'

'Yes, I like it,' said Nigel.

'Me too,' said Cassidy. 'We could shorten it to Beesfest.'

'Ooh yes, that's fab,' agreed Angeline.

Nigel looked around the table. 'Any objections to Beesfest?'

The Flints glanced at each other, and then Ian said: 'None from us.'

'Excellent! Beesfest it is. Motion passed.'

Cassidy got the feeling that if Nigel had a gavel, he'd be banging it.

As they talked, the event began to take shape in Cassidy's head: the inn's garden decorated with bunting, food grilling on the barbecue, the happy shouts of children. It all sounded wonderful. She felt a bright chink of optimism break through the dark clouds that had been lurking in her mind since the fire.

They took a break from working through the agenda when their lunch arrived, and Cassidy was just struggling through a painfully bland pad thai when they heard a horribly familiar voice.

'Well, isn't this a cosy little gathering! I assume my invitation must have got lost in the post.'

Sophia had materialised beside their table, coinciding with the air conditioning seeming to kick up a notch.

'Hello, Ian, Bettina,' she said, with a cold smile.

The Flints looked like teenagers whose parents had just caught them vaping with the bad kids.

'And, Nigel, it's wonderful to see you here! Can't keep away from our legendary Ploughman's Platter?'

He scowled down at his half-finished plate.

'How are you enjoying the food, Cassidy?' Sophia's tiny nose wrinkled. 'Oh, has nobody brought you any ketchup? I'm *so* sorry about that. I can ask someone to fetch if for you now...'

'Thank you, Sophia, but I prefer my pad thai without ketchup.'

'Of course. I just know how keen you Americans are on your tom-ay-to sauce!' She giggled at her joke. 'So, what's the occasion?'

Angeline, who appeared to be the least cowed by Sophia, said: 'We're organising this year's fête.'

'Oh goody! I do miss the village fête, such a shame we can't have it at the manor anymore, but the footfall was really making such a mess of the west lawn.'

Angeline had already told Cassidy that after Ned's tragedy Sophia had flatly refused to have the fête at the Manor anymore, although it had been nothing to do with the state of the lawn.

'So, where are you going to have it?' she asked. 'The village green?'

'In the Beeswhistle Inn's garden,' said Angeline. 'To raise money to rebuild the pub. There was a fire, you may have heard.'

'I did! Such a shame. I suppose that means you won't be able to open the pub for yonks, Cassidy? What rotten luck.' She pouted theatrically. 'But I hear the ever-gallant James Keating has come to your rescue! Don't go corrupting our reverend while you're staying under his roof, will you now?' She gave a brittle laugh. 'I presume you'll need me there to open the fête, judge the dog show and so forth. When will it be?'

Nigel grunted the date.

'Oh, that's a shame, I think Xav and I will be in Positano.

You may want to change the date so that I can be there? Or I suppose you could find another local celebrity to do the honours, but I'm racking my brain to think of anyone suitable.'

Ian finally found his voice. 'It's not really a traditional fête this year, Sophia, so I'm sure we'll be fine without those formalities.'

'Really? Sounds a little unconventional, but I suppose I know what you're doing... Oh, it's just *super* to see you all rallying around to help Cassidy. She really is flavour of the month, isn't she?'

Angeline discreetly lifted her brows at Cassidy.

'Anyway, I must get on, tons to do,' Sophia added. 'Bye all!'

The table let out a collective exhale as she left.

'That woman,' muttered Nigel darkly. 'She is absolutely—'

'Panic over!' Sophia had reappeared at their table. 'I've just realised we're leaving for Italy a day later, so I can be at your little fête after all.' She gave a fluttery wave. 'Can't wait!'

TWENTY-TWO

Nigel Lamb and his wife, Jennifer, lived in an old farmhouse on the outskirts of Dithercott accessed by an unmade track through the woods that apparently became an impassable swamp during bad weather. 'Keeps the undesirables out,' Nigel told Cassidy, as he showed her around.

In a village full of swans, the Lambs' house was the architectural ugly duckling, but it came with a lot of land and outbuildings, and it was in one of these that all the equipment necessary for putting on the village fête was stored. Nigel hadn't been inside the shed since the last fête four years ago and he had to get his shoulder to the door to force it open. It gave way with a weary groan that Cassidy could strongly relate to, and she involuntarily yawned in solidarity. Between planning Beesfest and helping Jasha, who'd been doing what he could on her non-existent budget to make sure the inn was at least structurally sound before the festival, she had been working around the clock.

Thankfully, the Dithercott village fête had clearly been run like a well-oiled machine and an army of volunteers had enthusiastically taken up the roles they had played in previous years.

Mrs Timothy started to prep for her jams and chutneys stall, Dithercott Primary volunteered the school band and, within days, the Flints had sourced an astonishing number of prizes for their tombola, including several boxes of sparkling wine from a local vineyard. A bouncy castle had been sourced and booked. Nigel had lobbied hard for the local Morris dancing troupe to perform, but Cassidy had argued that a load of hanky-waving, stick-bashing middle-aged men wouldn't suit the festival vibe, so instead, Ron Dunphy, the Elvis-impersonator partner of Dale from the Buttered Crumpet, would be performing a headlining set (and Dale had been so happy about this that he had offered to run a cake stall, so it was a win-win).

Not only was Cassidy deeply moved by the whole community's effort, all the support gave her time to focus on the catering. She couldn't remember ever feeling quite so much pressure on her cooking. This would be the first time most people in the village would taste her food, and she was well aware how important it was that they enjoyed it. In her more hysterical moments, it felt as if the future of the Beeswhistle Inn was entirely dependent on whether visitors to Beesfest enjoyed her lamb merguez flatbreads. It was ironic that she was trying to convince the village that she wasn't a fast-food cook when she would basically be cooking posh burgers for the event, but that couldn't be helped. She would just have to make sure they were delicious enough to convince people to try her more sophisticated offerings when the Beeswhistle finally opened.

As her eyes adjusted to the darkness inside Nigel's shed, Cassidy saw that the space was almost entirely full of boxes and plastic-wrapped paraphernalia, stacked from floor to ceiling. It was dingy and cramped, and when she heard a scuttling sound in the corner, her sleep-deprived mind instantly crawled with rats.

'Wow, this is... a lot,' she said, marvelling at the scale of the job ahead of them.

'The Beeswhistle fête was a very big deal,' said Nigel, proudly.

Producing a Stanley knife, he slit open the nearest box and fished out armfuls of rainbow-coloured bunting.

'Hand-sewn by the ladies of Dithercott Women's Institute. My wife, Jennifer, is president. You should think about joining, Cassidy, it's not all jam and Jerusalem anymore. They had a lecture on gender identity the other day. Very illuminating, apparently. Jennifer's even added her pronouns to her Facebook profile. Righto, what else do we have here...'

He started moving things round, muttering over labels and greeting the contents of boxes like old friends. 'Ah, lovely, here's our tombola drum – Ian and Bettina will be pleased, it still looks in excellent nick – and this is the candyfloss machine. And... a-ha! So *that's* where she's been hiding.' He stared to heave something heavy out from behind the boxes. 'You're going to like this, Cassidy...'

He dragged a large wooden contraption into view and presented it with a 'ta-dah!' gesture. It looked like a medieval instrument of torture.

'Um, what am I looking at, Nigel?'

'Death by a thousand sponges.' He tenderly dusted it down, as if it was a treasured antique dresser rather than a tool for tormenting peasants. 'Always one of our most popular attractions at the fête. Nearly everyone in the village has had a turn in these stocks over the years: vicars, head teachers, police officers – me! But it was Ned Bamford-Bligh's thing, really. Oh, Ned *loved* it. He'd be dressed up in his best tuxedo, like Dithercott's answer to James Bond but even more handsome, and he'd just be hooting with laughter while the local kids pelted him with wet sponges like billy-o! Bloody good sport he was...' Nigel's grin faded. 'Ned was such an integral part of the fête. He bought most of this stuff for the village; we couldn't have done it without him. Then there was the accident...' He sighed heavily. 'You know, sometimes I think that Ned died that day too.'

His words hung in the air like the dust motes lit up by the sunlight from the doorway.

Eventually, Nigel forced a smile and patted the stocks. 'Perhaps she should sit it out this year? The old girl is so indelibly linked with Ned, it would feel strange to have it without him.'

'I think that's a good idea,' said Cassidy. 'Although if Sophia insists on being involved, we could always lock her up in it.'

His boom of laughter echoed around the walls. 'Oh, I do like you, Cassidy.'

It took them the best part of the day to sort out what they would need for Beesfest and check it was all in working order. Ned had certainly been a lavish benefactor. There were stalls, trestles, a complete sound system, even a set of hand-carved Punch and Judy puppets. But then again, thought Cassidy, he could afford to be generous, seeing as how his ancestors had basically been handed a manor house for free. Not for the first time, she wondered how different her life would have been if Bertie hadn't been so rubbish at dice. Perhaps it would have been her winning hearts in the stocks instead of Ned.

When they had finally finished work, Nigel gave her a lift back to the vicarage, pressing a pack of pork chops into her hands as a parting gift. As she walked up the garden path, it struck Cassidy that all the people she liked most in Dithercott – Angeline, Mrs Timothy, James and now Nigel – adored Ned Bamford-Bligh. It made her regret that she hadn't met him before the accident. She had no interest in getting to know an angry recluse who liked to yell at children, but the pre-tragedy version of Ned sounded terrific.

TWENTY-THREE

The morning of Beesfest – the first of May – dawned stubbornly grey and rainy, as if the weather knew all too well that the entire village had its fingers crossed for sunshine. Cassidy hadn't got to bed until 3 a.m. as she'd been feverishly prepping the festival's food in the vicarage kitchen, and by the time she woke just a few hours later, there was already a flurry of messages on the committee WhatsApp group:

Nigel: Activate RCPP?

Angeline: RCPP???

Ian: Rain Contingency Planning Procedures (see p.32 fête handbook)

Bettina: Will bring additional gazebos plus waterproof ponchos

Nigel: Thumbs-up emoji

Angeline: Don't worry, folks, sun forecast from 11am onwards!!

Ian: Think extra ponchos and gazebos still
prudent

Angeline: Rolling-eyes emoji

James drove Cassidy to the inn after an early breakfast, the
boot and back seat of his car packed with containers of mari-
nating meat, vegetable garnishes and sauces, plus enough
pillowy rolls and pittas to fill the bouncy castle. Cassidy had
poured her heart and soul into the menu. She knew that the
visitors would probably be perfectly happy with a decent burger
– and she could certainly have delivered that – but when it
came to her food, she couldn't help pushing the envelope. Why
do a hot dog when you could do a coal-roasted aubergine wrap
with miso and coriander? 'I'll tell you why,' Mrs Arbuckle had
replied tartly, when Cassidy had said this to her last night,
'because most people prefer hot dogs.' It had been said with a
twinkle though, because the truth was that Cassidy had grown
on Mrs Arbuckle over the past few weeks, and vice versa.
Perhaps it was Cassidy's sustained charm offensive, or maybe it
was because the housekeeper had seen that their American
house guest was clearly doing all she could to move out of the
vicarage and get back to the inn, but whatever the reason, she
now greeted her with smiles rather than eye rolls and had
insisted that Cassidy call her Sally. The two women had
worked alongside each other in the kitchen last night.

'You know, I'm really enjoying this,' the housekeeper had
said as she minced a pile of garlic.

'Did you ever think about cooking for a career? You're
certainly talented enough to work in a professional kitchen.'

'Oh, you know, it would have been nice, but life got in the
way... Never say never, though.'

Cassidy had glanced at her. 'Well, you better watch out, or I
might poach you for a job at the Beeswhistle when it opens.'

And Sally Arbuckle had arched an eyebrow in a way that suggested that actually she might be quite happy to be poached, and Cassidy had tucked away this little nugget of information to take out and consider at some point in the future.

As James manoeuvred his car around the rainy country lanes, windscreen wipers working at full pelt, Cassidy glanced into the back of the car to make sure that nothing was in danger of tipping over. She scanned the containers like a worried mother hen checking up on her brood of chicks, and the jittery feeling in her chest cranked up a gear. Now that the opening of Beesfest was just hours away, Cassidy was beginning to have doubts about the food. Was the merguez too spicy? Did her honey-barbecue sauce for the pulled pork need a touch more sharpness? She was haunted by visions of festival-goers taking a bite and then grimacing.

'What time will you be getting to the festival?' she asked James, keen for a distraction.

'Around eleven-ish. I need to set up my Crockery Cricket stall.'

'You know, I still don't get what that is.'

'Oh, it's the most tremendous fun! It basically involves throwing a cricket ball at old china plates and cups to smash them.'

'And then?'

James glanced at her with a blank look. 'Well, that's it. That's the game.'

'So what do you win?'

'Nothing. That's not the point. It's about the thrill of the smash!'

'Huh. I see.'

But she didn't – not really. At least with a coconut shy you had a chance of winning a coconut. Cassidy filed it away under 'Bizarre English Eccentricities', just as she had done with Welly Wanging.

Still, it was impossible not to be carried away by the village's enthusiasm over Beesfest. People she'd never met before had been running up to her in the street, saying things like, 'Irene and I are on Splat-the-Rat!' And whenever it happened, Cassidy had felt the warm glow of being part of a community – something she'd never experienced in her life and didn't know she needed until she actually had.

Once James had parked outside the inn, Cassidy got out and gazed up at the front of the building, taking in the singed plaster, charred beams and the tarpaulins covering what was left of the roof. The rain had now petered out to a light drizzle; still, the Beeswhistle couldn't be a more miserable sight set against the flat grey sky. It was like looking at a much-loved face that had been scarred beyond recognition.

James came over to join her. 'She's survived worse,' he said. 'And if anyone can get her back to her best again, then it's you. You and the Beeswhistle are meant to be together, I feel that very strongly. You belong in Dithercott, Cassidy.'

Whenever James spoke to her like this, so calm and reassuring, Cassidy felt the worries that had been knotting up her insides literally dissolve away. She spent so much of her life trying to be strong for Nora that having someone tell her it would all be okay felt like sinking into a warm bath.

She turned to thank James, who was gazing up at the inn, and was admiring the sharpness of his jawline and how it ran parallel to the perfect swoop of his cheekbones when, to her surprise, she noticed a slight indentation in his earlobe.

'Have you got your ear pierced?' she blurted.

James's hand flew to his ear, his cheeks reddening. 'A friend did it for me at boarding school with a needle and an ice cube.' He glanced at her sheepishly. 'I was a big *Pirates of the Caribbean* fan.'

Cassidy laughed delightedly. 'And you made out you were such a clean-cut teenager!'

'I've never worn an earring in it, so it was a rather lame attempt at rebellion.'

'Hey, never too late to start.'

He arched an eyebrow. 'Gold hoop or diamond stud?'

'Oh either. You'd look good in both.'

'Thank you, Cassidy.' His cheeks dimpled with pleasure. 'Though I'm not sure Dithercott's quite ready for a pirate vicar.'

'I think the under-eights in the congregation would totally go for it.'

They smiled at each other for a long moment.

James opened his mouth to say something, then seemed to think better of it and returned his gaze to the inn.

'We better get on,' he said. 'Let's take a look at the garden.'

If the pub was still a depressing sight, the garden was putting on enough of a show for both of them. As they emerged around the side of the building, Cassidy stopped in her tracks, in awe at the transformation. The committee must have been working out here until the early hours.

'Oh my,' murmured James. 'How absolutely wonderful.'

Most of the stalls had already been set up, each one decorated with hand-painted signs and loops of rainbow bunting. Cassidy's cooking area, 'The Beeswhistle BBQ', was ready to go: there were two large gas barbecues and a coal Weber covered by one of Ian's emergency gazebos. The entire wall surrounding the garden had been draped with yet more of the Dithercott WI's bunting, while in pride of place was a giant 'BEESFEST' sign that had been painted by Nora and her friends. Hanging from the trees around the garden were glitter balls, pom-pom garlands and rainbow spirals, twisting in the breeze. And the flowers! Cassidy wasn't sure if they were weeds and wildflowers, but they seemed to have appeared out of nowhere, adding festive-looking pops of pinks and purples to the beds and paving cracks.

Cassidy and James began unloading the car. The electricity

still wasn't back on in the pub, so in the absence of a fridge, they unpacked the food into the stack of cold boxes waiting by the barbecues, also borrowed from village volunteers.

'I'm so impressed with you, Cassidy,' said James, as they got to work. 'A few months ago, you were a stranger and now you're virtually running our fête.'

'Oh no, it's all the work of the committee. I'm just in charge of catering.'

'Still. I'm very proud of you, if that's not an inappropriate thing to say.'

They worked on in companionable silence, although James seemed distracted. He dropped one of the bags, sending pittas tumbling out over the grass, and then tripped over a gazebo rope, while every now and then, Cassidy would catch him looking at her. Then, just as they were finishing up, he suddenly stopped and cleared his throat, as if about to give a speech at a wedding.

'Cassidy, I know you've got an enormous amount on your plate right now, but I was wondering, when things calm down a bit, if would you like to go out for lunch with me?'

'Oh! I—'

'Once you've managed to get on top of all the issues at the inn, obviously. I don't want to add to your to-do list!'

'Wow, that's such a—'

He jumped in again. 'I do hope you don't think me inappropriate! I just very much enjoy your company, and, um...'

Cassidy reached out and touched his arm. 'I'd really like that, James, thank you.'

His eyes went wide, as if he hadn't in a million years expected this response. 'Would you really?'

'I would. I also think you worry a bit too much about what's appropriate.'

'Ah! Probably, yes.' He chuckled. 'Goes with the territory, I'm afraid. Man of the cloth and all that. Anyway, I'm thrilled.

We can sort out a date nearer the time.' He clapped his hands together. 'Wonderful! Well, I'll let you get on. Lots to do. Goodbye, Cassidy. See you later.'

As she watched him leave, a spring in his step, she had a flashback to watching him and Nora play cricket on the vicarage lawn the other day. After one particularly impressive strike by her daughter, James had thrown himself into the air to catch the ball (despite his best efforts, Nora was still swinging the bat as if playing baseball) and he'd ended up half in the pond, leaving them both helpless with laughter.

A smile grew in her chest and then spread to Cassidy's face.

TWENTY-FOUR

Beesfest turned out to be a resounding success. The first people had appeared on the dot of midday and from then on there had been a steady stream of visitors, not only from Dithercott, but the surrounding towns and villages as well. Cassidy's barbecue wasn't far from the Crockery Cricket stall, and the sound of smashing plates and laughter was the happy soundtrack to her afternoon. Even if she still didn't fully understand the concept, she could at least appreciate the joy James's stall seemed to be generating. There was also a whole programme of entertainment: a Zumba demonstration from Jasha's ladies, the Dithercott Primary school band (mostly playing songs from *Encanto*) and, of course, Ron Dunphy performing as Elvis. Ron was dressed as a seventies-era Elvis, the flared white jumpsuit clinging to his large belly, but his voice was strong, and the crowd went crazy whenever he pulled out his surprisingly nimble moves.

'Thank-you-very-much,' he snarled at the end, to rapturous applause, and then added, still in his Elvis drawl: 'Battenburg slices and Viennese swirls now two-for-one at the Buttered Crumpet's stall. Uh-huh.'

As for her barbecue, the food couldn't have been better received. Cassidy's very first customer, a gruff-looking man in three-quarter-length hiking trousers, had been intensely suspicious – 'I don't like the sound of a whatever a merguez is' – but the look on his face after his first bite of pulled pork made all Cassidy's pre-match nerves disappear. She lived for that look as a chef: the doubtful first bite, followed by a slight frown and then a slow-spreading smile of delight that always made her want to punch the air. Word had obviously got round that she would be cooking at the Beeswhistle, and the number of people who came up to her promising to book a table and wishing her luck was quite overwhelming.

Cassidy kept half expecting someone to complain that the music from the steel band was too loud or that they didn't have the correct licences for serving food, but Nigel had been meticulous at making sure all the relevant permissions had been granted and the afternoon went off without a hitch.

The only slight cloud in an otherwise clear sky (quite literally, as the weather had behaved perfectly) was the presence of Sophia. She was with her children and a harassed-looking darkhaired woman, who, judging by the way Sophia was treating her, was the nanny. Sophia spent most of the afternoon on her phone, while the nanny tried to stop Cosmo and Mimi nicking coconuts from the coconut shy to chuck at each other.

The last event of the day was the dog show. Cassidy had sold out of food, so she and Nora wandered over to join the crowd who were standing three-deep around the show ring.

As the show's MC, Nigel Lamb was in his element, broadcasting a running commentary over the mic from his seat at the judge's table.

'And next, here's Jenny with Titus,' he said, as a stout little dog trotted around the ring with its owner. 'Titus is a three-year-old pug who likes bacon fat and belly rubs.' He flashed a grin at the crowd. 'You and me both, Titus!'

There was more laughter than the joke warranted, but then everyone was in an excellent mood: well-fed and happy after the afternoon's entertainment. In fact, the only sour face Cassidy could spot belonged to Sophia, who was standing at the front of the crowd on the opposite side of the ring. It didn't look like she'd brought her spaniel, probably because she didn't want him mixing with the local canine riff-raff, and Cassidy wondered why she was still here.

There was a huge number of categories in the dog show, including Waggiest Tail, Cutest Rescue Pup and Best Treat-Catcher, and it seemed as if most of the dogs had entered most of the categories in the hope of winning something. And the crowd were loving it, probably because most of them had dogs.

They were coming to the end of the show when Nigel made an announcement. 'We're lucky to have an extra-special guest with us to judge our final and most prestigious category, which is fitting, because this lovely lady is definitely Best in Show!'

The woman standing beside Nigel – Susan Dibble, the show's head judge and chairwoman of the board of school governors – muttered something at him.

'Why on earth not?' he said. 'It was a compliment!'

While this was going on, Cassidy spotted Sophia duck under the rope cordoning the show ring and start making her way towards the judges' table, waving at the crowd as she went. Ah, so that was why she was here. There was clearly no doubt in *her* mind who this mystery judge might be. She had almost got to the stage when Nigel finally spotted her.

A devious smile spread over his face. 'Everyone,' he said, his voice booming over the mic, 'please give a warm Dithercott welcome to our guest judge, our wonderful new landlady, Cassidy Beeswhistle!'

Sophia froze, her expression turning from shock to confusion to white-hot fury. A few people in the crowd laughed, but this was largely drowned out by applause for Cassidy.

'Go on, Mom, they're waiting for you,' said Nora, giving her a little push.

As the two women passed, Sophia gave Cassidy such a poisonous look, she was surprised it didn't turn her to stone. Cassidy smiled sweetly back.

She knew she was cementing the woman's animosity, but what harm could Sophia really do her?

None at all, Cassidy reassured herself, as she reached the judges' table. This would all just blow over, she was sure of it.

TWENTY-FIVE

The sun had dipped below the horizon when the last stragglers finally left Beesfest, waving to Cassidy, who was scrubbing down the grilles of the barbecues. Nearby, Nigel was up a ladder taking down the bunting, looping it round his arm like wool, while the Flints were methodically disassembling one of the emergency gazebos, which had happily proved redundant thanks to the day of unseasonably glorious sunshine. At the other end of the garden, Nora and Tilly were smashing the remaining crockery on James's Crockery Cricket stall. Cassidy could hear bursts of manic candyfloss-fuelled cackles after every successful shot. Nora would be out like a light at bedtime.

'Hey, Cass, check this out!'

Angeline was walking towards her, carrying a bucket that she'd been shaking at visitors all day, collecting loose change for the Beeswhistle repair fund. Judging by her posture and the jingle accompanying her steps, it was full.

She held out the bucket to Cassidy. 'Who knew people carried actual money anymore?'

'Wow, that is seriously impressive! I can't believe how generous everyone has been.'

Angeline gave the bucket a shake. 'Looks like there are quite a few notes in here too.' Frowning, she darted her hand inside and pulled out a piece of paper.

'What's that?' asked Cassidy.

'Think it's a cheque...' Angeline squinted, struggling to read the writing in the fading light, but even in the gloom, it was impossible to miss the sudden gleam of white as her eyes doubled in size.

'Ange?'

For a moment, Cassidy thought she hadn't heard her, but then her friend looked up and handed over the piece of paper. It was a cheque, and it was made out to Cassidy Beeswhistle, for the amount of ten thousand pounds.

Her mouth fell open and she glanced up at Angeline, exchanging looks of disbelief.

'Do you think it's a joke?' asked Angeline. 'Who's it from?'

'Um... Finca Investments Ltd.' Cassidy screwed up her face. 'Any idea who that is?'

'Nope. Did you see any rich people at the festival?'

'I don't think they make them wear badges, Ange.'

'Fair point. Hold up.' She took out her phone and started tapping away. 'Finca Investments Ltd... Give me a sec...' After a moment, she broke into a triumphant grin. 'Just call me Detective Berry,' she said, flashing her phone screen at Cassidy.

It was some sort of official record of companies. Cassidy glimpsed the words 'Finca Investments' and various numbers, but it was the company director's name that caught her attention. *Edward Bamford-Bligh.*

Cassidy looked around the garden, as if Ned might pop up from behind the coconut shy. 'Do you think he was here? Did you see him?'

'No, but with all the crowds, we could well have missed him. Nora and Tilly took the bucket round for me when I was helping Dale on the cake stall, so maybe he put it in then? Then again, I'm sure someone would have mentioned it if Ned had been here.'

Cassidy looked down at the cheque. 'I can't believe he would do this...'

'Why not? It's exactly the sort of thing Ned Bamford-Bligh *would* do. I know you have an irrational dislike of the guy, but—'

'He terrified Nora, refused to apologise and was then repeatedly patronising to the point of offensiveness. I'd say that's quite a rational dislike. And, on top of all that, he's a Bamford-Bligh! In fact, in a way, you could say that this cheque is just a fraction of what he should *actually* be giving me, seeing as his ancestors stole my family home.'

Angeline raised an eyebrow. 'Now you're just being unreasonable.'

'Maybe I am. But I'm the only person Nora has in the world, Angeline. That need to protect my daughter – it's deep in my core.' She pressed her fist against her stomach. 'I'd be letting her down if I didn't fight for her, because I'm all she's got. I've already uprooted her from everything she knew and moved her to the other side of the world and put her through all... all *this*' – she waved at the remains of the inn, her eyes swimming with tears – 'so the very least I can do is to make darn sure I fight her corner when she needs me to.'

Angeline put a hand on her arm. 'I get it,' she said gently. 'And if I thought someone had scared Tilly, then I'd feel exactly the same, but there's no fight to be had here. You caught Ned on a bad day, that's all. You need to put this whole misunderstanding behind you, stop being stubborn and give the guy another chance.'

Cassidy gaped at her. 'Me, stubborn? What about *him*?'

'I've no doubt he's just as bad.' She grinned. 'There, that's at least one thing the two of you have in common! The pair of you just got off on the wrong foot, that's all. I think you'd really get on if you sorted things out. And if this cheque isn't enough of an apology for you, lord knows what is. Besides, I know you're gagging to get a look inside the manor.'

Cassidy finally smiled. 'Okay, you've got me there.' She looked at the cheque again. Although she hated to admit it, she knew Angeline was right. 'I should go and thank him, shouldn't I?'

'I think it would be a very nice thing to do. I can give you a lift up to the manor tomorrow, I'll be heading that way in the morning.'

'Thank you. And thank you too for being such a wonderful friend.'

'Oh, stop it, you'll make me cry.' Angeline held out her arms. 'Come here, you, give me a hug...'

'Do you not own a dress?'

Sally Arbuckle was regarding Cassidy's outfit of denim shirt, black jeans and her least grubby pair of Nike Airs with the same expression she might a poorly risen fruit cake.

'I don't, no. I've never come across an occasion where a dress would provide any kind of advantage over pants.'

'You don't think going to Dithercott Manor, your ancestral home, jewel of the Sussex countryside, to charm your way inside, might be such an occasion?'

Cassidy shrugged. She was regretting asking Sally's opinion of her outfit, and indeed mentioning her visit to the manor in the first place, but she had actually put in some effort to her appearance today, braiding her hair and putting on mascara, and she'd been hoping for a compliment to help calm her nerves. She hadn't told Ned she was planning to stop by: Angeline had forwarded her Ned's phone number, but Cassidy didn't want to give him the chance to turn her down. And while she considered herself pretty fearless, the prospect of turning up at the manor unannounced (especially in light of some of the things she'd said to Ned the last time they met) was giving her severe butterflies. And not the exciting sort of butterflies. The ones that made you wonder if you were about to throw up.

Sally tipped her head to one side, still scrutinising Cassidy. 'I could always lend you a dress. It would be a bit roomy on you as you're such a skinny Minnie, but we could cinch it with a belt and sort of... blouse it over. The fashion lady on *This Morning* says proper frocks are very big this season.'

'Thanks, Sally, that's kind, but I think I'll stick with the jeans.'

There was the brisk toot of a car horn from outside.

'That'll be Angeline.' Cassidy grabbed her bag, the butterflies now flapping up a hurricane. 'I'll see you later.'

'Good luck! Do give Edward my regards, such a lovely young man, terrible tragedy what happened...'

'Yeah, yeah, whatever,' muttered Cassidy beneath her breath.

Was there *anybody* in Dithercott who wasn't a die-hard Ned Bamford-Bligh fan?

TWENTY-SIX

Angeline sped up the manor's driveway, revving the Fiat's engine as if it was a Ferrari, and then slammed on the brakes right outside the front porch. Cassidy shrank further into the front seat. She had been hoping to slip in unnoticed; fat chance of that now, with hip-hop blasting from the speakers and a deep slash of tyre marks in the gravel.

Her hands still gripping the wheel, Angeline turned to Cassidy with a smile. 'Play nice, okay?'

'I promise to be super nice. Unless Sophia is here. And then I will be just the right amount of unpleasant.'

'Excellent.' Angeline kissed her cheek. 'Go get 'em, tiger.'

Cassidy climbed out of the car, feeling as jittery as the deer the Fiat had spooked just moments before, and watched as Angeline spun around the parking circle in a spray of pebbles and throbbing bass and disappeared back down the drive, one arm stuck out the window in farewell. Even the statue of the Greek goddess in the middle of the parking circle appeared to frown its disapproval.

Once the sound of the car had finally faded away, Cassidy turned to face the manor. What a gorgeous sight it was in the morning light. Last time she'd been here, it had been too dark to make out much beyond its imposing bulk, but now she noticed little details, such as the scrolled turnbuckle handles on the windows and the stag weathervane on the central tower. Spring had brought the building vividly back to life: the vines covering the stone walls were now bursting with fresh leaves and exotic-looking violet blooms. From an open window, she could hear music; something gritty with throbbing guitars – the Rolling Stones, perhaps?

Cassidy rang the video doorbell and took a step back to wait. As the seconds ticked by, she decided that it would be good opportunity to get a selfie in front of the manor to send to Manon, who'd been badgering her for photos of her 'ancestral crib'. As Cassidy struck a pose – her fingers in a peace sign and tongue stuck out – the door opened behind her to reveal the same grey-haired woman who'd greeted her the last time.

She arched an eyebrow at Cassidy. 'Good morning. Miss Beeswhistle, isn't it?'

'Yes, hi, that's me,' she muttered, cringing with embarrass-ment. 'How are you?'

'I'm well, thank you. But I'm afraid Mrs Quill and her family left for Italy early this morning.'

Cassidy had to stop herself doing a celebratory fist pump. She'd completely forgotten that Sophia was going on holiday. 'I was actually hoping that Ned – uh, Mr Bamford-Bligh – might be home?'

One eyebrow raised a millimetre. 'He is. Just one moment, I'll let him know you're here.'

She was gone for almost five minutes. Cassidy supposed he might be busy at the far end of the grounds, in which case it would take him a while to get there. Or perhaps he was refusing to see her and the housekeeper was having to persuade him?

Finally, she heard a man's voice inside the house, getting louder. 'Thank you, Clara, I'll let you know.' And a few moments later Ned was at the door. 'Cassidy, hello. This is a surprise.'

And not just for him; Cassidy had to bite her lip to stop it falling open. This was a very different Ned than the one she had met previously. Though still only May, his skin was tanned dark gold and he was wearing a T-shirt and cargo shorts with a pair of Birkenstocks. He also seemed to have unclenched his teeth and found some hairstyling wax. The stand-offish English country gent had somehow transformed into an Ibizan DJ.

'Hi.' Cassidy shifted awkwardly. 'I hope you don't mind me dropping by unannounced.'

'Not at all. I had no idea that hell had frozen over, but I'm glad that it has.'

She reddened, ashamed at this reminder of their last conversation, though at least Ned was smiling – and it looked genuine too, not like before, when it had basically been one up from a scowl.

'I wanted to come over and thank you for the incredibly generous cheque.'

'My pleasure, it's an excellent cause. And I guess I feel it's my family's responsibility to help the village when we can.'

Cassidy felt inclined to leap on this as yet more proof as his arrogance, but she reminded herself to give him the benefit of the doubt. Perhaps it was actually just thoughtfulness?

'Well, it's very kind of you, and will be a big help. I have no idea what they thatch roofs with round here, but I remember the fairy tale about Rumpelstiltskin spinning straw to gold and I'm wondering if he might be on the payroll.'

Ned gave a soft, low rumble of a laugh, and the knot of tension in Cassidy's chest begin to unravel. 'Would you like to come in? That offer of a tour still very much stands.'

'I would love that, thank you.'

He stepped aside to let her in. 'I don't usually use the

manor's front entrance, this hallway always makes me feel as if I should be wearing a frock coat and long curly wig.'

'Well, if this was my place, I would always dress like that, but what do I know? I'm just descended from the sucker who was stupid enough to lose his home to you lot.'

'Which makes you, I presume, the great-great-great-grandsucker?'

'The very same.' Cassidy bobbed a curtsy. 'Delighted, I'm sure.'

Cassidy could see what Ned meant about the grandeur of the entrance hall. A vaulted ceiling supported by marble pillars soared at least two storeys over their heads, and there was a fireplace in which Angeline could easily have parked her Fiat, over which hung a number of stuffed deer heads, ranging from a tiny fawn to a fully-grown stag with a magnificent set of antlers.

Ned saw her looking at them. 'I think your relatives were responsible for those. They've been hanging here since before the Bamford-Blighs arrived.'

'Are you accusing me of having Bambi's blood on my hands?'

'I'm afraid so.' He gestured towards a glass display case, in which two gigantic stuffed owls were fighting over a stuffed baby rabbit. 'And Thumper's too.'

'Jeez... Though, to be fair, you're the weirdo who still has them on the wall.'

They grinned at each other, and Ned seemed as relieved as she was about their unspoken truce.

He gestured to an arched stone doorway. 'If you would step this way, madam, our tour is about to begin.'

There were just so many rooms, each one leading to the next in a procession of eye-popping grandeur. Cassidy couldn't believe this place was intended for just one family; it could have easily accommodated a dozen and still had plenty of space for visitors. And she had no clue what most of the rooms would have even been used for. How did a drawing room differ from a parlour? What on earth went on in the 'withdrawing room'? And as far as she was aware, a saloon was where you got drunk and had gunfights in the Wild West, but the room Ned showed her, with its crystal chandeliers, tapestries and gold-covered ceiling, was clearly meant for countesses, not cowboys.

Nevertheless, if you ignored all the wood panelling and tasselled curtains on the scale of theatre drapes, the manor still felt more like a home than a museum. Works of modern art and framed photos of the Quills hung alongside ceremonial swords, and Cassidy could have sworn she recognised an Ikea sofa amongst all the antiques. Try as she might, though, she couldn't spot a single photo of Ned. Were the rumours in the village about him being driven out of the manor by his half-sister really true? She hadn't cared one way or the other before, but now she found herself feeling almost sorry for him.

Ned barely lingered outside the rooms on the first floor – and Cassidy stopped counting after passing the seventh bedroom – but he came to a halt outside a particularly impressive panelled wooden door carved with garlands and swags of foliage. He turned to Cassidy with a smile. 'This is my favourite room in the house. The library.'

There certainly wasn't a trace of Ikea in this room. Bookcases covered every wall from floor to ceiling, even continuing above the doorway, entirely filled with leather-bound books. There was a library ladder nearby and, judging by the stack of books sitting on the top rung, it had obviously been used recently. Another pile of books was heaped haphazardly on an armchair.

Ned took a breath, inhaling the room's scent of old paper and leather as if appreciating a fine wine. 'I love spending time in here, it's the one place in the house where I know I won't be disturbed. My sister doesn't like it. Too "old and airless", apparently.'

He gave the tiniest shrug, giving nothing away. It was the first time he'd mentioned Sophia, and Cassidy was hoping he might say more, but he moved on.

'The library was built by Bertie's parents, Arthur and Jemima, who built up this collection over their lifetimes.' He ran his hand along the nearest shelf. 'The oldest books here date back to Tudor times. We get the occasional visiting academic who pokes around wearing white gloves, tuts a lot and tells us we need to install climate-control storage to protect the books.'

Cassidy was wandering around the room, entranced. 'And Bertie just... *abandoned* all of this when he left?'

'Oh yes. Apparently, all he took with him was a valise of clothes, his set of gambling dice and a silver-mounted Malacca cane.'

Cassidy couldn't help thinking back to her and Nora's speedy departure from Sacramento, and the paltry amount of possessions they had taken with them. 'I think Bertie and I have more in common than I'd like to admit.'

'Which reminds me!' Ned's eyes glinted. 'If you'd follow me please, our tour is about to get interesting...'

He led Cassidy through a door at the back of the library and up another staircase, which emerged into a corridor that was at least the length of the Beeswhistle Inn's garden. As she followed behind, Cassidy couldn't help noticing the objectively impressive V-shape of Ned's upper body. He had, she reflected, the muscular leanness of someone who'd got in shape chopping wood, rather than doing endless grunting reps at the gym. Never a fan of overly self-involved men, it was another surprising tick in the Ned Bamford-Bligh 'pro' column. Cassidy was having such a nice time, in fact, that she was struggling to remember any of the 'cons'.

They walked past a bathroom containing a wood-panelled bath with such high sides Cassidy imagined you'd need a stepladder to get into it. Next to it was a mahogany box, a round circle cut in the top, which she assumed was ye olde toilet. It was the first room she'd seen that looked like a perfect historical recreation. The only twenty-first century touch was the row of designer toiletries sitting by the sink.

'Are these rooms still used?' she asked.

'Yes, though only by guests. Most of the furniture here predates the Bamford-Blighs, so the rooms are largely as your family left them. Apart from the Jo Malone bath oil, of course.' He stopped outside a door at the end of the corridor. 'And this was Bertie's bedroom...'

Cassidy stood in the doorway, mouth agape. It appeared that her great-great-great-grandfather had been the eighteenth-century's answer to Elton John. Dominating the room was a four-poster bed (seven-foot square, according to Ned) swathed in purple and gold brocade. A candelabrum hung from the heavily embellished ceiling, its arms entwined like twisting vines, while dotted about the room was a gilt love seat uphol-stered in green silk, a pair of life-sized porcelain spaniels and a dressing table inlaid with what looked like Egyptian hiero-glyphs. And keeping watch over all this eye-watering opulence was a life-sized portrait of a man who Cassidy could only assume was the bedroom's flamboyant owner.

'Is that him?' she asked Ned, double-checking.

He nodded.

Cassidy turned back to face her distant relative. 'Hello, Bertie,' she murmured, entranced. 'It's great to finally meet you.'

He was standing in front of a sweep of scarlet drapery, his elbow propped on a low pillar, clad in a black frock coat, high-collared white shirt and a lavish cravat. In one hand he held a top hat, in the other a pair of white gloves. His quiff of dark hair spread around his face into extravagant mutton-chop sideburns, and, though clearly still young, he had the heavy jowls and ruddy cheeks of a hardened drinker. But it was Bertie's expres-sion that really caught Cassidy's eye: he was regarding her with the look of a scolded schoolboy who was trying his best not to snigger.

'I thought he was meant to be handsome,' she said, frowning.

Ned nodded. 'And bear in mind that portrait artists always flattered their subjects, so...'

'...So he really must have been an ugly sod,' she finished.

Ned grimaced apologetically at this reminder of what he'd said at their first meeting.

'Oh, it's fine, you were just stating facts.' Cassidy returned to the painting. 'It's weird coming face-to-face with him, though. I can't quite believe we're related.'

Ned took a closer look at the portrait. 'You know, I think you might have his nose.'

'I do?'

'It's a fine nose,' he added, quickly. He paused, then glanced at her. 'I have to say, mixing up the Beeswhistle gene pool has done wonders for its attractiveness.'

Cassidy blinked at him. Was that a compliment? Perhaps she'd got the wrong end of the stick.

After a long pause, Ned cleared his throat.

'Cassidy, the reason that I initially invited you here – well, in addition to the fact that getting to know a real-life Beeswhistle was too good an opportunity to pass up – was that I wanted to ask you something.'

'Oh?' His manner alarmed her. If she hadn't known better, she'd have guessed he was about to drop to his knee and propose marriage.

'I won't be remotely offended if you say no,' he went on, 'but I was wondering... if you would like to have Bertie's portrait?'

Cassidy gaped at him for a moment, and then burst out laughing.

Ned looked alarmed. 'You're right, it was a terrible idea, don't give it another thought.'

'No, not at all! I was just surprised. I have no idea where I'll put him, but I would love to take Bertie home, thank you. Plus any of those priceless Tudor books you've got lying around.'

It was a joke, but Ned's expression was grave.

'Cassidy, you don't resent my family, do you? For living in this house, I mean? I was concerned when things were rather tense between us previously... well, I'd completely understand if you *did* feel aggrieved. It certainly doesn't seem fair, the manner in which the Bamford-Blighs came into possession of Dithercott Manor...'

She considered this for a moment, gazing around the opulent room. 'It *is* a stunning house, and I'd be lying if I said I haven't thought about what it would be like to live here. My life would certainly be very different to how it is now...' For starters, she thought to herself, she wouldn't have to watch every penny. 'And I suppose I am a bit annoyed at what went on between our ancestors, but when all's said and done, Bertie was the idiot who suggested the wager. And the Bamford-Blighs have done an amazing job maintaining the place. It would probably be a shopping mall by now if Bertie had kept hold of it.'

Ned shot her a grateful smile. 'It's very gracious of you to see it that way. I'll ask one of the lads to help me get Bertie off the wall and then send him over to you. Now, shall we finish the tour?'

'Surely you don't have *more* rooms in here?'

He raised an eyebrow. 'You haven't seen my lair yet.'

To her horror, the roguish look he gave her instantly flushed Cassidy's cheeks pink. She covered up her embarrassment by gesturing him onwards – 'Lead the way!' – but she couldn't ignore the shiver of excitement she felt at the prospect of getting a look inside the enigmatic Ned's private world.

TWENTY-SEVEN

Cassidy and Ned retraced their steps back along the long corridor and at the main staircase took an immediate left through a small door she hadn't noticed before, then up another narrow flight of stairs that had such a low ceiling they both had to duck as they climbed up it. Cassidy could once again hear the music that had been drifting out of a window when she had first arrived at the manor, and it was getting louder.

At the top of the stairs, she found herself in another corridor, far more modestly proportioned than those in the rest of the house: narrow, and with just four doors leading off it. There was no wood panelling or decorative suits of armour here, just some ordinary stripy wallpaper and a very small watercolour of a dog. 'Sympathy for the Devil' was playing at top volume from somewhere very close by, so loud that Cassidy could feel the bass vibrating through her feet.

'Sorry,' shouted Ned, opening the nearest door, out of which burst a deafening guitar riff.

She followed him inside, hands over her ears, to discover a full drum kit, plus a couple of electric guitars, a keyboard and amps. One of the guitars was resting on an armchair, while drumsticks and sheet music were scattered over the floor.

Ned pulled a plug out of the wall and Mick Jagger fell silent.

'Sorry,' he repeated, tucking a lock of hair behind his ear, 'I don't get much chance to practise, and the house was empty, so I was making the most of it when you arrived. Give me a sec, I just need to straighten up.'

'You play all of these instruments?' Cassidy asked, astonished.

'I do. I had piano and cello lessons as a child, then picked up everything else over the years.' Clocking Cassidy's expression, he shot her a quizzical half-smile. 'What?'

'I guess I'm struggling to reconcile the tweed-wearing lord of the manor with the...'

'Frustrated rock god?' Laughing, Ned picked up the sheet music from the floor. 'One and the same. Though I can assure you, I have never worn tweed.'

As he tidied up, Cassidy looked around the room. It was cosy, but it was less than half the size of those on the floor below; certainly not what she'd have expected for the heir of Dithercott.

'Why don't you use the main bedrooms?'

'I used to, but it made sense to for me to downsize when Sophia and her family started spending more time here.' He propped a guitar back on its stand. 'They entertain a lot, and I'd rather keep out of the way. We move in different circles.'

He turned his back on her, as if putting a deliberate end to the conversation, which made Cassidy all the more curious why this widely adored golden boy who once had everything now chose to live like a hermit.

She scanned the contents of the room, searching for clues that might shed some light on its mysterious owner. The titles on the bookshelves ranged from thrillers to books on English history, some copies of *GQ* and a stack of vintage Beanos – so far, so typical thirty-something bloke – while the only photo was of a longer-haired Ned in a university gown standing next to an older gentleman who she presumed was his father, Humphrey. Where were the pictures of the woman whose death broke Ned's heart so completely that he was now, if the rumours were true, on the brink of renouncing his inheritance and moving out?

Then, across the other side of the room, she noticed Ned reaching up to a shelf and his T-shirt rode up, exposing a broad strip of tanned stomach, and Cassidy felt a shifting sensation deep inside her. It took her a few seconds to realise she was staring, but then she immediately looked away, frowning. As much as she was glad they were now getting on, she had no desire to join the oversubscribed Ned Bamford-Bligh fan club. She reminded herself how angry she had been with him, how unreasonably he had behaved to her in the past, yet for some reason, her fury could no longer find a foothold inside her. *Dammit.*

'Cassidy?'

She looked up to find Ned looking at her in a way that suggested she may well have been muttering to herself.

'Sorry, I was miles away...'

'I was just asking if you wanted to see the secret passage?'

'You're kidding. An *actual* secret passage? Like in *Scooby Doo*?'

Ned crossed over to the bookshelves and reached his fingers under the stack of Beano comics. There was an audible click, then he slid back the entire panel to reveal a stone passageway that seemed to end after a few feet in total blackness. A draught of cold air spilled out into the room.

Cassidy turned to Ned, who was clearly amused by her stunned expression. Her eyes lingered on his wide smile, his teeth shining dazzling white against his olive skin...

Way too many teeth, she told herself firmly. *Excessive. Like a great white shark.*

'This wing was originally the servants' quarters,' Ned was saying. 'Apparently, one of the less honourable of the Beeswhistles built this passageway to provide easy access to the house-maids' bedrooms without being seen.'

'Were *any* of the Beeswhistles honourable?'

'Bertie's parents were known as God-fearing folk, but beyond that... Perhaps it's wiser not to judge their behaviour by twenty-first-century standards.' He switched on his phone torch, gesturing for Cassidy to do the same, then held out a hand towards the entrance.

Cassidy was already sensing the first twinges of claustro-phobia as she followed Ned inside, then he pulled a lever inside the doorway and the panel slid shut, instantly plunging them into darkness. The beam of Cassidy's torch made wild patterns on the walls, her mind full of ghosts. It would be just typical of Bertie to have decided to have come back to haunt his old home, and she reckoned this passageway would be prime ghost real estate.

'I'm right here,' said Ned. She caught a glimpse of his face in the beam, his smile reassuring. 'You ready?'

'Mm-hmm,' she managed.

The corridor led to a narrow spiral stairwell, and they started to climb downwards. Cassidy was gripping the stone bannister and she yelped when her hand hit something slimy, hopefully just a bit of damp. It was probably only two storeys, but the stairs felt like they went on forever, the walls seeming to close in on her as they went, and Cassidy was hit by a wave of relief when they reached the bottom, only to be greeted by what looked like a solid stone wall.

'What now?' Her voice was high and jumpy.

But Ned was already reaching for a sconce high up on the

wall, which he yanked downwards, and Cassidy's eyes snapped shut against the sudden, dazzling daylight.

They emerged, blinking, onto a terrace at the rear of the house, the balmy spring air filled with the scent of flowers. Before them, the lawn sloped gently downwards towards a lake, which glittered in the sunlight, a pair of swans gliding picturesquely across the silvery surface. Nearby, a table covered with a cloth was laid with a silver tea service, along with some crustless sandwiches and a cake decorated with a thick layer of coffee-coloured icing inlaid with walnuts. The scene was peak English country house. All that was missing was a croquet set and some dogs, and fifty per cent of this was quickly rectified when Mungo, the old Labrador, came padding over.

Ned was looking at the table too. 'Clara,' he said, shaking his head with obvious fondness. 'Our housekeeper. She's clearly glad I have a visitor and wants to make sure I look after you properly.' He gestured to the table. 'Shall we?'

Cassidy still felt a little dazed by the contrast of the cramped, dark passageway with this dazzling scene. 'Is Clara the woman who answered the door?' she asked, taking a seat. She noticed the chair's cushion was embroidered with swans, and marvelled at the wealth of a place that could coordinate its garden furniture with the local wildlife.

Ned nodded, sitting in the chair next to her. 'She's been with us since I was a child. She's always been a second mother to me... an actual mother, I suppose, since my own died.' He poured the tea. 'Actually, it was Clara who delivered my cheque to Beesfest.'

'Why didn't you come to the festival?'

He didn't answer for so long, Cassidy thought he'd chosen to ignore the question.

'It's complicated,' he said eventually. He offered Cassidy the plate of sandwiches. 'I used to involve myself as much as possible in village life. Partly out of duty, because I felt that as the heir to Dithercott it was the right thing to do, but mostly because I enjoyed it. As I'm sure you've discovered, it's a wonderful village full of remarkable people.'

'They've certainly been very welcoming to me.'

Ned nodded, but then his eyes took on a glazed look. 'I loved being a part of the community, but a few years ago, I had to take a step back. Personal reasons. I left it too long to find my place in the village again, and since then...' He thought for another long moment. 'I can no longer be the person the village wants me to be, which means I can no longer take on that role.'

'But maybe the village wants you to be part of the community as *you*, rather than as some bountiful lord of the manor? We're not in the Middle Ages anymore, Ned.'

He looked pained. 'I wish it were that simple. You see, there are... conventions. Traditions passed down through generations, drummed into me over many years by my father. It's difficult to explain, but you're either lord of Dithercott, with all the privileges and responsibilities that entails, or you're not. You can't be half-in, half-out, and that's the end of it.'

She desperately wanted to ask why he no longer wanted that role, but Ned had very deliberately concluded the subject. Besides, he was right: she didn't have the first clue about the English aristocracy and their weird traditions. She would just have to take his word for it. Ned then steered the conversation onto Beesfest, forcing her to drop her dogged curiosity over his past, and for the rest of the meal they stuck to lighter topics, allowing Cassidy to relax and enjoy the surroundings – not to mention the unbelievably good cake.

After they had eaten, Ned said he wanted to show her the swans' baby cygnets, so they strolled down the lawn. From the terrace, it appeared as if the grass stretched in an unbroken sweep to the lake, but Cassidy discovered that there was a sunken wall about halfway down: a 'ha-ha wall', according to Ned, designed to keep the deer out of the formal gardens.

Ned jumped down first. 'Allow me,' he said, offering her his hand.

Cassidy smirked at him – the jump was no more than a couple of feet, after all – but in this alien world of lords and ladies, suits of armour and secret passages, it seemed the right thing to do. 'Thank you, sir,' she said, reaching for his hand.

She was acutely aware of his strength as he half guided, half lifted her down, and when he let go, her skin burned where he had touched her. Cassidy glanced at Ned's face, and when their eyes met, she felt a throbbing deep inside her. She let out a shaky breath.

As they walked on in silence, Cassidy gave herself a firm talking-to. The last thing she needed was to get a silly crush on Ned Bamford-Bligh. He had already made it clear that the only reason he had any interest in her was because of their shared family history. Not to mention the fact that he had made Nora cry and didn't seem in the least bit sorry about it. And if that wasn't enough, he was clearly still affected by the death of his fiancée. The man had more red flags than China.

'I must say, I'm very happy that you decided to move here, Cassidy.' Ned broke the silence. 'The Bamford-Blighs have always had a chip on their shoulders about how they came into ownership of the estate. My sister certainly does. But it feels absolutely right and proper that you're now part of Dithercott, not least because the inn was Bertie's favourite place in the village.'

Cassidy decided to bite the bullet. 'I don't think your sister likes me very much.'

'Join the club! Sophia and I are very different people, with wildly different opinions about the future of the estate.' He sighed. 'But enough about all that. What about you, Cassidy? What are your plans for the future?

'Well, I guess I'd like to open the Beeswhistle and make a success of it.'

'When's opening night?'

'Thanks to you and everyone else's generosity, hopefully in a couple of months. We raised more than enough to get the inn back on its feet before the insurance money comes through.'

'And how's your daughter finding it here?'

Cassidy's brow furrowed at the mention of Nora. 'She's very happy,' she said warily.

He hesitated. 'About your daughter... Nora, isn't it? I'm so sorry that I scared her that day. I was unnecessarily harsh. It's no excuse, but my people skills are out of practice.'

For some reason, Ned's apology sent a warm glow radiating through her chest.

'Thank you,' she said. 'And I know I probably went a bit mama bear on you, so I'm sorry for that.'

He smiled. 'Friends?'

'Absolutely. Like Bertie and Henry, but without the wild nights of sherry and gambling.'

Ned raised an eyebrow. 'Give it time,' he said.

Cassidy was in no rush to get back to the New Vicarage. It was a beautiful day for a stroll, and she had a great deal to think about. On balance, the visit to Dithercott Manor had been a great success: she and Ned were friends, he had apologised for upsetting Nora and she finally got why everyone was so fond of him. These were all Good Things. So why was she still feeling so, well, unsettled?

Perhaps, she thought, as she pressed herself against the hedgerow to avoid a car, it was because Ned was such a tightly closed book. Every time he came close to revealing even a glimpse of something personal, he clammed up. It was as if she was only getting ten per cent of the man, and she had a sense that beneath the impeccably mannered surface was a total stranger. She was convinced that she still hadn't met the real Ned Bamford-Bligh, and she reckoned that most of the occupants of Dithercott hadn't either. What had happened to him after his fiancée had died? What was he hiding?

Of course, none of this was any of her business, but as Cassidy turned into the vicarage's driveway, she realised she wanted to know more about him. She kicked at the gravel, cursing her curiosity. It would be so much more sensible just to stick with the charming ten per cent and leave Ned's hidden depths well alone.

As she approached the house, the front door opened to reveal a beaming James.

'Cassidy!'

He looked so delighted that she could almost believe he had been waiting by the door for her to arrive. She was struck by the contrast between James, who wore his every thought and emotion on his sleeve, with the secretive and shuttered Ned.

'I hear you've been up to the manor? I'm so thrilled you took Ned up on his offer. How was your visit?'

'Fascinating. Kind of overwhelming too.'

'I can imagine! Walking in the footsteps of your ancestors.'

James was still beaming at her, clearly keen to chat. After her morning at the manor, Cassidy was desperate to be alone with her thoughts, but she didn't want to be rude, so made the effort to continue the conversation.

'How's your day been?' she asked.

'Oh, you know, busy as ever. But the devil makes work for idle hands and all that!' He fiddled with his collar. 'Cassidy, I was wondering... the conversation we had yesterday. I didn't overstep the mark, I hope? By asking you to lunch?'

Cassidy was hit by a jolt of irritation. Hadn't she already *told* him she was happy to out with him? But she instantly let it go. James was just being considerate, after all.

'Not at all,' she said, softening her expression. 'I'm looking forward to it.'

'I'm so pleased.' He exhaled happily. 'Right, I'll let you get on.'

TWENTY-EIGHT

The weeks after the fire had been dark ones for Cassidy, despite the comforts of the New Vicarage. As much as she tried to be a glass-half-full sort of person, she'd been waking every morning expecting to discover that the glass had actually smashed overnight. She'd lost count of the number of times she'd nearly thrown in the towel when the challenges of fixing up the Beeswhistle Inn had overwhelmed her. On one particularly bad day, after the boiler had packed up and she'd had a blazing row with Jasha, she had even reserved flights back to Sacramento, only to cancel them after giving herself a firm talking-to. She had also apologised to Jasha, who had hugged her and said, 'It is tough, I know, but we will do it together,' which made her sob uncontrollably. He had then badgered her about why she hadn't been coming to Zumba, but as she had patiently explained to him, she had enough on her plate right now without trying to keep up with Bettina's cha-cha-cha.

Yet, by some miracle, a beautiful new Beeswhistle Inn was beginning to emerge from the ashes. The money raised by Beesfest had been enough to make good the fire damage and redecorate the interior, which meant Cassidy and Nora could finally move back in, plus the insurance money had started to trickle through so work could start on re-thatching the roof. As much as they both missed the New Vicarage (and of course James and Mrs A) it felt good to be back at the inn, for which Cassidy had grown to feel a deep, almost maternal protectiveness. With the help of Bert, she had found a younger (non-smoking) thatcher, who was making rapid progress and the inn now looked like a blonde bombshell midway through getting glamorous new hair extensions.

Cassidy was still braced for further catastrophe at every turn, but as the days marched on towards the scheduled re-opening date in six weeks time, on 15 June, she started to believe that it was actually going to happen. She would soon be standing in the kitchen of her pub, cooking her first meal for paying guests. Just thinking about this image sent a whoosh of hormones surging through her body that felt very much like falling in love.

Today, however, Cassidy's mind was occupied by something other than tile grout and damp-proofing. It was the day of her date with James; not that either party was admitting that it was such. 'An informal lunch to check in with the progress of renovations' was how James had described it when he had phoned to arrange it a few days ago. 'A catch-up with my former landlord,' Cassidy had told Angeline in a deliberately offhand fashion when she'd seen her for a haircut the day before, although her friend had pulled a face that implied she wasn't fooling anybody.

Cassidy took a final look in the mirror, pleased with the way the pink stripes on her top matched the newly dyed streaks in her hair. She was looking forward to seeing James and having a nice lunch, but there was none of the nauseous, sweaty-palmed anticipation that she usually associated with first dates. *And thank goodness for that*, thought Cassidy, as she scribbled on some eyeliner.

Just before midday, there was a knock at the inn's new front door: glossy black with a hefty brass stag's head knocker that Jasha had uncovered in a junkyard. Cassidy took great pleasure in the door's smooth motion as it glided open to reveal James, wearing a checked shirt and chinos, clutching a bunch of wild-flowers to his chest. No clerical collar, which was a relief. She still had niggling doubts over the ethics of dating a priest, though she assumed James would be across any formalities.

His face lit up in a very flattering way when he saw her. 'I'm not sure who's looking more lovely, you or the Beeswhistle.'

'Considering the amount of money she's had spent on her, I'd be disappointed if it wasn't the Beeswhistle – but thank you.'

James smiled as if he couldn't take his eyes off her, then remembered the flowers. 'Oh! For you. From the vicarage garden.'

He offered them to her with a tilt of the head, one hand held behind his back, and once again Cassidy marvelled at how different this first date was to the others she had been on. In her teenage years, they'd tended to involve a motorbike, a city bar and an undercurrent of dangerous unpredictability, while first dates as a single mom basically involved sitting in front of a stranger and being brutally judged on her appearance, person-ality and life choices for a few hours, then, more often than not, having to pick up the check for the privilege. She certainly couldn't recall a date ever bringing her flowers before. Cassidy felt like she might be about to embark on the first grown-up rela-tionship of her life, and she was absolutely here for it.

James gestured to his car. 'Your carriage awaits, my lady...'

He was a careful driver, flicking on his indicators to pull out of the parking space, even though there were no other cars around, and they set off slowly down the high street.

'So where are we going for lunch?' asked Cassidy.

'It's a surprise.'

'Ooh good, my two favourite things! Surprises and lunch.'

As the car followed the winding route through the fields, a warm breeze on her face and the murmur of classical music on the radio, Cassidy's eyelids drifted shut. She breathed out slowly, revelling in a rare chance to relax. She made a note to herself that she should listen to more classical music. Thrash metal was all well and good, but now she was an adult, she should probably expand her listening repertoire – and this was delightfully soothing. She sensed the car make a left turn and then start to climb, but it wasn't until they came to a stop a little while later that she opened her eyes and discovered where they were. Which was parked right outside the front of Dithercott Manor.

The bubble of calm in which she'd happily been floating instantly popped.

'Why are we at the manor?'

'We're going to have lunch here.'

What? She gaped at him, although James clearly mistook her expression for surprise.

'I called Ned and explained it was special occasion, and he was very happy to accommodate us. We're going to have a picnic at the folly in the grounds.'

James looked so thrilled with his plan that Cassidy made an effort to react in the way he had obviously been expecting – smiling and muttering 'how lovely' in that very English way – but her insides were clutching with embarrassment. Had James told Ned this was a *date*? For some reason, the idea of Ned thinking her and James were romantically involved made her sweaty-palmed with panic.

James had already climbed out of the car and was hefting a wicker picnic basket out of the boot, but she didn't move. She chewed her lip, fighting the urge to flee. *Come on, pull yourself together.* What did it matter if Ned thought she and James were an item? He hadn't been in touch since her visit to the manor a few weeks ago, after all. And why would he have done? They were little more than acquaintances, after all.

James's face suddenly appeared at the side window, making her jump.

'Ready to go?' he asked.

'I was just wondering... um... that sky looks a bit threatening,' said Cassidy, pointing at a single puffy cloud. 'You don't think we should perhaps have our picnic somewhere else?'

'Well, I'm sure Ned would be happy for us to relocate to inside the manor...' he suggested.

'No!' Cassidy almost yelled. 'It's fine, let's stick with the folly.'

She finally got out of the car.

'Super.' James beamed. 'This way!'

They walked around the side of the house – Cassidy hunched over and scuttling, as if that might make her invisible – and followed a gravel path bordering the walled kitchen garden, the roof of a greenhouse just visible above the bricks. James was chattering away about how the manor was requisitioned to house a military hospital during World War Two, oblivious to her unease.

The path led down a hill and then plunged into a thicket of woodland, the gravel underfoot giving way to trodden earth and twisted roots. It was shadowy and quiet here, the air filled with the scent of foliage, but as they crested a hillock, a sea of bluebells suddenly appeared in front of them, rolling out in all directions as far as the eye could see. Cassidy froze, open-mouthed, her worries of a moment ago instantly forgotten. It looked as if the entire forest floor had been carpeted in purple, with splashes of dazzling electric blue where the sun had filtered through the canopy of leaves overhead. She'd never seen anything like it in her life.

'This is just incredible,' she murmured.

James looked pleased. 'It's one of the reasons I wanted to bring you here. The bluebells are stunning at this time of year.'

The moment acted as a wake-up call for Cassidy. Why was she worrying about the opinion of Ned, a man who probably hadn't given her a thought since her visit, when James had gone to so much trouble for her?

Cassidy's steps felt lighter as they emerged from the bluebell woods onto another expanse of grass. As the ground began climbing upwards again, she spotted a small stone building on the top of the hill: the folly, Cassidy presumed. From this distance, it looked like a miniature classical temple, the sort of place where she could imagine ladies in long gowns with parasols strolling beneath the columns, but as they got closer, this romantic image faded. Rather than the charming summer house she'd been expecting, it looked like a mausoleum. There were no windows, just a single door that was barely visible in the gloom beneath the portico, and the stone walls were grim and unwelcoming. The place was giving out serious 'RIP' vibes.

James laid out the picnic blanket on the flat grassy area in front of the folly, and Cassidy gratefully turned her attention to lunch. From where they were sitting, the manor was completely hidden behind the trees. Perhaps now she could relax and enjoy James's company without feeling they had a telescope trained on them.

James (or more likely Sally Arbuckle) had gone to a great deal of trouble with the food. There were crustless cucumber sandwiches, a quiche studded with chunks of ham and cheese and a green salad with tiny jars of dressing, plus enough cake to feed the team of gardeners it must take to keep the manor's lawn looking like velvet.

As they tucked in, Cassidy started to relax. She always enjoyed talking to James; he was knowledgeable, and an excellent listener. He was also, she thought again, as he leant in to top up her elderflower cordial, very handsome. Now that he was out of his clerical gear, it was much easier to think of him as just another guy – albeit one who was a big Beethoven fan, phoned his mother every week and knew the Bible off by heart. In other words, the total opposite to her usual type. But then where had tattooed rockers and toxic bachelors got her so far?

After they'd eaten, Cassidy reclined back on her elbows, happily stuffed and sleepy. She glanced at James, who was sitting with his legs out straight, his arms propped behind him.

'Can I ask you a personal question?' she said.

'Fire away.'

'Why did you decide to join the priesthood?'

'Ah, now *that's* a question.' He gazed out at the view. 'I'd always thought I'd follow in my father's footsteps – he was a doctor – but as a child I was an altar boy at our parish church and our priest was one of the wisest, kindest men I knew. Anyway, one day he was reading out the Beatitudes while I was holding the cross, and I remember thinking, *Yes, I really do believe in all this*. It was a moment of revelation for me, although it wasn't until university when I did some volunteer work at a homeless charity that I decided my skills might be better suited to the Church than to medicine.'

'Jeez, I was getting drunk at gigs while you were feeding the homeless. You put me to shame.'

'We all have different paths, Cassidy, and mine is no better or worthier than yours. You have an incredible gift and it's important you use it.' James took a sip of his drink. 'My turn to ask you something, and please do say if it's none of my business, but I was wondering about Nora's father? Who he was, I mean.'

'I'm absolutely fine to tell you about it, although I should warn you it's not exactly PG-rated.'

James chuckled. 'I think I can cope with that.'

'Okay.' She sat up and rested her forearms on her knees, gathering her thoughts. 'Well, we met when I was living in New York. I was working at this very exclusive restaurant and there was a bunch of us who were all in our early twenties, so we'd work really hard and then when our shift ended, we'd go to a bar to let off some steam. Anyway, one night we ended up at a club where this band – kind of like Colombia's answer to Guns N' Roses – had played a gig. I met the drummer at the bar and... Have you ever met someone you just feel an instant connection to?'

'Yes,' said James, looking at her directly. 'I have.'

She lowered her eyes, smiling. 'Anyway, we hit it off over a bottle of mezcal and the two of us ended up having a brief relationship. And by brief, I mean – well – just the one night.' Cassidy gave a small shrug. 'By the time I discovered I was pregnant, the band had moved on. I contacted their management company and eventually got a message to him about the baby, but it was made very clear to me that he had absolutely no interest in being a father.' She flinched, feeling an echo of the choking sense of shame that the email from the drummer's reps had caused her. 'Anyway, despite the less-than-ideal circumstances, I knew I wanted to have the baby. My dad always joked that it was the best worst decision that I ever made.'

He was looking at her intently, as if really seeing her. 'Gosh, that must have been tough, raising Nora on your own.'

'I wasn't on my own, I had Dad. But, yes, it definitely would have been easier to have had another parent on the scene. I'll never regret having her, though, not for a single second. My life began the day Nora was born.' She glanced at James. 'Do you want to have kids?'

'Oh absolutely! I would love to be a father.'

'And that's okay with the Church?'

'Of course! I'm not a monk, Cassidy.'

He pulled a face and she laughed, happiness warming her like sunshine. It felt almost as if they were interviewing each other, feeling out the other's intentions, working out if they could be a good fit. Cassidy realised this must be the grown-up way to meet a partner, and she hoped her dad was looking down on her with pride. *Not so much of the Beeswhistle impulsiveness now, eh, Dad?*

When James began to speak again, his tone had changed. He had the manner of a man with an important item on the agenda. 'Cassidy, can I just say that I very much enjoy your company.'

'Thank you. Me too. Your company, I mean.' Things had been unfolding so naturally before, but she suddenly felt a little uncertain.

James shifted position and swallowed audibly. So they had clearly reached that point of a first date: the moment you decided whether it had legs, wasn't going anywhere or was set to end in a wild night of passion (although Cassidy doubted it would be the latter – it didn't seem like James's style). She waited to feel the throb of excitement that usually comes with the best of these moments, the burn of attraction and tingle of possibility, but there was nothing. That didn't matter, though, she told herself firmly; James might not light her up with wild and crazy desire, but Cassidy knew from bitter experience that wild and crazy desire made people *act* wild and crazy. Right now, she craved the sofa-snuggling sort of relationship, and she knew James could offer that in spades.

He edged closer towards her, perhaps intending to kiss her – 'Whoops, better move that hummus out of the way!' – but he seemed so nervous that all she wanted to do was pat the poor guy's hand and tell him it would all be okay.

'Cassidy,' he began, 'would you mind if I— Oh!'

Suddenly, a dog landed on top of them, all flying slobber and furiously wagging tail, jumping up and licking their faces with a passion that, to be frank, had been lacking a few seconds ago. Then, a moment later, they heard a man's voice – 'Tess! Come! Come, Tess!' – and Ned Bamford-Bligh burst out of the bluebell woods.

TWENTY-NINE

Ned tore up the slope towards them, his long, easy strides marking him out as a natural athlete. He was the last person Cassidy wanted to see, yet at his approach, her heart started beating like the wings of a trapped bird against a cage. No doubt it was her embarrassment at being caught here with James.

On seeing Ned, the dog bounded back over to him and sat at his feet, tail sweeping back and forth across the ground at full pelt, gazing up at her master adoringly. Ned attached the lead, then straightened up to catch his breath.

'I am so sorry,' he said. 'Tess is still in training and, as you can see, she's a terrible student.'

'Please don't worry!' James jumped up to shake his hand.

'I do hope we haven't ruined your picnic.' Ned's tone was stiff; he clearly felt as awkward as Cassidy.

'Oh no, not at all. Thank you again for letting us trespass.' James waved an arm at the view. 'It's such a stunning spot.'

'You're welcome any time,' Ned replied.

Cassidy was still seated, half hoping she would be ignored. Her cheeks were burning as hotly as if Ned had just interrupted her and James rolling around together on the rug. No such luck, though, as Ned addressed his next words to her.

'What do you think of the Beeswhistle folly, Cassidy? Apparently Bertie used to meet his lady friends from the village here.'

She couldn't help but smile at this, and when she looked up at Ned she discovered he was grinning too.

'Well, it's not the first place I'd choose for a booty call,' she said. 'It's a bit morgue-like.'

James chuckled nervously, muttering something about it being a 'charming building', but Ned's attention was fixed solely on Cassidy.

'Where would *you* have met your secret lover then?'

'The bluebell woods, without a doubt,' she replied.

'Wouldn't that be a little damp for a romantic rendezvous?'

'I guess it would depend on what you were getting up to.'

A lazy smile spread over Ned's face. 'I guess it would.'

Cassidy's mouth and throat suddenly felt dry, and she swallowed awkwardly.

James jumped in: 'Cassidy's making wonderful progress at the inn. I do hope you'll be able to pay a visit?'

'I'll certainly try. When's opening night?'

'June fifteenth,' she replied.

'I'll try to get the portrait to you by then. Sorry for the delay, I still haven't managed to get him down off the wall.'

'Which portrait is this?' asked James.

'I offered Cassidy Bertie, and I'm happy to say she's accepted.'

'Marvellous! The old rogue back at the Beeswhistle, right where he belongs. He'd have been thrilled.'

Ned asked James about the church, and they chatted briefly. Cassidy plucked a blade of grass and twisted it between her fingers, trying to calm the quivering she could feel inside her, but she could sense Ned's gaze still on her, which just made it worse. It made her feel exposed, as if he could see right inside her heart.

'Well, I'll leave you to your lunch,' said Ned. 'Apologies again for the interruption. Goodbye, Cassidy, and best of luck with the launch.'

James saw him off with a wave. 'Cheerio, Ned, and thank you again!'

But he was already halfway down the hill, the spaniel dancing at his heels.

'Right, where were we?' asked James, turning back to her.

But for Cassidy, Ned's appearance had changed the mood as dramatically as day turning to night. It was as if a switch had been flipped, and the feelings she'd had for James just moments before – that their friendship could (and should) lead to more – had been abruptly turned off. And as she watched Ned disappear into the woods, the realisation hit her like a punch to the guts. It wasn't James she wanted to be sitting here with. It was Ned.

A chain reaction of thoughts tumbled through her mind. Of course you couldn't fall for someone just because they were sweet and kind! There had to be a spark that made you want to be more than friends, and, while she wished it wasn't so, her relationship with James was undeniably spark-less. There was obviously no chance of anything happening with Ned – he was still mourning his lost love – but as her dad always said, the heart wants what the heart wants, and Cassidy had to face up to the fact that her heart wanted Ned Bamford-Bligh.

She was still reeling over this revelation when she realised James was speaking.

'Sorry, what was that?'

'I was just saying that I was about to ask you something before we were interrupted by Ned.'

Her eyes darted around as if searching for an escape route.

'The thing is, Cassidy,' James went on, 'it's been so wonderful getting to know you over the last few months, and I was hoping, if you feel the same way, that we could perhaps—'

'James?' The word shot out of her like a bullet.

'Yes?'

She took a breath. 'You've been such a good friend to me since Nora and I moved to Dithercott. In fact, it's thanks to you that I didn't chuck in the towel and run back to Sacramento. I'm so grateful for your friendship and, well, everything else. I really feel deeply lucky to have met you.'

James placed a hand on his chest. 'Honestly, Cassidy, it's been my pleasure.'

'The thing is, though, I'm not sure that I'm ready for...' She stumbled over the word. 'A relationship.'

'Ah.' His face sagged. 'I see.' Then rallying, he added: 'I'm a bit out of practice with all this, so if there's anything I've done or haven't done...?'

'No, no, it's not that at all, I just... Could we possibly just keep things between us the way they are? As very good friends?'

James hesitated, but then released his breath. 'Of course. I know you've been through a lot over the past weeks and now probably isn't the right time, but you're an amazing woman, and you and Nora will always hold a very special place in my heart.' He put on a brave smile. 'Now, Sally won't forgive us if we don't finish off this food. How about a slice of cake?'

To James's credit, they enjoyed the rest of the picnic without any sense of lingering awkwardness; in fact, they had a wonderful afternoon, strolling together around the estate once they had finished the food. Perhaps, thought Cassidy with a surge of hope, a spark might appear between them given time? After all, she loved James's company and certainly found him attractive; on paper it should definitely work. But, no, it would hardly be fair to embark on a romance with James when she had feelings for someone else. He needed to be with a woman who adored him as much as he deserved.

And as for Cassidy, she needed to work out what to do about her disturbing new feelings for Ned.

THIRTY

'Welcome-to-the-Beeswhistle-I'm-Lance-and-I'll-be-your-server-tonight.'

Cassidy's new waiter – Jasha's former building apprentice – mumbled with all the enthusiasm of a football fan being forced to cheer for the opposition.

He looked up at Cassidy and Angeline for their verdict.

The women, who were sitting at a table role-playing customers, glanced at one other.

'Maybe take it a little slower,' said Angeline.

'And with more pizzazz,' added Cassidy.

Lance narrowed his eyes. 'Pizz-what?'

'Pizzazz!' Cassidy did jazz hands. 'There's an element of theatre to working front of house. In a way, it's sort of a performance.'

Lance's eyes narrowed even further. 'I thought this was a waiter job. You didn't say nothing about no performance.'

'Of course it's a waiter job,' said Angeline, soothingly, 'and we know you'll be brilliant at it, but what Cassidy was saying is perhaps could you try introducing yourself in a more friendly manner?'

Lance rubbed his jaw. 'The thing is, it don't feel very natural. It's not the sort of thing I'd say. Like, why am I telling these people my name? It's weird.'

Angeline thought this over. 'I suppose it is quite an American way of greeting customers. We tend to be a bit less chatty over here.'

'Fair point,' conceded Cassidy. 'How would you prefer to greet diners, Lance?'

'Um, well...' The teenager ran a finger around the collar of the white button-down shirt that he hadn't wanted to wear. 'How about... "All right"?'

Angeline glanced at Cassidy, whose brows lifted slightly in response.

'Don't worry, Cass, I can take care of things out here,' she said softly. 'You get back to the food.'

'Thanks, hon. And, Lance, just remember to smile and you'll be brilliant.'

On her way back to the kitchen, Cassidy checked the clock behind the bar. In just two hours, the new Beeswhistle would be opening its doors to customers for the first time. She swallowed down the shriek of excitement that rose inside her.

The pub was fully booked tonight; in fact, they could have filled the place three times over with the number of people who'd wanted to come. They planned to open on a part-time basis for the time being – five evenings a week, closed on Sundays and Mondays – then, once they got into the swing of things, they would keep more traditional pub hours, although Cassidy had already told Mrs Timothy that she was welcome to stop by at any time for half a milk stout.

Her mind was already back in the kitchen, but when Cassidy reached the doorway, she made herself stop and take one final look at the dining room. Usually, her eye would immediately go to anything that wasn't quite right, be it a scuff on the paintwork, or a table that was slightly askew. But today all she

felt was the same sense of awe that other people got from
museums and cathedrals.

Before they'd redecorated, the dining room had still had the
white walls and black timbers of a traditional Tudor inn, which,
though charming, wasn't exactly cosy. The low ceiling and
heavy timbers had made it feel like you were dining inside the
ribcage of some giant sea creature. Jasha had been horrified
when Cassidy had suggested painting the entire room a warm
cream colour, beams and all, but even he'd been forced to admit
that it was a vast improvement.

She had chosen simple wooden tables and chairs and
commissioned earthenware jugs and pots from a local ceramics
artist to decorate the room, while Jasha had got the lighting spot
on: not too gloomy, yet not so bright that you could perform
open-heart surgery under its glare. The end result was a room
that was still proudly Tudor but felt like somewhere you actually wanted to sit and relax, rather than taking an audio tour
before exiting through the gift shop.

Surveying her little kingdom, Cassidy had to literally pinch
herself. It was silly, but she needed help believing this was actually all real. Less than a year ago, she had been broken and
jobless, and now she was about to open her own gastropub in a
village full of her new friends. As she turned and headed for the
kitchen, she couldn't stop the smile growing across her face.

'I've done it, Dad,' she whispered, fighting happy tears. 'I
just wish you were here to see it.'

In the kitchen, James's housekeeper, Sally Arbuckle, was
prepping vegetables, her dress protected by her favourite fruit-
decorated apron. Working alongside her was the Beeswhistle's
other new recruit, a newly graduated catering student named
Ollie, whose lanky figure, clad in chef's whites, was hunched
over a pan. He had been introduced to Cassidy by Dale from
the Buttered Crumpet, who was in a portrait painting group
with Ollie's mum. Ollie wasn't much of a talker – in fact,

Cassidy couldn't even remember seeing him smile – but he worked with the focus and precision of a sushi master, while his seasoning always was spot on. And when it came to her kitchen brigade, she'd take culinary skill over charisma any day of the week.

The kitchen was as silent as a library, except for a pan sizzling on the stove and the rat-a-tat of a chopping knife. Cassidy's heavy-metal playlist had been vetoed by Sally, who'd declared that it was her or Metallica, and Cassidy had happily given up her favourite soundtrack because, quite frankly, the woman was a godsend. She was everything you could want in a sous-chef: calm, efficient, dependable and with a wealth of culinary tricks up her Country Casuals sleeve. If a hollandaise split or a sauce curdled, Sally could fix it. She was still working at the New Vicarage, but, as James had told Cassidy, looking after him and the house was a part-time job at best, and one that hardly made the most of her talents. So, with James's blessing, Cassidy had offered Sally a job helping her in the Beeswhistle's kitchen and she had jumped at it.

Meanwhile, Angeline was managing the front of house and Tash was manning the bar. Tash had already proven herself to be a natural mixologist, creating a signature cocktail of gin, Campari and pineapple juice called 'Bertie's Ruin'. Completing the team, Lance was waiting tables, along with his on-off girlfriend, Lauren (currently more on than off, judging by the amount of covert kissing going on). Cassidy knew all too well that a good team could be the difference between a successful establishment and one that closed after a month, and she couldn't be more confident in her small but perfectly formed squad. Like a crack team of military operatives, she knew that everyone was performing at their highest ability, and she was pretty sure that Lance would get the knack of smiling eventually.

'How are we, troops?' said Cassidy, going over to check on her lamb. 'Everything okay?'

'Oui, Chef!' barked Ollie.

Sally threw a weary glance up to the heavens.

'Just "Cassidy" is fine, Ollie,' she said.

But Ollie didn't reply. And if it made him happy to pretend he was cooking at Le Manoir aux Quat' Saisons, then it so be it. As long as he didn't start insisting on wearing a toque. There was barely room for the three of them in the kitchen, let alone a foot-high chef's hat.

There was a brisk tap on the door and Dale came in carrying a stack of Tupperware boxes.

'Cooee! The pudding fairy is here!'

'Amazing, thank you so much, Dale.' Cassidy helped him offload the containers. 'Wow, that treacle tart looks incredible...'

'Serve each slice with a quenelle of clotted cream, remember?'

'Of course.' She beamed at him. 'Don't worry, I'll make sure it's all plated exactly as we discussed.'

It had been one of Cassidy's better ideas, asking Dale (the best winner *The Great British Bake-Off* never had) to be the Beeswhistle's off-site pastry chef. There wasn't space in the kitchen for a dessert station, and Dale had been thrilled at the idea of expanding his baking repertoire to include puddings. The recipe-testing phase had been an education for Cassidy, who had never before met a jam roly-poly or rhubarb trifle, let alone a spotted dick... But Dale's classic English puddings perfectly suited the homely yet refined style of food she hoped the Beeswhistle would become famous for.

Once Dale had left – 'Break a leg, darlings!' – Cassidy got back to work, the fire in her belly fuelled by weapons-grade adrenaline. She'd barely slept last night, and the only time she'd eaten today was testing the food, yet she was so hyped up she could almost believe that if she jumped off a roof, she would fly. It helped that she was confident in the menu she'd created for opening night, which was, as she'd told Angeline that morning, 'all killer, no filler'. Yet amongst the elegant dishes, she was also sneaking a burger onto the menu in honour of her dad. Joe's Burger, however, was about as far from fast food as you could get, consisting of a venison patty (a nod to the stag on the Beeswhistle family's crest) topped with homemade bacon marmalade and local cheddar. In taste tests, Jasha had declared it 'the best burger I have had in my whole life' and Bettina Flint, who insisted on eating it with a knife and fork, had literally groaned with delight. Nora had scrunched up her nose and left half of it, but Cassidy knew there were few things her daughter loved more than a standard quarter-pounder with cheese.

As if conjured by this thought, Nora's head popped around the kitchen door. She and Tilly were having a sleepover upstairs so that Angeline wouldn't have to worry about childcare while working. Cassidy had a feeling this would become a regular occurrence, a prospect which made her very happy indeed.

'Can Tilly and I watch a movie?'

'Sure thing.'

'And can we please have a midnight feast?'

Nora's idea of a midnight feast was a bowl of ice-cream at 8 p.m.

'Of course you can, just help yourself, honey.'

'Cool, thanks.'

Nora disappeared, but a moment later she was back, and this time she came over and threw her arms around Cassidy, smooshing her face against her chest.

'Good luck tonight,' she said.

Cassidy leant down to kiss her head. 'I love you so much, honey. I couldn't have done this without you.'

Then Nora had given her a squeeze. 'I'm proud of you,

Mom,' she whispered. 'I wish Grandpa Joe could see our pub, I bet he'd be super proud too.'

Something melted inside Cassidy and the bustle of the kitchen faded away, leaving just her and Nora in their own bubble, the warmth of her daughter's arms and the scent of her hair filling her to the brim with happiness. At that moment, she felt like part of Joe was there with them too.

'Oh, me too,' she replied softly. 'Me too.'

Seven frantic hours later, Cassidy fell into bed. The night Nora had been conceived had been one of the best of her life, and this was how she remembered feeling in the aftermath: exhilarated, exhausted and as blissed out as if she was somehow existing on a higher plane. This time, however, it had been a perfect night of cooking at her new gastropub rather than a sexy Colombian drummer who had helped her reach nirvana.

Over the course of the evening, a succession of empty plates had come back to the kitchen, accompanied by accounts of lavish praise and compliments to the chefs. It helped, of course, that they had been playing to a home crowd: guests had included Mrs Timothy, Dale and his partner, Ron, the Flints and Nigel and Jennifer Lamb. But there were names that Cassidy hadn't recognised, people who must have found her through social media word of mouth.

'Outsiders,' Mrs Timothy had muttered darkly, as one of many friends to pop into the kitchen to congratulate her.

James had come too, accompanied by his mother, Helen, a lovely lady who had her son's ready smile and golden colouring. He had introduced Cassidy to her as 'one of my dearest friends', and she had felt like crying for what must have been the hundredth time that evening.

The night had been chaotic and stressful at times, of course, but the prospect of doing it all over again tomorrow made Cassidy feel like the luckiest girl in the world. She stared into the darkness, reliving the moment Angeline had dragged them all out of the kitchen at the end of the night for the customers to give them a standing ovation. It had been so unexpected that Sally had cried and even Ollie had managed a smile. Cassidy grinned to herself at the memory of it. It was a moment she would never forget.

She rolled over onto her side to check the clock. Gosh, it was late, she really should get to sleep... But how could she when she was buzzing as fast as if she'd been hooked up to a nuclear reactor?

In need of distraction, Cassidy reached for her phone. She hadn't switched it on since that morning, and now a flurry of messages from well-wishers filled the screen. As she scanned through them, one name in particular caught her eye. It was Ned – and he had sent her a series of messages. Intrigued, she clicked on the first.

> Best of luck tonight. I'll be rotting for you.

> Sorry, not rotting! Rutting.

> NO

> ROOTING! I'll be rooting for you.

> Apologies, clumsy thumbs! But all good wishes for a successful opening night. Ned.

Cassidy could just imagine him bent over his phone, cursing the typos. She giggled at the image.

> Thanks for thinking of us. It went really well. Hope you'll come and dine with us sometime.

It was late, but he'd get the message in the morning.

Cassidy lay down and closed her eyes. After a few moments, a muffled beep made her reach for her phone again.

I'd love to. Goodnight Cassidy.

THIRTY-ONE

Nearly two weeks had passed since the Beeswhistle had first opened its doors and by any measure it was an unqualified success. They had a full house every night, customers were raving about the food and then a five-star review from a respected food blogger had got everyone even more excited.

Angeline had burst into the kitchen to read it to Cassidy.

'This is not just a burger, it's an ecstatic gourmet experience. I took a bite and heard angels singing. After eating half of it, I decided to propose marriage to the chef (is it un-PC to add that Cassidy Beeswhistle is seriously hot??).' At this, Angeline had looked up and sniggered. 'And when I had finally finished this dish from heaven, I immediately ordered another. Yes, the Joe's Burger at the new Beeswhistle Inn is THAT GOOD, folks.' She had looked at Cassidy, grinning. 'Didn't I tell you it was an amazing review?'

'Wow.' Cassidy had given a stunned chuckle. 'Who did you say wrote it?'

'This blogger called Eddie Eats Everything. He's a bit of a knob, but he's got tons of followers. This is major, Cass. It could really put us on the map.'

Sure enough, the following day they'd had a call from their biggest local newspaper, *The Sussex Star*, who'd seen the blogger's review and heard about Cassidy's personal story – the return of the long-lost Beeswhistle to Dithercott – and wanted to interview her for the paper. It was arranged for a few weeks' time, and in the meantime, Cassidy had to stop herself getting overexcited about what the exposure could mean for the inn's future. In her wilder moments, dreams of Michelin stars and features in food magazines gave her kid-at-Christmas chills.

Yet Cassidy had been working in restaurants long enough to know that you couldn't have rainbows without rain, and it was on their second Saturday that the downpour finally arrived.

The evening's service had not begun well. Lance and Lauren had been having relationship problems and neither of them had got the memo about leaving personal issues at home. Ten minutes before the first customers were due, Lauren was in tears, her mascara running in black rivulets down her cheeks, and Lance (who Cassidy suspected was either drunk or high) was refusing to come out of the toilet. Somehow, Angeline had managed to get them both ready by the time the doors opened, but the glares they were shooting at each other across the pub were as subtle as if they'd actually been hand grenades.

Then, just after 8 p.m., Angeline appeared at the kitchen door, her face grim. 'Sorry to be the bearer of bad news, but the Wicked Witch of Dithercott Manor and her flying monkey are dining with us tonight.'

Cassidy's stomach dropped. 'Sophia Quill?'

'And Xavier.'

Cassidy stifled a curse. 'What are they doing here?'

'Checking out the opposition, I presume.'

'I really hope they don't cause any trouble.'

'Well, they've already asked to change tables twice and complained about the taste of the tap water, so I'm guessing they're not here to relax and enjoy a pleasant evening.'

'Okay, well let's just kill them with kindness.'

'Or we could just kill them,' said Ollie, in a tone that made everyone look round.

'Um – thanks, Ollie, but let's stick to Plan A,' said Cassidy.

With a shrug, he turned back to the onions he was chopping, the 'LONE WOLF' tattoo on his wrist a blur as his knife raced through the pile at lightning speed. Sometimes Cassidy worried about the character of their new recruit, although there were no such concerns over his cooking.

A little while later, Lauren came into the kitchen, notepad in hand.

'Cass, the couple at table three has asked if the duck can be served rare, rather than medium rare, and they would like the root vegetable rosti with that rather than the croquettes. Is that okay?'

'Sure,' said Cassidy.

She knew exactly who was sitting at table three.

'And they want to have the pork with the sauce on the side, and with plain carrots not creamed spinach.'

'Okay.'

'Oh, and the lady says she's gluten-free.'

'Bullshit,' muttered Cassidy, who clearly recalled seeing Sophia tuck into a doughnut at the fête. 'That's all fine, thank you, Lauren. Are you okay?' she added to the girl.

Lauren nodded, lips pressed together as if she was about to cry, and then ran out.

Young love, thought Cassidy wearily, getting back to work.

Moments later, Lauren was back.

'Table three's changed her mind and wants a watercress salad with the duck instead of the croquettes. Can we do that? It's not on the menu.'

'No problem.'

Perhaps, thought Cassidy, as she went to the fridge in

search of watercress, now that the Quills had made their presence felt, they might enjoy the food and then leave quietly.

Soon after their order had gone out, however, Lauren was back.

'Sorry, Cass, the lady at table three wants to speak to you.' She dropped her voice. 'She's being a total bitch.'

Biting back her anger, Cassidy wiped her hands on a cloth, then went through to the dining room. She allowed herself a moment's pride in seeing the pub full of happy customers before heading towards the corner where the Quills were seated at the best table in the house.

Sophia was prodding at something on her plate, nostrils flaring, while Xavier was sprawled in the chair, his legs blocking the gangway, staring at his phone. Cassidy noticed that the plate in front of him appeared to have been licked clean.

'Oh, Cassidy, hello,' said Sophia, her voice oozing regret, as if she felt *really* bad about all this.

'Hi, Sophia, Xavier. I hear there's a problem?'

'I'm afraid so. This duck is so undercooked, it's inedible.'

'I understood that you wanted it served rare.'

'Well, yes, but this is so rare that it's quite literally quacking at me.'

Cassidy's felt a flash of rage.

Don't lose your rag.

'I'm so sorry,' she said, plastering on a smile. 'Would you like me to cook it a little longer?'

'Gosh, no, I hardly think that would improve matters! What I would like is to order something else.'

'Of course.'

Cassidy went to fetch a menu, stepping over the oblivious Xavier's legs to do so.

'I assume the duck will be removed from the bill,' asked Sophia when she returned, 'and that I won't be charged for its replacement?'

'Absolutely.'

'Then I'll have the steak, thank you.'

'Actually, that dish is meant for two to share.' Cassidy pointed at the menu. 'You see? It's a large rib-eye, too big for one person.'

'I can't help that.' Sophia held out the menu, eyeballing Cassidy as if daring her to refuse.

'I'll get it out to you as quickly as I can,' she muttered.

'And I'd like it cooked *very* well done.'

Cassidy gritted her teeth. Sophia would have known how much it would pain her to have to ruin a beautiful (not to mention expensive) piece of lovingly raised meat by cremating it, but what choice did she have? The idea of telling the Quills to get the hell out was tempting, but it was hardly going to help the Beeswhistle's reputation.

'Of course,' said Cassidy, hurrying back to the kitchen before she did something she regretted.

Shortly after it had been served, the steak was returned to the kitchen barely touched. Apparently the lady at table three had 'lost her appetite'. Cassidy had heard horror stories of chefs taking revenge on tricky customers by doing unspeakable things to their food, but she'd never dreamt of doing anything like that herself – not until a pudding order came through from table three and it took every ounce of her willpower not to swirl on the sticky toffee sauce with a toilet brush.

At the end of the evening, Angeline came into the kitchen with a sheepish expression. 'Sophia's making a fuss about the bill.'

'What on earth can she have a problem with? We didn't charge her for either of her mains!'

'She says the service has been disappointing.'

Cassidy closed her eyes, leaning both hands on the counter. 'Just take off the service charge.'

'Right you are, boss.'

A few minutes later, Angeline's head popped around the door again. 'They've gone.'

'Praise the lord,' muttered Cassidy.

She had a nasty feeling, however, that this wouldn't be the last they heard from Sophia Quill.

Early the next morning, Cassidy tried to exorcise her remaining fury by going for a run. She hadn't said anything to the team, but she was worried about Sophia Quill. Although she couldn't prove it was Sophia who had persuaded the Flints to tip off the council about the renovations at the inn, she was ninety-nine per cent sure that she was behind it – and the Quills' visit last night had cemented her suspicion that Sophia was out to cause trouble for her. It certainly didn't seem likely, as she had hoped, that Sophia's hostility would fade when she realised Cassidy was only focused on the Beeswhistle and had no interest in staking some wild historical claim on Dithercott Manor. Cassidy even considered speaking to Ned about it, but that felt like a last resort. Although the pair of them didn't seem at all close, they were family, and it might even make things worse if Sophia found out she had been telling tales to her brother.

Cassidy was running back down the lane when she felt a vibration in her pocket. Grateful for an excuse to stop, she slowed to a halt and pulled out her phone to check the message.

> Morning, Cassidy, I hope all is well. I was wondering if you had a day off any time soon? Ned.

Cassidy's heart soared. It was the first time she'd heard from Ned since his message on the Beeswhistle's opening night, but when she closed her eyes at night, his face was the first thing she saw. As much as she'd tried to dismiss it as a silly crush, she couldn't get the enigmatic lord of Dithercott out of her head.

> Hey. I'm actually free tomorrow.

The Beeswhistle was closed today as well, as it was Sunday, but she'd set aside the day to spend with Nora.

Cassidy stared at the sequence of dots showing Ned was writing a reply. They stopped, before starting up again a few seconds later. This went on for some time. Either Ned was writing an essay, or he was choosing his words extremely carefully.

Cassidy was about to put her phone back in her pocket and get back to her run when his answer flashed up.

> Would you have time to meet for a coffee?

A smile spread across her face.

> Sure.

> Great. 11 a.m.?

> Thumbs-up emoji. Where shall we meet?

That rotating sequence of dots again. Ned was obviously thinking hard.

> How about the bluebell woods by the manor?

Cassidy's eyes were on stalks. Was it a coincidence that he'd named the very place she mentioned when he'd asked where she'd have a – what were his words? – a romantic rendezvous?

See you there, she typed, resisting the urge to sign off 'your secret lover'.

THIRTY-TWO

Dark clouds were gathering as Cassidy trudged up the driveway towards the manor. It had been sunny when she had left the inn, but the sky had been growing increasingly more threatening during her walk and there was now an eerie stillness in the air that she hoped wasn't the precursor to a storm.

In a way, though, the atmosphere suited how Cassidy was feeling: as if something big could be about to happen, something dramatic and exciting and potentially a little dangerous.

Since getting Ned's text yesterday, she had been turning over all the possible reasons he might want to meet with her. Her first thought was that he wanted to arrange delivery of Bertie's portrait, but why would he need to do that in person? He could have just sent a text. In fact, in almost every scenario she could think of, a phone conversation would have sufficed. All except one, and it was this that she kept returning to like a scratch she couldn't help but itch: that Ned liked her, and he had asked her here today to tell her that.

At the sound of an engine, she looked up to see a large black car speeding down the drive towards her. Judging by its sleek lines and the little statue on top of the bonnet, it was expensive. Cassidy stepped onto the grass as it swept by and caught a glimpse of the driver and passenger: a man and a woman in their seventies, elegantly dressed, with matching sombre expressions. She spent a brief moment wondering who they might be, before her thoughts were inexorably drawn back to the meeting with Ned, which was now just ten minutes away. Cassidy picked up her pace; she didn't want to be late.

It was dark under the leafy canopy of the woods today, and as she passed beneath the ancient oaks, she felt acutely aware of her insignificance. The bluebells had all but died away now, with just a few faded stragglers remaining. Life went so fast, thought Cassidy – all the more reason to grab it with both hands. Then, between the trees, she spotted Ned. He was sitting on a fallen log with Mungo, the sweet old Labrador that never left his side. He kept the dog so close, it was almost as if he was still trying to hold onto Tamara, and Cassidy's steps slowed at this reminder of his fiancée, but then Ned turned to her and his smile drove away any doubts.

'If it isn't Sussex's new culinary superstar!' He stood to greet her. 'I'm honoured you've made time in your busy schedule to see me.'

'I've only got ten minutes before my *Vogue* interview, so you'd better make this quick.'

He grinned. 'I won't keep you long, I promise.'

Cassidy scratched Mungo under his chin and then turned to face Ned, who was still hovering a little awkwardly. She thought he was about to hug her, but instead he rubbed his hands together.

'Let's sit! I gambled and guessed you'd prefer coffee to tea?'

'Yes, please.'

'Wonderful, coming up.'

Ned busied himself with the Thermos while Mungo settled down at the base of the log with a contented grunt.

'So, it sounds as if everything is going well at the inn,' Ned said, handing her a cup.

'Yeah, it's been quite overwhelming. Everyone's been so lovely about the food.'

'So I've heard. I'm looking forward to coming to try it for myself.'

'I'm not sure Bertie will be very happy with the prospect of having a Bamford-Bligh on the premises. I can't promise he won't haunt your soup.'

'Well then, could you perhaps do a takeaway?'

'Only for my sworn enemies.'

Ned laughed. 'Yes, I suppose that's what we should be really, considering our families' history.'

'I'm happy to declare a truce if you are.'

'Agreed. Let's shake on it.'

His grip was warm and firm. Was it Cassidy's imagination or did he keep hold of her hand a little longer than necessary?

They talked more about the Beeswhistle, the conversation unfolding with the same easy rapport they'd had when she visited the manor. Still, her mind couldn't stop returning to the question of why Ned had asked to meet with him. It didn't help that they were sitting so close that she was hyper-aware of his presence: his tanned arms, the shadow of stubble across his jaw and those hypnotic eyes, which made her stomach flip at every glance.

Ned was telling Cassidy about the restoration work that was being carried out in the grand saloon, during the course of which a centuries-old wall-panel had been uncovered that depicted riders hunting a stag through a forest. He mentioned it casually, but it sounded like the sort of thing you'd find in a museum. It reminded Cassidy of something that had occurred to her when she had first visited the manor.

'I have a question,' she said.

'Shoot.'

'I get the impression that most stately homes in Britain struggle to afford the upkeep. Like, they have to rent out their ballrooms for weddings or put on visitor tours to cover costs. But Dithercott Manor is so beautifully maintained, and I was wondering...'

'How we pay for it all?'

'Pretty much. Is that a bit direct? I know you Brits like to dance around sensitive subjects like money.'

Ned grinned. 'Not at all.' He took a sip of coffee. 'So, when my ancestors came into possession of Dithercott Manor—'

'You mean when they *stole* Dithercott Manor,' she teased.

Ned smirked. 'When my ancestors *won* the manor, the Bamford-Blighs were in fact already very wealthy. Henry B-B was a lawyer in London, but he came from a long line of gentleman farmers and the family owned a large estate in Gloucestershire. When Henry took possession of Dithercott, he sold the Gloucestershire house, but retained the accompanying land, which turned out to be an extremely profitable decision. Today, some of our land is still occupied by tenant farmers, but most of it has been developed – which, as you can imagine, brings in quite an income.'

'Is that why your sister is so keen to take over the estate? For financial reasons?'

Thankfully, Ned didn't seem at all perturbed by the personal question. 'Partly, but she was very well looked after in our father's will. It's more the status that she's after. You may have noticed that Sophia is rather keen on being lady of the manor, with all the prestige that affords. You have to remember that for my sister everything comes down to image. She lives for her Instagram account and her appearances in the society pages of *Tatler* magazine. And Xavier is basically penniless, so he's happy to go along with whatever she wants, as long as someone foots the bill for his boozy lunches and shooting weekends.' This was said with weariness, rather than bitterness, and

Cassidy was deliberating whether she could get Ned to further open up when he said: 'Now it's my turn to ask *you* something. Do say if it's none of my business, but I was wondering what's happening between you and James Keating?'

This caught Cassidy completely off-guard. 'Oh! Well... we're friends.'

'I get the distinct impression that he'd like to be more than that.'

'Yeah. He's a really lovely guy, but...'

'I understand.'

Ned was looking down at the cup in his hands and frowning slightly. Why would Ned be asking about her relationship with James unless he was interested himself? It seemed like just the sort of gentlemanly thing he'd do, checking the coast was clear before making his move. Cassidy's heart started to race.

There was a rumble in the distance and what had been the odd drop of rain suddenly increased. Ned reached for an umbrella from behind the log and put it up to cover them.

'Didn't I tell you that this place was a little damp for a romantic rendezvous?' he said.

Cassidy held her breath. On the surface, it was a light-hearted comment, but from the way Ned was looking at her, it was obvious there was a deeper meaning behind the words.

'Is that what this is?' she asked.

Ned didn't reply, but his eyes locked intently with hers. Even with the rain drumming on the umbrella, Cassidy was aware of a hissing in her ears. Their faces were close enough for her to see the dark fan of his lashes, a tiny moon-shaped scar high on his cheek and the cushiony curve of his bottom lip. There was a stirring deep inside her, a bone-deep urge to reach out and touch him.

A rumble of thunder sounded in the distance.

Ned's voice was hoarse. 'Cassidy, I...'

Then all at once they were reaching for each other, the

umbrella thrown, forgotten, to the side. Their lips met and suddenly they were kissing with the same urgency as the rain pounding against their skin. Ned's hand was in her hair, pulling her to him, their bodies pressed against each other. Cassidy heard a low, animal moan that she realised must have come from her. It was as if all the repressed desire was now exploding out of her. Ned moved his mouth to her neck and her skin sparked with electricity wherever his lips touched her, setting off a dizzying series of shocks deep at her core. It felt like she was falling and flying at the same time, her insides soaring and tumbling through space.

But then as abruptly as it had begun, it was over. Cassidy was aware of a sudden chill on her wet face and she realised that Ned had pushed her away. It was as sudden and shocking as a car slamming on its brakes. Gasping for breath, she looked at him for an explanation and the expression on his face stung her like a slap.

'Ned? What's wrong?'

'I'm sorry, I shouldn't have...' He made an anguished noise, then ran a hand through his hair. 'It's just all so complicated. Christ, that sounds clichéd... Let me explain.'

But there was no need for him to do so, because Cassidy could see exactly what had happened. In those moments before they kissed, she had felt almost possessed, as if she had to have Ned no matter what. Although she couldn't remember how it started, it was crystal-clear now that she must have lunged at him – literally thrown herself at the poor guy – and he had been too polite to stop her. Shame oozed over her like thick, black tar.

There was a rolling crash of thunder that echoed around the woods. The trees felt like they were closing in on her, trapping her in this disaster of her own making. She had to get out of there.

'I'm so sorry,' she said, grabbing her bag. 'I should go.'

'Cassidy, please, just listen,' said Ned, reaching out a hand towards her. 'There are circumstances... things you don't know about.'

'Ned, it's fine.' She already knew he was still in love with Tamara; she didn't need to hear him say the words. 'I know this was a mistake.'

Ned's eyes went round. He opened his mouth to speak, then closed it again. After a moment, he nodded, his face grave. 'Of course. I'm so sorry.'

'It's really not your fault.'

'Can I at least give you a lift home?'

But she had already turned to leave, getting away as fast as she could without breaking into a run. 'I'd prefer to walk, thank you,' she called over her shoulder.

'At least take the umbrella!'

'No need, thank you.'

The storm was overhead now, the thunder punctuated by flashes of lightning, and she barely heard him when he shouted: 'I wanted to apologise for taking so long to get Bertie's portrait to you!'

And there it was: confirmation that he had asked her here to talk about the painting. Cassidy's insides crumpled and twisted. God, she was such an idiot! She would have to text him to say she didn't want the portrait anymore. It would be far too painful to have it on the wall, reminding her of Ned every time she looked at it.

THIRTY-THREE

The journalist from *The Sussex Star* came to interview Cassidy for the newspaper's weekend section. He was a well-spoken man called Louis Blunt, and his eyes were on stalks behind his glasses.

'So you really didn't have a clue about your family's connections to Dithercott until you found this email from the local vicar in your late father's papers?'

'Nope, none at all. And then when I did some digging and found out the Beeswhistle Inn was for sale...' She spread her hands. 'I guess you could say it was fate.'

Louis slumped back in the chair. 'Incredible... It's like the plot of a movie! I can see the headline now' – his hands made a frame in the air like a film director – 'From downtown LA to Downton Abbey: how a shocking family secret led an American chef to discover her aristocratic roots in the Sussex countryside!'

He looked so pleased with himself that Cassidy decided not to point out that Los Angeles was nearly five hundred miles from where she actually came from.

The interview's allotted hour was nearly up, and Cassidy was feeling happy with how it had gone so far. Louis was a keen foodie and had asked lots of intelligent questions about things like provenance and seasonality – subjects she could happily talk about for hours. She had made him a sausage roll that she was testing for their new bar snacks menu (a blend of pork belly, apricot and nuts), and he had polished it off with an enthusiasm that was impossible to fake. Despite being in a state of high alert for most of their chat – paranoid she would say something stupid and it would end up being the whole focus of the article – Cassidy's shoulders had started to ease from where they had been jammed up around her ears.

Louis checked to see that his phone was still recording their conversation.

'So how did the other villagers respond to an American buying their pub?'

'Really well.' Hermione was winding himself around her legs and Cassidy leant down to pet him. 'To start with, there was an understandable concern over whether I would respect the Beeswhistle's incredible history. I'm an outsider after all, and the pub has been here for nearly half a century. But I think they now see that I care as deeply about this place as they do. And the inn was in a bit of a sorry state when I first arrived, so it's been lovely to be able to work with the community and bring it back to life.'

'So you had a warm welcome from the locals?'

'Oh absolutely. Everyone couldn't have been nicer.' No need to mention Sophia's frosty reception, noted Cassidy. 'I feel very lucky to have found such a wonderful place to call home.'

Louis noticed Hermione slinking by, but when he put out his hand towards him, Hermione recoiled with that affronted look cats sometimes get, as if to say: 'In your dreams, buddy.' Cassidy was surprised. Hermione was usually so friendly they had to shut him in Nora's bedroom while the pub was open to stop him jumping on diners' laps.

Shrugging, the journalist went back to his questions.

'I understand it's not all been plain sailing though. There was a fire soon after you moved in?'

'Oh yes, that was devastating. The roof was destroyed. If it hadn't been for everyone's help, I'm not sure I'd even still be here. The whole village pulled together and we put on a festival – Beesfest, it was called – to help raise funds to restore the inn. It was a fantastic day and I'll always feel indebted to the community for their generosity.'

'I see.' Louis rubbed the immaculate stubble on his chin. 'There've been rumours about the fire...'

'Rumours?' Cassidy was suddenly on guard.

'Yeah. That it was started deliberately, so that you could use the insurance money and donations to give the inn an upgrade.'

Cassidy's mouth went slack. 'But I'd almost finished renovating the inn with my own money when it caught fire.'

'Sure, but from what I understand, you couldn't afford to replace the roof out of your own pocket?' Louis took in her dazed expression. 'I'm a journalist, you understand why I need to ask the tough questions.'

'Sure, but... I have absolutely no idea where you've got that from.'

'It was mentioned in a review of the Beeswhistle Inn on Tripadvisor.'

A chill swept through her. 'It was?'

'Yeah, hang on a sec, I'll show you.'

As he reached for his phone, Cassidy's heart was racing. She had no idea what he was talking about. She tried to avoid reading reviews (if they were good, they made you complacent, while the bad ones knocked your confidence), but she assumed Angeline would have flagged up anything important: such as, for example, being accused of arson.

'Here it is,' said Louis, passing her the phone.

Cassidy read the review, her chest getting tighter with every damning line. Not only did it imply she was guilty of criminal behaviour, it tore apart every aspect of her pub. 'The food was inedible, the atmosphere non-existent and the service utterly inept,' the reviewer concluded. 'Avoid this hell-hole at all costs.' It was so brutal, and so utterly unfair, that although Cassidy was pretty sure this was Sophia's handiwork, she was horrified to feel on the verge of tears. She handed back the phone, too shocked to know what to say.

Louis was scrutinising her. 'That sounds like it was written by someone who might hold a personal grudge against you. Have you made any enemies since you moved to here?'

Keeping her voice light, Cassidy said: 'I thought we were going to be talking about my food, not my Mafia connections.'

He immediately started writing on his pad.

'You do know that was a joke?'

Still scribbling, Louis didn't look up.

'The thing is,' Cassidy went on, desperate to get the interview back on track, 'I've been a chef for long enough not to let one bad review bother me. Besides, I'm not here to make friends – I mean, that would be nice, but my job is to focus on cooking the best food I possibly can.'

'Strictly speaking, it's not just the one bad review.'

Cassidy opened her mouth to speak, but nothing came out. What the hell was happening? One minute they had been having a really interesting discussion about kale, the next Louis was lobbing bombs at her.

'And as to your point about you being a chef,' Louis went on, 'how would you respond to local concern that now their pub has reopened as a restaurant, the villagers have no place to drink? In the words of one reviewer, you've –' he checked his notes again – '"turned a cosy Tudor boozer into a soulless eatery more suited to London than the Sussex countryside". I do get that as an American you probably don't understand how important pubs are to us Brits, but—'

'Believe me, I understand,' she said firmly. 'And it's not a restaurant, it's a gastropub. I've always planned to open the Beeswhistle along more traditional pub hours in due course and with space to come just for drinks too, but we've only just opened our doors. It's what we call in the trade a "soft opening".' She forced herself to take a breath. 'Listen, I'm not sure where you're getting your information, but I can promise you that I'm making every effort to make sure the Beeswhistle Inn remains the heart of the village. I did a heck of a lot of research into the history of the village before starting renovations to make sure I retained the inn's character. It's very important to me, not only as the inn's owner, but as a Beeswhistle. It's my name over the door, after all.'

'Yes, about all this "research",' Louis made finger quotes, 'is it true you've been digging around for the so-called "Lost Deed of Dithercott" in the hope of taking the manor back from the Bamford-Blighs?'

'That is utterly ridiculous! First off, the lost deed is just a legend, as I'm sure you're well aware, and second of all, I have zero interest in Dithercott Manor.' Then she muttered under her breath: 'Which is ironic, because one of its inhabitants appears to have an obsessive interest in *me*.'

'Sorry, what was that?'

'Nothing important.'

'It's fine, I'm sure the voice recorder picked it up.'

Damn it.

'Well, I think I've got everything I need.' Louis' smile put her in mind of a crocodile. 'Thank you, Cassidy, that was very interesting. The article will be in the weekend's paper and on the website in a few weeks. I'll let you know the date once the editor has made a decision.' He reached to shake her hand, as if the assassination of the past few minutes hadn't even happened. 'I'll see myself out.'

As the door closed behind him, Cassidy dropped back into her chair and stared blankly at the wall. She felt like she'd just done twelve rounds in a boxing ring. She was still sitting there when Angeline arrived for work ten minutes later.

'Hey! How did the interview go? Are they going to say nice things about us?'

Cassidy looked up at her. 'I don't think so.'

'*What?* But why?'

'The journalist mentioned some bad reviews.'

The look on Angeline's face made Cassidy even more worried.

'Angeline? What haven't you told me?'

Angeline hesitated, then took the seat next to Cassidy. 'It's only been in the last few days, but there's been a few really nasty reviews on Tripadvisor. It started with a particularly spiteful one, which had Sophia's grubby fingerprints all over it—'

'Is that the one that accused me of setting fire to the pub?'

'That's it. I've already been in touch with Tripadvisor to ask them to take it down, as it's pretty much libellous. But, since then, they've just kept coming. I'm positive they're fake, partly because they're generally pretty vague, just basically saying the Beeswhistle's crap, without any details – but also because the reviewers haven't published anything else on the site.'

'You really think Sophia would have gone to all that trouble to get at me?'

'I think that's exactly the sort of thing she'd do. Or perhaps get some friends to do her dirty work for her. Bottom line, though, I'm confident they're not from genuine customers.'

Cassidy got up to find her phone. 'I need to see them.'

'Cass, there's no point, they're all bullshit!'

'But other people don't know that though, do they? They're going to read them and then avoid the Beeswhistle. I need to know what's being said.'

It was as bad as Cassidy's worst fears. The most recent review on the site, from a 'Mrs Smith', claimed to have seen a 'suspiciously large rodent' run across the pub's floor. Another reviewer said they had 'been on the toilet all night' after eating undercooked pork, and strongly recommended that people eat at the Quill instead (which Cassidy thought was a nice touch). After every review, Angeline had left a polite comment asking the disgruntled diner to get in touch to discuss their concerns directly, but apparently not one person had got back to her.

Cassidy was numb. She knew Sophia felt threatened by her – over her personal links to the manor as well as in business – but if these reviews really were written by her, then this would seem to be nothing less than a coordinated campaign designed to destroy her. Speaking to Sophia wouldn't work: she would deny she had anything to do with it – and perhaps she hadn't, Cassidy really couldn't be sure. Angeline was less concerned, assuring her that it would blow over, but Cassidy had worked in the industry long enough to know how fragile an establishment's reputation could be, especially one that was still only a few weeks old, and, once the rot had set in, how tricky it was to slow the spread.

Cassidy was still wading through the swamp of negative comments when a message notification flashed at the top of her phone's screen. She glanced at it, and her stomach turned over at the sender's name. Ned.

She hadn't heard from him since their meeting in the bluebell woods two weeks ago. In fact, she was trying to convince herself that it had never actually happened, as that was preferable to the horrible cramping sensation she got whenever she remembered the stricken look on Ned's face as he'd pushed her away.

Cassidy's finger hovered over the screen. She'd rather not read his message at all, but it was better to do so now, quickly, before she immediately deleted any trace of him from her phone and moved on with her life.

> Hello Cassidy, I hope you're well. I feel I should explain myself. Could we possibly meet?

Before she could change her mind, she replied:

> Thank you but no need.

She was pretty sure what Ned would have to say: that he was sorry about what had happened, but he was still mourning the loss of his beloved late fiancée. Or perhaps he would tell her that as much as he enjoyed her company, he would prefer to just be friends, or claim that he was too busy for a relationship. However he dressed it up, Cassidy knew for sure that the underlying message would be thanks, but no thanks.

A reply appeared almost instantly.

> I understand. I'll be in touch about the portrait.
> Take care, Ned.

Cassidy was quite sure, however, that she would never hear from him again.

THIRTY-FOUR

A blast of rain rattled the windows of the New Vicarage. From her seat at the kitchen table, Cassidy looked up to see the leafy branches of the birch tree whipping around like streamers. It was July, but the English weather clearly hadn't got the memo.

Inside the vicarage, however, it was perfectly snug and cosy. The huge oak table bore evidence of the long lunch the room's four occupants had just enjoyed, the clutter of empty plates and glasses pushed to the side to make way for the game of Cluedo now reaching its nail-biting conclusion.

Nora was knelt up on her chair to survey the board. She tapped her pencil against her chin, thinking.

'I know who did it,' she announced. 'Reverend Green with a candlestick in the kitchen.'

James gasped theatrically. 'Speaking as a man of God, Nora, I am personally affronted on Reverend Green's behalf.'

Nora giggled. 'He was a *bad* vicar, James. Not like you.'

'Why, thank you, Nora,' he said with a smile.

'Let's check the envelope, shall we?' suggested Sally Arbuckle, who was still wearing her apron. Cassidy wondered idly if she perhaps slept in it too. Sally looked through the cards inside. 'Revered Green... Candlestick... Kitchen. Oh, well played, poppet!'

Nora punched the air.

'Congratulations, sweetie,' said Cassidy. 'Shall we play another round?'

'Can I go and practise the piano instead?' asked Nora. 'If that's okay with James...'

'Of course.'

'Cool – thank you!'

'Hold up, Nora, do you want some chocolate mousse?' Cassidy had made the pudding as her contribution to supper.

'Later, Mom!' she called over her shoulder, running from the room.

As Cassidy served bowls of the mousse to the adults, they could hear the opening chords of the White Stripes' 'Seven Nation Army' being slowly picked out.

'Well, I don't know about you,' said Sally, twirling the little metal candlestick between her fingers, 'but if I was going to kill someone, I certainly wouldn't use this.'

'How would you do it?' asked Cassidy.

'Poison, obviously,' she said smartly. 'Which reminds me, Reverend. Do you remember that murder-mystery party they had up at the manor one Christmas?'

'Oh yes! I was given the character of a "disgraced bishop",' he told Cassidy, 'Ned's idea of a joke, I think...'

'I made him a mitre out of cardboard and a bishop's staff from an old broomstick,' added Sally.

'It was a quite brilliant costume, Mrs A.'

'I said to James at the time, "Are you sure you won't get in trouble for dressing up as a church superior?"' She chuckled. 'I think we've got some photos of that evening somewhere. I remember one of you with Ned's lovely fiancée in that amazing sparkly dress. She went as a showgirl, didn't she?'

'Gosh, you've got a good memory.'

'And then, just a few months later... Well, enough about that.' Sally took another spoonful of mousse. 'And now, of course, Ned's leaving Dithercott...'

James looked up sharply. 'What?'

'Yes, apparently he had an appointment with his solicitor to discuss handing over the estate to that godawful sister of his.'

James looked as shocked as Cassidy was feeling. The thought of seeing Ned again after what happened between them was mortifying, but the prospect of him leaving for good? It just felt so final.

'Where did you hear this?' James asked.

'Clara told me.' Sally turned to Cassidy. 'She's the house-keeper up at the manor.'

'Yes, I met her.'

'So I heard,' said Sally, with a cryptic little smirk that made Cassidy wonder what else had she had been told. 'Can you imagine, walking away from that beautiful house? You've got to worry for Ned's state of mind. And it'll be bad news for Dithercott too, having that dreadful Quill woman at the helm.'

'Gosh, this *is* sad,' said James. 'And just when I thought we were finally starting to get the old Ned back again.'

Cassidy's mind was darting all over the place. Had Ned already made the decision to leave before their kiss in the blue-bell woods? Or did the fact that she'd thrown herself at him push him over the edge? Well, it didn't matter now. Ned was leaving Dithercott and that was that.

Cassidy pushed her pudding bowl to the side, her appetite vanished.

There was the sound of running feet in the hallway and then Nora burst back into the kitchen.

'Did you guys hear me play?'

'We certainly did,' said James, smiling. 'And jolly good it was too.'

'Will you come and do the "Chopsticks" duet with me, James?'

'It would be an honour.'

He got up and walked around the table to where Nora was standing in the doorway.

She grabbed his hand. 'Mom, Sally – you better listen!'

'Don't worry, we will,' said Cassidy.

'I do love a bit of "Chopsticks",' added Sally.

Cassidy watched the pair of them leave, hand in hand, chatting away together. *Thank goodness for James*, she thought. After turning down his advances at the folly, she had feared it would ruin their friendship, but it had continued to be as warm and easy as ever – possibly even more so. This was the third Saturday in a row he had invited them to the New Vicarage to join him and Sally for supper, which made her feel like they were part of a real family unit. And then there was something he had said to her earlier that afternoon, when he had tried the chocolate mousse.

'You know,' he had said, brandishing his spoon for emphasis, 'if you ever changed your mind about just being friends, then I would certainly be open to your thoughts.'

She had brushed it off as a joke, but thinking about it again now, Cassidy wasn't so sure. Perhaps it was actually James's way of letting her know that the door was still open?

From the living room came a sudden burst of laughter.

Sally chuckled. 'Those two are just adorable together.'

'They certainly are,' said Cassidy with a smile.

THIRTY-FIVE

Cassidy had been checking her emails before walking Nora to her activity camp, school having broken up for the summer, when a new message popped up. To her delight, it was from Manon, and it was headed: 'I know I told you to stick with it but...'

She could hear Nora putting her boots on by the front door, but Cassidy lingered at her laptop, intrigued by Manon's cryptic opener. Perhaps it had something to do with their conversation the other day? She had phoned her friend to ask for advice in dealing with the bad reviews of the Beeswhistle ('Ignore them,' had been Manon's brisk response), but the two of them had gone on to chat for well over an hour, and after the call Cassidy had felt lighter than she had in weeks. As much as she'd made wonderful friends in Dithercott, she and Manon had years of shared history – plus, of course, she fully understood the pressures of working in the restaurant industry.

'Mom, are you coming?' Nora's voice, edged with irritation, drifted up the stairs. 'It's water fight day at camp and I can't be late as I need to make sure I'm on a good team.'

'Be right there, honey...'

Cassidy glanced at her watch – if she was quick, she could probably skim Manon's message. She clicked on the email and started to read.

> *Darling Cass. I've been agonising over whether to send this to you. It feels selfish to do so, especially now Nora is so settled and you're making a success of things at the Beeswhistle (and a few mean reviews don't change that, OK?), but after much soul-searching I've decided it's best if I lay all my cards on the table and let you know about my offer, on the understanding that I'm fully expecting a 'no' in response.*

'*Mom!* We need to go – now!'

With great reluctance, Cassidy dragged her eyes away from the screen. 'Coming,' she called downstairs, closing her laptop.

As soon as she had dropped off Nora, Cassidy reopened the email and read it as she walked back through the woods.

Manon was writing to tell her that the Spring Street Smokehouse had been bought out, and the new owners, who already ran a string of critically acclaimed restaurants, were virtually handing out blank cheques. 'They've refurbed the kitchen and bought top-of-the range EVERYTHING!' she wrote, her excitement leaping off the screen. She went on to detail all the amazing changes that would be happening under the new regime (not least that Mario was being replaced as manager) and then abruptly dropped her bombshell.

> *I know I said you should stick it out in England, no matter how tough things get, and I still stand by that advice. But here's the thing. We desperately want you back at the Smokehouse. Not just me (though I miss you like crazy, both as a friend and colleague) but the entire kitchen team. It's not the*

*same without you here, Cass – plus, of course, you cook like a
goddamn dream.*

Manon was proposing that the pair of them share head chef
duties, meaning they would be working less hours, yet would
still each be paid a full-time salary: 'the dream scenario', as
Manon put it. Not only that, but she had a friend with a two-
bedroom apartment near the restaurant who would apparently
be looking for tenants later in the year.

*There's no rush to make a decision, although feel free to fire a
'thanks but no thanks' straight back at me, but if by some
miracle you are interested, we'd be looking at a start date of
just after Christmas. There's a space by the stove with your
name on it, honey! Manon x*

*PS. I'm still not sure I'm doing the right thing in sending this
to you, but screw it. Too late now, right??*

Cassidy sat down on a mossy stump by the stream and re-
read the email, then lowered her phone and stared blankly
ahead of her. It was the sort of opportunity that rarely came
along: more money for less work, with a team she loved. It
would be, as Manon put it, a dream. The Beeswhistle was her
baby and she felt proud of everything they had achieved, but
she couldn't deny it would be a relief to have someone else
worry about overheads, budgeting and all the other tedious jobs
that took up so much of her time, freeing her up to focus solely
on cooking. It had become glaringly obvious that she wasn't cut
out for the business side of restaurant owning. Just that morning, she had received an alarmingly high invoice from the
ceramics artist who'd she'd commissioned to make the restaurant's jug (then promptly forgotten about) and she had no idea
how she was going to pay it.

Cassidy watched as a moorhen launched itself into the water. As tempting as Manon's job offer was, however, she knew there was no way she could accept it. Not after everything she had put Nora through to establish their lives here. She had already uprooted her once this year already – and it would be far worse this time round, because Nora was so happy in Dithercott. Just the other day, she'd announced that Dithercott Primary was even better than Hogwarts, although that could well have been because they'd spent the last week of term having outings to the seaside and adventure park.

The morning was already getting hot, and Cassidy shrugged off her jacket, enjoying the feeling of the sun on her skin. It was such a gentle, polite warmth compared to the heat back in Sacramento, which seared your eyeballs, flayed your skin and wrung the sweat from your body. She tipped her head back to look up at the trees, some of which had probably stood here for hundreds of years, and Cassidy could imagine the whisper of the leaves overhead telling her to stay.

Angeline was probably right: if it was Sophia Quill who was trolling the Beeswhistle, then she'd surely get bored soon enough; they just needed to hang in there and weather the storm. Besides, Louis Blunt's article was coming out in the *Sussex Star* this weekend, and in the days since their interview, Cassidy had begun to think that she'd got her fears over his line of questioning totally out of proportion. The vast majority of their interview had been really positive; it had only been in the final few minutes that things had got weird. Hopefully, the article would be a fair reflection of their conversation, in which case it would be some much-needed good press for the Beeswhistle and go some way towards countering the bad reviews.

Cassidy replied to Manon, thanking her for the offer and assuring her she'd think about it. An immediate 'no' would have been rude; she wanted her friend to know that she had given it serious consideration, even though it was out of the question.

Cassidy knew she had made the right decision – the *only* decision – but as she started the walk home, she couldn't shake the lingering sense of 'what if'. Just thinking about Manon's job and how much easier her life would be if she took it made her entire body feel light. She would have more money, more time to spend with Nora – and no Sophia sticking her nose in things.

From somewhere on the other side of the stream, Cassidy heard the distinctive honk of a pheasant. It snapped her out of her daydream; there was no point wishing over what could be, she would just have to make a success of the Beeswhistle instead.

As Cassidy turned onto the village green, she caught a glimpse of St Andrew's church tower standing amongst the trees and she had a sudden urge to see James. He always made her feel strong and capable, and she could do with a dose of his reassuring presence after her resolve being ruffled by Manon's offer. She checked her watch: yes, James could well be at the church right now. Instead of returning to the inn, she turned in the opposite direction and headed across the green.

Cassidy made her way through the lychgate, the roofed entrance to the churchyard. James had told her that in the Middle Ages this was where corpses would be placed, wrapped in a shroud, until the day of burial, and since then she always hurried under it, glad to be back in the sunlight when she was out the other side. And then, up ahead, standing on the path, she saw James.

Smiling, she picked up the pace. He was talking to someone – a woman, considerably shorter than he was – but he had his back turned, blocking her view of who it was. Cassidy hesitated, reluctant to crash what could well be a personal conversation with a parishioner, but a burst of laughter suggested this was a casual chat, so she continued up the path and, after a few steps,

she realised the mystery woman was none other than Miss
Poppy, Nora's lovely school teacher. She was wearing a floral
dress and her neat chestnut bob was gleaming as if it had been
polished.

'Hi there!' called Cassidy, pleased to see her.

James and Miss Poppy both spun round, the smiles from the
conversation they'd been having lingering on their faces.

'Cassidy!' James held up a hand in greeting as she
approached.

'Hello!' Miss Poppy's pretty smile lit up her face. 'How's my
sweet Nora?'

'Missing you already. She's been at holiday camp this week,
so that's taking the edge off a bit.'

'Aw, I miss them all too. In fact, I'm actually here to see the
reverend on school business. Has Nora told you about their
summer homework?'

'Oh yes, the "My Family Tree" project is a very popular
topic of conversation in our house right now. Nora's excited
about getting started, especially in light of our connection to the
village.'

'That's wonderful to hear. I came here this morning to ask if
James would be happy for me to bring the children to visit the
village archives next term, and I'm delighted to say he's agreed.'

James beamed down at Miss Poppy, who was almost a foot
shorter than he was. 'I think it's a wonderful idea,' he told her.

'I'm so glad,' said Miss Poppy, smiling back at him.

'Poppy and I were actually about to take a look in the
archives and come up with a plan of how to present things to
the children,' he told Cassidy. 'There are so many documents in
there, some rather more interesting than others. For instance,
I'm not sure how fascinating ten-year-olds would find the 1894
burial lists!'

'Oh, I don't know,' said Miss Poppy. 'Imagine if one of the
children could discover a distant relative on one of those lists?

How incredible would that be? I don't think we should discount anything at this stage.'

'You're absolutely right, Poppy, of course. And I've got a quiet morning, so we can spend as long as you need getting everything in order.'

She briefly touched his hand. 'Thank you, James, that's extremely sweet of you.'

The pair's eyes locked, and as the moments ticked by, Cassidy began to feel decidedly gooseberry-like. The atmosphere between James and the pretty teacher seemed almost... *flirtatious*.

Shaken, Cassidy was about to make her excuses and go, when James suddenly seemed to remember she was there.

'Sorry, Cassidy, did you need to speak to me about anything in particular?'

'Oh, I was just passing and thought I'd say hello. I don't want to interrupt your plans.'

Miss Poppy looked concerned. 'Are you sure? I'd be happy to wait in the vestry.' Cupping her mouth, she dropped her voice to a stage whisper: 'Don't tell James, but I know where his custard creams are hidden...'

James laughed and gave her a little push, while she brushed his hand away, giggling.

'Well, I'll let you guys get on,' said Cassidy quickly. 'Good luck with the archives.'

James didn't try to dissuade her. 'Thank you, Cassidy, I'll see you soon. Give my love to Nora.

'Mine too!' added Miss Poppy.

'Will do,' replied Cassidy, but the pair had already resumed their conversation.

As she headed back down the path, she heard Miss Poppy giggle again, and her girlish voice drifting down the path: 'Oh, James, you're *such* a silly goose...'

Cassidy realised her mouth was hanging open and abruptly

closed it. Judging by what she had just witnessed, if there wasn't anything going on between James and Miss Poppy, then there soon would be. She knew she should be pleased about this; if anyone deserved happiness, it was James, and the pretty teacher was perfect for him. Why, then, as she hurried back down the path, did she feel an urge to aim a swift kick at a nearby gravestone?

The sight of James and Miss Poppy made her regret all over again what might have been between them. He would have made such a perfect stepfather for Nora, and Cassidy was hit by a wave of misery at the thought that she had let her daughter down by depriving her of yet another father figure.

By the time she had reached the village green, however, Cassidy had started to see this was an absurd way of thinking. Her feelings for James had never been much more than platonic; she only had to contrast them with the lurching sensation she got deep inside her whenever she thought about Ned Bamford-Bligh to realise that. James was a dear friend, and she was happy for him. She was just being silly and jealous because he hadn't been at her beck and call waiting to make her feel better about herself – which, as a grown woman, she should really be able to manage to do herself.

Turning along the high street, Cassidy pushed back her shoulders and walked on. She would get back to the inn, put on her apron and get stuck into doing what she did best: cooking delicious food.

Or you could accept Manon's job and go back to Sacramento, came a treacherous little whisper in her brain.

THIRTY-SIX

The next morning, after returning from her run, Cassidy headed straight for her laptop without even bothering to change out of her mud-spattered leggings. It was publication day for her interview, and as she clicked on the website for *The Sussex Star*, there was a trembling in her limbs that had little to do with the seven miles she'd just run.

It's just one article, she told herself firmly, as she navigated the newspaper's homepage. What was the phrase Angeline had used? 'Today's news is tomorrow's chip paper.' Cassidy had never heard this British expression before, and it made her smile – although it wasn't actually much comfort, because while newspapers were short-lived, the internet had a far longer memory. Besides, hopefully Louis Blunt focused on their conversation about food and her aims for the Beeswhistle, rather than her personal story.

Cassidy knew it was going to be bad, however, when she saw the headline.

Beeswhistle or Bust? How a steely blonde American has been ruffling feathers in the Sussex countryside.

Steely blonde? Cassidy snorted. She was about as steely as a marshmallow. And if you had any interest in the facts, her hair could best be described as 'mousey with a touch of pink'.

She read on.

It's a long way from LA to Dithercott, but chef Cassidy Beeswhistle is at the centre of a tale that wouldn't be out of place in a Hollywood blockbuster. Since the glamorous Californian – a direct descendant of the original owners of Dithercott Manor – bought the centuries-old Beeswhistle Inn earlier this year, there's been a mysterious fire, a wild grudge against a prominent local family and decidedly mixed reviews of her new venture. But as Cassidy herself bullishly declares: 'I'm not here to make friends.'

Her mouth fell open. She had already guessed from Louis Blunt's line of questioning that he wasn't planning to write a cosy piece about her hunt for the perfect local Cheddar, but this read like the episode notes for the season opener of *Billions*. And was he really allowed to misuse a quote like that? He'd taken it completely out of context to paint her as a ruthlessly ambitious bitch.

Cassidy thought about closing her laptop and leaving the rest of the article unread, but on balance she decided she would rather know the worst of it rather than torment herself by imagining what it contained. Besides, everyone else she knew was going to read it, and forewarned was forearmed.

Like ripping off a particularly stubborn plaster, she sped through the remainder of the article. As she had feared, it was a total hatchet job. Cassidy's cooking and the pub were mentioned briefly, but the focus of Louis Blunt's story was the way in which a back-stabbing newcomer was trampling over the village of Dithercott and its residents' wishes for her own personal gain. Worst of all, he had included her furiously muttered comment about Sophia Quill, and spun it to sound like *she* was the one with the crazed grudge.

> *Cassidy's ancestors lived at Dithercott Manor until the 1800s, when Albert Beeswhistle gambled it away to the Bamford-Bligh family. The attractive mum of one's expression grows guarded when the estate's current owners are mentioned, who she appears to blame for at least part of the inn's troubles. 'One of Dithercott Manor's inhabitants seems to have an obsessive interest in me,' she claims, with a wariness perhaps teetering on the brink of paranoia.*

Letting out a howl, Cassidy dropped her head in her hands. What if Ned saw this and thought she was talking about *him*? Perhaps she could complain to the editor and get the article taken down from the website? No, that wouldn't work. True, it was almost entirely fiction, but Louis Blunt had been careful to write it in such a way that made it almost impossible for her to make concrete objections. It was all vague insinuation and conjecture. Besides, the newspaper would already be in the shops.

Convinced that Sophia must somehow be involved, Cassidy typed 'Louis Blunt' into her search engine. Sure enough, amongst links to other articles he'd written, she found one entitled, with typical wordiness: '*The Quill: Birds of a feather should stick together and fly to this fab gastro-gem in the heart of Sussex!*' And at the top of the review was a photo of Louis Blunt with Sophia and Xavier, their arms around each other, beaming chummily at the camera in a way that strongly suggested this wasn't the first time they'd met.

Cassidy closed her eyes and slumped back in her chair. If only she'd done this research *before* the interview... But there was no point wasting any time on that line of thought. The damage had been done.

. . .

Over the following few weeks, the flood of bookings at the Beeswhistle slowed to a stream and then petered to a trickle. Cassidy reassured her team this was entirely normal, that things always calmed down after the initial flurry of interest, and that August could be quieter in the restaurant trade, but privately she knew that the plunge in enquiries was much too dramatic to be explained by a simple levelling-off. It was becoming hard to ignore the fact that increasingly few people from beyond Dithercott – Mrs Timothy's so-called 'outsiders' – were wanting to dine at the Beeswhistle.

After the soft launch, Cassidy had always intended to open the Beeswhistle as a full-time pub and had been looking forward to seeing it make a triumphant return to its rightful position as Dithercott's much-loved village boozer. Yet as the number of bookings dropped thanks to the bad reviews, so did the balance in her business account, meaning she couldn't afford to pay the extra staff she needed to open for longer hours, which in turn prevented her making more money and getting more genuine good reviews to counteract the bad. Trapped in this vicious circle, Cassidy became increasingly preoccupied and snappy, which put everyone else in the pub on edge as well. Minor hitches that usually wouldn't have fazed her, such as a late delivery from a supplier, sent her into total meltdown.

Angeline kept reassuring her that it would all blow over – 'just keep your head down and cook' – but *she* wasn't the one whose character had been ripped apart in the local paper. No doubt she was being paranoid, but every time Cassidy went out in Dithercott these days she got the feeling people were muttering about her when she walked past, believing the lies in Louis Blunt's article.

She repeatedly turned down James's invitations to join him at the New Vicarage for Sunday supper, as she felt terrible about how moody she'd been with Sally at work and imagined she wouldn't want to see her out of work as well. This had left Nora in tears because she didn't understand why they couldn't go and so Cassidy was struggling with 'mom guilt' on top of everything else.

She was so desperate to lift her mood that she even went back to Zumba, thinking physical exercise might help. Jasha was delighted to see her, giving her a bear hug and lending her his favourite jingle-trimmed scarf, but even Bettina's kind words about Cassidy's cooking and Mrs Timothy's promise to pass on her secret recipe for her greengage chutney failed to banish the clouds, and when she got back to the inn, the appearance of yet another one-star review tipped her further into a spiral of depression.

The final straw was a visit from the council, who had been tipped off by a 'concerned citizen' about the Beeswhistle's alleged rodent problem. They were, of course, given a clean bill of health – in fact, the officer had complimented them on their hygiene practices, but the message was clear: they were under attack.

With takings falling steadily week on week and the one-star reviews multiplying like a particularly nasty virus, Cassidy knew there was only one way ahead. She would have to fight back.

THIRTY-SEVEN

Rain had been thundering down for the two hours that Cassidy had been standing in the middle of a shopping precinct handing out flyers – or rather thrusting them in people's faces while they did their best to dodge them.

Earlier that morning, she had taken the train to Brighton, the nearest city to Dithercott, armed with two thousand glossy leaflets offering twenty per cent off a meal at the Beeswhistle. Cassidy had thought it would be a good way to drum up new business, but she had realised within minutes that it was going to be an expensive waste of time.

Despite it being the middle of summer, the rain had started as soon as she found a promising-looking place to stand. She had brought along a golf umbrella, having checked the forecast before she left the inn, but she hadn't appreciated how tricky it would be to get the flyers into people's hands while holding it. She didn't care if *she* got soaked, but her precious leaflets – featuring a photo of the Beeswhistle looking like the perfect destination for a special night out – were quickly turning into papier mâché.

The problem, Cassidy quickly discovered, was that people

really didn't like flyers. Even when she'd shouted 'FREE MONEY!' while waving them in the air, most passers-by actively went out of their way to avoid taking one. And if by some miracle someone did, it would invariably go straight in the nearest bin or get shoved in a pocket unread.

As the drumming on her umbrella grew louder, Cassidy looked hopelessly around the square. She still had over half her flyers left, but the crowds had thinned out so much that she wondered whether she should just cut her losses and head home. She watched as a woman pushing a pram in her direction clocked the leaflets and then abruptly headed the other way.

'I'm just trying to save my business and support my child!' Cassidy yelled after her rapidly disappearing back. The woman turned and shot her a look that she probably deserved.

'So there you are!'

Cassidy swung round to see a dishevelled middle-aged man approaching her. He wasn't even trying to shield himself from the rain and his hair was plastered to his head as a result.

'Damn it,' she muttered.

She'd already had to move locations to avoid this guy. He'd seemed pleasant enough at first, though she could smell the alcohol on his breath, and Cassidy had been happy to chat as he'd seemed lonely. It was only when he'd started badgering her to go for a drink with him that she had politely made her excuses and found somewhere else to stand.

'Hello again,' he said, edging so close that his head pressed up against her umbrella. 'You forgot to tell me your name.'

'Uh – I'd rather not.'

'No need to be like that, darlin'.' His words were slurring together. 'Jus' trying to be friendly.'

Sighing inwardly, she told him.

'Natalie?'

'*Cassidy.*'

He screwed up his face. 'That's a boy's name, innit?'

A man in a suit walked past; Cassidy thrust out a flyer and he actually took it. *Yes!* Then dropped it on the ground.

She bent to pick it up and waved it at him. 'Sir? You dropped this.'

He ignored her and hurried on, hunched against the rain.

'So, Natalie, are you married?'

She sighed. 'That's really none of your business.'

'Ooh, touchy! Must have hit a nerve, eh?' The man elbowed her, briefly putting her off balance.

Cassidy dug her teeth into her bottom lip. 'Will you please leave me alone,' she said tightly.

'You should smile more, love. You're pretty when you smile.' He swayed on the spot. 'How about we go for that drink now?'

'No thank you.'

Then he grabbed her arm. The primitive part of Cassidy's brain instantly seized control. 'Don't you touch me!' she screeched, shaking him off and storming away.

Through the rain, she spotted a policeman sheltering under the awning of H&M and headed in his direction. She'd had just about enough for one day.

'Excuse me? That guy over there is harassing me.'

The policeman looked over to where the drunk man was now slumped on a wall. When he saw Cassidy pointing at him, he blew her a kiss.

The policeman made no attempt to move. 'Can you tell me what happened?'

'Well, I was handing out flyers and—'

'Do you have permission?'

'I'm sorry?'

'Did you apply to the council for a licence to distribute leaflets?'

She gaped at him. 'You've got to be kidding me. I just told you I was being harassed and you—' Cassidy stopped herself. 'You know what – *forget it*. I was leaving anyway.' She shoved a flyer at him. 'Here, if you fancy a night out. Better make it quick, though, as we'll probably be out of business in a few weeks.'

Then she stalked off in the direction of the station, muttering savagely to herself. She had wasted an entire Saturday morning when she could have been hanging out with Nora, baking cookies or jumping in puddles on a walk – and for what? The Beeswhistle might get a couple of extra bookings out of it, but that was hardly going to help her shortfall of thousands of pounds.

Passing a coffee shop, she looked longingly through the steamy window at its cosy interior, but three pounds on a flat white was an extravagance she couldn't afford. This past week she had started to get stroppy messages from suppliers whose invoices were overdue, and as the money ran out, so did her hopes of using only local, organic produce in the Beeswhistle's kitchen. It had broken her heart when she'd realised she had no choice but to bulk-buy ingredients from Costco.

The flyer scheme hadn't been Cassidy's first attempt at marketing. She had already spent hours on Instagram researching and then contacting influencer accounts to offer a free meal in return for a shout-out for the Beeswhistle. A few (generally the accounts with the least followers) had responded positively, but others had asked her to send an email stating her proposal in detail, and it all became so complicated that Cassidy had given up. She wanted to be spending her time cooking, not quibbling over exactly how many drinks she was offering to some entitled twenty-year-old who couldn't even spell 'shampain'.

Cassidy spent the entire thirty-minute train ride back to Dithercott whipping herself into a froth of anger. She knew she was partly to blame for the Beeswhistle's troubles, having naively assumed that just because she was a good chef she would automatically be a successful restaurant owner, but though her business and financial management skills might not be up to scratch, most restaurateurs didn't have the additional challenge of having to battle against a barrage of fake reviews.

Cassidy had done everything she could to try to find out who was posting them. Despite her strong suspicions that Sophia Quill was to blame, she and Angeline had discussed each of the reviews with the front-of-house team, poring over the details to tally them with interactions they'd had with genuine guests, and they had concluded that most – if not all – were pure fiction. Who else other than Sophia could be behind such a smear campaign? Cassidy certainly wasn't aware of anyone else who wanted her out of Dithercott (and would resort to dirty tricks to achieve it) and Sophia's link to the newspaper journalist Louis Blunt was a definite red flag. Would she get bored of trolling her like Angeline thought? Or was she so intent on driving Cassidy away that she would keep going until the Beeswhistle's reputation had been so thoroughly trashed that they were forced to close?

By the time they pulled into the station, Cassidy was almost vibrating with fury. This was all Sophia Quill's fault.

Rather than taking the road back to the village, she swerved towards a taxi that was idling outside.

'Where to, love?' the driver asked.

She jumped in the back, ignoring her worries about the cost of the fare. 'The Quill gastropub, Dithercott Road.'

There was nobody in the lobby when Cassidy arrived, so she took the remaining flyers from her bag and put a stack of them by the reception desk. No doubt they would be removed as soon as anyone noticed, but at least it made her feel she was fighting back in some small way.

A woman appeared and greeted Cassidy with a smile. 'Are you dining with us today?'

'No, I was hoping I might speak to Sophia Quill.'

The woman took in Cassidy's sodden hair and clothes, which were dripping on the parquet floor.

'I'm so sorry, she's having lunch right now. Can I take a message for you?'

'No need,' said Cassidy, 'I'll give it to her myself.'

As she headed into the restaurant, the receptionist called after her – 'Excuse me, you can't go in there!' – but Cassidy ignored her. She spotted Sophia across the other side of the room sitting at a table with Xavier and two other smartly dressed couples and picked up her pace, immune to the curious looks from the other diners as the receptionist continued to call after her.

On seeing her approach, Sophia's face briefly hardened, but then she delicately dabbed at her mouth with her napkin and broke into a broad smile.

'Cassidy. To what do I owe this pleasure?'

'I need to speak to you,' she snapped – but then made herself check her fury. 'If it's a convenient time.'

'As you can see, it's not.' Sophia turned back to her guests, conversation clearly over.

Cassidy stood her ground. 'Then I'll wait in reception until it is.'

Irritation flashing in her eyes, Sophia pursed her lips, weighing up her options. After a moment, she pushed back her chair and stood up. 'I'm so sorry, everyone, I'll be back as soon as I've dealt with this... matter.'

Cassidy followed as Sophia headed towards a door marked 'PRIVATE', her heels clacking angrily across the floor. Inside, there was an office, with a desk and sofa, but Sophia made no move to sit. Instead, she folded her arms and glared at Cassidy.

'What do you want?' she said.

'I want you to leave the Beeswhistle alone.'

'I have absolutely no idea what you're talking about.'

Cassidy forced herself to take a calming breath. 'There've been a lot of fake reviews of the inn online, and I'm pretty sure that you're behind them.'

Sophia's eyes went wide. 'That is an outrageous accusation! I did post an honest review of my own disastrous experience, as I felt it only fair to warn people, but I wouldn't dream of making things up.' She glanced at the door. 'Is that all?'

'No, it's not,' said Cassidy, struggling to keep her voice level. 'I know you're behind this, Sophia. What the hell is your problem with me?'

Sophia raised an eyebrow. 'The only problem I have is that you're keeping me from my guests. And if you continue to make these wild allegations then I will have no alternative but to speak to my lawyer.'

To her horror, Cassidy felt a forming lump in her throat. She dug her fingernails into her palms, desperate not to cry, but it felt like the Beeswhistle was slipping through her fingers and she was powerless to keep hold of it. With nothing left to lose, she parked her dignity and decided to beg.

'Please, Sophia, I need to make the Beeswhistle work. For my daughter, as much as for Dithercott. I don't know if you're worried I'm going to try to steal the manor from you, or muscle in on the Quill's business, but I swear that's not the case. All I want is to be left in peace to try to make a success of the inn.' She looked at Sophia beseechingly, hoping to appeal to her better nature. 'There's no need for us to be enemies. We might even be able to help each other! We could – I don't know – have some joint promotions between our two businesses? Just please, I'm begging you, leave the Beeswhistle alone.'

Sophia's nostrils flared as if there was an unpleasant smell in the room. 'Like I said, this is absolutely nothing to do with me,' she said icily. 'If your establishment is receiving bad reviews, then I suggest you take a look at the standard of your food and service, rather than blaming other people for your shortcomings. That may be the way you do things in America, but it's unacceptable here. Now, if you've finished, I need to get back to my guests.'

Sophia held out an arm towards the door. Cassidy hesitated, racking her brain for some other way to convince her, but she knew it was hopeless. Sophia clearly didn't have a better nature to appeal to. Feeling like a shamed child being sent out of class, she sloped towards the door, catching Sophia smirking triumphantly as she left. She knew this had been a long shot, but she wanted to try everything she possibly could to save the inn before finally admitting defeat. Now, all that remained was the nuclear option, and as she walked out into the rainy car park, not even bothering to put up her umbrella, Cassidy realised she had no choice but to hit the button.

THIRTY-EIGHT

Cassidy put down a plate of French toast, extra-crispy bacon and blueberry maple syrup in front of Angeline, then laid a starched napkin over her friend's lap with a theatrical flourish.

'Voilà! The Beeswhistle breakfast special and a flat white, just as madam likes it.'

Angeline rubbed her hands. 'Well, this was definitely worth getting out of bed at six a.m. for,' she said, reaching for the cutlery.

'Yeah, sorry about the early start, but I wanted to have a chat with you before Nora was up.'

Angeline waved her fork. 'Chat away – I'm going to be too busy eating to do much except listen.'

Taking a seat opposite her friend, Cassidy had a sudden flashback to another occasion, many months ago, when she had cooked Angeline a special meal because she had something important to talk to her about. This time, however, she had a feeling their conversation wouldn't go quite so well.

'So what's this about?' asked Angeline. 'Something to do with the inn, I presume?'

Cassidy nodded. 'Takings are down week-on-week and the

THE ACCIDENTAL INHERITANCE

bad reviews keep coming. I went to see Sophia to try to reason with her, but she threatened me with legal action.'

'What a surprise.'

'It's looking bleak, Ange. So much so, in fact, that... well, I'm wondering whether I should sell the inn.'

Her friend froze in the middle of cutting up her French toast. 'You couldn't even let me have one mouthful before ruining my appetite?'

'Sorry.'

She put down her knife and fork. 'You can't be serious.'

'I've spent hours agonising over the best way to deal with this, believe me, but I can't see any other option. Not only is Sophia destroying our reputation, I can't afford the extra staff we'd need to open the Beeswhistle full-time. In fact, I don't think I can even afford to stay open for much longer. I just don't see how I can make this work.'

'Come on, Cass, I know things have been tough lately, but, like I've already said, Sophia will get bored and bookings will pick up again after the summer break. It will get better, I'm sure of it. You just need to hang in there.' She grabbed Cassidy's hand and gave it a squeeze. 'You can't let Sophia win!'

'But I'd rather let Sophia win than Dithercott lose. The village needs its pub back, and, as much as it pains me to admit it, I can't give it to them. I think it's time to let someone else take charge, someone who knows what they're doing. I'm sure the new owners would be happy to keep you on as manager – in fact, I'll make it a condition of the sale.'

Angeline chewed her lip. 'If you need to wait a bit longer to extend the opening hours, then everyone will understand. What you've achieved at the Beeswhistle is nothing short of miraculous – and if you can do that in a few months, with all the odds stacked against you, imagine what you can do in the next few years!'

It was fighting talk – just as she would expect from her dear friend – and Cassidy wished she could find encouragement in Angeline's words, but this was just one obstacle too many.

'I'm so sorry, Ange, but I've not got any fight left in me. Not to mention any money.'

Angeline stared at her for a moment. 'So what will you do instead? Go to work at the Quill? In case you hadn't noticed, there isn't a huge demand for cordon bleu chefs around here.'

'I've been offered a job back at my old restaurant,' said Cassidy, avoiding her gaze.

Angeline frowned. 'I don't understand. Which one?'

'The one in Sacramento.'

In the long silence that followed, Cassidy could hear voices in the street outside.

'You're not serious,' said Angeline eventually.

'They've offered me the head chef job with an increase in salary and reduced hours. It's too good an opportunity to turn down.'

Angeline stared at her. 'I don't believe this,' she said, shaking her head. 'What about Nora? She'll be devastated.'

'Don't you think I know that!' Cassidy instantly regretted snapping at her. 'I'm sorry, it's just... I know Nora will be heart-broken at the idea of leaving Dithercott, and it's eating me up inside, but I'm the grown-up here – I need to decide what's best for us as a family. I know that Nora is far happier here, but what good is that if I can't support us financially? And kids are resilient, aren't they? I'll do everything I possibly can to help her deal with it. I'll be working shorter hours with this new job, which means I'll be able to spend more time with her, and perhaps we can even take Hermione back with us to soften the blow.'

'You can't take Tilly though, can you? Or Olive or Harry or any of the rest of Nora's friends.' Angeline's tone was hostile. 'You've been in Dithercott for little more than six months and now you're chucking it in without giving it a proper shot.'

'I *have* given it a proper shot, but it's not exactly been a smooth ride.'

'When does life ever guarantee you a smooth ride? This looks a lot like you're running away because things got a bit tough for a while.'

'That's unfair.' Cassidy had known this was going to be a difficult conversation, but she hadn't expected Angeline to be quite so resistant to the idea. She needed to make her friend understand what an impossible situation she was in. 'What chance does the Beeswhistle have when Sophia Quill seems determined to get us closed down? I can either sit around waiting for her to drive the inn's reputation into the mud, or I can leave on my own terms, when there might still be a chance to get back some of the money I invested. It wouldn't be running away, it would be making the best of an impossible situation. Nobody can accuse me of not having tried my best.'

There was a creak and they both looked up to see Nora, still in her pyjamas, standing on the stairs. Judging by her expression, she had overheard at least some of the conversation.

'Mom? What's going on?'

An icy chill struck at Cassidy's core. Terrified at what Nora may have heard, she leapt into damage control. 'Good morning, honey! How did you sleep?'

'I heard you say something about leaving. We can't leave here, it's our home.'

'Oh no, Angeline and I were just chatting through some ideas about the inn. Nothing to worry about at all.'

Cassidy felt terrible lying to her daughter, but she couldn't face telling her truth yet, as she knew all too well that it would devastate her.

Nora's eyes flicked between the two women. 'I love it here, Mom. I don't want to *ever* leave, okay?'

'I know that, sweetie... Now, why don't you go back upstairs and watch some TV while we finish up our boring business chat and then I'll make you pancakes for breakfast. How's that sound?'

After an agonising few seconds, Nora's fearful grimace relaxed into a smile.

'Okey-dokey. Tilly will be at camp today, right, Angeline?'

'We'll see you there. Maybe we could all grab an ice-cream together afterwards?'

'Cool!'

Nora turned and ran back upstairs and shortly after they heard a door close.

Cassidy let out a long exhale, slumping back in her chair. The prospect of telling Nora that not only were they leaving Dithercott, but also moving back to Sacramento, suddenly felt a whole lot harder. The rush of guilt made her feel physically sick. She closed her eyes, dropping her head in her hands, and a moment later Angeline came over and wrapped her in a hug. The two women stayed like that for a while, Cassidy clinging onto her friend's arm, and when they broke apart again, Angeline's expression had softened.

'I know how hard this decision must have been for you. And I do appreciate it's a very tough situation. I'm sorry if I was unsympathetic, I'm just going to hate to see you and Nora go. But if you really believe this is for the best, I'll support you however I can.' Angeline sat back down heavily. 'God, this all seems so... *final*. Surely there must be another way...' Her face suddenly brightened. 'How about trying to find an investor? That would at least help with the financial issues.'

'Maybe, but that still leaves the problem of Sophia. And who in their right mind would want to invest in a failing business that's had terrible reviews?'

Angeline chewed her lip. 'True. But would you at least give it some thought?'

'Of course,' said Cassidy, although mentally she had already dismissed the idea as yet another undoubtedly fruitless task that she didn't have time for. 'And thank you. You've been such a wonderful friend to me, Ange. The thought of leaving you and everyone in the village...' She finished with a shrug, aware she was about to cry again. She seemed close to tears most of the time these last few days.

Angeline glanced at her abandoned plate of food. 'Funny how that seemed so delicious a moment ago,' she said, grimly. 'When would you go?'

'I have to discuss it with my old boss, but I think she wants me to start back after Christmas.'

'Okay, so we've got a bit of time. And perhaps some miracle will happen in the meantime and you'll be able to stay.'

'Yeah, maybe I'll win the lottery and Sophia will emigrate to Australia.'

'We can only hope,' said Angeline, with a sad little smile.

THIRTY-NINE

Cassidy had spent the morning at her laptop, taking the first steps to put the wheels in motion for the sale of the pub and their return to Sacramento. Nora was at camp and the Beeswhistle's team wasn't due in for a couple of hours, which meant she was free to make calls without the risk of being overheard. She didn't want the news about their move to spread any further until her plans had progressed to the point of no return. Her resolve was so flimsy since yesterday's conversation with Angeline that Cassidy didn't think she'd be strong enough to resist a further barrage of pleas to stay unless the move was a done deal.

From her favourite spot at her desk next to the bedroom window, Cassidy could see a pair of jays squabbling and chasing each other around the inn's walled garden. Hermione was dozing on her lap, though rather than curled in a ball, he was draped over her knees, legs dangling in mid-air on either side. She gave the cat – who usually spent hours at the window monitoring the birds – a gentle nudge. 'Hey, buddy, you'd enjoy watching this.' He raised his head, blinked sleepily, then went back to sleep.

Cassidy took a sip of the milky tea that she'd grown to love these past months. *Home.* That was the word that came to mind right at this moment. Indeed, the Beeswhistle felt more like home than any place she'd lived before. So why was she leaving?

Taking a deep inhale, Cassidy once again forced down the doubts that continued to plague her, especially when she thought about how Nora would react when she finally broke the news. Moving back to Sacramento was the best option, she told herself for what must have been the hundredth time – the *only* option, all things considered. She remembered a quote she'd once read: 'The right thing and the easy thing are never the same'. And Nora would be fine. Cassidy would make sure of it.

There was a knocking downstairs – no doubt the delivery of vegetables she'd been expecting – so she lifted Hermione onto the bed and went to answer the door. When she opened it, though, it wasn't Geoff, the cheery delivery guy who called her 'Mrs B'. It was Ned Bamford-Bligh.

Cassidy froze, her mind instantly flashing back to the moment he had pushed her away after she'd shoved her tongue down his throat.

'Hello, Cassidy. I hope this isn't a bad time?'

Her automatic response was to say yes, it was actually a very bad time because she wasn't wearing any make-up, her hair was greasy and she hadn't even brushed her teeth yet, but instead she just mutely shook her head.

'Everything going well at the inn?' he asked.

'Not bad, thank you,' she said, raising her hand to her mouth to discreetly check her breath.

In the awkward silence that followed, Cassidy was desperately trying to think of a polite way to get rid of him when Ned suddenly said: 'Your hair is different.'

Cassidy's instantly hand shot to her hair, horrified that it must be looking greasy and unwashed, but then she remembered that in a particularly bleak moment last week she had asked Angeline for a dramatic change in colour. Her friend had suggested 'steely blonde', which had made Cassidy laugh for the first time in ages, and she actually liked the result, even though Nora had told her she looked like Draco Malfoy's mother.

'It really suits you.' Ned rubbed the back of his neck. 'Look, I'm sorry to turn up unannounced, but I have something to give you. Don't go anywhere...'

He stepped out of sight and then Bertie's portrait loomed in the doorway, her great-great-great-grandfather's smirk seemingly levelled straight at her.

Ned's face popped around the side. 'Surprise!'

Cassidy couldn't help but laugh. 'Will that even fit through the door?'

'I hope so, because I'm not taking him back again.' He sized up the space. 'We'll need to turn him on his side, but I reckon we'll be able to get him through...'

Sure enough, they managed to shuffle the painting through the doorway and then carried it through to the bar. Even though they were having to work together, Cassidy got the feeling that Ned was trying to avoid physical contact with her as much as she was with him, the memory of what had happened last time they met looming over them. They propped the portrait up against the wall in the bar, opposite the fireplace, and then took a step back to so see how it looked in situ. As convinced as Cassidy had been that she no longer wanted Bertie, thanks to his painful association with Ned, now that he was here, he looked right at home.

'Propping up the bar, just as he would have wanted,' said Ned.

'You know, I could swear I just saw him smile.'

'I think that's entirely likely.'

She looked at Ned, who was standing alongside her, and the sight of him triggered a pulse of desire inside her. She had somehow forgotten just how handsome he was. Her heart clearly still hadn't got the memo, despite being repeatedly told so by her head, that Ned wasn't interested in her.

'Well, thank you very much for delivering him personally,' she said, hoping he'd get the hint and leave.

'Not at all. I – um – was actually wondering if I might have a word with you? I saw your interview in the newspaper.'

Cassidy dropped her face in her hands. 'I'm so sorry, the journalist completely twisted my words and took things out of context. That quote about one of the manor's occupants having an obsessive interest in me...'

'Don't worry, I guessed it was my sister you were referring to. And I'm well aware of what she's been up to, trying to sabotage the inn. In fact, I've spoken to her about it.'

Cassidy gawped at her. 'You have?'

Ned folded his arms. 'Yes, but I'm afraid it didn't go very well. She denied having anything to do with the negative reviews, even though Xavier had already let slip to me that it was her.'

'Well, thank you for trying to sort it out.'

'It's no excuse, but Sophia's threatened by your family's historical connection to the manor. She has this deep-seated fear that you're going to usurp her position on *Tatler*'s best-dressed list.'

Cassidy looked down at her outfit of Nora's Hello Kitty sweatshirt, which was baggy on her ten-year-old daughter but alarmingly snug on her, plus some very crumpled dungarees. 'I hardly think there's much danger of that. I just want to be left in peace to cook good food.'

'I know that.' Ned had an odd glint in his eyes. 'Which is why I thought *this* might be of interest.'

He crossed over to the portrait and shuffled it around, so the back of the canvas was showing. A sheet of brown paper had been stuck on it, and Ned gently peeled away the tape holding it in place to reveal several blocks of writing on the canvas.

Intrigued, Cassidy came to get a closer look. The writing obviously dated from around the same time as the portrait, because it was in the same ornate style as Bertie's letter, and a mess of inky smudges and fingerprints suggested it had been finished in a rush.

Cassidy peered at it. 'What exactly am I looking at here?'

'What would you like it to be?'

She looked back at Ned. 'Well, obviously the Lost Deed of Beeswhistle.'

He just raised his eyebrows.

'You're kidding.'

'I'm not.' A grin burst out of him, as if he'd been struggling to keep it inside. 'When I finally got Bertie down off the wall this morning, I found the writing on the back of the portrait, as plain as day! Either nobody has bothered to read it before, or they did and made the decision to keep it quiet. It turns out the old rogue has been keeping quite a secret over the past couple of hundred years.'

Cassidy could only shake her head, lost for words.

'See' – he pointed to the bottom lines of scrawl – 'those are Bertie and Henry's signatures, with the names of what I presume were a couple of witnesses.' Ned looked back at her, eyes sparkling. 'This really is it, Cassidy. The Lost Deed of Beeswhistle. It's actually real.'

Before she could think, Cassidy threw her arms around him. For a split second, she was swept away, lost in the feel and smell of him, until he gave her an awkward pat on the back that snapped her back to reality. Cassidy pulled away and flashed him a quick smile, which thankfully he returned.

'I don't believe this,' she said, turning back to the portrait. 'I was so sure it was just a story.'

'We all were. Part of me always suspected, though, there might be more to it than that.'

Cassidy's head was spinning. If this really *was* the Lost Deed of Beeswhistle – a document confirming that ownership of Dithercott Manor would pass back to the Beeswhistle family after two generations – it would mean that she would have a claim on the ownership of the estate. For the first time, it occurred to her just how generous Ned had been in showing this to her. He could have easily made an excuse not to give her the portrait and then she would have been none the wiser.

Of course, she would never dream of trying to put the deed into action: the idea of attempting to force the Bamford-Blighs out of their home was unthinkable. Besides, it hardly seemed possible that a centuries-old agreement on the back of a painting would carry any legal weight. Ned wasn't to know that, though. And yet he was looking as delighted as if *he'd* just been given this amazing gift, rather than the other way round.

'Thank you so much,' she said. 'I really appreciate you bringing me this.'

'You really are most welcome. Do you want to see what it says?'

'Absolutely.'

She bent down and started to read.

This agreement between Albert Charles Phillip Beeswhistle and Henry George Carruthers Bamford-Bligh is hereby entered into on the date of the 7 July, 1842.

Thanks to the cramped handwriting and archaic language it was slow-going, and many of the words were indecipherable, but Cassidy could certainly get the gist of it. She felt as if she had stepped back in time and was listening directly to the voice of her great-great-great-grandfather. If she was honest, she'd always had a slight niggle over Bertie's actions – blithely giving away his descendants' birthright on the roll of a dice – but her feelings towards him softened on discovering he hadn't been as reckless as everyone had assumed.

Cassidy had got about halfway through, however, when her smile abruptly vanished. She re-read the same sentence over again, her stomach sinking as she took in its meaning. 'But I don't understand.' She turned to Ned. 'This isn't—'

He held up a hand to stop her. 'I know, but hear me out. I have a plan.'

FORTY

At the end of that evening's service, Cassidy was tidying up the kitchen with the help of Ollie and Sally. It had been a disappointing night – three bookings hadn't turned up, including a table of six – and Lance had mixed up a table's order, leading to complaints, but James had stopped by after an evening out to collect Sally, and it was a pleasant distraction to have him chatting away as they cleared up. He was squeezed into the gap between the fridge and cabinet so that he wasn't in their way, eating the remains of a broad bean risotto straight out of the pan.

'Gosh, this is stupendous,' he said. 'I didn't even think I *liked* broad beans.'

Cassidy had wanted to ask where he had been that evening, but the opportunity hadn't arisen. Judging by his outfit, though, it had been a case of pleasure rather than business, and Cassidy found herself hoping he had been with Miss Poppy. Having got over her brief green-eyed moment, the thought of them together felt perfectly right.

There was a sudden hammering at the back door and everyone in the kitchen turned their heads towards the noise.

Sally narrowed her eyes. 'What in the name of all that's holy is that?'

They heard raised voices and then, moments later, Sophia Quill burst into the kitchen in an explosion of sequins, eyeliner and hairspray. She looked as if she'd come straight from the Oscars, although, judging by her expression, someone had just dropped their gold statuette on her toe.

'Sorry, Cass, I couldn't stop her,' said Lance, who had followed her in.

'Not to worry, I'll take it from here. Sophia, how are you?'

'How do you *think* I am?' she hissed.

Cassidy turned to the others in the kitchen. 'Sorry, guys, could you please give us a moment?'

'You sure you don't want me to stay?' asked Ollie, eyeballing Sophia.

'I'll be okay, but thank you.'

'We'll be just out here if you need us,' whispered James, as he passed her.

Once the kitchen was empty, Cassidy turned to Sophia. 'So, how can I help you?'

'Don't play the innocent with me,' she scoffed. 'I got a call from my brother in the middle of a charity gala at the Dorchester, which *I* helped to organise, and he told me all about his ridiculous discovery.'

'Oh, you mean the Lost Deed of Beeswhistle?'

Sophia's eyes were blazing. 'I *knew* this was why you came to Dithercott! I saw straight through your innocent act.' She affected a whiny American accent. '*I don't know anything about a lost deed! I just wanna cook burgers and suck up to all the locals!*' Sophia snorted. 'The other idiots might have been taken in by you, but I knew this was your plan all along: to get your grubby hands on the manor and drive my children out of their home.'

'Strictly speaking, your home is in London, and I can assure you I've got no interest in that.'

'You listen to me,' snarled Sophia, pushing her face right up to Cassidy's. Up close, her breath smelt of stale champagne and there were smudges of mascara beneath her eyes. 'The Bamford-Blighs have lived at Dithercott Manor for two hundred years. If you really think some ancient scrawl on the back of a painting will stand up in court, then you're an even bigger moron than you seem.'

Rage surged inside Cassidy, her heart thundering, and she forced herself to take slow breaths, determined not to lose her cool. 'Well, you obviously think it might, otherwise I doubt you'd have interrupted your gala to drive down all the way down here at this time of night.'

Sophia looked as though smoke might start pouring from her ears.

'You are right, though,' Cassidy went on. 'I very much doubt the deed *would* stand up in court. And, believe it or not, I've got no interest in putting it to the test.'

Sophia's eyes were slits. 'I don't believe you.'

'It's true, I've got no interest in taking the manor off you.' Cassidy paused, her brows bunching together. 'It is a pretty good story, though, isn't it? The discovery of a secret legal document that throws the Bamford-Bligh family's claim on Dithercott Manor into dispute. I mean, I guess it would imply that rather than *you* being lady of the manor, it should actually be, well... me!'

Sophia gasped, her hand clasping her chest as if she'd been physically wounded.

'Yeah,' Cassidy went on, 'I suppose it could appear a little *dishonourable* if it came to light that our ancestors made an agreement the manor should return to the Beeswhistle family, yet the current occupants were refusing to abide by it. People might even start to question the legitimacy of the Bamford-Bligh family's social status. And I can certainly imagine more than a few raised eyebrows if the story somehow made it into the press or social media. I've noticed how much you Brits love reading about badly behaved aristocrats. I guess it might even make the national papers!'

Sophia was glowering at her, breathing heavily. 'What is it that you want? Money?'

Cassidy's gaze was steely. 'What I want is for you to stop trying to sabotage the Beeswhistle Inn.'

She didn't even try to deny it. 'Done. What else?'

'That's it. But if I find out that you've done anything else to jeopardise my inn, I'll immediately make a photo of the deed public.'

'Fine,' she spat. 'Xav and I are thinking about selling the Quill anyway and buying a restaurant in London, where people actually understand quality. You're welcome to this godforsaken backwater.'

'Great! I'm so glad we could have this conversation.' Cassidy beamed at her. 'Friends?'

Scowling, Sophia turned on her heel and flounced out of the kitchen, slamming the door behind her.

Once she had gone, Cassidy dropped her hands to her knees, feeling as if she had just completed a triathlon.

A few moments later, there was a tentative tap at the door, and then James's head popped through the gap.

'Cassidy? What was that about?'

She beckoned him in, indicating for him to close the door behind him.

'Ned found the Lost Deed of Beeswhistle.'

James gawped at her. '*What?*'

'It was on the back of Bertie's portrait. He discovered it when the painting was taken off the wall.'

'I... I don't believe it...' James ran a shaky hand across his brow, his gaze feverish. 'But this is incredible! So it really exists?'

'Yup, it's the real deal. Signed by both Bertie and Henry.'

'Well! I can see now why Sophia was so angry.'

'I'm afraid I threatened to make the deed public if she didn't lay off the inn.'

'Quite right too,' he said, stoutly. 'Gosh, if only Joe were alive to see this! Cassidy Beeswhistle, rightful heir to Dithercott Manor!'

Cassidy sucked in her bottom lip. 'Well, not exactly.'

'What do you mean?'

She hesitated, but after all James's help it felt right to give him the full picture. 'It turns out the rumours about the lost deed weren't entirely accurate. You see, Bertie and Henry didn't agree that the estate should revert back to my family after two generations. In fact, the deed doesn't even mention Dithercott Manor at all. What it actually concerns is the ownership of the Beeswhistle Inn.' She thought for a moment. 'I suppose the clue is in the title, really – the Lost Deed of *Beeswhistle*.'

James frowned. 'I'm afraid I don't understand.'

'It turns out that Bertie had actually bought the inn a few years before he gambled everything away. Ned had already mentioned to me that it was his favourite place in the village, so it makes sense. Anyway, as the pub was part of his estate, it went to the Bamford-Blighs along with everything else, but Bertie must have got cold feet about it, because shortly afterwards he obviously asked for an agreement confirming that after two generations the Beeswhistle Inn should pass back to his family.' She raised an eyebrow. 'That was Bertie's main concern. Not where his descendants would live, but where they would *drink*.'

James was hanging on her every word. 'Well, I never...'

'But it adds up, right? The more I heard about Henry Bamford-Bligh, the more unlikely it seemed that this shrewd lawyer would ever agree to return ownership of the manor. But the *pub*... That must have been worth a fraction of the estate's value. You can imagine Henry's thinking: "Silly old Bertie, let's agree to his ridiculous deed if it means we get to hang onto the rest of the estate..." I think the Bamford-Blighs must have sold the inn soon after, because Ned doesn't have any record of his family ever owning it.'

'So this would make you the rightful owner of...'

'The Beeswhistle Inn, yes. Or, at least it would have, if it hadn't already been sold on to someone else.'

'Gosh, this is quite astounding...' James was chuckling to himself, then abruptly stopped. 'But what about Sophia? If the deed concerns the inn, surely she wouldn't care about its discovery?'

'Ah, but Sophia hasn't seen the entire deed. Ned told her that he'd been delivering the portrait to the inn when the writing came to light. He sent her a photo, being careful to crop it so she couldn't see the passage referring to the inn, and told her that its contents were just as had been rumoured.'

'And she believed him?'

'Oh yes. Ned tells me that Sophia thinks he's so boringly honourable that she'd never suspect him of lying. Apparently she yelled that he cared more about "doing the bloody right thing" than protecting their family's legacy.'

'So you're sure she'll leave you and the inn alone?'

'Absolutely. There's no way Sophia would risk the deed going public.'

'Well, this is terrific! No harm done, and you can now focus on the Beeswhistle without having to worry about Sophia's meddling.' He beamed. 'A fresh start!'

'A fresh start,' Cassidy repeated.

But the smile on her face felt forced, the memory of the phone calls she'd made about selling the inn looming in her mind. As thrilled as she was that Sophia had surrendered, those damning one-star reviews were still online for anyone to read. It would take time and money to repair the damage to the Beeswhistle's reputation, both of which were rapidly running out. She couldn't continue to run the place as a restaurant, let alone fulfil her promise to open as a full-time pub, unless business suddenly picked up.

FORTY-ONE

Cassidy turned over in bed, kicking her feet out from the tangle of sheets, and checked the time. Only 4.42 a.m.! She dropped her head back on her pillow with a huff. The last time she had looked at her phone it had been just before 2 a.m., which meant she'd only got a couple of hours of sleep at most. She'd been sleeping so badly lately it reminded her of when Nora had been a baby and she used to tot up the snatches of sleep she'd managed to get each night to convince herself that she she'd actually had five or six hours in total. Now, though, it was fears rather than feeds that were keeping her awake.

At the root of her insomnia was her decision to accept Manon's job and going back to Sacramento – which was ridiculous, as it was *clearly* the best option for both her and Nora. She had even put together a list of pros and cons to make sure it was right. The 'pros' were certainly persuasive, including 'more time to spend with Nora', 'shorter working hours', 'purely creative role', 'more job security', 'unnecessary to wear woolly socks in bed' and so on. The 'cons' of the move, however, were largely emotional: 'Dithercott is nicer than Sacramento', 'Nora has lots of friends here', '*I* have lots of friends here', 'I don't want to leave the Beeswhistle' and in small letters at the bottom (which she later crossed out) 'Ned B-B'. Mindful of her tendency towards rash and emotional decision-making, this time Cassidy had been sure to follow her head, not her heart. She had done things *properly*.

Why, then, was she still worrying whether she'd made the right choice? As she lay awake each night, she was aware of something niggling at her, a vague uneasiness at the edge of her consciousness. It wasn't anything concrete, but it had been enough for her to have delayed telling Manon that she was planning to accept the job at the Smokehouse, despite her friend messaging her with a gentle nudge for her final decision.

In the silence, Cassidy could hear the soft murmurs and sighs of the inn. The noises had quietened down since the renovations, but the ancient building still seemed like a living thing, muttering to itself in its sleep.

Cassidy sat up. There was no point just lying here, tossing and turning for another hour. She would go for an early run: give her poor, restless mind a break and let her body take the strain for a change.

As always, Cassidy looked in on Nora before she left the house. Her daughter had thrown off her duvet in the night and was on her side, curled in a ball. Hermione, who was lying next to her on the pillow, raised his head, yawned, and then settled back down again.

Cassidy hesitated in the doorway. Watching Nora sleep always triggered a huge surge of love inside her, making her feel like her sole purpose on earth was to protect her precious girl. Today, though, this was followed by a thundering wave of guilt. It wasn't just Manon who didn't know about her decision to return to Sacramento; she still hadn't told Nora either. Softly closing the bedroom door, she vowed to do it today, after she got home from camp.

Locking the back door, Cassidy slipped out into the pre-dawn stillness of the inn's garden. The dewy air instantly worked like a sedative, softening the lines in her face and unravelling her knotted nerves. The sun wasn't up yet, but there was a residual warmth lingering from the previous day, and she left her light jacket back on the porch before heading around the side of the inn.

After a few stretches, she started to run along the high street, falling into an easy rhythm, her arms pumping at her sides. Angeline's upstairs curtains were still closed, although Cassidy knew she would be up soon for her morning yoga practice. She noticed a large stick whittled to a point, like a spear, outside Angeline's front door: Tilly must have brought it home from summer camp, as Nora had an almost identical one by her bed. In fact the pile of clay figures, stones and leaf pictures in Nora's bedroom had been getting so unmanageable that Cassidy had sneaked a few things into the bin, assuming one rock looked much like another, but Nora had noticed immediately. 'You can't throw out *Nigel!*' she had said, clutching a grey stone stuck with googly eyes to her chest.

The curtains were drawn in the Old Post Office too, although there was a light on downstairs; perhaps Ian or Bettina was getting a head start on the day. She noticed Dale had put a life-sized inflatable flamingo in the window of the Buttered Crumpet, which made her smile as she jogged past. Cassidy thought back to her first day in Dithercott when it had felt as if the shuttered windows on the neighbouring houses had been frowning at her. Now they were as comfortingly familiar to her as the people who lived inside them.

Having reached the break in the hedgerow leading to the footpath across the fields, Cassidy hurdled the stile in one swift move. She had perfected it now: one hand gripping the top bar, legs swinging up and over. It was about as athletic as she got and always made her feel strangely proud; it was just a shame there was never anyone around to see it, apart from a few crows and the odd rabbit.

The hay had just been harvested in the fields and the air smelt pungent and grassy, triggering a long-forgotten memory of playing in her grandparents' barn as a kid. Overhead, the sky was deep navy, casting the landscape in a bluish light, and the moon was still full and white, but there was a peachy-gold glow on the horizon, announcing dawn was on its way. It was the time of the day when Cassidy felt closest to her dad. Joe had always been an early bird, getting up at 5 a.m. or often even earlier: 'Tackle the day before it tackles you,' he liked to say. She'd been highly sceptical in her younger years, when late nights and hangovers had made lie-ins mandatory, but now she got it. It was a magical time to be out in the world. Forget wishing on a star, wishing on a sunrise seemed a far more sensible idea. *And what would you wish for?* She knew the answer instantly. She would wish they didn't have to leave Dithercott. This wasn't a fairy tale, though, and she had to deal in hard facts rather than dreams.

The ground started to climb upwards, and Cassidy made herself stop thinking and focus on her breath as she tackled the steepening incline. It was tough-going, and for a while all she could do was concentrate on moving forwards. She glanced up, checking how far she had left to go, reminding herself it would be worth it when she reached the summit and could take in her favourite view. Just a few more steps now – jeez, why didn't this ever get any easier? – and then suddenly she was at the top of the hill, and at that moment the sun peeked over the horizon, flooding the valley with light.

Spellbound, Cassidy gazed at the world laid out below her, her hands planted on her hips as she caught her breath. The lush greens fields of early summer had mellowed to a sun-baked gold, while across the other side of the valley stood Dithercott Manor, its windows glinting silver in the sunlight. Apart from a couple of small farms, from up here it was the only visible sign of human habitation, and it occurred to Cassidy that this sight must barely have changed since Bertie Beeswhistle was alive. There was something very special about the idea of seeing the world through her ancestor's eyes, and Cassidy sat down on the grass to take it all in, not wanting to move on just yet. She took a deep breath, wallowing in the beauty of her surroundings, and thought about Bertie. No matter how bad his problems, how could he have decided to leave this wonderful place for good?

Cassidy frowned. This thought shifted something inside her. For the first time, it occurred to her that perhaps that was exactly what *she* was doing: running away, hoping she could escape her problems simply by moving location. If she'd learnt one thing over the past few months, it was that you couldn't outrun problems: they had a nasty habit of following you wherever you went. And Bertie's situation had been way worse than hers. It wasn't as if she was destitute and homeless – well, not just yet, anyway...

Her phone vibrated, jolting her out of her head. It was a message from Manon, although that wasn't surprising, as she often heard from her friend in the early hours thanks to the time difference.

> Hey honey, just to keep you posted – that friend of mine I mentioned with the two-bed apartment has just leased it to someone else. Sad-face emoji. So sorry. Won't be a big problem though, we'll find you somewhere else fabulous to live if you decide to take the job. On that note...?? x

Cassidy stared at the screen; well, that was spooky timing. Just as she'd been thinking that the move back to Sacramento might not be as smooth as she had assumed, Manon had texted her to say that their accommodation had fallen through. If she'd been superstitious, she might even have seen it as a sign.

Replacing her phone in her pocket, Cassidy looked back at the view, trying to recapture her previous train of thought. She had been on the edge of some revelation about her dilemma before being interrupted by Manon's message, she was sure of it, but it had slipped away. If only her dad was here to give her advice. Closing her eyes, Cassidy tried to summon his presence.

What should I do, Dad? I don't want to leave here.

At first, the only sound was a jangly burst of birdsong, but then in the silence she heard it.

So don't leave then. Stay and fight.

Cassidy blinked her eyes open. It wasn't Joe's voice she had heard; it was her own, and it was loud and clear. It sounded so sure of itself, in fact, that Cassidy was mystified that she hadn't heard it before. Was it because Manon's offer had given her an easy way out? Or had she just not believed in herself enough to seriously consider it? Perhaps she just needed to be in the stillness of this moment to hear it. But, whatever the reason, Cassidy was certainly listening now.

A trembling started in her belly. Could she do this? Staying in Dithercott was the tougher option, for sure: the Sophia problem might have been solved, but the lack-of-funds problem most definitely had not – and a lovely sunrise hadn't magically changed that. Yet something *had* changed, inside her. Cassidy now felt as if she was strong enough to face up to the challenge. It was as if she had just discovered she had superhuman powers – and perhaps, in a way, she had. True, it wasn't shooting webs or lifting buses, but believing in yourself was clearly a powerful force.

She thought back to Angeline's advice: *try to find an investor.* Cassidy slapped her head – how could she have been so stupid! Of *course* she should do that. She'd instantly dismissed her friend's suggestion before (another mountain she had felt too exhausted to climb), but in this new frame of mind,

Cassidy knew that she owed it to both her and Nora to at least try.

She jumped up, her entire body fizzing with energy. Rather than 'doing a Bertie' and running away, she needed to do everything she could to make their lives work here. Flinging out her arms towards the horizon, Cassidy closed her eyes, beaming as the sun warmed her face. Maybe she wouldn't be able to find an investor, in which case she would accept Manon's job and go back to Sacramento, but she was definitely going to give it a go.

One last throw of the dice.

FORTY-TWO

'Woah, this place is *sick*,' murmured Nora, tipping her head back to admire the imposing grey-stone facade of Dithercott Manor. 'Like Wayne Manor in *Batman*.'

Standing beside her, Tilly planted her hands on her hips. 'I can't believe your family used to live here, Nora. It's so unfair. Your family tree project is going to be way better than mine.'

'Come on, Till, we've got some good stuff in there,' said Angeline, who was standing behind the girls with Cassidy. 'What about Great-Grandad? Being a fighter pilot in World War Two is really interesting.'

Tilly tutted. 'Yeah, because that's *so* much cooler than having relatives who lived in an actual castle.'

The little group was here at the manor as part of Nora's research into the Beeswhistle family tree. Cassidy had forced herself to get over her awkwardness around Ned and had messaged to ask if she could bring Nora to visit, and he had replied almost instantly, not only saying he would be delighted to show them around, but also inviting her to bring a friend. Cassidy wasn't sure who was more excited: Nora at seeing the manor for the first time, or Angeline at seeing Ned.

There was the clunk of the door being unbolted from the inside and the girls jumped to attention. Cassidy was expecting to see Clara, but instead the door opened to reveal a figure dressed in a frock coat, stockings and breeches, topped off with a black curly wig and fake moustache.

'Greetings, peasants!' He struck a pose in the doorway, one hand resting on a cane.

Nora and Tilly gasped.

Cassidy's mouth fell open. 'Ned?'

'No, 'tis I, Henry Bartholomew Bamford-Bligh.' He gave an elaborate bow. 'And I have just won this house in a game of dice from an old friend of mine, Albert Beeswhistle!'

Having got over their shock, the girls played along.

'Boo!' jeered Nora. 'You probably cheated!'

'And your wig looks stupid!' added Tilly.

Cassidy pushed her fist to her mouth to stifle a laugh.

'That may well be, child, but I am also the new lord of Dithercott Manor, and there's nothing you or anyone else can do about it! Mwah-ha-ha!'

As the girls heckled him again, the women swapped amused glances. Leaning in, Angeline whispered: 'Now do you see why he was so popular in the village?'

'Absolutely,' muttered Cassidy. It was easy to imagine *this* Ned in the stocks at Dithercott fête being pelted by wet sponges by local kids.

Ned swept an arm towards the door. 'And now, if you'll step this way, I believe you lowly village folk wish to see inside my magnificent new home?'

With a yelp of excitement, Nora and Tilly rushed inside. Cassidy could hear their excited shrieks as they took in the scale of the grand entrance hall.

Angeline stepped forward, looking unusually coy. 'Hi, Ned, thank you very much for having us.'

'Angeline! So lovely to see you again.' He clasped her hands inside his. 'How are you? And Tilly?'

As the pair of them caught up, Cassidy breathed in the now familiar scent of furniture polish and woodsmoke and marvelled all over again at the height of the vaulted ceiling. In a way, she thought, it was a relief that the lost deed had turned out to relate to the inn, because while she would never have dreamt of challenging Ned for ownership of the manor, Cassidy imagined she would have been left wondering at what might have been if she'd been named the rightful heir.

She was just wondering how Ned could possibly even consider leaving this place for good, when he came over to greet her. 'Miss Beeswhistle,' he murmured, with a tilt of his head, regarding her from beneath his brows with such a wicked glint that it sent a ripple of excitement through her, even though she knew it was all part of the performance. The urge to touch Ned hadn't faded in the slightest, she was dismayed to see.

'I really appreciate you going to all this trouble,' she said, trying to keep her voice light.

'Honestly, it's my pleasure. Any excuse to get in a pair of breeches.'

Just his mention of the word 'breeches' was enough to send colour flooding to her cheeks, making Cassidy cringe, but thankfully Ned had already turned away.

Getting back into character, he strode over to the girls, who were crouched by the display case of stuffed owls. 'Ah, I see you admiring these fine examples of taxidermy.'

Tilly pulled a face. 'They're owls, aren't they? Not taxiwhatever.'

'Taxidermy, you philistines!' boomed Ned, making the girls snigger. 'The art of preserving a creature's body for the purpose of display. We Victorians had a fascination with natural history, you know, and such exhibits were a way to showcase not only our wealth, but also our refinement and sophistication. All of

which I have in spades.' He tossed his curls over his shoulder.
'And now, if you'll follow me, our tour is about to begin.'

Seeing the manor through her daughter's eyes turned out to
be even more rewarding than Cassidy's first time here. Nora
and Tilly noticed details that she'd missed, such as the stag and
eagle from the Beeswhistle crest carved into the bannisters and
the bee motif inlaid in the marble floor.

Ned was a brilliant guide, keeping up a running commentary about the manor's history, yet bringing it so vividly to life in
the character of Henry Bamford-Bligh that the girls didn't get
bored. He seemed to have a sixth sense about what would
appeal to ten-year-olds, at one point taking the ceremonial
pistols down from the wall for them to examine.

As Tilly swung the barrel towards them, Angeline instinctively ducked. 'They're not loaded, are they?' she asked,
nervously.

'Oh no, I'm sure they're not,' said Ned. A pause, and his
brow creased. 'Maybe don't touch the trigger, girls, just in case.'

Cassidy had been worried about Nora seeing Ned again
after their encounter in the woods, although when she had
tentatively broached the subject before their visit, she had
barely shrugged. Either Nora had forgotten about it or she had
accepted the fact that he'd apologised and moved on. And now,
as Ned swept her around the saloon in a waltz to demonstrate
'the Victorian equivalent of one of your TikToks', while Nora
laughed so hard she had a coughing fit, you would never have
guessed they had ever been anything other than great mates.

Their next stop was the guest wing and, while Ned showed
the girls the two-hundred-year-old toilet, to shrieks of wonder
and disgust, Angeline drew Cassidy back into the corridor.

'When are you going to talk to Ned?' she asked quietly.

'I'll try to grab a moment with him after we've finished the
tour.' Cassidy glanced at her. 'Are you sure this is a good idea,
Ange?'

'For the hundredth time, yes. What's the worst that could happen?'

'He laughs in my face and tells me to leave?'

'Then you leave.' She gave her a hard stare to underline this. 'Okay?'

Cassidy felt more confident knowing Angeline was in her corner, even if it was her heart that was on the line.

They moved on to Bertie's bedroom, where Cassidy was surprised to see a painting of a young woman hanging where his portrait had previously been. How lovely to be so rich that you had spare gigantic antique paintings just hanging around – although she supposed they were the aristocratic equivalent of family photos.

'Who's that?' she asked Ned, nodding to the painting.

'That's Jemima Beeswhistle, Bertie's mother.'

'She looks just like you, Mom!' said Nora.

'You know, I actually think she does,' mused Angeline. 'Copy her pose, Cassidy.'

Jemima had been painted in profile, arranging roses in a vase, and Cassidy struck a similar stance. 'What do you think?'

Angeline laughed. 'That's uncanny!'

Grinning, Cassidy glanced at Ned for his verdict and was struck by the way he was studying her. There was a furrow between his brows and his jaw was set in a way that seemed almost disapproving. She instantly dropped the pose, feeling stupid. When she looked back at him after a moment, however, she found him looking at her again in that same stern way, and she suddenly wondered if she'd done something to offend him.

Cassidy was thinking back over the morning, trying to remember if she'd said something stupid, when Ned cleared his throat. 'I don't suppose anyone here would be interested in seeing the manor's secret passage?' he asked, to squeals from the girls.

As they walked back down the guest wing corridor, Cassidy

put the moment behind her. She was probably just being over-sensitive because of her nerves over the difficult conversation ahead. No doubt the poor guy had simply been taking a well-deserved break from entertaining them for the past couple of hours.

They finished the tour back in the entrance hall, where Ned took an old-fashioned handbell from the sideboard and rang it a couple of times. A moment later, Clara appeared wearing a mob cap and a long gown with an apron.

'I can't believe you made Clara wear that costume,' Cassidy muttered to Ned.

'This was all her idea!'

'You rang, mi'lord?' said Clara.

Nora and Tilly gaped in wonder.

'Ah, yes,' said Ned, getting back in character. 'My guests and I will be taking tea and cakes in the blue drawing room.'

Clara bobbed a curtsey. 'If you would be kind enough to come with me, ladies...'

Angeline shot a quick glance at Cassidy, who responded with a nod. She was well aware this could be her last chance to get Ned on his own. As he turned to follow Clara, she touched his arm.

'Ned, could I have a word in private?'

'Of course. Clara, we'll catch you up.'

'Right you are, Lord Henry.'

Once the others had disappeared, Ned gestured back in the direction they had just come. 'Let's go through to the parlour, we'll be more comfortable there.' As they walked along the corridor, Ned ripped off his moustache and then pulled off the long curly wig. 'Gosh, that was itchy,' he muttered, ruffling his hair so vigorously it stuck up in all directions. It made him look as though he'd just got out of bed, and the sudden image Cassidy got of waking up next to Ned did nothing to calm the nerves churning in her belly.

FORTY-THREE

The parlour was a cosy little room that showed little evidence of the Quills: no glossy coffee-table books, white pillar candles or bikini-clad photos of Sophia on a tropical beach. The furniture was tatty and well-loved, and despite the fine weather, there was a fire in the grate.

Cassidy perched on the overstuffed sofa, while Ned took the tartan armchair next to the fire. Mungo appeared and clambered onto the sofa next to Cassidy. He looked up at her adoringly as she gave him a scratch, then settled by her side with a huff of contentment.

'I hear Sophia paid you a visit at the inn,' said Ned, with an apologetic grimace.

'It was fine. She agreed to lay off the Beeswhistle, which is the main thing.' Cassidy glanced at the door. 'She's not here today?'

'No, she and Xavier have decided to stay in London for the time being. I get the impression she's been rather spooked by the discovery of the deed.' He shot her a complicit grin. 'Anyway, what did you want to talk about?'

'Right.' Cassidy sat up straighter, trying to remember the

speech she had rehearsed with Angeline that morning. 'It's about the inn. As you may know, we're currently operating on reduced hours, but after everything the community did to help me after the fire, I'm very keen to open full-time. The village deserves to have their pub back again, rather than just a part-time restaurant.'

'I quite agree,' said Ned.

'The problem is because of our teething problems, I can't afford to hire the staff I'd need to open for longer hours.'

'And by teething problems I presume you mean my sister's meddling?'

'In part, yes. But also I've blown through my initial capital and it's getting to the point where I can't afford to stay open for much longer.'

She felt a stab of shame at having to admit this to Ned, especially after his generous donation at Beesfest.

'I see.' Ned sat back in the chair, steepling his fingers. 'Forgive me for interrupting before you've finished, but what I think you might need, Cassidy, is an investor.'

Her eyes went wide. She opened her mouth to speak, then closed it again.

'Someone who can inject some cash into the business,' he continued, 'so you can hire the extra manpower and take off some of the pressure in these early months. Might that be something you'd be prepared to consider?'

Still wondering how on earth Ned had managed to guess exactly what she'd been going to ask him, Cassidy managed to recover her voice. 'Funnily enough, I'd had the same thought.'

'Interesting.' A smile twitched at Ned's lips. 'And supposing you found someone who would be prepared to invest in the Beeswhistle. What terms would you be proposing?'

'A ten per cent stake in the business in return for a share of the profits.'

'Okay...'

'Plus I could throw in some free beer.' She couldn't help but break into a grin, her heart lifting. 'If you know of anyone who might be interested.'

Ned rubbed his chin. 'You know, *I* might be interested in a proposal like that.'

Cassidy couldn't quite believe how well this was going, but she was anxious not to pressurise him. 'Ned, you've already been so generous. Please don't feel obliged to agree to this.'

'I don't. But I think it's an appealing investment opportunity, and you know I like to support the community when I can. I'm also very happy to back *you*, Cassidy. What you've achieved at the Beeswhistle these past few months has been very impressive.'

'Thank you,' she said, with a flush of pleasure.

'We'll obviously have to discuss it further, but for now let's say I'm definitely interested.'

Cassidy would have jumped up and kissed him if she hadn't made that mistake once already. She knew this was far from a done deal, but if she had Ned's backing, she would be able to finally open the Beeswhistle as a proper gastropub. It would take the financial stress off her shoulders, so she could focus on her cooking rather than haggling with suppliers over every potato. And most importantly, it would mean she and Nora could stay in Dithercott.

'Thank you so much, Ned,' she said, the words feeling pathetically inadequate. 'Especially as I appreciate the timing probably isn't great, in light of your plans.'

'Plans?'

'Yes, I heard you're leaving Dithercott.'

'Who told you that?'

The expression on his face made her hesitate. 'Oh, you know, word on the street.'

'And what were these words exactly?'

Cassidy was beginning to wish she'd kept her mouth shut.

'Something about you speaking to a lawyer to arrange the transfer of the estate to your sister.'

'I see.' After a long moment, Ned propped his elbows on his knees and leant forward. 'Cassidy, I know you said there was no need for me to explain my personal situation to you, but if I'm going to be your business partner, then I think you have a right to know.'

'It's really none of my business,' she said quickly, wary of venturing into personal territory with him.

'Actually, in a way it is.'

Cassidy hesitated. After all he had done for her, the least she could do was listen. Besides, she spent an unhealthy amount of time thinking about Ned, and perhaps if he filled in some of the blanks in his story it would help put an end to her silly obsession.

She signalled for him to go ahead.

'Thank you. Well, I'm sure you'll have heard that three years ago the woman to whom I was engaged died in a road accident.'

'I did, and I'm very sorry.'

He dipped his chin in acknowledgement. 'Tamara was the eldest daughter of my father's best friend. Our future together was essentially decided when we were children.'

'What – like an arranged marriage?'

Incredulous, Cassidy couldn't help blurting this out, but thankfully Ned didn't seem offended.

'Not as such. If I'd said to my father that I hadn't wanted to marry Tamara, he wouldn't have forced me to do so, but for as long as I could remember, our marriage had been discussed as a done deal. I loved my father dearly. Humphrey was a kind, decent man and the most fabulous parent. But I was also raised with an acute awareness of my responsibilities as the heir to Dithercott. The English aristocracy and their archaic tradi-tions...' There was a bitter note to his voice. 'I suppose I felt that

I didn't have any other option *but* to marry Tamara, even though it was never put to me quite that bluntly.'

'You must have loved her though, to go through with it?'

Ned's face clouded. 'Tamara was beautiful and accomplished, ideal "lady of the manor" material, but we had nothing in common. She liked shopping, entertaining and socialising. What she *didn't* like was the countryside, or any activity that involved flat shoes.' He managed a low chuckle. 'Soon after we started dating, I invited her on a walk around the estate and from the look on her face you'd think I'd suggested a fifty-mile hike in a blizzard. It was quickly apparent that we were tremendously ill-suited. Most troubling of all, for me anyway, was that Tamara wasn't at all keen to live at Dithercott once we were married. She wanted to move to London, or even New York, anywhere other than being "stuck out in the sticks", as she put it. Looking back, I think we both felt trapped by the engagement from the start.'

Cassidy was confused. From what she'd heard, Ned had so adored Tamara that her death had destroyed him, but the way he was talking about her now it didn't sound like they'd ever even been in love.

'Why didn't you call the wedding off?'

'Duty, I suppose.' He gave a helpless shrug. 'I know this must sound ridiculous to you.'

'Well, yes, but we do come from very different backgrounds.'

'It's ridiculous whatever your background,' he said, firmly. 'Anyway, one afternoon shortly before the wedding, we had the most terrible row. Tamara had been drinking heavily that day. She'd always loved a cocktail, but it was no longer confined to nights out. She'd start on the martinis at lunchtime and was drunk by most evenings. Looking back now, I wonder if it was because she was struggling with the idea of our marriage as much as I was. That day, we ended up yelling at each other, all sorts of terrible things, and then, before I could stop her, Tamara rushed out of the house, jumped in her car and...' Ned ran his hand over his eyes. 'It was hushed up by our families to avoid a scandal, but the police told us that she'd been several times over the limit.'

'God, I'm sorry, Ned...'

'I've had to live with the knowledge that if we hadn't had that argument, she might still be alive.'

His eyes were glazed, as if caught up in his memories, and Cassidy had to fight the urge to rush over to comfort him.

'You can't think like that,' she said.

'It's true though,' he said. 'Her parents were devastated, as you can imagine. My father made me promise that I wouldn't have another relationship for at least five years as a mark of respect to Tamara and her family, who I believe had asked him as much, and I felt so utterly wretched that I would have agreed to anything. Then, six weeks after the accident, my father had a heart attack and died. I was wracked with guilt, grieving my father, and then one morning I just... couldn't get out of bed. I felt as if I'd let everyone down – that I'd failed in my duties as heir. So I shut myself away from everything.'

Cassidy opened her mouth to speak, but Ned held up a hand.

'Soon after my father's death, Sophia turned up at the manor. She told everyone that she'd come to look after me, but I knew full well she was taking advantage of the situation to advance her own interests. I was well aware how desperate she was to be lady of Dithercott and have the manor as her and Xavier's "country seat" to entertain their London pals, and quite frankly I was so sick of this antiquated system that had, as far as I was concerned, contributed to Tamara's death and my misery, that I didn't try to stop her. I decided that once the five years were up and I'd fulfilled the promise to my father, I would leave Dithercott Manor.'

'But why? You told me yourself – you love it here.'

'I do, but I also feel trapped by it. When you're the custodian of a place like this, responsible for upholding its reputation and hundreds of years' worth of history... at times the weight of everyone's expectations can feel suffocating. Do you remember when I saw you in church that morning? The moment I walked in I felt as if the entire congregation was talking about me.' Cassidy clearly recalled this, because she'd got the same impression. 'I find that sort of attention very uncomfortable. I know that my upbringing has given me a slightly skewed outlook on life, but the idea of being anonymous, of not worrying about people judging my actions – well, that feels absolutely liberating. So, even though the manor would always be where my heart was, I thought it better to trade in all the responsibilities in exchange for a quiet life. And if that meant leaving Dithercott, it was a price I felt willing to pay.'

Cassidy didn't know what to say. She had hoped that hearing how much he loved Tamara would help blunt her fixation, but instead, hearing of his desperation and his feelings of being trapped, made her want to throw her arms around him and cover him with kisses.

'Anyway, your mole was quite right,' Ned continued. 'I did speak to a lawyer the other day. But it was nothing to do with handing over the estate to Sophia. I'm not leaving Dithercott, Cassidy.'

Her head jerked up. 'You're not?'

'No.'

'So... what's changed?'

'Three things, really. First of all, I've started looking into rewilding the estate, which has given me a purpose again and made me feel like rather than just being a rich kid who's simply been handed everything on a plate, I can actually make an important contribution to the estate's future.'

'Rewilding? Help an urban Californian out here...'

'It's when you allow the land to return to its natural state and let nature do what it pleases without human interference. The idea is to get native birds and insects returning to the land. In similar projects, seriously endangered species have re-emerged.'

Ned's eyes were dancing, and Cassidy warmed to his enthusiasm. 'What a fantastic idea.'

'I'm glad you think so. Secondly, I've managed to pull myself far enough out of my self-absorbed hole to realise that Sophia is, in fact, the last person who should be in charge of this place. I've had quite enough of her treating the manor as her weekend party pad, and I've told her as much. That conversation was just as lively as you might imagine.'

Cassidy giggled. 'And the third thing?'

Ned paused, then grew very still. 'The third thing, Cassidy, is you.'

FORTY-FOUR

Cassidy blinked at Ned. A moment ago, she'd been the sympathetic listener, but now the focus had suddenly and unexpectedly shifted slap-bang onto her. She felt as if she was on stage in a spotlight in front of an audience and hadn't a clue about her next line (a scenario that was her go-to panic dream).

'Do you remember the first time we met?' asked Ned.

'You mean when I stormed up to the manor and yelled at you while you ignored me?'

'That's it.' He looked amused. 'I get the impression you went away from our first encounter thinking, "what an asshole".'

'Yep, pretty much word for word.'

He gave a snort of laughter. 'I, however, was left with a very different impression. At the risk of sounding like the stuffy, tweed-wearing aristocrat you seem to think me to be, I found you extremely captivating.'

As his words sank in, Cassidy became aware of her heart thumping in her chest.

'It wasn't just because you were a Beeswhistle, although to start with, meeting one of Bertie's relatives was admittedly part of the appeal. But I thought you were... well, absolutely gorgeous.' He paused, his words hanging in the air. 'Even though you clearly felt differently, I wanted to see you again.'

Cassidy was sitting perfectly still, terrified the tiniest movement might interrupt Ned's story, but inside, her mind was racing, trying to reframe their meetings in the churchyard and by the river in light of what he had just told her. Had she been so determined to see him as the enemy that she'd completely misread the signs?

Ned fiddled with his cuffs, shifting position. 'I couldn't stop thinking about you, but at the same time I had my father's voice in my head, reminding me of the vow I'd made to Tamara's parents. I hadn't even looked at another woman since her death, but suddenly here you were in all your wonderful pink-haired glory, someone I could really see myself being with, and there was nothing I could do about it because of that promise. I realised I needed to explain the situation to you – to lay all of my cards on the table – which is why I asked you to the bluebell woods that day.' He ran a hand through his hair. 'But then that very morning I had an unexpected visit from Tamara's parents.'

Cassidy thought back to the black car she'd seen speeding away down the drive when she'd been walking to the manor.

'It was the most terrible timing. They tended to drop in every now and then – I think it was a way for them to help keep her memory alive – and that morning they were going on about Tamara, and how grateful they were that I was respecting theirs and my father's wishes, so when I saw you soon after and we kissed...' He bit his top lip, his face etched with misery. 'That was why I pulled away, Cassidy. It was my conscience stopping me doing something I would regret.'

The word 'regret' hit her like a bucket of ice-cold water. It was suddenly obvious to her how this was going to play out: Ned was going to tell her that although he liked her, it couldn't go any further. She knew enough of the man to know he'd never break the promise to his father.

'I understand,' she managed, pain stabbing in her chest.

'Just hear me out,' said Ned. 'That moment you walked away from me in the rain – that was when I realised that I had to find a way to be free of all the guilt and expectation so that I could finally move on with my life. I decided to set up a charitable scholarship at Tamara's old school in her name. It was an idea that had occurred to me before, but this time I actually did something about it. And, as I subsequently explained to Tamara's parents, that would do far more to honour their daughter's memory than me not going on any dates. That's why I've been speaking to a lawyer, Cassidy. To set up the scholarship, not hand over the estate to Sophia.'

The silence that followed was broken only by the crackle of the fire. Ned was clearly waiting for her to speak, but Cassidy was struggling to make sense of what she had just heard. Her heart had been catapulted up and down so violently she felt she had whiplash.

'So what you're saying is...' She tailed off, hoping Ned would fill in the blanks.

'What I'm saying...' He rubbed his jaw, thinking. 'As you Americans might put it, what I'm saying is that I dig you, Cassidy.'

Despite the tension gripping the room, she laughed. 'We don't *ever* say that, Ned.'

'Even so, I very much do,' he said, his eyes gleaming. 'You're funny and fascinating and brilliant, and just being around you makes me feel like my old self again. I mean, you're the only person I'd wear this ludicrous costume for.' He looked at her with a lopsided smile. 'I don't want to waste any more time, Cassidy – I need to live again. So even if I've made a complete fool of myself, I'm still glad I've told you how I feel. And I just hope that despite what you said about our kiss being a mistake—'

'But I only said that because I thought I'd just thrown myself at you without reason!'

He broke into a slow grin. 'I think it was probably more that we threw ourselves at each other.'

Cassidy could feel the air between them crackling like static.

'In that case,' she said, 'maybe we should have a rematch. Just in the interests of fairness.'

Ned's eyes locked on hers and she caught her breath as he got up and walked over to where she was sitting on the sofa. She looked up at his face, taking in the strong lines of his face and his full, slightly parted lips, and her heart jittered in her chest. Mungo was still hogging most of the space on the sofa and Ned gave him a little shove, but the dog ignored him.

'Down, boy,' he muttered. 'Come on, Mungo, now's really not the time.'

The dog grumbled in his sleep and twitched a leg, but didn't move.

Turning his gaze briefly upwards, Ned reached out his hand and gently pulled Cassidy onto the rug in front of the fire so that she was on her back. He lay down next to her and then propped himself on his elbow, his face just inches above hers, staring down at her as if he couldn't believe his luck. She could feel Ned's breath on her skin and caught his scent, warm and mellow like sun-baked fields. Cassidy had no idea how long they stayed like that, locked in each other's gaze, but then Ned lowered his head and his lips brushed hers, sending a million tiny jolts shooting through her, sparking at her fingertips and toes.

He pulled back to look at her again. 'Bertie Beeswhistle may well have been an ugly sod, but his great-great-great-great-granddaughter—'

'Too many greats,' breathed Cassidy, her voice barely a whisper.

'Not possible,' he said, his fingers tracing her jawline, triggering a pulsing at her core. 'As I was saying, his *descendant* is the most beautiful woman I've seen in my entire life.'

And then, all at once, their mouths were pressed together, their hands grasping for each other. Ned wrapped his arms around Cassidy's back and swung her over so that she was on top of him, the heat of their bodies mingling, and as he murmured her name, she let out the gasp that had been gathering inside her. She felt Ned's hands tangle in her hair and the stubble on his jaw rasping against her cheek, sending shockwaves of sensation through her. She knotted her fists in his clothes, pulling him closer, wanting to consume every bit of him. He broke off to bury his face in her neck, breathing in her scent, and then his lips found hers again, agonisingly gently at first, and then with total abandon. Heat flooded through Cassidy's body, and she felt as if she was climbing to the very top of a rollercoaster. She was readying herself for the wild plunge and scream that would surely follow when the clock on the mantelpiece started to chime.

It was a wake-up call, and with huge effort and reluctance, the two of them broke apart. They lay wrapped in each other's arms for a while, their breath slow and jagged, the only movement the rise and fall of their chests. Cassidy's body felt deliciously heavy and fluid, as if her limbs were full of molten gold, but there was a smile on her face that she thought might never fade.

Ned pulled back to look at her, shaking his head in wonder. 'You really are quite something, you know,' he said.

Cassidy stroked the contours of his cheekbones and then trailed her fingers down his neck. 'Somehow you even look hot in this ridiculous outfit,' she said with a smile, fingering his lacy cravat. 'What do you think Henry would say if he could see you now?'

'Oh, probably something along the lines of "what took you so long, old chap?"'

'Well, we got there in the end.'

'We did. And I couldn't be happier about that.'

Cassidy lifted her head to kiss him. As their lips touched, she felt herself spiralling away again, but she forced herself pull back. 'We should probably get back to the others,' she said, her voice husky.

Ned hesitated, as if debating whether to try changing her mind, and then reluctantly acquiesced. He looked towards the door, where something seemed to catch his eye. 'Stay right there,' he said, getting up. 'I want to show you this first.'

There was a small box-frame hanging by the door that Cassidy hadn't noticed before and she watched as Ned took it down from the wall, opened up the back and removed whatever was inside. Coming back to join her on the rug, he held out his hand to reveal two small dice the colour of old ivory.

'They belonged to Henry,' he said. 'In fact, they're rumoured to be the very dice he used in that fateful game with Bertie, although that might be poetic licence. For as long as I can remember, they've been hanging over there with a little plaque explaining their significance.'

Ned dropped them in Cassidy's hand and as she rolled them between her fingers, marvelling at how the lives of two families had been completely transformed by these tiny objects, an idea took shape in her mind.

'Remind me what game Bertie and Henry were playing?'

'It was Hazard. A popular nineteenth-century gambling game.'

'Do you know how to play it?'

'No, I'm afraid not.'

She thought for a moment. 'Well, if Hazard's out, how about the first one to roll a double takes the estate?'

Ned laughed. 'Now that *would* be a plot twist,' he said. But then he frowned, registering in her expression. 'You're not serious...'

'I think it's only fair you give me a chance to win back the manor back and restore my family's honour.'

Ned scrutinised her for a long moment and then raised an eyebrow. 'Okay, Beeswhistle, let's do this.'

'Winner takes all?'

He nodded. 'The estate, the house, my heart – the lot.'

Cassidy threw her arms around him and kissed him again. 'You're on.'

She blew on the dice, then began to shake them in her clasped hands.

'Here goes nothing...'

A LETTER FROM CATE

Dear reader,

Out of all the fabulous books available, it feels an immense privilege that you chose to read one of mine. So a huge, sparkly THANK YOU from the bottom of this happy author's heart for picking up, borrowing or downloading *The Accidental Inheritance*. If you enjoyed it and would like to keep up to date with my latest releases, just sign up at the following link. Your email address will never be shared and you can unsubscribe at any time.

www.bookouture.com/cate-woods

In a way, *The Accidental Inheritance* is a bit of an accidental novel. I'd just written two books set in Vermont, which is where my parents live, and I'd always intended there to be a third in the series, but then Covid struck and took a wrecking ball to everyone's plans, including mine. My husband, two kids, dog and I were based in London at the time, but, like many of us, lockdown made us take a closer look at where and how we were living, and after alarmingly little research or thought (almost as little as Cassidy before she moved to Dithercott, in fact!), we upped sticks and headed for the Sussex coast.

We've ended up in a gorgeous spot sandwiched between the wide open space of the South Downs and the wider open space of the sea and, although it hasn't always been plain sailing, we haven't regretted it for a moment. I've always been influenced by location in my writing, so as soon as we moved here, I knew I wanted to set a novel in Sussex, and, while the characters are all fictional, the Beeswhistle Inn, Dithercott village and the manor are based on very real places. I'd be happy to supply details if you're interested, just get in touch via the social media links below.

Looking back now, I do wonder how much of this book was inspired by my own experience of moving to a new place. It certainly wasn't conscious, but with hindsight I can see the warmth of the welcome I found when I moved in the way that Angeline, Mrs Timothy and the rest of the Dithercott embrace Cassidy. I think there's something very life-affirming about the notion of being accepted into a community where you don't know a soul, regardless of who you are. I know there will always be the occasional Sophia Quill to deal with, but with all the bad news around right now, I think it's good to be reminded of the essential niceness of most people.

I do hope that you enjoyed reading about Cassidy's adventures. If you did, I'd be hugely grateful if you could write a review. Not only would I love to hear what you think – I still find it mind-blowing that people actually want to read my stories – but it makes such a difference in helping new readers discover my books for the first time.

In the meantime, if you have any questions or comments, please do get in touch with me via social media, as I do love hearing from readers.

With all best wishes,

Cate xxx

KEEP IN TOUCH WITH CATE

facebook.com/catewoodswriter

twitter.com/catewoodswriter

instagram.com/catewoodswriter

ACKNOWLEDGEMENTS

Huge thanks to my brilliant editor Lucy Frederick, who is to editing what Marcus Rashford is to football (deliberate Man U reference there!), and to the entire Bookouture team. My eternal gratitude also goes to my agent, Rowan Lawton, for all her wisdom, encouragement and guidance, and for reminding me to believe in myself. Thanks also to Sally Bigland for answering my fire-related questions and the excellent plotting advice; to the Real Housewives of Hove (you know who you are!) for making me feel so welcome; and to my A-Team, Oliver, Daisy and Bear. Finally, thank you to YOU, dear reader, as without you I wouldn't have a writing career, just a very self-indulgent and time-consuming hobby. I couldn't be more grateful for your support.

Printed in the USA
CPSIA information can be obtained
at www.ICGtesting.com
LVHW050159180823
755595LV00008B/346